THE SHEIKH DOC'S MARRIAGE BARGAIN

SUSAN CARLISLE

THE SURGEON'S CONVENIENT HUSBAND

AMY RUTTAN

MILLS & BOON

First Published in Great Britain 2019
by Mills & Boon, an imprint of HarperCollins*Publishers*
1 London Bridge Street, London, SE1 9GF

The Sheikh Doc's Marriage Bargain © 2019 by Susan Carlisle

The Surgeon's Convenient Husband © 2019 by Amy Ruttan

ISBN: 978-0-263-26972-7

MIX
Paper from
responsible sources
FSC C007454

This book is produced from independently certified FSC™ paper
to ensure responsible forest management.
For more information visit www.harpercollins.co.uk/green.

Printed and bound in Spain
by CPI, Barcelona

THE SHEIKH DOC'S MARRIAGE BARGAIN

SUSAN CARLISLE

MILLS & BOON

To Becky,
your Aunt Susan loves you!

CHAPTER ONE

DR. LAUREL MARTIN placed the test tube into the rack with great care, her pulse racing in anticipation. This could be it. The breakthrough she'd devoted her career to finding. The process to stop the mutation in the factor IX gene in the X chromosome. If it could be tested for during pregnancy and corrected then thousands of lives could be changed, in some cases even saved. The key was discovering that link.

To find the answer she had to have funding. That money was difficult to come by. She'd already been put on notice that hers was running out. Still she held out hope that would change. She'd submitted another grant application and should hear about it any day.

The study of hemophilia had become her life's calling. In medical school it hadn't taken her long to realize her comfort zone didn't include interacting with patients and their loved ones. She didn't like to tell them bad news. Being an introvert further hindered her ability to do so. Research had become her safe spot.

A tap on her lab window drew her attention. She pushed up her goggles in an effort to adjust them on her nose. Stewart, the director of the lab, stood on the other side of the glass. His medium height was dwarfed by the tall, lean man standing beside him.

Oh, my. Laurel's heart jumped then adjusted. She stared. The stranger was gorgeous. She hadn't had that type of reaction to a man in years. Not since college when she'd first seen her ex-boyfriend, Larry. A college football player, he'd been shockingly good looking as well. She'd learned the hard way that good looks didn't always equate with being a kind person.

The man beside Stewart looked as if he might be of Middle Eastern decent. His skin had a warm pecan tint as if he spent a great amount of time in the sun. His proud bearing gave him an aura of authority, as if he knew his place in the world and had no trouble holding it. The black tailored suit jacket covering his broad shoulders matched his hair and his equally dark, meticulously groomed beard screamed wealth and power. His gaze locked with hers.

To her surprise his eyes weren't like ink. Instead they were chestnut, reminding her of the color of a racing stallion she'd seen once as a girl. One of his well-shaped brows rose slightly as if he suspected the effect he had on women and wasn't surprised by her reaction.

His look bored into hers, making her feel like one of her petri dish specimens under a microscope. The devil of it was, he was the kind of man she'd always been attracted to. The type of male who had always looked past her mousy, too-serious and impossibly intelligent personality in favor of a tall blonde, with perky breasts, long legs and an engaging giggle that stood just behind her. Laurel was wallpaper and his sort was interested in the chandeliers.

Men like him didn't seriously consider her worth noticing. The one time someone had, she'd been trauma-tized. Larry had damaged her that much. So much so she'd sworn off men and had stuck to that vow for ten years. Long enough to become so absorbed in her work she had little life outside it. Laurel mentally shook her head. None of that had anything to do with the man be-fore her.

The wave of Stewart's hand, indicating he wanted her to come out of the lab, drew her attention away from the arresting stranger. Laurel checked her test tubes again and pushed the rack further away from the edge of the table before rolling her chair back. She exited the room door with a swish of the airlock seal behind her. In the outer room she removed her goggles and adjusted her glasses. She pulled her mask, gloves and gown off, leav-ing her in a simple round neck T-shirt and jeans.

Shrugging into her starched lab coat, she touched the bun at the back of her head, making sure it was in place. She glanced over her shoulder. The stranger's intense gaze remained on her. A ripple of heat went through her, disconcerting her even more. What was he seeing? Thinking?

Shaking off the response, she moved with cool pro-ficiency into the main lab. It wasn't until she'd almost reached the men that she noticed the two larger ones standing a few paces behind the man. How had she missed those intimidating figures? Because she'd been so absorbed by her reaction to the man front and center. These guys were larger, with bulkier shoulders and had even grimmer faces, if that was possible. Their hands were clasped in front of them and legs apart as if ready to move into action. Who were these people and what did they want with her?

Laurel's hands trembled. She shoved them in the pockets of her lab coat. Had she done something wrong? Her eyes narrowed and she gave Stewart a questioning look, relieved to have an excuse to break off eye contact with the others there.

Stewart's voice shook slightly as he said, "Laurel, this is Prince Tariq Al Marktum, and he would like to speak to you." Stewart enunciated the man's unusual name carefully, as if he'd been practicing in order not to stumble over it.

Prince? What would a prince want with her? A "lab rat", according to her siblings. Astonishment made her blurt, "About what?"

"I'll be glad to share that in private," Prince Tariq answered in a deep smooth voice like velvet with a thread of steel running through it. His accent made Laurel want to hear him say more.

She wrinkled her nose as alarm washed through her. "Stewart, what's this about?"

"I'll let the Prince explain. Why don't we go to my office?" Stewart turned and started toward the swinging doors separating the main lab from the offices. The Prince stepped aside, allowing her to precede him. Acutely aware of him and his security men, she walked stiffly. At the doors, he quickly stepped ahead of her and held one open. Laurel gave him a quick glance as she passed. His inscrutable look revealed nothing. She wouldn't want to deal with *him* on a daily basis. How could she ever discern what he was thinking? Feeling?

As they walked down the tiled hall her low sensible clogs made a tap-tap but there was no sound behind her. How did such immense men move with such agility? That thought didn't comfort her.

Stewart swiped his card and pushed the office door open. She entered, expecting him to follow, but instead Prince Tariq joined her and closed the door behind him. The already small space shrank in proportion to his large presence. She faced him and shoved her hands into her lab coat pockets, bracing herself.

"Please, Dr. Martin, have a seat." He indicated the chairs in front of Stewart's desk.

"No, thank you. I need get back to my lab as soon as possible." She wanted to return to her safe place. "How can I help you?" Laurel couldn't imagine how but it seemed like the right thing to say to hurry this along.

"Sit, please." The Prince's tone implied she had no choice.

She hesitated but eased into a chair, noting too late that it put her into closer proximity to him. To her surprise he took the other chair. At this point she fully expected he might try to lord it over her. After all, he acted as if he owned the place. Stewart didn't allow just anyone to take over his office. She clasped her hands in her lap and waited for the Prince to speak.

"Dr. Martin, I would like you to come to Zentar with me."

"What?" she yelped, leaping to her feet. Had this man lost his mind? Why had Stewart allowed this crazy person into their lab?

The Prince raised his hand. "Just hear me out for a moment. Please."

Laurel eased back into her chair more from shock than trying to please him. She glanced at the door.

"I assure you, you are safe. What I meant to say is that I would like to offer you a position. And chance to further your research."

Laurel shook her head in confusion. That sounded completely different than his earlier statement. She already had a place to do research, one in which she was very close to a breakthrough. Her family lived near. She already had a settled and secure life and cared nothing about working somewhere else. Where was Zentar anyway? She had no intention of going anywhere with a stranger. "Thank you, but I already have a position here."

"I understand you are the top researcher in the field of hemophilia. I am the Minister of Health for Zentar. I have overseen the building of a state-of-the-art laboratory. I intend for my country to be a leader in finding a cure for hemophilia."

Really. That was interesting. She couldn't help but have her curiosity piqued.

"I have vetted you and you come with the highest of recommendations."

"Thank you but I have no idea who you are." Why was the Prince of some nation she'd never heard of focusing on hemophilia? "I appreciate your confidence in me but I'm happy here." She wasn't the adventurous type and she'd had that fact driven home in no uncertain terms. The idea of even living in another state, much less some far-flung country, terrified her. "I don't even know where Zentar is."

Finally, there was a spark of emotion in those dark penetrating eyes. Was it pride? "It's an island in the Arabian Sea. We have beautiful white beaches and stark mountains that are amazing in their own right. We are a small independently wealthy country and progressive in many aspects. My brother, the King, worked hard to make it so. Still, we remain very traditional in others."

What would it be like to have a man talk about her

with that same admiration? She shook that shocking idea away. "It sounds nice but I have my work here."

He leaned forward. "I can offer you anything you desire. The best of equipment, assistants and endless funding."

"But why me? Why hemophilia?"

He paused, looked away from her so long she felt uncomfortable. "I have my reasons." That sounded like a dismissal more than a confession.

Laurel started to rise.

His expression still remained shadowy when he turned back to her. "Hemophilia is a problem in my country."

Laurel now knew what drove him. "I see."

Those eyes pierced her with a look. "I am not sure you do. In my country the number of children born with the disease is increasing. As the Minister of Health I must find out why. You can help me."

Apparently he'd believed she would accept without question but it wasn't going to happen. Just the idea of getting on a plane made her shudder. She could not and would not pick up her entire life and move to a faraway country. "I can't go."

"Is there something keeping you here?" His brows formed a V.

"No."

"Then why not?" He watched her too closely.

"I don't fly."

His silent steady examination lasted a heartbeat too long. "Ever?"

"More like never."

"You would be taking my private plane. Every luxury would be afforded you. All I ask is that you come and have a look at our facility. Then you could decide."

Laurel appreciated him thinking so highly of her but she had no interest in going to Zentar. She wasn't a daring person. Her work, her life, her security was here. She stood and he did as well. "Thank you for the offer but I cannot accept. So I really shouldn't waste any more of your time. If you'll excuse me, I need to get back to my lab now."

The Prince's lips thinned and his eyes were emotionless again, more telling than if they had held some. She'd just refused a man who was clearly used to getting his way. It took a great deal of willpower, but she stepped between the chairs into his personal space. A whiff of his citrus aftershave tickled her nose. A shiver ran along her spine as she hurried to the door. She was unsure if her body's reaction was in response to his close proximity or from the irritation gusting off him.

"Dr. Martin."

Laurel turned.

In a low, even voice he informed her, "I make a point of getting what I want."

That evening in his hotel suite Tariq poured himself a finger of whiskey. Perplexed, he pondered where his interview with Dr. Martin had gone awry. She had proved intelligent, but more than that she was forthright to a fault. He rather liked that quality in a person. Few people he was around did not have an agenda and said what they meant. Dr. Martin had impressed him with her directness. More than that, she had dared to refuse him!

To his great vexation her shy green eyes had captivated him, too. Behind those silver wire-rimmed glasses they had been wide and clear, as if they had never hidden a secret. Otherwise she was a nondescript slip of a woman.

He was both irritated and intrigued. In his world, no one other than the king would tell him no, yet a wallflower doctor who lived most of her life closed up in a glass laboratory had done so. He was confounded. What had gone wrong in the meeting he'd so carefully planned? Worse, why did that haunted look he'd glimpsed in her eyes before she'd come out of the lab still disturb him?

Leaning back in his chair, Tariq stretched his legs out and crossed them at the ankles, swirling the transparent copper-colored liquid in his glass. He'd done his homework. In fact, he'd even called a couple of research facilities to verify she was the person he should focus his efforts on. It had never occurred to him she would turn down his offer. What research scientist wouldn't want to head their own lab and have access to all the funding they wanted? Apparently he had overlooked some pertinent fact about Dr. Martin. He didn't have a Plan B formulated but by evening's end he would. He wanted Dr. Martin in Zentar and he would have her.

After his brother's death in a car accident, Tariq had taken over the responsibility of his sister-in-law's and Roji's welfare. Tariq would give anything to have Roji grow up with his father there. That wouldn't happen now, but if Tariq had anything to do with it no more of his family would have to endure what Roji would. The future members of the royal family would be free of hemophilia. The cure was out there and he'd built a lab in which to find it. Now he needed the right person to lead it, and that was Dr. Martin.

He would never put a wife and child in the same position as Zara and Roji. Despite being the only male in his family who did not have the malformed gene, he refused to take the chance on having a family. He didn't deserve one when the others had to deal with the disease. As a doctor he understood that the ailment was thought to be passed by the female. What if he picked the wrong woman? He already lived with enough guilt.

As a small child he had seen the suffering his brothers had gone through. Always having to have intravenous injections of replacement factor after an injury. Yet that had not helped his brother when the bleeding could not be stopped after the accident. Even with his fancy Harvard medical degree, Tariq had still been unable to save his brother's life. That weight became heavier with each passing day.

Medical advances were being made but not fast enough. Now Roji took the IV factor every three days prophylactically. Still a boy should be able to run and play and have no worries. Tariq wanted that for his family and others with the disease. To do that he needed Dr. Martin, yet she'd made it clear she had no interest in his offer. He must come up with some way of convincing her, make her an offer she could not refuse. Besides, he never took no for an answer when he had his mind made up.

He had some phone calls to make. Dr. Martin must have something she wanted badly enough that he could use it to make her agree.

Two days later Laurel picked up the phone in her lab on the second ring.

"Laurel, when you can get away I need to see you in my office," Stewart said.

Was the Prince back? She'd thought of little else since his visit. For some reason he'd stuck with her. It wasn't as if she would ever see him again yet he'd had an effect on her. "Okay, I'll be there in about ten minutes."

She knocked lightly then entered Stewart's office. They'd had a strong, friendly relationship since she had joined the lab staff five years earlier. Stewart had always left her to do her work and she'd appreciated that.

"What's up?" Laurel asked, both relieved and disappointed the Prince wasn't there. She took the same chair she had sat in during that interview. This time the office felt less suffocating. Stewart didn't generate the larger-than-life aura the Prince possessed.

"This isn't good news, I'm afraid. The grant was denied."

Laurel's heart and hopes plunged into despair. "Your work was an add-on here. I'm sorry, you can't continue." Sympathy rang throughout each of Stewart's words.

Laurel couldn't breathe. Her heart fluttered. Her life's work. What was she going to do? She might have been hit in the chest for all her ability to say a word. She groaned. A breakthrough was so close. "Why, Stewart? I almost have an answer. My research is important."

The older man nodded his head in understanding, his eyes filled with compassion. "I know. But others' work is equally important. Money is always an issue where research is concerned. You know that."

"Isn't there some other way?" There must be. Lives were at stake. "I can't stop now. I'm too close."

"As much as I hate to say it, it's not going to happen at this lab." He paused.

She leaned toward him. "This isn't right! What about the people I'm trying to save?"

"I wish I could tell you there might be hope down another avenue but I would only be giving you false hope. Maybe you should consider the Prince's offer after all.

From what I understand, it was an impressive one. It might not be too late."

Her face twisted in disbelief. She couldn't do that! Travel to a foreign land with a stranger. Where she knew no one.

She leaned forward and gripped the edge of the desk. "Isn't there something else you can do?"

"As of right now, no. I would hate to lose you, but the best I could do is put you on another project."

This couldn't be happening. Panic welled in her. The timing seemed off. The Prince had shown up and the next thing she'd learned was that she no longer had funding. He'd made it clear he got what he wanted. No, he didn't have that much clout. She narrowed her eyes at Stewart. "The Prince didn't have anything to do with this, did he?"

"Not that I know of. I'm sure he knows people on the committee, though. You know most researchers would be glad to be offered such a wonderful opportunity."

"I don't want to move. I know nothing about Zentar or Prince Tariq. I'm a home body."

"Maybe it's time you stepped out of the bubble. Just think what you could do with all that research money at your disposal. A chance like that doesn't come along more than once in a lifetime."

Phrased like that, she had a hard time disagreeing. If only it wasn't so far away. And she wasn't so affected by the Prince. She would have to guard herself where he was concerned. She had no intention of repeating her mistakes. "I like the way things are."

"I know you do, but maybe it's time for a change. For you to get out of the lab and live a little. This could be your golden chance. Sometimes change can be a good thing." Stewart was looking and sounding like the father figure she privately considered him to be.

"I don't want adventure or change. I want to find a way to help hemophiliacs."

Stewart looked over the rim of his black glasses at her. "You do realize the Prince is offering you an opportunity to do just that? You could go until funding comes through."

Could she do it? Step out of her comfort zone? She had done it once before in college and still wore the scars. Yet she was so close. Only months away from finding the key to unlocking the secret to the gene. With the Prince's offer it might be sooner. She really wasn't left much choice. Laurel looked at Stewart for a long moment before releasing a resigned sigh. "Do you know how to get in touch with the Prince?"

Tariq had been expecting Dr. Martin's call. He had known the night before she would not be receiving her funding. He had done nothing to make her lose it but he could not say he was not pleased. What he had done was put the word out that she had funding elsewhere so that no one else would step in and she would have to turn to him.

"Mr. Al Marktum…uh… Prince, this is Dr. Laurel Martin."

"Yes."

She sounded out of breath. "I…uh…was wondering if you were still looking for someone to oversee your lab?"

"I am." He waited.

"I might be interested after all. And I'd like to meet to discuss it." The words came out fast as if she was hurrying so not to stop herself.

"I am flying out first thing in the morning so we will need to talk tonight."

"I guess that'll have to work."

She sounded unsure. Was she reconsidering? He could not have her do that. Tariq leaned back in his chair. "I'm at the Chicago Hotel. Come up to the Presidential Suite. We will not be disturbed while we talk."

There was silence.

"I can tell by the pause that you are thinking of refusing. I would suggest the bar but I think it will be noisy and I do not know the area well enough to propose another place. My assistant is with me so you will be safely chaperoned."

"I don't require a chaperone. I'll be glad to meet you."

He smiled slightly. Had she bolstered herself to make that statement? "If you say so."

"I'll see you in an hour."

"I look forward to it, Dr. Martin."

As good as her word, one of his bodyguards announced her arrival right on time. That alone he could appreciate about her.

Meeting Dr. Martin at the door, he escorted her across the room to one of the two sofas in the center. She was a tiny thing. Not tall and leggy like the women he usually found attractive. He mentally shook his head. This was a business meeting. He needed her to run his lab and that was it. The color of her eyes or the length of her legs did not matter. "May I get you something to drink?"

"No, thank you, I'm fine." She shifted her large bag cross her like it was a shield.

"Please, sit."

Dr. Martin gave him a timid nod, then took a seat next to the arm of the sofa. She looked as though if he said boo she would run. That did not matter. What did was how good she was at her job. Tariq sat on the sofa across from her and crossed one ankle over the knee of his other leg. It was time to get down to business. "I understand you want to talk about my job offer."

"Uh… I wanted to see if you'd consider a compromise on the position you offered me."

"I'm listening." He watched her. Her hair remained tightly pulled back and her glasses had slipped down her nose. She wore almost nondescript clothing and the big black bag remained hugged to her chest. Not a single piece of jewelry was visible. She seemed to dress not to be noticed. Did this woman live in a hole and crawl out to go to work in a lab?

"I have lost my funding. I was wondering if you'd consider putting funds into the lab here where I can continue my work with the understanding that your country would have first access to any of my findings."

He stared, shaking his head before she'd even finished. "That will not do. I want someone working in my country. With my people."

Her voice contained a tight, desperate tone. "But I can't do that."

"Why? I will see you have a place to live. A driver. All the comforts." He leaned forward, watching her closely. She did have interesting eyes. There were tiny flakes of gold in them.

"I can't just fly off to some place I don't know."

"We have already had this discussion. I am offering you a chance to continue your research. I do not think you will be disappointed in the lab I have set up. Wouldn't you like to continue your research?"

She tightened her arms around her bag. "I would. It's important. I'm very close to a breakthrough."

Laurel wasn't sure to what he was referring. She wasn't planning to stop her research. Her new discovery was so close. Did he know something she didn't? Quitting now would be impossible. She narrowed her eyes. "Why are you asking that?"

"It was you who came to me saying that you needed funds to continue your work."

"That doesn't mean that I am giving up. I can't. I'm too close to an advance. I'll find funding somewhere since you won't consider providing it."

"I am sorry, I cannot. My funds are my people's. I don't have any to give you."

He must be a wealthy man. After all he was a prince. "You don't have personal funds that could be used?"

"I do not. They were invested in the lab. You should reconsider coming to Zentar."

She glared at him as panic grew. Why couldn't he understand? "I cannot. I have explained that."

"I have only heard excuses. I have what you need. You no longer have a lab to work in here and I am offering you one. I do not understand the problem. Perhaps you do not care as much as you say you do."

That statement couldn't have hurt more if he'd slapped her. Okay, that did it. He'd gone too far. She jerked to her feet, mindful of the fact this was his hotel suite. Keeping her voice low, she asked, "How dare you?"

His look remained steady. "I dare because I need you leading my lab. There is important work to be done."

Laurel had been on the verge of losing her temper. The idea of going halfway around the world terrified her. What would her parents say, her siblings, about her living in Zentar? She just couldn't do it. Or could she? The Prince wasn't leaving her any choice. Laurel released a heavy breath.

"We can agree on the need for more research. Since you'll not relent I will come to Zentar and set up your lab. In return you will see to it that I get to do a study of your families that have two generations of the disease. Beyond that I make no promises."

"Excellent." His smile reminded her of a conquering hero's. "I will delay my return one day so that you can get your affairs in order."

She gaped at him in disbelief. "One day?"

He put his foot on the floor. "I am sorry but that is all the time I can allow."

Her lips formed a tight line and her gaze went to somewhere over his shoulder. She had so much to do.

"My assistant can help you with anything you might need."

She blinked. "I won't have time to see my family."

"I'm sorry. Once the lab is operational you may return for a visit." At least he sounded sincere.

Straightening her shoulders, Laurel moved to the edge of the cushion. "Well, if I'm to be ready to go then I need to be headed home. I have a lot to do."

Tariq followed her toward the door. "There is just one more matter."

She looked at him. "Yes?"

"You will need to marry me."

CHAPTER TWO

"WHAT? ARE YOU CRAZY?" Laurel stood with her mouth gaping open. There was no way she was going to marry him! It was taking all she had in her to even travel to Zentar. Marrying some man she didn't know was out of the question. "What do you mean, I have to marry you?"

"My country still holds to traditional values. They expect a single woman to be under the care of a man. No one is going to answer your personal health questions without you having a man's name associated with yours. Our social rules have not changed that fast."

"You have to be kidding." Her bag swung at her side.

He gave her a direct look. "I assure you I am not."

"You don't want to marry me." Laurel couldn't believe the turn this conversation had taken.

"It's true. I had no plans to marry. Ever." His words came out flat and to the point.

"Then why would you marry me?"

"Because I know your work is important and I know what must be done to get you to come to Zentar."

"And you're willing to put your personal life on hold?" This man was unbelievable.

"If that is what is necessary."

She watched him closely. "If I agree, this will be a

marriage in name only. You understand?" The idea of getting tangled up with the Prince made her shudder. She was so out of her depth. Once before she'd been in this position and she'd vowed never to go there again. Who would have thought lightning would strike twice in the same place?

"I would expect nothing less."

He made it sound like the thought had never crossed his mind to treat it as a real marriage. Or had it? Laurel wasn't sure she liked being dismissed so easily. The hot sizzle of attraction she felt apparently didn't go both ways. That suited her just fine, or did it? "Couldn't we just *say* we're married and not make a further deal of it?"

"No. If the media discovers that, my people would feel deceived."

"They want this way?"

"How I live in my home is my business. They need not know."

She couldn't do that to her parents. "Can I at least tell my family? They can be trusted."

"No. The media may ask them about it. I don't want them to be forced to lie or for their faces to show something different from what our Minister of Communication may have put out."

Her chest hurt with the thought of her mother and father. "My parents are going to be so hurt."

"In time you can explain it to them." He sounded determined rather than sympathetic.

There was no way they would ever understand. Maybe she could slip off and be back before they had to know much about what was going on. She could just tell them she would be out of town for a while for work. "What's *your* family going to think when you show up with an American woman they have never heard of?"

"The King knows who you are. The others I will tell that I have chosen you as my wife and that will be it." He said that like a man who didn't make a habit of answering to anyone.

"You say your country is very traditional. Will they accept me with no questions?"

"I did not say there would not be questions. Many, I am afraid. But in the end it will not change my decision."

"Me coming with you is that important?"

"It is. We are agreed?"

Laurel pursed her lips then finally nodded.

"Then I will make the arrangements. We marry as soon as we arrive in Zentar."

Two days later Laurel gripped the armrest of the luxury airplane seat and squeezed her eyes tight. She questioned her sanity for the thousandth time, leaving all she had ever known for a far-flung kingdom in the Middle East to work for a man she hardly knew in a lab she'd never seen. And to top it off—marry him. What had happened to her happy, ordered life?

"We are in the air now," the Prince said from the seat across from her. The mirth in his voice rang clear. "You can open your eyes."

"I'd rather not."

"So what is your plan? To spend the next ten hours with them closed?" His humor had turned to disbelief.

"Maybe." She sounded childish but she didn't care.

His hand came to rest over hers for a second. A shiver of awareness zipped through her. "You do not want to miss this view of Chicago."

Laurel opened an eye a slit. She met the Prince's look.

"Look out here." He nodded toward the oval window but made the statement with enough authority she didn't dare not do as he requested. With her eyelids raised only enough to make out the window, she leaned toward it.

Her fingers remained glued to the leather arms of the seat. To have recognized the material covering the chair was making progress with her terror. For the last thirty minutes she had been almost comatose. Slowly she opened her eyes until she had clear vision then peeked out the window.

He was right. The view was amazing. Below was the sparking blue of Lake Michigan. Along its bank were the glistening skyscrapers of Chicago in the afternoon sun. She could make out the river running through the center of the city. The picture was like nothing she had ever seen before. Her breath caught—in a good way.

She glanced at the Prince.

"Aren't you glad you took a chance?" His eyes didn't waver.

Was he talking about something more than looking out the window? "I am."

He gave her hand a pointed look. "Do you think you could let go of my seat? I'm afraid you're going to crush it to sand if you do not."

She quickly clasped her hands in her lap until her knuckles hurt.

"I was just kidding you, you know," he said in a dry tone.

Laurel hadn't known. Had no idea what this man considered humor. They were strangers. The Prince studied the view out the window as well. It was dizzying to think that he would try to joke with her. He looked far too serious most of the time. She had seen a couple of breaks in his unbending expression but they were rare. He usually looked as if he supported the weight of the world on his shoulders. As the Minister of Health, he must carry a heavy burden.

"Prince Tariq, are you making fun of me?"

"No Dr. Martin, I'm trying to ease your mind."

"Thank you, I think." Had he really been that concerned about her?

"Try to sit back and relax, Laurel."

She like the nuances of her name on his lips too much. He made it sound exotic and a little bit naughty. Until he'd used it she'd thought it a simple name and too sweet.

"By the way, you may call me Tariq when we are in private. I know my title is a mouthful. Would you like to have something to drink? Some crackers to settle your stomach?"

He had even realized that? "Yes, that would be nice." Laurel wasn't much of an alcohol drinker and she certainly didn't need to start now at ten thousand feet in the air with a man who had such an effect on her.

Tariq lifted a finger and the steward came to stand beside them. "Dr. Martin will have some—"

"Ginger ale, please."

"And I will have the same. Please bring crackers as well."

The steward nodded and left as quietly as he had approached.

Having relaxed a little, Laurel looked around the plane. It was decorated in pale gray with darker gray curtains on either side of the windows. Her fingers rubbed the arm of the seat. The leather felt ultra-smooth. She looked across the aisle at another seat. On the headrest was what she guessed was the Zentar coat of arms. It consisted of a blue emblem with a yellow dragon over it. Since this was her first time on a plane she had no others to compare it to but she thought this one had to be one of the most luxurious ever built.

Lauren couldn't fathom living in a world like this all the time. The expense of it alone boggled her mind. Her upbringing didn't allow for that kind of lifestyle. She was so out of her element. *What was she doing here?*

The steward returned. He didn't have the expected can of soda. Instead he held a silver tray with two clear glasses and a china plate holding crackers. He unfolded a small table from within the arm of the seat. After placing a napkin on it, he put her glass and the plate on it. He did the same for the Prince then quietly backed away.

Could she feel more out of place? She glanced at Tariq. He had opened his laptop. Without looking up, he said, "Dinner will be served in a couple of hours. Feel free to roam the plane. There is a bedroom at the back if you would like to lie down. I have work to do so you will need to entertain yourself."

Nothing like being dismissed. He'd gotten what he wanted in her coming with him to Zentar so he apparently felt no need to keep her happy any further. Not that he'd really been trying anyway. Most of their interaction had gone his way and not hers. With a sigh, she closed her eyes. It was just as well anyway.

*Tariq. W*ould she ever get used to calling him that?

The last twenty-four hours had been a whirlwind of activity. Nasser, Tariq's driver, had seen her home after her meeting with the Prince at the hotel. She'd phoned her parents and explained where she was going but had strategically left out the part about getting married. She hated lying to them by omission but she couldn't find another way that made the situation any better. They had sounded confused, concerned and a little excited for her. She assured them she would video-chat regularly. Her brothers and sister were more enthusiastic. They all asked if they could come for a visit. Especially if the Prince would agree to send the plane for them. Laurel assured them she wouldn't be asking him to do that.

She'd spent the rest of the day on the phone, arranging things and packing. Tariq had insisted that his assistant take care of the business end of her departure so she could handle the personal. Overwhelmed by the time crunch, she'd agreed. Once again he had gotten his way.

Winter was approaching in Chicago, where it could be bitterly cold, and now she was off to a hot, arid climate. What few clothes she owned that might suit, she'd stuffed into her ancient suitcase. She didn't plan on being gone long so she would make do with what she had. Her heavy coats she left behind. She had to admit she wouldn't miss the freezing windy weather of the upper mid-west.

By the time Nasser had pulled to the curb in front of her apartment just after midday, Laurel had been standing on the sidewalk with two suitcases and a box of books ready for him to load into the car. As a reluctant voyager off on a grand adventure, she had watched her apartment get smaller in the window.

Sometime later, a large warm hand on her shoulder shook her awake. Laurel jerked straight. She'd been asleep. As emotional as she had been about flying, and equally disturbed by being in Tariq's presence, she wouldn't have thought she could have fallen asleep. "Uh. What?"

"Dinner is being served when you are ready." Tariq

stood at her right shoulder. "The bathroom is down the hall toward the rear of the plane if you need it." He moved away.

She looked back at him. He pulled out his phone and sank into a chair beside an elegantly set table, with the silent steward standing attentively nearby. Even high above the earth he ate well. Had the man ever had a hamburger?

Making her way to the bathroom, Laurel discovered it was twice as large as the one her family had shared growing up. Even this room was elegant, with gold fixtures and plush towels. Returning to the cabin, she took the chair across from Tariq.

The steward efficiently served their meal. She smiled. To her humor and amazement the food being offered was less sophisticated than practical. There was breast of chicken, roasted potatoes and steamed broccoli with a roll. Despite the simplicity of the menu it was tasty and filling. Since she'd missed her other meals that day, the food was welcome.

Tariq was a charming dinner companion. He kept a light dialogue going about what he had done and seen while in Chicago, asking her small insignificant questions about her favorite things to do there. When he had finished with his meal, he leaned back in his chair.

Her body heated as he studied her with his piercing look. "So, were you able to get your affairs in order without difficulty before we left?"

"I did. It required numerous phone calls and asking two neighbors to take my plants." She raised her starched linen napkin to her lips.

"Did you work things out with your parents?"

"I did." Not that she liked deceiving her family.

His attention focused on her. "Tell me about them."

To her further amazement he sounded as if he genuinely wanted to know. This part of his personality she'd not expected. She cleared her throat. "They live about an hour outside Chicago. Dad is a factory worker and my mother a schoolteacher. They're very happy together. I have two brothers and a sister. I wish I'd had time to see them. I'll miss them."

"You obviously care about them. I am sorry I could not have allowed you more time. If you had taken the job when I first asked, you would have had it."

So much for his charm. He was right, but she didn't like him pointing it out. "Are you trying to start an argument?"

His mouth lifted slightly at one side. "I am not. Just stating a fact. So how is your family taking you being away?"

"To say that my parents were surprised is an understatement. Along with concerned, and maybe just a little excited for me. They've been telling me for years I need to get out more." Why was she telling this dark, brooding man that? He should be the last person she would confide in.

"I too am sorry you did not have time to see them, to have been able to say a proper goodbye. Family is important."

She lowered her chin and gave him a narrow-eyed look. "I appreciate that but I don't plan to be gone long."

His expression didn't waver and he said nothing. What was he thinking? She turned her attention to her plate. "My brothers and sisters were jealous. They all wanted to come with me." She leaned back as the steward removed her plate then the Prince's. "About us getting married, are you sure there is no other way?"

The question hung in the air as the steward put a plate down in front of them with a decadent-looking chocolate cake on it.

"Positive."

After the steward left, she said softly, "Sorry."

"He is loyal and knows that nothing he sees or hears is to be repeated. But you should still be careful what you say."

Laurel picked up her fork and concentrated on the cake. "I will be."

"Good." Tariq just looked at her a moment with those unreadable eyes. He blinked. "Did you have to give up any other commitments to come to Zentar?"

"You're asking that now?"

"I just wanted to make sure some man wasn't going to show up unannounced and create a problem."

"You don't need to worry about that happening." She refused to let him know why it wouldn't be an issue.

"That's good to hear. I suspect you live for your work."

That might be true but she didn't like the way it sounded out loud. He didn't think she had a personal life? His attitude made her think too much of her childhood years when she had been made fun of for reading all the time. She glared at him, which she seemed to be doing a lot of. "It would be my guess we both tend to do that."

"Agreed." He dug into his cake.

He made it sound like she had given him a compliment. "You mean I actually have something in common with a prince!" Laurel made her tone as cynical as possible. Who was she kidding? She had little in common with him and never would.

Tariq smiled. Her breath caught. Having it directed

at her made her feel special, all warm and gooey inside. "It sounds like we do."

This laid-back, easygoing aspect of his temperament she could learn to like.

"You know, I've been wondering about where I'm going to be living. Do I need to rent a car? Can I just walk to the lab?"

"You will be my wife. You will live on the palace grounds, in my apartments. All you have to do is ask for anything you need."

Live with him? At the palace? She hadn't thought this through. A palace wasn't where she belonged. She wouldn't fit in with royalty. She wasn't like them. "There's no other arrangements that can be made?"

"Not if you are my wife. There are plenty of rooms in my apartment. You will not be disturbed. Nasser or one of the other drivers will always be available to take you to and from the clinic."

"Am I going to need an escort for some reason?" Was there something going on she needed to know about?

"You do not." He almost sounded hurt. "Zentar is a very safe country. You are welcome to wear Western dress but be aware of the sun. It can often be very strong so you may want to consider a hat and sunglasses whenever you're out. Cover your fair skin in the middle of the day."

It gave her a peculiar feeling to have him note something as personal as her skin. As if she mattered to him. That wasn't possible.

He continued, "I think you will find that everything you might wish for will be at the lab, which will be fully under your direction. I've already hired six highly qualified employees. They have impeccable qualifications."

"Okay." She wanted to do research, not wrangle people, and she had no intention of starting to do that now.

"The lab is housed in the same building as our public clinic, which will be opened five days a week. You will find that it is extremely busy. Anyone who comes to the clinic with hemophilia will automatically be referred to the lab for testing." His voice took on a certain ring of excitement as he spoke. "The lab will also handle any special cases, like cancer." His phone buzzed and he frowned at the screen.

"I don't know if you have made any notations in your paperwork or talked to people who know me, but I'm not a manager. That's part of the reason I went into research. I don't give orders well."

He glanced at her. "That is hard to believe. You have had no difficulty making it clear to me what you like or dislike."

She leaned forward in her seat. "Even you have to admit this is an extraordinary situation. Or do you demand women marry you all the time?"

"I do not. You are the first. I think you will be fine in the lab." Tariq's attention went back to the phone.

"I don't want the responsibility of telling people what to do." That was an aspect of her personality that had always been a struggle.

"You should not have a problem. I have hired professionals who know their jobs. If you do have an issue, let me know."

"You can bet I will," Laurel murmured. "My research comes first."

His attention was on her now. "And I fully intend that it should be."

"Is there anything else you expect from me?"

Tariq studied her a moment too long, his eyes not wavering. Laurel shifted in her chair. Was Tariq thinking about what they were discussing or had his focus shifted to them being husband and wife? Once again she wished she could have a hint of his thoughts.

"No, I just expect you to do what you have been brought here to do and nothing more." He stood. "It's another seven hours before we land. Feel free to use the bath and bedroom. I'll have the steward wake you an hour before we arrive. There is a TV in the bedroom that you are free to watch. If you are interested in tracking our flight, turn to Channel Three. Now, if you will excuse me, I have a matter to handle." With that he walked to an office area toward the front of the plane.

Laurel hadn't felt at ease about this job arrangement or fake marriage from the beginning. Her recent discussion with Tariq hadn't improved her attitude. Unease filled her. *Tariq.* She had no business calling a prince by his first name alone. This entire situation was surreal.

Maybe a shower and a little reading would help settle her nerves. It had turned dark since she had fallen asleep earlier.

She found her small bag sitting beside the bathroom door. Apparently the steward had placed it there while they'd been having dinner. After a hot shower in the roomy bathroom she dressed and crossed the hallway to the bedroom.

After locking the door, she tested the bed like Goldilocks, sitting on it and giving a little bounce. It was as plush as the rest of the plane. Somehow it was unnerving to think of sleeping in Prince Tariq Al Marktum's bed. How many others had? That wasn't her business.

She needed rest if she planned to have her wits about her when they landed.

Curious about where she was in the world, she turned on the TV. Finding out that she was over the center of the ocean didn't reassure her and she quickly turned the TV to another channel. Finding little interest in any show, she turned it off and slipped under the covers. Where the Prince planned to sleep she had no idea.

Laurel ran her hand across the ultra-soft material. What would it be like to sleep in such luxury all the time? With Tariq? She shuddered. Where had that impossible thought come from?

She was jolted awake by a knock on the door and the steward announcing it was time for her to rise. Choosing a blue suit over a pale pink knit top, she quickly dressed, hoping she appeared confident and professional. Blue flats finished her outfit. She would need that self-confidence to face what was coming her way today. Laurel rubbed her hands along the front of her jacket. This wasn't what she'd dreamed of wearing to her wedding. But hers wouldn't be a real one so it really didn't matter.

She found Tariq already sitting at the dining table with a plate of eggs in front of him. The smell of strong coffee circulated in the air.

She stopped short.

He was no longer dressed in a Western business suit. Instead he wore a white robe. Over it was a long mint-green vest with a wide decorative braid running the length of the front opening. His beard had been meticulously trimmed under his neck and at the hollows of his cheeks, creating a thin chic fashionable look that only emphasized the ruggedness of his appearance. He was every bit the picture of a desert prince. A lightning bolt of awareness shot through her core.

Trying to ignore the sudden warmth in her nether regions, she managed, "Uh…good morning."

"Join me." The sound of his deep voice ran across her nerve endings like a bow over a violin string. As usual his request was more of a statement than an invitation. Her awareness of his virility was so acute, his simple demand had her hands trembling. She swiftly sat across from him, grabbed the napkin and twisted it in her lap. This surreal physical reaction to Tariq had to stop.

The steward came to stand beside them.

"What would you like for breakfast?" Tariq asked.

Laurel looked at the steward. "Toast and a cup of tea will be fine."

"I fear that you'll need more than that for today," Tariq commented as he continued to look at the papers spread out on the table. "Some eggs with that, please."

The steward nodded and stepped away.

"I don't know how you expect me to be intelligent enough to run your lab if you don't think I know my mind well enough to order what I want to eat."

He looked at her, a brow cocked, and nodded. "I apologize. It will not happen again."

"What? I actually get my way for once?" For the brief time she'd known Tariq every disagreement had gone his way. This tiny victory she planned to savor.

There was a twinkle of something in his eyes that looked suspiciously like mirth. "It would appear you have. I trust you slept well last night."

"I did." She smiled.

"Excellent." He moved a paper and picked up another beneath it. "I wanted to share today's schedule."

Laurel hadn't stepped off the plane and he'd already planned her day. Would he always be controlling her time? When was she supposed to do her research? Between his calendar and managing the lab, how was she supposed to get anything done?

"We will be arriving midmorning Zentar time. From the airport we will go straight to the palace. We will have a small ceremony there. A few of my family will attend. Afterwards we will visit the lab then we will return to the palace. I have a late afternoon meeting I must not miss."

Nothing like marrying and running. Didn't sound much different from what Larry had done to her. After all, he'd gotten what he'd wanted and gone on his way. The Prince was manipulating her as well. But in return she was getting something she sought too, the chance to continue her research. For that she would do anything.

"Laurel, are you listening to me?" Tariq sounded put out. From the look on his face he didn't make a practice of repeating himself.

She looked at him.

"After that your time is your own. Take it from an experienced traveler that you should rest. Jet lag is a real thing." He let the paper he'd been reading flutter to the table.

"I'll be fine, I'm sure." She'd had enough of him dictating to her. "I'll want to get to work at the lab as soon as possible."

As usual his eyes revealed nothing of his emotions. "That is your choice, but I fear you will pay dearly for that decision. You need not concern yourself with being there before the day after tomorrow."

"I'll be there first thing in the morning. I was close to

a breakthrough in my research and I want to get started again as soon as possible."

"As you wish." He went back to his papers.

Her breakfast arrived. While she ate, Tariq continued reading. Occasionally he would make a note on one of the papers or look at his phone. When she put her fork down for the final time, his gaze met hers. She cheeks went warm. Despite not wanting much food, she'd cleaned her plate. The fact Tariq had been right about her appetite irritated her.

He stood. "Come and have your first look at Zentar." He indicated the window she had looked out the night before.

Curious about the place she would be calling home for the next few weeks, for that was all she planned to stay, she went to the seat she'd occupied the evening before. Gripping the armrest, she slowly leaned toward the window.

"I see you have not overcome your fear." To her astonishment there was a note of sympathy in his observation.

"No, I haven't. I doubt I ever will." About many things. However, making this trip was a huge step toward doing so. She couldn't deny the pride forming in her chest for having found the courage to come to Zentar.

"I promise you will be glad you looked if you only will." His beautiful voice seductively coaxed her.

Fortifying herself, Laurel rested her head against the side of the plane. Below she could see the sapphire Arabian Sea.

"See that small white dot in the distance? That is Zentar."

Laurel jumped and glanced around to find Tariq's head close. Too close. Her lips were an inch from his face. His citrus aftershave filled her nose. He had a hand braced against the bulkhead, leaning over her, as they looked out the same window.

Laurel wasn't sure which made her dizzier—Tariq's nearness or the sensation of the plane skimming over the water toward the small crystal jewel ahead. Tariq remained where he was, his breath ruffling her hair. Yes, he was much too close.

"You must learn not to flinch every time I am near or when I touch you. My people will think you do not like me. That will not do."

What *his* people didn't know was that she reacted too much to their Prince for her comfort. "Maybe you should leave some distance between us so they'll not notice."

"I am not sure that will be possible." Had his lips touched the top of her head?

Laurel forced herself to focus on the sight outside the window. Zentar grew larger, turning into a pallet of off-white with spots of green here and there. The plane banked to the right. Laurel hissed and grasped the seat with both hands.

Tarik laid a gentle hand on her shoulder. "It's okay. We're just lining up for our approach."

His soothing voice and touch reassured her. "I bet the pilot thought that was a lot more fun than I did."

Laughter deep and full rolled from his throat. "I will remind him next time not to be quite so dramatic with his banking when you are on board."

Again she looked out the window, fascinated by the land below. Now she could make out buildings. Some were a pale pink while others were yellow and blue. High on a rise off to the north was a sparkling mass of buildings that overlooked the others.

"That is the palace off on the horizon. It is beautiful, is it not?"

It was. That they could agree on. How would it feel to have a man like Tariq speak about her with such pride and love? Squelching that unacceptable idea, she heard a distinctive ding ring throughout the cabin.

Tariq moved to take the seat across from her. "It is time to prepare for landing. You need to buckle up."

Laurel shivered as she settled into her seat. It was suddenly cool in the cabin without Tariq so near. Fumbling a moment, she finally secured her belt.

The plane started its descent and she clasped her hands in her lap, closed her eyes and pushed her head back into the chair. She didn't like the landing any better than she had the take-off.

"It is painful to watch you. You must stop. I want to wrap you in my arms and hold you."

Her eyelids whipped open. The Prince's intense stare held her captive.

"That is better." His words were gentle and encouraging, easing her anxiety. "At least I shocked you out of the misery you were in."

He had only said that to help her? Why did that disappoint her? In a tight voice Laurel said, "Please don't make fun of me."

"I would never do that. I believe you are very brave, to leave all you know and for your first trip to be one halfway around the world when you have experienced so little of it."

She'd never thought of herself as brave. It was rather a heady experience to hear Prince Tariq say she was. As a child she had always been afraid. She'd accepted early in her life that her only way of coping with being the butt of her classmates' cruelty was to hide in her books. The only time she'd felt accomplished had been when she'd made good grades. Which in turn had added something more for her peers to use against her.

In college she hadn't faired any better. After Larry had dumped her she'd overheard a couple of his buddies laughing about the "brainiac" Larry had laid to win a bet. Instead of facing them and telling them she was a person with feelings, she'd slipped away. They never knew she'd been there. She'd vowed not to trust a man again. Now here she was with her entire world dependent on one she didn't really know or trust. This time she would guard her heart more closely.

Even after becoming a licensed physician she hadn't had the strength to venture further than two hours away from where she'd grown up. It had been a major event to move to Chicago by herself and she'd only managed it because of her burning desire to continue her search for a cure for hemophilia. She'd attended only those medical conferences that were close to home. Even though she'd made the flight to Zentar she wasn't so sure it had as much to do with courage as it did with how badly she wished to have access to a lab. Her research was what drove her. Aware she had a number of admirable traits, bravery wasn't one of them.

Seconds later the tires touching the tarmac with a screech of brakes made her tense again. Tariq placed a hand over hers. His look held hers as heat shot through her.

Soon the plane was rolling slowly and smoothly to a stop. She was safe on the ground. Tariq removed his hand. Laurel watched him nonchalantly release his seat belt and stand. Without a word he walked toward the back of the plane.

Through the window Laurel observed the heat haze just above the tarmac and the low tan-colored building that was the airport terminal. It looked simple yet modern. A flag flew above it that held the same emblem adorning the seats of the plane. Beyond the airport were buildings after buildings. None were over two stories high. In the distance stood the sprawling, gleaming pearl—the palace. The place she would call home, at least temporarily. She was out of her league. Fitting in here would be harder than it had been when she'd been a child.

The whoosh of air when the steward opened the door brought her back to the present. She hurriedly unlatched her seat belt.

Tariq reappeared. He'd placed a white headdress with gold braid on his head, and it flowed around his shoulders.

Laurel stared. As striking as he was in Western wear, this island Prince's attire made him more appealing.

"I am expected to look the part of the royal family when I arrive home after official trips. It is the King's way of reminding the people that we honor our traditions. As Minister of Health I have a position to uphold."

Why did he feel he must explain his choice of clothing to her? In the last few days he hadn't seemed to take any notice of her feelings or concerns. When did what she thought of him start to matter?

"I understand. I just didn't expect..." She shut her mouth and waved at him in frustration. Laurel wasn't about to tell Tariq she hadn't planned on him taking her breath away with his Arabian Nights good looks, charm and impressive lifestyle.

"Expect?" He watched her too keenly for comfort.

"I, uh…don't know. I guess I just assumed you always wore Western clothes."

"Most of the time I do, but the reporters will be here. I must look the part."

"I get that." For him this attire was like when she'd pulled on her lab coat to meet him. It was the uniform that specified status.

He stepped near and took her elbow. "It is time to go. We have a schedule to keep."

She was too aware of that. Getting married to him was at the top of the list. The mere idea made her middle flutter like a flock of birds taking off. Laurel suddenly wished she hadn't eaten so much breakfast.

Tariq's hand remained on her elbow as they walked down the stairs that had been precisely placed at the open cabin door. The Prince greeted the group of people waiting at the bottom with a wave.

Laurel had never dreamed the press would be interested in her. She was so out of her element. A couple of cameras flashed. She closed her eyes and turned her head.

Tariq raised a hand and everyone quieted. "This is Dr. Laurel Martin. She will be heading our new research lab as well as becoming my wife. We will be having a small family ceremony this afternoon at the palace. A celebration will be planned for a later date."

The crowd gasped. Cameras flashed.

He didn't let that deter him. "Please be kind enough to give her a warm Zentaran welcome. Also hold all questions for later. We've had a long flight and have much to do today."

Laurel had never identified more with Dorothy arriving in Oz than she did at that moment. What had she gotten herself into?

CHAPTER THREE

Tariq escorted Laurel to the limousine waiting nearby. He had had to nudge her arm twice before she moved. Her body trembled. She was terrified. In hindsight he should have told her about the press. When he had seen how much she hated flying he had worried she would not get off once they landed if she knew the media would be there to greet them.

Had he made a mistake by bringing her so far from home? Insisting that she marry him? One was stressful enough but both might be too much for Laurel. Never in his wildest imaginings had he believed a woman of her intelligence and reputation would be such a novice where the world was concerned. Yet it was refreshing to see each new experience replace her fear with excited amazement. It made him see life in a different light.

Pride swelled his chest at her reaction to her first sight of Zentar. Her appreciation of its beauty was the same as his own each time he returned home. Sharing it with someone was nice. He never had before.

With Laurel settled in the backseat of the car, he instructed Nasser to take them to the palace. Normally he would be busy on his phone but Laurel enthralled him. He turned to her. Seeing her fascination with the city he loved had become more important than some email about an issue he needed to resolve.

She was busy looking out the windows of the car from one side to the other, as if trying to take it all in on one drive. He had no idea if she was aware of his presence until she said in reproach, "You should've told me that the press would be waiting, instead of ambushing me."

"I was afraid you would not get off the plane."

Laurel looked over her shoulder at him. "And that statement about us marrying?"

He shrugged. "It must be announced." He leaned back into the cushions of the seat, enjoying the snap in her eyes. At least they were not panic-filled, as they had been earlier.

She turned to him. "I guess that's true. Are you still sure it's necessary?"

"Marrying? Yes."

Laurel resumed watching the scenery but the air around them now held tension. They said little the rest of the way. He had anticipated her reaction to the onion-domed palace but it was more flattering than he'd expected.

They were pulling in front of the palace when Laurel said with a whispered awe, "You've lived here all your life?"

Again wonder filled her face. He had looked at the palace almost every day of his life but thanks to her he was seeing it anew—its white walls, arched entrances, high battlements with shiny tops and flags flying—the grand scale of it. "Well, most of it. I lived abroad when I was at university and a few years after that."

"I can't imagine growing up in a place like this. My

family had a three-bedroom, two-bath home. My sister and I shared a room until I went off to college."

They really were from two different worlds. He had learned long ago that was the case with almost everyone when you were a prince. He rather liked the sound of the low-key quality of Laurel's life. "The size of a house has nothing to do with the closeness of a family."

The car pulled up in front of the arched doors of the official entrance to the palace.

"I'll get the door," he said to Nasser as he stepped out and offered his hand to Laurel. She hesitated a moment, then placed her soft, small, shaking fingers in his. The inescapable comparison to their hand sizes had a peculiar effect on him. There was such a marked difference between them in so many ways.

Laurel quickly pulled her hand away and raised her chin to look at the massive ornamental exteriors of the palace state rooms. "We're getting married here?"

"Yes."

She gave him a worried look. "In an office?"

"No. The Grand State Room."

"This isn't right," she hissed, looking around as if she feared someone was listening.

"I am a member of the royal family, and we do not have a lot of time. So it is the way it must be done."

Her lips pursed before she burst forth with, "You know I've just about had it with you pushing me around about everything. We have no business getting married." She pointed to the palace. "Much less doing it here and in front of your family."

"Laurel…" Tariq lowered his voice to the one he used when trying to reassure a skittish filly. "I think you are right."

She stared at him as if confused. "You do?"

"Yes, but plans have been set in motion that cannot be changed. Come, it will be over soon and then we will go to your lab." He took her hand and rubbed his thumb over the top. If he was in her position he would not like feeling out of control either.

"I still think this is a bad idea but I'll go along with it for now."

He smiled. "I am glad to hear it."

Tariq placed his hand at her waist and directed her toward the entrance. As they approached, a man in a uniform opened the door and they entered the dim and refreshingly cool stone building.

"Oh, wow." Laurel's whisper carried across the worn marble floor. "It's so beautiful."

Zara, with Roji in hand, came toward them and drew Laurel's attention. Her body stiffened beneath his palm. "This is Zara. She is my sister-in-law and is here to help you dress."

"Dress?" Laurel looked down at herself. "I hadn't even thought about that."

Tariq was not surprised. Her mind remained on one track, her work. As important as he believed it was, she still needed to step outside her glass box. It also pricked his ego that Laurel thought so little of their marriage she had no concern for what she wore. Did not all women want to look nice at their wedding? Even if it was a marriage of convenience?

At that moment Roji broke away from Zara and ran to him. Going down on his knee, Tariq met the five-year-old with open arms.

"Uncle Tariq, I rode my horse today."

Tariq lifted the boy, who had already lost so much in his short life, into his arms. "You did?"

Roji nodded. "He leaned over the fence and touched me here." Roji placed his hand on top of his head.

"He did? It must have thought you were something good to eat." Tariq tickled Roji's stomach, earning a giggle.

Tariq glanced at Laurel, who watched him intently. Seconds later Zara joined them. "Roji, leave your uncle alone. He is busy."

"Zara, he was just telling me about his day."

"You spoil him, Tariq. We take up too much of your time."

"You and Roji are family and family always comes first." Tariq meant that. He put Roji on his feet then said, "I wish you to meet Dr. Laurel Martin."

Zara extend a hand and Laurel offered hers. "It is a pleasure. I am glad Tariq has found someone to love." The women released hands. Zara looked at him. "Even though he kept you a secret."

Laurel's gaze met his. He gave her a reassuring smile. "Go with Zara. I must speak to someone and I will see you again in a few minutes." He feared Laurel would balk but instead she went with Zara, who held Roji's hand.

Laurel looked around her without truly seeing. It was far too overwhelming to take it all in. The beauty of the place, the vastness and the fact she would be married to Tariq in only minutes. She'd always been so practical until Tariq had entered her world and now she walked around in a daze as if she no longer understood her own mind. Here she was following some beautiful woman to put on clothes she'd never seen. Life had become surreal in a blink of an eye.

Zara pushed open the thick wooden door and entered. She motioned for Laurel to follow. "This is the royal lounge of the palace. We use it for these types of occasions and meeting dignitaries of state."

The room had a high ceiling with whitewashed walls and a large stained-glass window. The light from the outside reflected colors off the wall, reminding Laurel of a kaleidoscope.

Zara didn't add any confidence to her feeling of inadequacy. The tall, dark, willowy woman dressed in a perfectly tailored dress that flowed around her legs made Laurel feel self-conscious of how little attention she'd paid to her appearance in the last few years. Laurel admired Zara's English, which was as flawless as Tariq's. He and his sister-in-law shared a similar accent but Zara's wasn't near as sexy as Tariq's. Having no Arabic in her vocabulary, Laurel felt at a disadvantage.

"These women are here to help me dress you." Zara indicated the women standing at attention near a tall mirror. "Roji, I need you to play nicely. I brought you cars. They are in a bag over there." She pointed across the room. The boy eagerly headed after them.

Laurel had watched the sweet moment between Tariq and Roji with a smile on her lips. The boy obviously adored his uncle and Tariq returned the admiration. How wrong she had been in her first impression of the lordly Prince. The more she learned about him, the more she found to appreciate. She had no doubt he would be a doting father. Her stomach took a dip. Why would she be having a thought like that? About him?

In an effort to gain some control in the situation Laurel said, "Princess, I don't need help dressing."

"Please, call me Zara. And I think you will be surprised." She waved at the women and they moved behind a nearby screen.

Laurel nodded, sure that she wouldn't be seeing Zara often enough to ever be on that friendly of terms.

One of the women returned with a long gown draped across her arm. It was made of a wispy fine cream fabric embroidered in tiny gold flowers. The other carried a matching headpiece.

Laurel's breath caught. It was the most stunning piece of clothing she had ever seen, even in pictures.

Zara moved beside her. "It is beautiful, is it not? It was Tariq's mother's and hers before her. He wishes you to wear it."

Tears filled Laurel's eyes. If the guilt wasn't heavy enough where her family was concerned, it was compounded now. After all, she and Tariq were frauds. They had his family believing this was real. It was wrong. Laurel shook her head. "I can't wear that."

Zara ignored Laurel's words and took her hand. "Tariq waits. You must meet him in something besides what you have on. We will see how it fits."

Over the next few minutes Laurel did little more than stand there as Zara and the women fussed over her, removing her clothes and replacing them with the elegant traditional costume. With great reverence Zara placed the headdress on Laurel. It covered most of her forehead, and the veil landed at her elbows.

Zara stepped back and studied her. "Perfect."

The two women smiled and nodded in agreement.

"Now, come and see." Zara led Laurel out to the mirror. She turned her around.

Laurel couldn't believe the woman looking back at her was her. Where had that plain person gone? Laurel's shoulders straightened. She not only looked beautiful but for the first time in a long time she felt it as well.

Zara gave her a light squeeze. "Tariq will see it too."

Laurel wasn't sure what that cryptic statement meant but she didn't have time to ask before Zara announced, "It is time." She hustled Laurel out of the room and back the way they had come. "I will walk with you to the door then I will leave you to meet Tariq by yourself."

Laurel almost grabbed her hand and begged Zara not to abandon her. But how would that look for a bride to not want to meet her groom?

As they walked Zara whispered, "You are marrying a great man with a large heart. He has taken care of Roji and me since my husband, Rasheed, died. It was hard on Tariq as well, as they were the best of friends. Maybe now that you are in his life he will move on, not carry the pain so heavily. Not fear the disease will take all he loves."

Laurel glanced at her. "Disease?"

"My husband had the bleeding disease. He was in a car accident and they did not find him in time. Now enough of the sad talk. It is a happy day. I leave you now to go to Tariq."

Laurel stopped as Zara hurried to the front of the room where seats were set in rows. When Laurel no longer heard the clip of her shoes she forced herself to take a step forward. Tariq stood tall and strong ahead of her, looking so sure while she was a puddle of insecurity. He'd exchanged his headdress for a gold one. His gaze captured hers as he extend a hand. On shaking legs and with trembling hands, she walked toward her make-believe groom.

Not soon enough for Laurel, the ceremony was almost over. She wasn't sure she could have remained standing if it hadn't been for Tariq holding her securely to him. For that she was grateful. Finally, the moment she hadn't let herself think about arrived. Tariq turned her to face him. His gaze meet hers, held, then questioned. With an expression so serious it was as if he had made a decision of state, his mouth slowly found hers.

She assumed it would be a peck just for show, and it was at first. Yet with exquisite gentleness their kiss turned into a joining that sent warmth cascading throughout her body to leave a throb of desire deep within her. She returned it. Too soon, Tariq pulled away. Laurel's eyes rose to meet his. Satisfaction that reminded her too closely of Larry's look when he'd climbed out of bed and announced he was done with her filled Tariq's eyes. He had been testing her?

As they ended the ceremony, she said, "May I see the lab now?"

His lips thinned as his jaw hardened. Had she hurt his feelings? How? They had agreed this was in name only.

"As soon as I introduce you to my family and change. You look lovely, by the way." But the words seemed stiff, as if he was forcing himself to say them.

It stung. What would it feel like to have a man like Tariq actually believe she was pretty? "Thank you. The gown is beautiful. I hope I didn't shame it by wearing it for this type of marriage."

"Enough of that talk. We must meet my family."

Tariq led her to the small group of people assembled a few steps away.

Zara gave Laurel a quick kiss on the cheek.

"Your Majesty." Tariq bowed his head before both men stepped into a hug, slapping each other on the back. Was this the same serious Tariq who'd had such a fortress around him just moments ago? She was having a difficult time meshing the two.

Tariq stepped back and gave the King an appraising look. "It is good to see you, brother."

"Now you have made me rude. Who is this lovely woman you woke me to tell me you were marrying?"

The King wore a warm, welcoming smile. With his hand extended, he came forward to greet her. "Dr. Martin, or should I be the first to say, as you might in your country, Mrs. Tariq Al Marktum, we are glad to have you in Zentar and a part of our family. How like Tariq to bring home a bride without telling anyone." He gave Tariq a stern look that would have weakened a lesser man. "I have heard much about you from Tariq before he left. He was excited at the thought of meeting you," the King added with a winsome grin.

He had been? What had Tariq told him about her? That she had refused to come at first? That she had lost her funding? Had he confided that the marriage was a sham? That she only wanted to do research, not be a member of the royal family. She managed to squeak, "He was?"

"Yes," the King continued, "he speaks very highly of you and your skills in the medical field. As usual he failed to mention he had fallen in love with you as well."

"That was a surprise to us too." Laurel managed to make that sound sincere.

"This is my wife, Loulisa." A pretty but shy woman with streaks of gray in her hair stepped forward.

"It is nice to meet you," Loulisa said. "Those…" she

pointed in the direction where Roji was playing with an older boy and girl "…are our children. They had a day away from lessons so they are very excited to have you here."

Laurel smiled. "I'm glad I could help them out."

A cry of anguish echoed through the pillars of the spacious room. All looks flew to where Roji lay on the floor.

Seconds later Zara rushed in his direction, quickly followed by Tariq.

"What has happened?" Laurel asked, joining them. Zara held Roji in her arms.

"He slipped and hit his head. He is bleeding!" Zara sobbed, barely getting the words out.

Why such a reaction over a simple fall? Laurel looked at Tariq, who was pulling a length of cloth off his waist and going down in a squat beside them. Seconds later he applied the cloth to the gash. He appeared equally concerned.

Tariq spoke to Zara as he swiftly picked up his nephew. "I will call Nasser. Have him meet us at the side door with the car."

Zara rose with the King's help and took a seat in a chair. Tariq placed the boy in her lap.

Laurel stepped forward. "Easy, Roji. Be a brave boy and let me have a look. I'm a doctor."

With a loud snort, Roji collected himself and wiped his tears. To Tariq she said, "Let me see the injury."

"He has hemophilia. There is some emergency factor in my purse." Zara pointed to the chair where she had sat earlier. One of the older children went to fetch it.

Laurel looked at Tariq, who still held the cloth to Roji's head. His face was as still as stone. "He'll be fine," she assured Zara. To Roji she asked, "May I touch you for a minute? It may tickle."

The boy sniffled, but nodded his agreement.

Laurel gently ran her hands over the boy's head, checking for any pooling of blood. "Where does it hurt?" Roji placed a finger on his head.

"Anywhere else?"

The boy put his hand on his shoulder. Zara removed his shirt enough for Laurel to see the bruise that had already formed.

She first lifted one eyelid and then the other. "His eyes aren't dilated. Which is good."

"Yes, I know," Tariq said impatiently. "I have a medical degree as well."

Her eyes flashed with surprise. "You never said so."

He gave her a piercing look. "There are many things I do not say."

The King's son returned with Zara's bag. She fished in it and pulled out the container with the factor and items needed to give it with a shaking hand. "I do not think I am able to give it."

Tariq went down on one knee.

"Uncle Tariq, make it not hurt." Roji's tear-filled eyes were begging him.

He ruffled the boy's hair. "I plan to, but I have to admit I am out of practice."

"May I?" Laurel placed her hand on Tariq's shoulder with complete confidence. This was her area of expertise. He looked at her. "I do this every day." She smiled at Roji. "Will you trust me not to hurt you?"

Roji nodded but his grip on his mother's hand tightened a bit.

With quick efficacy Laurel pulled out rubber gloves

from the container and looked for a good vein in Roji's arm. "This is going to be a little uncomfortable but it shouldn't last too long." She located the rubber band as well and tied it around the boy's arm so that his veins rose. "So, do you have a dog at home?"

"Yes."

"What is his name?" As she asked she placed the tiny butterfly needle in his most prominent vein.

"Czar."

A few minutes later Laurel had the factor in his blood system.

Zara grabbed her hand. "Thank you, Laurel."

She gave them a wry smile. "I'm glad I could help. He still should be seen at the hospital."

"He will be. Nasser is just outside." Tariq picked up Roji. "I will go with him. I do not want the media alerted."

Laurel didn't understand why he was being so secretive about the boy. After all, his illness wasn't something he should be ashamed of.

Zara soft words carried. "You have a wife to worry about now."

Tariq glanced back at Laurel as if he had forgotten about her. "Meet me at the hospital. The car will return for you." With that his strides lengthened as he left the room.

Laurel excused herself from the King and the rest of the family so she could change. The two women whisked the gown off her and led her to the door through which Tariq had exited, where Laurel waited by herself for the return of the car. Her worst fear had come true. She was in a strange country alone. Thankfully the car soon arrived and fifteen minutes later Nasser escorted her into a hospital.

A woman behind a desk said something Laurel couldn't understand as they passed. Nasser nodded and continued down the hallway. A few doors down, he stopped. "The Prince is here."

"Thank you, Nasser." She gave him a weak smile as she walked past him. Inside the room she found Tariq, leaning over Roji's bed. The boy must have been sedated because he was so still. Zara sat in one of the chairs, looking concerned, with her hands clasped so tightly the knuckles were white. The part of Laurel that had made her go into medicine took over and she went to the bed. "What can I do to help?"

Tariq looked up. "I did not hear you enter. His BP is up. I am concerned there is bleeding we cannot see."

"You have ordered tests?"

"A full blood panel, X-rays of his abdomen and joints. A CT scan of the head. The preliminary results show nothing meaningful but my gut tells me I am missing something."

More than once that feeling had led her as well. The only time it had failed her had been where Larry was concerned. Then she had gotten nothing. "Has a second dose of factor been administered?"

"Yes. As soon as we got here."

She lifted the bandage off the boy's head. "The blood flow has slowed so the factor must be working." Laurel walked to the other side of the bed so that she stood facing Tariq. "Have you done a thorough hands-on exam yet?"

"No. I was just getting ready to do that." He placed his hands on Roji's head.

"I'll start with his feet and work up." Laurel lift a leg.

Tariq's fingers were running over Roji's neck when he said, "Laurel, see if you feel the same thing I do."

She placed her fingers over the spot behind Roji's neck that Tariq indicated. There was some swelling but the most telling information was the heat coming from the area. "It's hot."

"That's what I thought as well."

"What's wrong?" Zara came up behind Tariq.

"All is well, but we need you to go and get a nurse." Tariq voice held that no-argument tone. Roji's mother rushed out again.

Laurel looked at Tariq's concerned face. "He must have hit here first then rolled forward and hit his head."

A nurse hurried in and right behind her was Zara.

Tariq didn't waste any time, demanding, "We need a dose of rapid-clotting concentrate, stat. Also, order another to be here ready in case it is needed. Order another CT, for the back of Roji's neck this time."

"Yes, Your Highness."

Laurel looked at him. "Good catch."

He nodded.

The nurse soon returned with an IV set-up.

"I'll take that." Laurel put out her hand, palm up.

The nurse glanced at Tariq and he nodded. She handed it to Laurel, who went to work placing a cannula in Roji's arm. As soon as she had it in a vein she said to Tariq, "You can start pushing that now."

He lost no time doing so. Before he had finished, a staff member with a portable X-ray machine arrived. After he left, Roji was moved to a hospital room. Tariq sent Zara home for clothes because Roji would be spending the night in the hospital.

Tariq remained beside Roji's bed, taking his blood pressure every fifteen minutes.

"It has stabilized." He put the cuff back on the rack.

"That's good news," Laurel said, going to the side of the bed.

Tariq looked at her. "I am sorry our ceremony ended like this."

"I am not surprised. Our relationship has been a rather interesting one so far."

His smile flashed, the sincere one. "On that we can agree. Now, to keep my promise. As soon as Zara returns we will visit the lab. Soon my country will learn about the remarkable woman I have married."

Laurel couldn't ignore the pleasure that flowered within her at his words.

CHAPTER FOUR

TARIQ TURNED SO that his back was in the corner of the car seat to better watch Laurel as they rode through the streets of Zentar. She had looked beautiful in his mother's gown, and so fragile as she'd come to him. So much so, his chest had ached. Her hand had been shaking as he'd taken it and he'd pulled her close to support her, something he'd been surprised he'd wanted to do.

He had seen to it that they'd had an official who spoke English well to perform the ceremony. Laurel had made it clear she felt manipulated. He did not want that during the ceremony. Her words had been spoken softly. He'd had to concentrate to hear them, which had centered him.

When it had been time to kiss her he had intended to give her a perfunctory one, but the second his lips had touched hers it had changed. Just the initial timid hint of her soft lips against his had made him want more. Tariq had not missed her sigh, or the way her body had been drawn to his. Her fingers had flexed on his forearms. She had been as stirred as he.

At first he had been shocked that she had returned his kiss, then he had become aroused. The kiss had deepened and he'd had to remind himself where they were. He had received a number of reactions to his kisses but never one that had disturbed him like Laurel's. She had placed some spell on him. Afterwards her eyes had been bright and shining.

He could have lived in that moment forever but she'd blinked then asked about the lab. Other women's responses had reassured him he was more than an able lover so why had Laurel acted as if it was no big deal to receive his attention? His ego did not appreciate it. Anger had flashed through him that had soon turned to hurt.

Now he was just confounded. For a moment there he had believed Laurel might be interested in making theirs a real marriage. Instead she had questioned him about her work. Maybe he had misread her and all she wanted was to keep their relationship professional. Well, at least he was going to see that she saw her precious lab. Hopefully someday soon he would have a chance to kiss her again and she would admit to her desire.

At this moment he would concentrate on their business relationship. "When did you become interested in hemophilia?"

She did not look his way. He was not sure if it was because she was interested in the sights outside or because she could not meet his eyes. "I cared for a middle-schooler who was a hemophiliac. His case fascinated me. I'd never known anyone with the disease before that. The boy wasn't an easy patient. It was summer break and he wished he was anywhere but in the hospital."

Tariq loved the enthusiasm in her voice. She was passionate about what she did and why. It was just another confirmation that she was the right person for his lab. Where passion existed in one area of her life, surely it did in others too. He needed her to be passionate about her work, nothing more.

"I started asking the attending doctor questions about the boy's care. He told me if I was that curious I should consider research and that he had a friend who ran a lab in Chicago. So when I finished my residency I contacted him."

"You were impressive with your IV placement ability. It would not have been a pleasant experience for either Roji or me if I had done it."

She gave him a small smile. "Don't tell him I got all my practice on mice."

He chuckled. That drew an odd look from Laurel so he explained. "For a small boy that might be an exciting thought."

A smile formed on her lips. It changed her entire face, showing him a hint of the beauty he had seen the moment he'd looked up to observe her dressed in his family heirloom gown and coming to join him. She mysteriously peaked his interest. Quiet, blend-into-the-crowd women had never been his thing. In fact, far too often the King had hauled him on the carpet because Tariq had been in the tabloids with some flashy woman. Laurel was the type of person who had always been his girlfriend's assistant. Not seen or heard.

"Why didn't you tell me you were a doctor? It seems to me you might lead with that information if you were trying to convince another doctor to work with you," she said.

"I was meeting you as the Minister of Health." He liked it when her ire was up. At least she was not dismissing him, like she had earlier.

"Where did you do your training?"

"I studied at Harvard."

Her eyes widened. "One of the best in the country."

"Yes, but now I do more administrative and public appearance work than practice medicine." He wished it was the other way around.

"I'm sure what you do administratively is very important."

He surveyed her. Her fingers were long and narrow with fingernails neatly trimmed, which would be necessary in her profession. Then he added, "But I do miss caring for people. When I get the clinic and lab open and running, I plan to put in some time actually working there." Part of his push to help was for selfish reasons. The research would benefit his family.

"The other day you didn't strike me as being a particularly humble man."

He gave her a narrow-eyed look. No one, other than the King, had dared speak that freely to him since he'd been at school. Her shocked look and pink cheeks made him chuckle. He laughed more often since she had arrived.

"I'm so sorry. Sometimes things just come out of my mouth without me thinking. The downside of working in a lab all day by myself."

"Apology accepted." Had he come on so strongly she had been intimidated by him? Maybe he had. He'd been so focused on getting the best person to lead his clinic it had never occurred to him that Laurel might not want the job. After all, she had not been looking for the position. He had just assumed she would never refuse his offer since she had no other funding. Then he had made it worse by insisting she marry him.

A few minutes later he escorted her through the automatic sliding doors into the coolness of the building. Pride flowed anew through him. It was like being a new parent, showing off his baby for the first time to somebody he wished to impress.

"To the left is the clinic. There is an additional entrance on that side where the majority of the patients enter. This section…" he pointed to the hallway running down the center of the building "…is the administrative offices. You will have an office there. This way to the lab."

They stopped before a solid door on the right side of the building. Tariq pulled a plastic card out of his pocket and swiped it. The door clicked open. He allowed Laurel to enter ahead of him then led her down a short hall to a glass door. There he put his forefinger on a reader, then swiped his card again.

Tariq's attention returned to her lab. A far more comfortable subject. "There is three-step entrance security to your lab. To get into it will require a retinal scan. The security is state of the art. A guard also patrols twenty-four hours a day. You will be issued a card tomorrow." The door slid sideways.

"Impressive." She sounded as if she meant it. There was far more enthusiasm in her tone than there had been when they had been reciting wedding vows.

His chest swelled a little larger. "Your lab is this way."

The door closed behind them. They walked down a hall with glass-walled rooms on either side.

"Those working with you will report tomorrow. I wanted them to start under your leadership, not mine."

Laurel gave him a long inscrutable look.

He returned it. "Is there a problem?"

"No. Just thinking that was considerate of you."

From her tone he was confident that was not what she had been thinking. "I hope I am most of the time."

She huffed.

"What is that supposed to mean?"

"I doubt that's true." She observed each room they passed.

"You may be right. My job doesn't often afford me that pleasure." He stopped in front of a door to a lab twice the size of the others. "This is yours." He put his eye next to the retina scanner. The door opened with a swoosh. They stepped into the outer chamber. He was in the process of removing sterile covering when Laurel stopped him.

"Don't do that. I'll go inside tomorrow."

Tariq nodded. "Here you will have to use your card again to enter. Once you are inside no one can enter without you allowing them in. The system will recognize that there are two people coming in at the same time and will not allow that unless you unlock it with a code. This is to be changed daily by you."

Her attention was less on what he was saying and more on the room in front of her. In fact, she had gone off into her own world and seemed to have completely forgotten he was there. That bothered him, but it was still fascinating to see her in her element. He could imagine the excitement that bubbled in her. Never had he been so alert to a woman's emotions. Laurel definitely had a curious effect on him.

"This is amazing. It lacks for nothing. You even have a couple of machines that are considered the latest diagnostic equipment."

"Did I not promise you state of the art?"

She placed her hand on the window. "Yes, but I've been made promises before."

And had been disappointed, Tariq assumed, based on the manner in which she made that statement. How would she react when she learned it had been him who'd stalled her chances of funding in the States?

"There's even a whiteboard to write on. For some reason, I had to fight to get one of those at the university." Amazement and pleasure flowed in her words.

Tariq smiled. The simplest things pleased her. "My planners and I tried to think of everything."

She turned. "All seems in order. I look forward to starting my work. I have a box of books and things that need to be brought here from the palace."

"I'll see that Nasser takes care of it tomorrow. Now I think it is time you get some rest. You have had a tiring day."

He checked his watch. "We must go. I have a meeting at the palace."

While they were retracing their steps to the front of the building Laurel asked, "When were you going to tell me about Roji and your brother having hemophilia?"

"I thought it would come out. Zara told you about Rasheed, did she not?"

"She did. But why not mention it earlier? Didn't you think it would be of interest to me?"

He looked at her. "That is the problem. Too many people are interested."

"The media?"

"Yes. Some things even royalty has the right to privacy about."

"But you have built a lab to help find a cure. You brought me here. Don't you think the media might help shine a light on the issue of living with hemophilia? And that I could keep the information about your family confidential? Your words and actions are contradictory."

"I do not mean them to be. Some people react negatively to my family's disease." A couple of times Tariq had shared with close friends about his family. They had acted as if they were contagious. Even some of his past relationships with women had died because he had stated he never wanted children because of the medical issues in his family.

"And you thought I would?"

He did not like being forced to explain himself. "Truthfully, old habits die hard and I did not want it to look like I was hiring you to come to Zentar just to aid my family. There are too many others in my country who will benefit from your work. I want the focus to be on them. Start with them."

Laurel walked through the door opening into the lobby. "Okay, I can sort of understand that line of thinking. By the way, I was sorry to hear about your brother. That must have been difficult."

"Very." Rasheed had been the middle son and Tariq's closest friend. Their oldest brother had been busy with duties as the successor to the crown and later as the King. Free of that hereditary load, he and Rasheed had had a chance at a more casual life and had made the most of it. Tariq missed him daily.

"Do others in the family have hemophilia?"

"The King and his son."

She stared at him. "And you have it as well." Her words were a thoughtful statement, not a question.

He wanted this conversation to go away yet he was left no choice but to answer. "No. I'm the only male in the family who does not. Apparently my father's genes were more involved in my creation than my mother's."

She pursed her lips and nodded thoughtfully. "Your family is an interesting case. I've never had an opportunity to study an entire family. I must study yours while I'm in Zentar."

His jaw tightened. By the look on Laurel's face he had no chance of talking her out of it.

"Is there a problem? All that would be involved is some blood work and a few minutes of conversation."

"My family has many obligations."

"Surely they aren't so busy they wouldn't want to help discover a cure. You make it sound as if finding a therapy for hemophilia is important to you yet you barely let me in on your family secret. It doesn't make sense. What are you afraid of?"

"Nothing. I just cannot speak for other members of my family."

She threw him an irritated look. "Really? After you brought me here to do research on the disorder?"

"It is not something that we discuss outside our family."

Was he serious? "I guess, based on our show today, I'm family now. So I'd be the perfect person for them to discuss it with. I don't understand you stonewalling me on this. It seems to me that looking at your family history would be a logical place to begin my study."

He raised his chin. "The royal family must not show weakness."

Her mouth dropped in disbelief. "Would the people of your country really see the royal family as doing that? There shouldn't be a stigma around hemophilia in this day and age."

"Some do. I am working to change that attitude."

"As you should. No one has to know I am studying the family. I could start with you."

"But, as I told you, I don't have hemophilia."

Laurel's eyes narrowed as she considered him a moment. "Could the reason you're putting up this resistance have something to do with you feeling guilty about not having the disease?"

A pain as if a vice squeezed his chest made him come to an abrupt halt. She saw that.

"I'm sorry." She stepped up to him, laying a hand on his arm.

Tariq looked away and bit out, "There is nothing to be sorry for. It is a good thing I do not have the disease."

"It is. It must be difficult to be the outsider."

"Not as hard as it is to live with the disease." His retort came out flatly.

"That's true." She rubbed his arm.

He took a step back, out of her reach. Her pity he was not interested in.

Laurel's hand dropped. "We'll find a cure."

The tense moments between them ended when his phone buzzed. He answered, "Prince Tariq."

He listened for a moment and then spoke swiftly in his native language before hanging up. "That was Zara. Roji is well. Running around as if nothing had happened. The resilience of children is amazing."

Her fingertips brushed his arm briefly. "I am glad to hear it."

Tariq appreciated her touch of reassurance this time. Laurel had discovered his secret so easily. He had worked hard to keep his guilt at bay and she had seen right through him. As far as he knew, no one else recognized his burden. Tariq's gut had clenched to see the fear in his nephew's eyes when he had been told he would have to go to the hospital. The research that would come out of the new clinic would one day mean that fewer children like Roji would have to be rushed away every time they had a simple fall.

Roji looked so much like Rasheed. The boy was a daily reminder of what Tariq had lost. He had no intention of letting him suffer the same fate as his father, was determined to see advances made in the knowledge of hemophilia. Laurel was right. Their family should be more open about having the disease. He had been protecting them for so long, and in turn himself, it was difficult to let go of that mindset.

Laurel watched him with that same intent expression she had worn when they had been at the lab. The one that made him believe he had gone up in her estimation.

"You really care about your family, don't you?" She still considered him closely.

"It is the way we were taught. You care for yours. It comes through when you speak of them. We have another thing we can agree on."

She smiled. One that he would enjoy seeing again. "I would've thought it impossible but we do." Her astonishment rang clear.

"And there is another. We have medicine." Why did he care if they had anything in common? She was here to work, nothing more. Friendship was not even necessary. Yet he wanted her to like him or, if she did not, at least respect him. "Nasser waits. We should be on our way to the palace."

Minutes later they were on their way back in the car. As they approached the palace Laurel peered out the window. "It's so beautiful. And intimidating."

"You will soon learn your way around."

"I won't be here that long," she said, as much to herself as him.

Why did the idea of Laurel leaving before she had given them time to get acquainted make his gut clench? He should concentrate on something besides her. "We are passing the state entrance, where we were earlier. It is only used for visiting dignitaries."

"And, apparently, weddings," Laurel murmured.

"The main family entrance is on the west side of the palace. The King and his family have one on the east."

She craned her neck to look up. "How many people live here?"

"There are over a hundred staff members. Each member of the royal family has their own apartments."

Nasser turned under an archway into a courtyard and pulled to a stop in front of the door. Tariq helped Laurel out of the car. "Welcome, Princess."

The shocked look on her face made him chuckle. "I see you had not thought of that. Yes, you are considered a princess now." He cupped her cheek briefly. "I think you will make a lovely one."

Stunned, Laurel walked into the cool of the palace entrance. The tingle of Tariq's caress still lingered. Her fingertips brushed briefly over the spot he had touched. What was this reaction she was having to him? It needed to go away.

Her heart had broken for Tariq earlier when she had discovered what he hadn't wanted to reveal—his guilt. What an unnecessary weight he carried. The self-contained man didn't want her sympathy, hadn't intended her to see what he considered his weakness. Did his family know?

An opportunity like the one the royal family offered didn't come around often in medicine. Laurel tingled at the thought of the advances that might be gained from her research. Maybe through her work she could ease Tariq's pain, whether or not her work was done in America or here.

Laurel looked down the long passage of whitewashed walls and dark wood flooring. She stood in a palace. *A palace.* She was a princess. Her siblings would laugh themselves silly at the idea. Although she had never been overly impressed with splendor and wealth, the grandeur of the place awed her. It was so unlike anything she had ever seen before. Just the age and design alone was fascinating. Laurel couldn't shake the silly notion she was Cinderella and something special was happening to her. She pushed that notion away. Wasn't she here to do a job? Not pretend she was someone she wasn't.

"This way, Princess." Tariq indicted with a hand.

"Please just make it Laurel. I don't think I'm princess material."

"I believe you might find differently."

Tariq escorted her through a network of hallways until they came to wide arching double doors with a pointed flourish at the top. He opened them, revealing a jewel-blue-toned room. A huge canopy bed set in the center of the room, covered with a dark blue spread laced with silver threads. The drapery above and around the bed was also silver. Windows echoing the door design flanked the bed. The bedside tables were laden with lamps, the shades of which were trimmed with beaded braid.

A couch and two chairs created a sitting area on one side of the space. A blue oriental rug covered the white marble floor beneath the furniture, including a cabinet she suspected concealed a TV behind its ornate doors. On the other side was a large cream-colored desk complete with lamp and visitor chairs before it. Laurel couldn't believe all of this splendor was hers.

The room was the most luxurious she'd ever been in. Her father worked in a manufacturing plant in a small town. He could never have afforded anything like what she was seeing. Even with her medical degree she didn't make enough money to have the funds for such a fine living space. "This is wonderful."

Going to one window, she looked out. Below was a lush green paradise. This place she could learn to like, if she planned to stay, which she didn't. This wasn't her world. Outside her research this was all make-believe, storybook stuff.

"Your bath is through here." Tariq indicated a smaller door on the same side of the room as the desk.

Laurel entered to find a gleaming gold-plated, free-standing footed tub with a white plush mat in front of it. The vanity was white marble with gold hardware. Behind a silk screen with an outsized blue bird embroidered on it was the commode. Laurel had never been in a more luxurious bathroom. She had to remind herself she was in a palace.

"I hope you will be comfortable here."

She turned to Tariq in amazement. "I can't imagine why I wouldn't be."

He nodded. "Now I will show you how to get to the garden. The pool is at your disposal. Also, you are free to have your meals here or come to the dining room where something is always available."

"I don't imagine I'll spend much time here. I'll probably eat most of my meals at the lab." She was uncomfortable with the idea of people waiting on her.

"If not, all you have to do is pick up the phone and let

whoever answers know you wish for food and tell them what you want."

Just like that. There was a short-order cook always on call?

"Now let me show you the garden."

They exited the suite, going along the hallway and down a few steps. From there they came to a door that opened to the outside. She could only describe what she saw as an oasis of lush green leaves, chirping birds and bright flowering plants. A heavenly scent filled the air. It was the most divine place she had ever been in. She followed Tariq along a stone walk around a curve to an oval pool sparkling in the late afternoon sunlight.

"This is amazing." She didn't try to keep her awe out of her voice.

"The family uses the pool and you're free to as well, of course."

She was considered part of the royal family? *Unbelievable.* When had her life turned into a fairy tale? The minute Tariq had walked into her lab.

Nasser approached. "Sir, they are ready for you."

"I am on my way. You have my papers?"

Nasser handed him a folder.

To her Tariq said, "Can you find your way back to your room?"

She gazed around at the lovely place, hating to leave it so soon. "I can, but I think I will stay here for a while."

"You are welcome to. I shall see you this evening." He gave her one last unreadable look and swiftly walked away. His flowing robes made him look every bit the royal he was.

Nasser nodded and quietly disappeared behind him.

Half an hour later Laurel took one more longing look

around the garden before going to her room. The walk convinced her that if she ever deviated from her original path she would surely be lost. Who would she call? Anyone who cared about her was thousands of miles away. Straightening her shoulders, she decided she wouldn't think about that now. Soon funding would come through and she would be back where she belonged.

In her room she found that her bags had been unpacked and all of her clothes put away. Thankfully, there was a tray of food waiting. She freshened up and pulled on her nightgown and robe then settled on the sofa to make a few notes about what she wanted to accomplish the next day at the lab.

As the sunset turned rosy her eyelids drooped. Apparently the jet lag that Tariq anticipated had found her. She would just close her eyes for a few minutes and rest.

Tariq tapped on Laurel's door. No answer. Was she exploring the palace? Nasser had not mentioned her requesting anything.

His meeting had gone longer than planned. Before he started on yet more work that evening, he wanted to assure himself Laurel was happy with her room and let her know he would be going with her to the clinic the next morning.

He knocked again. Still there was no answer. Now he became worried. After rapping a third time, he called her name. No response. What if something had happened to her? Had she fallen?

Tariq opened the door, Laurel's name on his lips, to see her curled into a ball asleep on the sofa. Relieved, he should have backed out but went to her instead. After a hard day she would sleep better in the bed.

As he drew near, he glimpsed a hint of her full breasts in the lace-lined V neckline of her pale teal, nylon gown. Although robed, most of her curled legs were exposed. They were beautiful. Temptation to run a finger along one silky-looking thigh and calf almost overrode common sense.

Tightening his lips, he scooped her into his arms, bringing her against his chest. Laurel weighed almost nothing. Murmuring something, she burrowed her cheek against him. He laid her on the turned-down bed, careful to nestle her head on a pillow, and pulled the covers over her enticing body.

Laurel's eyes fluttered open. "Tariq?"

"Yes, *habibti*, it is I. I am putting you to bed."

She muttered something incomprehensible and pulled a pillow close.

Tariq tucked her in and backed away. He would be a very lonely groom tonight. In no mood to face the stack of paperwork on his evening agenda, he decided an exhausting swim and then a cold shower was what he needed.

An hour later he made another turn in the pool and went into the breaststroke. He was punishing himself, but Laurel's face, so sweet and innocent in sleep, he could not get out of his mind. Her slim body had fit so perfectly against his, it felt as if she were made for him. Which was impossible. He should not, did not, deserve a woman like Laurel. What he had learned about her upbringing and family made him believe she would want the same for her children. He could never offer her that. He needed to keep in the forefront of his mind why Laurel was in Zentar. She was here to do crucial medical research, which was far more important than his baser needs. He needed to focus on his job as Health Minister. His family's future and that of his country depended on it.

Tomorrow the clinic would open for the first patient and Laurel's work would begin again. He should prepare, ensure everything was in order. However, he needed to put distance between him and his wife. The wife he had never planned to have. Even now he was surprised he had insisted that he be the one she should marry.

But it was in name only. Otherwise he would be in bed with her right now, awaking the passion he was positive was just below her surface.

Laurel woke at sunrise in the luxurious bed with its deep mattress, plump pillows all around her. How had she gotten here? *Tariq.* She thought she had been dreaming of being in his arms. It had felt so good, so right. He had called her something. What was it? *Hab*…something? What did it mean?

All night she had relived that moment he'd kissed her after the ceremony. The instant his mouth had claimed hers, all else had faded away. It had only been the two of them in the world. She had seen the desire burning in his eyes. Felt the heat of him against her. Tasted his lips as his beard had brushed her cheek. The feel of being alive and wanted had swirled through her, tugging her into the vortex that was Tariq.

She longed for that whirlwind to sweep her away and for her to ride it to its natural conclusion, but she would never allow Tariq to know that. Instead she had spent her wedding night alone. She couldn't risk giving in to her body's reactions to Tariq's virile attentions.

When Larry had shown her the same kind of interest, it had been so new and exciting she'd fallen hard, and had been sure she was in love…only to discover to her horrified humiliation that his interest had been a heartless act. He had felt nothing for her during their brief relationship and he had cruelly stated that moments after he'd gotten what he'd wanted from her.

She would never recover if she let her guard down and fell victim to Tariq's wiles.

To be used and discarded, which Tariq would surely do, wasn't something she could live through again. She would keep her mind clear, do her work and stay out of his way. He was busy enough with all his royal responsibilities that he wouldn't have time for her if she kept out of his sight.

Laurel shook her head and threw the covers back before jumping out of bed. It was time to go to work. Tariq wouldn't be kissing her again. She would see to that. Going to the phone, she picked it up. A heavily accented male voice answered in English, "How may I help you?" Embarrassment filled her at having to have someone wait on her. That was a foreign concept for her. "This is Dr. Martin. May I have a muffin and tea brought to my room? I promise to find the dining room this evening."

"Right away, Princess Laurel."

Princess Laurel. She would never get used to that title. "Thank you."

She hurried to take a quick shower. She was wrapping her hair in a towel when there was a knock on the door. Pulling on her robe, she called, "I'm coming."

Fully expecting one of the staff with her breakfast, her jaw dropped and she stood speechless when she saw Tariq standing there. There was a small lift to the corner of his lips as he surveyed her from the top of her twisted towel to her red-painted toenails. Then he drawled, "Good morning, Laurel."

Heat flashed through her and she didn't need a mirror to know her cheeks were bright pink. She stammered, "Wh-what're you d-doing here?"

He glanced down and her attention followed to the small tray in his hand. "I brought you breakfast."

Why was he doing that? "Aw…thank you."

"I was headed this way and I offered to bring it."

"Oh."

Tariq looked amused. "May I set this down or would you rather eat right here in the hallway?"

"Uh, yeah." What had she just done? She'd invited Tariq into her bedroom. "Just put it on the table."

Tariq wore a crisp white shirt, collar open, and light tan pants with a thin dark belt at his trim hips. His hair was combed back and his beard sculpted. He was as devastatingly handsome as ever, possibly even more so.

There she stood in a wet towel and no clothes beneath her robe. Laurel stayed by the door to keep as much space between them as possible. "Yes, thank you for thinking of me."

"I've been doing too much of that lately."

"Excuse me?" Was he blaming her for something? She hadn't been the one to take their kiss to a place they shouldn't have gone.

"For what?" He gave her a sly look as he came toward her.

Laurel had the urge to move out into the hallway but she wasn't dressed to do so. What if someone saw her? She took two steps back, unsure if it was because she didn't trust him or herself. These feelings weren't something she had much experience with.

Moving did her no good. Tariq stopped in front of her. "By the way, you look quite lovely after a morning shower. I hope you slept well."

"I did." Laurel couldn't meet his look. "Thanks for getting me to bed."

"You are welcome. It was my pleasure."

She dared to look at him. Had he added under his breath, "and pain"?

"I will be waiting in the car for you in thirty minutes. Nasser will take us to the clinic."

He left, leaving Laurel with mouth gaping. He was flirting with her. She might be rusty in the relationship department but she did recognize that. But she must not fall for it. She had before, and she couldn't survive it again.

Laurel left her tea to steep and went to dry her hair. She returned to eat. The fruit added to her order was delicious. Finished with her meal, she returned to dressing. With five minutes to spare she closed her bedroom door. She questioned locking it but that would be ridiculous because who would be interested in her belongings when they could have the...royal jewelry?

She giggled as she went down the hall, concentrating on remembering how she'd come the day before. Proud of herself, she opened the courtyard door to bright sunshine. It was early and already on its way to hot. Mercifully she had chosen a simple lightweight dress. Inside her bag she had stuffed a sweater. Sometimes it could be cool in an air-conditioned building.

The car was waiting just as Tariq had said it would be. Nasser stepped up beside her and opened the back door.

Laurel smile brightly at him. "Good morning and thank you, Nasser."

He nodded. "Good morning, ma'am."

She paused a second when she saw Tariq sitting there. He glanced up from the papers in his hand and smiled. "I like a woman who is punctual."

"Good morning to you too, Your Highness." She made the words sound syrupy sweet.

He gave her his full attention and lowered his chin. "I do not like that address coming from you." His voice was tight with reproach. "You make it sound like it is something that tastes bad."

Laurel smiled. "I'm sorry. It wasn't meant that way."

Tariq's gaze locked on hers. "I wish I could believe that."

She took her seat beside him, making sure they did not touch. Moments later Nasser was in the driver's seat and they were leaving the courtyard.

"I am not going to jump you," Tariq said, low enough for only her to hear. "So relax."

"No, you are not."

"You look ready to run for the mountains. I am sorry if I have made it uncomfortable between us. That was not my intent."

"Just what was your intent? To play with me?"

A troubled look came over his face. "No. I do not play games."

She studied him a moment. This man didn't strike her as someone who ever took action without first understanding the motive behind it. He was deliberate about his decisions. So, was he saying he was genuinely attracted to her?

"Again, I apologize. I will honor our agreement. Our marriage is in name only."

Laurel appreciated the sincerity of his words but

couldn't ignore the disappointment that came with them. The high from being in his arms wouldn't happen again. It was just as well. Not to mention a relief. Even if he was truly attracted to her, which she seriously doubted, nowhere in her scenario of life did she see herself with Tariq forever.

Their bumpy conversation was effectively ended when Nasser pulled up to the same door of the clinic they had used the afternoon before.

"I will introduce you to the lab staff and let you get started. I will then go and see how the opening of the clinic is progressing. Zara and Roji are to come in for his checkup."

Laurel hadn't even thought to ask about Roji this morning. "If you don't mind, I would like to examine him as well."

Nasser already had her door open. As she slid out and stood Tariq stated, "You must remember he is a little boy, not some test subject."

Laurel was caught off guard by how much Tariq's remark hurt. "Has anything I've done indicated that I would treat him like one?"

CHAPTER FIVE

TARIQ COULD NOT believe that not once but twice Laurel had put him in his place. First about their kiss and now about her handling of Roji. He did not like it, and more than that he did not appreciate her being right. Which she was. "No."

"Thank you. Just so you know, I've no intention of starting to now."

"I didn't think you would."

"That's not what you implied." Laurel walked ahead of him into the building.

He went after her, touching her elbow to get her attention and then letting his hand fall away. She was rightly angry with him. "We will go to Security first and get your badge so you can open the doors."

Minutes later they were on their way to the lab and Laurel's card was in her hand. Over the next hour he introduced her to all six of the lab techs. They each congratulated Laurel and Tariq on their marriage. He placed a reassuring hand at her waist but she said all the right words, keeping the conversations short, before she asked them about their work. With that done, he escorted her to the clinic.

Laurel stepped to the window of the reception area. "Wow, look at all these people. I can't believe it."

It always amazed him as well. From old thin men who could hardly walk to infants in their mother's arms they were lined up out the clinic door. It was already hot outside and they would wait all day to see a doctor. "Now you can see why we need a clinic so desperately. What we have been doing in the past has not been enough."

"You have done a good thing here." She gave him an admiring look.

Tariq did not think himself overly proud but Laurel's affirmation of his work made him hold his head higher. It shocked him that her positive appraisal mattered as much as it did. He had never felt the need for a woman's support. They had always just been a pleasurable pastime.

Laurel walked toward the door and looked down the awning-covered walk where people sat, stood and leaned in a ragged line. "Will it be like this every day?"

Tariq stepped beside her. "I hope it will ease with time. That people will learn they can come when they first need to and not wait until the problem is bad. Our country has too few doctors and clinics. I am working to change that. In the past we have not had a central facility in the city so now all of the doctors and people are coming here. We are also in the process of building satellite clinics throughout the country. I travel regularly to check on those. Until recently we have been very backward in some ways. The King and I are trying hard to change that. This clinic and its satellites is the first big step."

Laurel said with what sounded like conviction, "I'm sure it will be a success."

Her words of confidence bolstered him. "Many of our citizens are not comfortable with Western medicine. We must change that for the health of the country. Today, unfortunately, I cannot lend my medical services to the clinic because I have other state obligations that will not wait."

Laurel looked out the window once more then back at the waiting room, where people filled the chairs and the floor. "Then I will take your place."

Tariq studied her in disbelief. "Why? I know you are anxious to get to your research."

"Because I can't imagine what it must be like to wait so long for your sick baby or elderly mother to be seen by a doctor. I'll help get this under control then I can work in my lab tonight."

"I understood you do not like to do clinical work." He did not understand this woman.

"I don't, but that doesn't mean I don't know how. Now introduce me to the director so I can get started."

Tariq located the director and made the introductions.

As Laurel shook hands with the man she said, "I see you are busy today. How can I help?"

The director looked like he might fall at her feet with appreciation. "Your Highness, I will be delighted to see that you have an exam room." With a nod to Tariq he said, "When you are ready."

"I'm ready," Laurel assured him. "Please, call me Laurel. You may send me the first patient now."

The man pointed to a room on the left and walked away with a smile on his face.

Tariq watched in amazement. This was yet another facet of Laurel he had not anticipated. "Thank you for this. I know it is not what we agreed on."

"No, but my parents taught me to do what has to be done." She entered the room and looked around.

He followed her. "I would like to meet them one day."

"I'm sure they would like to meet you as well," she said off-handedly, frowning. "Excuse me, I must borrow a stethoscope." She started to leave.

He stopped her with a hand on her arm. "Laurel, do you know how to get to your lab from here?"

"Yes. Thanks for asking but this building is not quite as intimidating as the palace."

"You will learn your way around there soon, I'm sure."

"Maybe, if I'm here long enough."

He wanted her to stop saying that. Again her focus was not on him. He watched her stop at the reception desk and start talking to one of the employees. Thankfully it was someone who spoke English.

Thirty minutes later he left Laurel busy seeing patients and oblivious to his presence. Was this the same doctor who had stated so emphatically she wasn't coming to Zentar and she didn't see patients? Zentar needed Laurel and, for some unknown reason, he believed Laurel might need Zentar. Or was it just him wishing she needed him?

Laurel had little time to think about Tariq during the day. It seemed like the patients would never stop coming. She only had one brief break when someone brought her bread, fruit and cheese for a very late lunch. As she ate, she pondered the personal burden Tariq carried for his family and the even heavier one he had voluntarily assumed for his country. Clearly there was more to His Highness then the regal manner, domineering ways and sexy exterior.

Her unexpected husband was revealing charms she wasn't immune to and that frightened her. She tried to resist him but the longer she was around Tariq, the more she liked him. He loved his family deeply, had a heart for his people, took pride in being honorable and more than once had honestly apologized to her when he had been in the wrong.

The more she learned about him the more difficult it was to believe Tariq was anything like Larry. That Tariq was someone who would, if given half a chance, callously use and discard her, not caring one bit for her fate once he was done with her. Did she dare let her guard down?

What confounded her even more was what to do about her physical reaction to Tariq. The best solution she could come up with was staying out of his way. The other was to find funding as soon as possible and return to America. She wasn't sure being thousands of miles away would dampen her wayward feelings for the Prince, but it would eliminate the temptation to act on them. Larry had traumatically taught her the difference between sexual attraction and love. She was too practical to waste time dreaming that anything other than lust could develop from her sham marriage to Tariq.

Not long after she'd finished her meal one of the nurses stuck her head into her exam room and said that Princess Zara and Prince Roji had arrived and were asking for her.

"Please send them in next." Laurel returned to caring for the patient she was seeing.

A few minutes later the same nurse escorted Zara and Roji into the room. Zara looked as elegant as ever with her dark hair flowing around her shoulders and her vivid yellow dress. Roji was bright-eyed and looked the picture of health.

"Hello, there," she said to Roji. "How are you doing after your tumble?"

Zara, with a hand to his back, nudged him toward Laurel. She bent to the boy's level. He watched her closely. "How're you feeling, Roji?"

He shrugged his shoulders.

"He is acting normally," Zara offered.

"Do you hurt anywhere?" Laurel asked the boy.

He shook his head.

"Can you do this?" Laurel rolled her shoulders.

Roji did the same.

"That's good. Now, can you do this?" She turned her head to one side and then the other.

This time he did it with a smile on his face.

Laurel stood. "Good. Now, can I look in your eyes and ears? And listen to you?"

Roji said, "Yes."

Zara joined them. "Come on, Roji. I will help you up onto the table."

The boy lifted his arms and his mother sat him on the examination table.

"He seems to have recovered nicely." Laurel smiled at Zara.

"Thanks to you." Zara held Roji in place as the boy squirmed.

Laurel prepared to look into Roji's ears. "I didn't do much."

"When you are a mother, anyone who helps your child has done a lot."

"I was glad I could." Laurel's attention went back to Roji. "Now it's time for a tickle." She checked his ears, eyes and throat. "Can you hold the stethoscope for me while I give you a listen?"

Roji put his hand on the bell.

Laurel moved it over his heart. "Right here is where

it goes. You sound perfect to me." She tickled him and he giggled. Laurel helped him off the table. She spoke to Zara. "He looks fine to me. It's good to see you both again."

"I'm sure we will see each other often." Zara took Roji's hand, stopping him from jumping up and down. "I am glad you are here. I know Tariq is glad to have you to help him. He admires you. Admiration is not something he gives lightly."

"Thank you." Was Zara trying to tell her something?

"This is the first time I've been in the clinic. It is very nice." Zara looked around the room. "I know Tariq takes great pride in it."

"He should. He did an excellent job in putting together an up-to-date facility." Laurel hadn't found any fault in it. In fact, she wished there were more clinics like it in the US.

"He is passionate about many things. Not just his work and the clinic."

Laurel was super-conscious of the woman's intense gaze. What was Zara not saying?

As if changing the subject, Zara commented, "I understand from Tariq that you would like to study our family medical history."

"He told you that?" Laurel couldn't conceal her surprise. Yesterday afternoon he had made it sound like she would have to fight him tooth and nail to get him to agree for her to study his family.

"He did when I spoke to him a little while ago."

Excitement filled Laurel. So Tariq had arranged it. "Yes, I would. All that's involved is you answering a few questions and having some blood drawn."

"That will not be a problem." Zara started for the door.

"Tariq doesn't like the idea of me studying the family."

"He is very protective of us. I think more than he should be. Still, it is nice to have someone to care about you, is it not?"

It was, if the person really cared and wasn't just after a fling. Laurel forced a smile.

Roji pulled on his mother's hand. "Ice cream."

Zara laughed. "I know. I promised, did I not? Laurel, we must be going now. Let me know when you are ready to do your study work."

"If you have time, maybe you could have the blood drawn today. It would just be a matter of going down the hall for a minute."

"That would be fine."

"Then I'll write the order." Laurel hurriedly wrote on a pad. Tearing the sheet off, she handed it to Zara. "If there is a problem with Roji, send for me. I will come do the draw."

"That I promise." Zara walked Roji out.

"Thank you for being willing to help me."

"You are welcome. Tariq will come around as well, I am sure."

Laurel wasn't as confident. "You know him far better than I do."

Zara turned and gave her a piercing look. "He admires you. Likes you. He knows he can trust you. That says much about your character."

"Thank you for saying so." This conversation had taken a turn into an area Laurel wasn't sure she understood or was prepared for.

Zara left, smiling at her serenely.

Laurel was also smiling. She had made a friend. It was a nice feeling.

* * *

By the time the director closed the door for the day, Laurel's back and feet hurt. Not since her fellowship had she spent such long hours on her feet. Yet the day had been rewarding. More so than she had imagined. For years she had avoided patient contact and today she had discovered she rather enjoyed it. Other than asking for the next patient to be sent in, she had given few orders. The nurses knew what they needed to do almost before she asked.

Exhausted, Laurel still had work to do in her lab. She needed to set up some tests so she could get an early start in the morning. The staff she passed on her way out smiled broadly at her. She'd worked alone for so long she'd forgotten what being a member of a team was like.

Laurel had no idea how long she had been in her lab when the phone rang. She jumped when the sound shattered her concentration. Grabbing the receiver, she took a deep breath in order to say in a calm voice, "Dr. Martin."

"It is Nasser."

"Is there something wrong?" Had something happened to Roji? Tariq?

"No, ma'am. I am here to drive you to the palace."

"Now?" She hadn't called him.

"The Prince said to come and get you at midnight if you had not called."

"It's midnight?" She had been so adsorbed in her work she'd no idea it was so late.

"Yes. The Prince says I must stay here until you are ready to go."

Laurel had no doubt the loyal man wouldn't move until she came out. After all, the Prince had given his orders. "I will be there in a moment."

How had Tariq known she was still at the lab at this hour? Did he have a spy checking on her? She quickly removed her sterile covering, scrubbed and went out to meet Nasser. She fully expected to see Tariq sitting in the back seat of the car but was disappointed.

"Nasser," she said as they rode, "I'm sorry. I had no idea that it was so late. You must want to get home to your wife and family."

"No wife and family."

"Still, I kept you out late."

"I was on the way home from taking the Prince to the airport."

Tariq wasn't at the palace. Why did that disturb her so? Panic started to fill her but she tamped it down. She was being silly. "Where did he go?"

"To the other side of the country for meetings."

"Oh. So, how did you know I was at the lab?"

"The Prince said you would still be there."

So the man thought he knew her that well. She tightened her lips. Maybe he did. She had been right where he'd told Nasser she'd be.

Laurel tried not to ask the question but she had to know. "Will the Prince be gone long?"

"A week or more."

Laurel's chest fell. So long? Tariq hadn't said anything about leaving or even goodbye. But why should he? There was nothing between them.

Except that kiss.

Tariq took another strong stroke in the palace pool. With gratifying fluidity of motion he put one arm over his head and then the other with hardly a ripple as he pulled through the water. Swimming was his way of unwinding. Tonight, however, it was not working as well as he wished.

He had been gone for over a week. The issues at the two new clinics had taken him away longer than he had planned. He always disliked being away from his family, but this time he had wanted to come home almost the moment he had left. He had never been so anxious to return to the palace. He had tried to convince himself he should be home overseeing the main clinic, be on hand in case he was needed.

But the truth, he had finally realized, was that he did not like being away from Laurel. The easy justification was that he feared she would leave if he was not close. The honest fact was that he was attracted to her. Wanted to get to know her better. They had only known each other for a few days yet they shared something. It sparked between them anytime they were together.

Tomorrow he planned to check in at the clinic and see how things were progressing. There would also be a stop in the lab to see Laurel. He missed their sparring. She made him laugh and there was not enough of that in his life. Laurel spoke her mind. And there was that kiss. Heat flared in him whenever he thought of kissing her again. He was losing his mind where Laurel was concerned.

Maybe it was good he had been gone so long. If he had stayed near her, he might have done something he would regret. Her reaction to his kiss had been unsure and untutored, almost fearful. He had scared her with his ardor, and that was the last effect he wanted to have on her. Why was she so skittish? Surely someone her age had had relationships. Or had she always hidden herself behind a glass window?

To appease his guilt at having left without telling her,

which he had done only because of Laurel's insistence they were merely business associates and he did not owe her an account of his movements, he had sent her a gift of a new stethoscope. He'd had Nasser see to the purchase and delivery, but Tariq had taken the time to write her a note before he'd left. He had labored to keep it as impersonal as possible.

Thank you for helping my countrymen.

In her line of the medical profession she would rarely use a stethoscope so he doubted she had brought one with her. Especially since she had asked to borrow one that day at the clinic.

Nasser had provided him with daily reports. He had said Laurel seemed pleased with the gift. He also said she had been keeping long hours at the lab and that more than once he'd had to insist she leave at midnight.

Tariq worried she would burn herself out or become ill. He could not remember ever experiencing this much concern for anyone besides his family. Perhaps he felt responsible for having brought Laurel halfway around the world, away from all she knew and loved. Whatever the reason, he was not comfortable with these new feelings whirling in him.

He had corralled his temptation to go to Laurel's room when he had arrived home tonight, believing it was too late to disturb her, plus he did not want to appear overly eager to see her.

So, to burn off some frustration he had decided to come to the pool. He slowed to an easy glide. If he could not shut his mind down then maybe his exhausted body would override it.

The rustle of leaves and a movement to his right caught his attention. He trod water, watching the spot. A person stepped into the moonlight. *Laurel*.

His heart beat extra quickly, much to his dismay. He was a grown man who had seen and experienced enough of life that he should not be reacting to a woman this way. As one normally in command of his emotions and any relationship, this was a new situation for him. Around Laurel, though, he was off the path as if following a special star in the desert sky, unsure where he was headed.

She turned to go back the way she'd come.

"Don't go."

"Tariq?" She stepped closer.

"Yes."

"I was not told you were home." There was a note of confusion in her voice, but there was also an unmistakable tone of excitement.

"I got back about an hour ago." He swam closer to her.

"Oh."

"I would have let you know, but it was so late." She looked amazing in the moonlight. A sleeveless long dress with a scooped neck clung to her curves. If he were to guess, she was braless. "I thought you would be asleep."

"I love this garden so, I come here for a few minutes each night before I go to bed. It's so lovely." She advanced to the edge of the pool in a tentative manner. "I'm usually alone."

"Would you like me to leave?" He waited for her answer, watching her closely.

"No. After all, it's your pool."

That wasn't the answer he had been hoping for, but he would take it.

She stood over him. "Thank you for the stethoscope. It

was really thoughtful. Now I won't have to borrow one. I will pay you back."

He had wanted to do something special for her. Could she not understand that? "Can you not accept a gift?"

She focused on something behind him. "I can, but I don't generally get them from employers."

Tariq crossed his arms on the deck of the pool. "I am more than that. I am your husband, if only in name. If that is not sufficient reason, then accept it from a friend."

She looked down at him. "I would like for us to be friends."

Her soft words flowed in the sweet fragrance of the air. "Come and join me, Laurel."

"I didn't think to pack a swimsuit."

He wanted to tell her she did not need one but that would frighten her away. "At least sit on the side of the pool and tell me about your week."

Laurel regarded him a few seconds, her moonlit face giving no hint of her thoughts, before she gathered her long dress up and around her thighs. She had amazing legs. Maintaining her modesty, she sat, letting her bare feet dangle in the water.

From his vantage point Tariq determined he had been right. She wore no bra. Her nipples pushed against the fine knit fabric. His manhood twitched in reaction to the teasing view.

Laurel swished her feet back and forth. "It's so cool."

"It is so because it is fed by a spring. This used to be the palace well. The palace was built here because of it. Modern improvements have made the palace increasingly efficient, reducing the amount of water diverted from the spring's source. Now there is enough to keep the pool refreshingly full."

"Your ancestors were smart."

Tariq moved back in the water so he could see her clearer. The only light came from underwater illumination around the pool and the moon. "I like to think so. I understand you interviewed my brother and his family while I was gone. Zara and Roji as well."

Her shoulders straightened. "Yes. The King invited me to dinner. Everyone seemed open to my questions. Thank you for seeing to it. I know it wasn't your wish."

"I also understand that it was the only night you actually came home from the clinic at a reasonable hour."

Even in the dim light he could see her eyes narrow. "Has Nasser been informing on me?"

Tariq swam toward her. "It's part of his job to answer my questions."

"Nothing about you is repentant, is it?"

Tariq cupped her heel in his hand. She hissed softly but did not pull away. He brushed the pad of his thumb over her ankle bone. Her attention remained on his hands as he answered, "I have nothing to be repentant for. I was concerned about you, Laurel." He waited until she looked at him. "I missed you."

Laurel's heart beat at the same rate as one of her spinning blood test machines. She contained a moan just behind her lips. Tariq's wet hand moved up her calf then slid back to her foot. She gripped the edge of the pool to quell the impulse to slip into the water with him. Tariq lifted her foot out of the water and placed a kiss in the arch.

"What're you doing?" The words came out as a squeak.

"I'm showing you I desire you. So soft. So smooth." His hand repeated its travels.

"You don't desire me. I'm just convenient. I'm not even your type."

"Normally I would agree. But the fact is you interest me, Laurel Al Marktum." He put emphasis on the last name. "A great deal."

"The great bachelor Prince could only want me for one reason."

"And that would be?" His voice was deep and sultry like the warm night air.

"As a conquest." She'd been that before but never again. She wanted a love for a lifetime.

"Laurel, what happened to make you so cynical?"

"Let's just call it college life." This was a subject she had no interest in sharing with anyone, especially him. She had only confided to her roommate and her sister what Larry had done to her, and hadn't talked about it in all the years since.

"It can sometimes be difficult." Tariq let go of her foot and moved beside her. Seconds later he lifted himself out of the water, twisted his hips and sat beside her in all his bare-chested glory.

Her hand craved to touch. She bit the tip of her tongue to keep from licking a rivulet of water from his shoulder. Laurel had never seen a more enticing man. Tariq's muscles rippled under his dark skin with every movement. His broad shoulders tapered to lean hips where his swimming trunks rode low, leaving no doubt he was all male. His thighs were thick and his athletic calves narrowed to sculpted feet.

He was the complete package of what Laurel believed a man should look like. Why was she so superficial that she would let his looks affect her so? She knew well that appearances could be deceiving. A wolf in sheep's clothing. She was no Red Riding Hood anymore.

Water sluiced off him. She shifted, pulling her dress out of the way of a stream of water. "You're getting me wet."

"Stop evading the question. What happened when you were in college?"

"Nothing I wish to share." Using her big toe, she splashed water into the center of the pool.

"I would like you to tell me, since it affects me too."

She glared at him. He watched her, eyes unreadable. "Just how does it affect you?"

"Because you are projecting whatever happened onto me. Not giving me a chance."

Had she really been doing that? Was she keeping Tariq at arm's length because of Larry? "Very well, since you insist."

"I do."

Laurel couldn't believe she was about to confide in Tariq of all people. Maybe it was because she knew of his secret guilt over not having hemophilia, or perhaps it was her belief he was an honorable man, but regardless she was only going to tell him the big-picture parts. "My college boyfriend was on the football team. I never understood why he had picked me. The girl with the glasses who studied all the time. Nevertheless, I was crazy about him and he acted the same about me until I went to bed with him. He dumped me that very night and had no further use for me. I later overheard some guys on his team laughing about how he had won a bet because he had taken my virginity."

The tendons in Tariq's arms stood out from him gripping the ledge of the pool so tightly. He said something in Arabic that she guessed was a foul word. She had no idea what the expression meant but she would agree. "Now are you satisfied?"

"Satisfied? I will not be until the day I punish him for hurting you. So you let this idiot of a man-boy dictate to you how you see all males?"

"No."

"I think you do. You do not trust me because of this. You judge me by him. Because of this reptile you have hidden away in a lab and missed out on life. You are afraid to trust."

"That's not true." Laurel looked into the pool, watching the ripples from a slight breeze. She hadn't been doing that, had she? Wasn't she just dedicated to her work?

"Then prove it. Spend the day with me tomorrow. We both have earned a day off. I will show you Zentar City. We will have dinner, just the two of us. I will show you how a man treats a woman. With respect."

"I don't think that would be a good idea." She was afraid to spend time with him. Not because she didn't trust him but because she didn't trust herself.

"I promise that it will be because I wish to be with you and not because I have made some juvenile bet."

"Why would a man like you want to spend time with me?"

With his index finger under her chin he turned her head so she had no choice but to look at him. His gaze met hers. "You really have no idea how refreshing you are to be around, do you?"

She shook her head. "I guess not."

"You are. Let's go tomorrow and have a good time and see where it leads. We will go to the marketplace and I will show you the sites around the city. What do you have to lose?"

Her heart? He studied her with a sincere expression she recognized as genuine. Could she give him a chance? "Okay. As friends."

"For as long as you want it that way."

In one lithe movement Tariq stood and offered his hand. She took it and he pulled her to her feet. Her body brushed his as she moved. He put some space between them. "I will see you in the morning in the dining room for breakfast and then we will start out. Now, off to bed with you."

Laurel headed down the path, even though her body begged to stay and be held against his. As she started through the foliage Tariq called, "Do not forget your sunscreen and a hat. Goodnight, *habibti.*"

CHAPTER SIX

Tariq sat at the table the next morning, finishing his second cup of coffee. He had waited for Laurel long enough to start wondering if she would show up. Had she gone to the lab without letting anyone know? He checked his watch once more. If she did not make an appearance in ten minutes he would send for her. He was already debating whether or not to go to her room.

"What are you so nervous about? She will come." Zara buttered her bread with a smile on her face.

"I'm not nervous." Tariq came close to snarling. He was not used to anyone commenting on his emotional state. In fact, he generally concealed it.

Zara's grin grew wider. "Tariq, you forget I have known you for a long time. This woman matters to you. I'm glad to see it. Rasheed would be too, if he were here."

"He would also find humor in my actions." Tariq's brother had often made unmerciful fun of him.

A sad smile covered her lips. "That he would."

The soft pad of feet in the hall drew his attention. Laurel came through the doorway. Her hair was pulled back, as always, but it was loose otherwise and bounced becomingly about her shoulders as she walked. He itched to see it down and flowing over her slender, pale shoulders.

Those dreams were better left in a locked box in his mind. Today was about showing her that all men were not brutes.

She wore a simple T-shirt, jeans and flat, functional shoes. Her ever-present oversized bag hung over one shoulder and she carried a wide-brimmed hat. Behind her glasses her large eyes were glowing with eagerness. Her shirt was tight enough to accentuate her full and tempting breasts. If he did not harness his libido now, he would be in trouble. Laurel had no idea how attractive she was, despite her lack of attention to her appearance.

He had carefully calculated their day, wanting to show her all the sights and sounds of his city. Then he had a nice dinner planned for them. Tariq resisted the urge to coax more than that from Laurel. His goal was for her to start trusting him.

"Good morning." He stood.

"Hi," came her shy reply. "Sorry. I slept in. Which I never do. Hello, Zara."

"Good morning." Zara looked at him, then at Laurel and back again. "I should check on Roji." She took her bread and went out the door.

Zara would have some teasing comment when next he saw her, he was sure. To Laurel he said, "You have had a busy week."

"I guess I was more tired than I thought."

"Come and have a seat." He held a chair for her next to him. "Are you ready to see my city?"

She sat. The smell he loved so much surrounded her. "I believe so."

Laurel put the wide-brimmed hat in the empty chair next to her.

"I see you followed directions about a hat. Did you put on sunscreen?"

She nodded. "Don't let that go to your head. The me following your directions part."

"I am sure you will manage to see that it does not." They were bantering, he realized with amazement. Since when did he do that with a woman outside his family? Why did being around Laurel make him act oddly? "You need to eat a hearty meal this morning because we will be doing a lot of walking."

One of the staff entered with a cup of tea in one hand and a muffin in the other.

Laurel smiled. "Thank you, Marcus. How's your wife feeling?"

Why did it not surprise Tariq that Laurel would ask the man a personal question in the presence of a member of the royal family? She did not stand on ceremony.

Marcus glanced at him. Tariq nodded. Trying to conceal his relief, Marcus said with subdued politeness, "She is much better, thank you, Your Highness."

Laurel looked at Tariq as she picked up her muffin. "I saw Marcus's wife at the clinic the first day. They're expecting a baby."

He looked at Marcus. "I did not know. Congratulations."

The man grinned. "Thank you, Your Highness." He slipped quietly out of the room.

"Do you mind if we stop by the lab for a few moments this morning?" Laurel popped a piece of muffin into her mouth.

"I do. I have a busy day planned that does not involve work for either one of us." Tariq leaned back in his chair and picked up his coffee cup, expecting fireworks from the chair next to his.

"Not even thirty minutes? I have tests to check."

"No, not even that. Your work is important. I wish for you to do it, of course, but it is just as important that you take time for yourself as well."

She picked up her tea cup and gave him a direct look. "So says the Prince who jets all over the world and is never without a stack of papers in his hands."

"So we are going to start our day in an argument?" Tariq liked debating with her, enjoyed seeing her eyes flash with emotion. Sometime very soon he would like to see passion in her gaze when she looked at him.

"No, I was just stating a fact."

Tariq looked at her over the brim of his cup. "Yes, but I believe I also told you I make sure to take time off."

They lapsed into a silence he found surprisingly comfortable.

When Laurel had finished her muffin Tariq pushed back his chair. "We should be going. The market will be hot if we wait until the middle of the day."

A few minutes later they were making their way down the hall. As they walked he asked, "Is there anything special you would like to do that you have heard about?"

He was on the verge of repeating himself when Laurel said, "I'd like to see the seashore. I miss Lake Michigan."

"I will put that on the schedule."

They exited into the courtyard. He had asked Nasser to have his personal car brought around.

"Are we going in this?" Laurel's voice held a note of awe.

Tariq put on his sunglasses. "It is my car. So yes."

Laurel trailed a finger down the side of his shiny black two-seater convertible.

"It's gorgeous. I've always wanted to ride in one."

Tariq chuckled and opened the passenger door. "Then get in."

Laurel continued to surprise him. She looked at the car in the same way he sometimes caught her looking at him, as if he were a piece of her favorite candy. He was not sure he wished to share that with a car. He preferred being the center of her attention.

As they headed into town he glanced over to see Laurel with chin up and eyes closed, a blissful look on her face.

"My brothers and sister will be so jealous," she said, as much to herself as to him. As they neared the center of the city Laurel looked at him. "Aren't you worried about the people noticing you?"

"Some will but I have always come and gone among them so they are used to me."

"Then why the bodyguards in America?"

Tariq shrugged. "It is not my idea. The King does not want to take any chances."

He made a couple of turns and parked. "We will have to walk a couple of blocks from here."

Laurel looked him up and down. "You wore jeans today. I hadn't expected that."

Smiling, he grabbed his cap out of the back seat and pulled it on. "And a baseball cap."

"Mighty casual clothes for a prince."

"Today I am not a prince. I am Tariq, showing his date around."

"I thought we agreed we're just friends." She opened the car door.

"You do not think friends ever go on dates?"

"I guess some do."

"Then that is us." He went around the car and joined her on the sidewalk.

Laurel put on her hat and sunglasses. "You're just going to leave your car here like this?"

"Yes."

"We would never do that at home."

Tariq took her hand. "Where could it go on this island that someone would not recognize it as mine?"

She pursed her lips for a second and bent her head to one side. "You have a point there."

He grinned and led her down the sidewalk. "Come, let us see what we can find at the market."

"I've heard talk about the market. It sounds like fun. I'd like to find some gifts to take home to my family."

Tariq frowned at her talk of going "home" to America. At least she had not mentioned going to the lab again. "How is your family?"

"They're fine. I've talked to one or another of them about every day I've been here. They miss me, knowing I am not close." She sounded wistful.

"Maybe they can come for a visit soon." He desperately wanted to hear happiness in her voice. "You have told them of our marriage?"

"No. My family doesn't travel in the same circle as yours. I just hope they don't hear about it before it's over."

Over. Tariq did not like the sound of that. "You are that eager to be done with me after only a week of bliss? I must do a better job of being a husband." He pulled her to him and gave her a swift kiss on the lips before releasing her. Before she could say anything he took her hand and led her down the street.

They reached the market area with all its bright-colored awnings, tents and bustling people.

Laurel looked at him with wide, eager eyes just as he had hoped. "This is wonderful."

"I thought you might enjoy it. As boys, my brothers and I would sneak off and come here. Our parents always knew where to find us."

"You miss your brother, don't you?"

She was watching him too closely. Tariq had to look away. "Every day."

"I'm sorry." She gave his hand a gentle squeeze, reminding him they were still holding hands. "Did your parents worry about your brothers all the time?"

"To an extent, but they mostly let us be boys. My father's mother was so overprotective that my father refused to be the same. My mother had a more difficult time. I saw her crying more than once."

"And you?"

Why did Laurel have such insight where he was concerned? This was a subject he did not discuss. "I watched over them both. Enough of that. We have gifts to look for. You lead and I will follow." He did not have to tell her twice. She headed for the nearest stall.

Over the next hour Tariq watched Laurel move along the line of booths. Mostly he stayed nearby while she haggled with the sellers. Every once in a while she would look over her shoulder with a quizzical look on her face. He would step in to translate.

A couple of times the merchant recognized him and wanted to give Laurel the item, but she would insist on paying. He was stopped often by people he knew well. After a brief exchange, he would quickly excuse himself. This was Laurel's day and he intended to concentrate on her.

They strolled by a stall with beach paraphernalia. He caught Laurel's hand when she was about to go in a different direction. "We need to look here."

"Why?"

"I wish to buy you something." He led her over to the rack of bathing suits.

"You don't need to do that."

"I know, but I want to. Pick out one." He looked at the hot pink bikini hanging on the side of the tent. That one he would like to see Laurel in.

"I will get one, but I'm buying it." She looked through the rack, pushing suits around, and pulled out a black one-piece. Holding it up, she studied it one way and then the other.

Tariq took it from her and hung it back on the rack.

"Hey, what are you doing?"

"That is not the one for you." Tariq gained the stall-holder's attention. "I would like to see that one." He pointed to the one he had admired.

The man used a stick with a hook on the end to lift it down. He handed it to Tariq.

Laurel's mouth opened as surprise then indignation came over her face. She shook her head. "I'm not getting that. It's two pieces of string. It isn't my style."

Tariq grinned. "Maybe it is and you just do not know it. It would show off your beautiful figure."

"I don't have one." She huffed.

He caught her hand and said for her ears only, "I have had a glimpse of a beautiful one when you're not trying to hide it."

Laurel glared. "Now you are making fun of me again."

He gave her a direct look, capturing her absolute attention. "I would never make jokes about that subject. Get the bikini, Laurel."

The moment hung between them. She broke it with a shake of her head. "And I would never have the nerve to wear it." Turning on her heel, she walked off.

Tariq gave the man some bills and stuffed the suit in his pocket. It was worth the outrageous price because now that he had bought it, Laurel might be coaxed to try it on for him in private.

Laurel felt Tariq's presence behind her before she saw him.

When he caught up with her he asked, "Would you like to stop at a café for a drink?"

"That'd be nice. I've gotten more exercise this week than I've had in a long time."

They walked a few blocks then turned into an alley. Tariq said, "This is my favorite place."

There were bright strips of red, yellow, and orange cloth hanging from between two buildings, creating a shaded area. Small wooden tables and benches set beneath them. Large plant pots filled with foliage created a tranquil atmosphere. Laurel was thoroughly enchanted.

Tariq gestured as only a prince would toward the dining area. "Have a seat. I will get our drinks. Are you adventurous enough to try the specialty?"

She smiled. "Why not?"

He ducked as he entered the dark interior.

There were only a couple of other people there. While Tariq was gone she settled on a shaded table near the wall of the building where it was coolest. She would always remember Zentar's heat when her funding came through and she left. And, of course, Tariq.

She'd had a splendid time at the market. It had been long years since she had been around so many people. It had been invigorating. Why had she hidden herself away for so long? Not all people were jerks like Larry or her schoolmates. Surely some of those kids who had been so cruel to her in school had matured into decent human beings.

Tariq returned with their drinks. He placed a tall glass filled with something orange in front of her and sat on the bench beside her.

She twisted the cool glass in her hand. "This looks good. What is it?"

"It is Omar's special. He does not share the recipe."

Laurel took a sip. "It is delicious." There was a taste of orange and melon and something else she couldn't name.

"I thought you would like it." Tariq appeared satisfied with himself. "So, did you get all the gifts you needed for your family?"

"I did. They'll be so excited. I really enjoyed the market. It's been a long time since I've been to one."

Tariq leaned back against the wall and crossed his ankles. He looked every bit at home there in that simple café as he did in the palace. Maybe more so. "I'm glad you had a good time."

A man, smiling broadly with few teeth and dressed in a multicolored striped robe, shuffled toward their table as if his limbs weren't co-operating well.

Tariq sat forward. "Laurel, I would like you to meet Omar. He is a long-time friend and the owner of this establishment."

"It's nice to meet you, Omar." She raised her glass. "Your drink is very good."

Tariq translated for her then said, "I have told him you are my wife and a doctor in our new clinic."

Laurel hated lying to this man and misleading the rest of the country about their marriage. It was wrong. But she had agreed in order to do her research. For the sake of her work she would make a small sacrifice of minor ethics.

"He says congratulations. It is about time Prince Tariq found a woman," Tariq said.

Laurel smiled and said, "Thank you."

"Omar has hemophilia," Tariq said.

Laurel looked at Omar anew. "He does?"

"Yes, I have the blood disease. I must be careful all my life," Tariq translated.

Now she understood why Omar walked as if in pain. Hemophilia had damaged his joints, severely she guessed from his awkward gait. "I see."

Tariq spoke to her. "Omar has agreed to talk to you if you would like."

"Yes, I would like that." She hated being excited about meeting someone with a disease. Still, her research was important. "Could you ask him if he would mind coming to the clinic one day and answering some questions? I would also like to take some blood."

Tariq spoke to the man. "He has agreed to come this week."

Omar nodded and backed away.

"Thank you, Omar," Laurel called, watching him limp away.

With the man gone she turned to Tariq. "Omar has agreed to come in, what about you?"

"When would you like me to be there?"

His casual response was a marked contrast to his earlier reaction. What happen to the man who had fought her a week ago? "That easily?"

"You are right, I brought you here for that purpose." Tariq finished his drink as if their tense "discussion" had never happened.

Laurel looked at him. "I can understand why you would be weary of someone asking personal questions. You are a private man. I respect that. Could you come in Monday?"

"I'll make it work. Now, how about we go and see the beach?"

"That sounds wonderful." Laurel emptied her glass. "That was good. I'll have to remember how to get here."

Tariq stood and offered his hand. He seemed to want to always be touching her. She liked the thrill it gave her when he did. "I would be glad to bring you anytime."

Laurel allowed him to help her to her feet just for the momentary pleasure of physical contact. They strolled back to the car. Tariq answered her questions about items in stalls as they passed. He took time to explain everything. He made the perfect tour guide.

She loved riding in his little sports car as he maneuvered through the narrow streets of the city. The scenery turned rural after a while and they had to stop a few times for farmers to herd livestock across the road. As they continued downward on a winding narrow road she caught glimpses of water and white beach. The shoreline came into view. A few minutes later they were traveling parallel to it. "It's beautiful."

"It is not the only thing that is beautiful."

Laurel looked at Tariq. He was watching her. "I think you need glasses."

Tariq turned his attention back to the road. "I see more clearly than you think."

Did he see her insecurity? How little confidence she had where men were concerned? That she was out of her element and floundering to find stability?

They continued down the road a few miles before Tariq pulled off to the side in a spot hardly large enough for his car. Huge rocks broke the view of the sea.

"The royal beach house is not far from here but this was my brother's and my favorite stretch of beach. The boulders were our fort when we played pirates."

Laurel liked hearing him talk about his childhood. His voice and demeanor relaxed as his mind traveled through pleasant memories. This Tariq she didn't see enough of. Wanted more of.

He stepped out of the car. "Come this way." He offered his hand once again and helped her stand on the seat and cross to the other. Losing her balance when she put her feet on the ground, Tariq's steady hands pulled her against a solid wall of male chest. The sensual aroma of citrus and coffee, and something special that was him alone filled her head. His hold tightened. She looked to see him watching her, questioning. In his dark, usually inscrutable eyes she saw clearly desire burning for her.

What would it hurt to have just one more kiss? To see if time would stand still again?

She leaned forward and his mouth found hers. That fire in his eyes sped along her nerves to burst into fireworks at the ends. All she could do was hang on. Tariq's lips were firm and commanding. He brought her tighter.

The long soft moan bubbling in her throat brought her back to reality. She couldn't do this. He was the wrong type of man for her. She'd made that colossal mistake before. Never again, she had promised herself. Gathering the few wits she had left, Laurel pushed against Tariq's torso.

His lips left hers with exquisite slowness. So much so she was tempted to return for another kiss. But she hadn't come to Zentar to become part of Prince Tariq Al Marktum's harem. Her work was her sole focus in life. Nothing else mattered. She put space between them, murmuring as she moved away, "Thanks."

"For the kiss or seeing that you did not fall?"

"Both."

"That is what friends do." The rich timbre of his voice had gone deeper.

What friends didn't do was leave her wanting to cling to them, begging for more kisses.

Going to the trunk of the car, Tariq opened it and removed a basket and a bag. Handing the bag to her, he offered his hand. After a prolonged second she took it.

Laurel studied his large hand securely holding her much smaller one. They were so different yet they had so much in common. All day Tariq had either taken her hand or offered his and she hadn't once pulled away or denied him. What was happening to her? Was she under a Zentaran spell or just under Tariq's?

He led her down a path circling the rocks and out to the water. The Arabian Sea was a blue-green jewel before them. She kicked off her shoes and wiggled her toes in the grainy sand. Tariq removed his as well.

"This is only the second time I've ever been to a beach. My family couldn't afford to travel so far. I love it."

"When my parents were alive we came here every weekend we could. This was my second home."

"I'm so jealous." She walked toward the water. What

would it be like to have this opportunity all the time? She could learn to love it here.

"Don't be. You speak of your family as if they are wonderful." He joined her.

She turned in a circle with her arms out wide. "They are. I wish they could see this."

Closer to the water, Tariq put down the basket and took the bag from her. He pulled out a blanket and spread it on the ground then placed the basket on it. "A walk first or food?"

Laurel rolled up her pants. "A walk." She strode into the gently lapping waves and played until Tariq reached her. He had removed his shirt. Laurel could hardly think of anything but his toned chest and muscled arms. How would he react if she touched him? Just traced the dark line of hair down his chest with a swift fingertip?

"If you continue to look at me like that, our friendship will be over."

"Then you shouldn't be so handsome." Laurel couldn't believe she had just said that out loud. She hurried ahead of him, splashing at the water's edge. She was on a deserted beach with a man she was attracted to and she'd just blurted out something very suggestive. Trouble she couldn't handle was headed her way.

Tariq caught up with her. Grinning, he took her hand and kissed her palm. They continued down the beach.

She was experiencing those same out-of-control feelings she'd had when Larry had seduced her with actions and gifts. Forgetting who she was and who Tariq was wasn't wise. She wouldn't be treated that way again. What else could Tariq want but a fling? He would use her while she was here and be done with her when she was gone. She needed more out of a relationship.

Yet the day had been wonderful so far. Laurel didn't want to give up this feeling right now. She was enjoying it too much. Glancing at Tariq, she'd never seen him look more peaceful. With the amount of stress that must go with his job he needed time like this. She wouldn't ruin the day by being a naïve ninny. What she'd said was the truth. All the man had to do was look in the mirror to confirm it.

The warm water on her feet, the sun on her face, and her hand in Tariq's made for a perfect moment. She was going to hold onto this feeling for as long as she could. Something in her had come alive again when she'd met Tariq.

"You are having a good time?" It was both a question and a statement from Tariq.

She dared to look at him. "I am. The best."

"Excellent."

They walked a little further before he tugged on her hand and they headed back the way they had come. "I am hungry. Let's go see what the cook packed."

When they arrived at their belongings they dropped to the blanket.

Tariq opened the basket. "So what do we have?" He removed a plate with dates, grapes, olives and small pieces of bread. Next came a bowl. He unwrapped the covering and they found olive oil in it. Then came a small cooler that held a plate of cheeses and sliced meats.

"This looks wonderful." Laurel had never seen a more delicious picnic. Tariq, the place and the food were all conspiring to make her fall in love with Zentar.

"These are all things produced on Zentar," he said. "Help yourself."

Laurel popped a date into her mouth. "Mmm." She

glanced at Tariq. He watched her with an unnerving absorption, as if she were the most fascinating person in the world. His intensity sent a zip of excitement through her that made her pulse hum. "Shouldn't you be eating? You said you were hungry."

"I am."

His answer clearly suggested he meant hungry for her. That blaze in his eyes burned brightly. Her center throbbed.

Tariq blinked and the look disappeared. He calmly picked up a piece of bread, dipped it in the oil and popped it into his mouth. While he ate, he opened a bottle of wine. Holding a glass like the expert she was sure he was, he poured.

Laurel chose one of the large olives then took a bite out of it. She wanted to know more about this man who seem to have two different sides. "Did you go off to school when you were a child?"

Tariq looked out at the water. "No, we had tutors come to the palace. My brothers and I showed them no mercy."

"I can imagine what three young boys can do to a person. My brothers and sister are younger than me. They used to gang up on me."

A small smile curved his lips. "We did that and more. Mice, garter snakes, spiders. If you can think of it, we did it. Mother and Father threatened to send us to boarding school, but we knew they did not mean it. They wanted us close. Especially the Heir Apparent and Rasheed."

She had just unlocked another element of his personality. "You felt left out, didn't you?"

"Somewhat, but I understood. They were special."

"I'm sure your parents didn't think you were any less special." Laurel felt for the little boy who might not have gotten the attention his brothers had. It had shaped him into the man he was. Tough on the outside and vulnerable on the inside.

CHAPTER SEVEN

Tariq had had enough of this conversation. This day was about relaxing, not resuscitating old feelings. "It is my turn to ask questions. Has there not been any other man in your life since that jerk?"

Laurel's face reddened. She looked away. He wished he hadn't asked. Apparently she was as touchy about this subject as he was about his childhood. But the question was out there now.

"No."

She said the word so softly he could barely make it out over the lap of water. That was difficult for him to believe. "Why not? Has no one asked you out?"

"They've asked." She picked up a rolled piece of meat and bit into it.

Tariq settled on his side, legs crossed and his head propped up on his hand. "You know, you cannot run away all your life."

"Okay, great wise Prince, then tell me why you're not already married? A family man? From seeing you with Roji I know you love children."

The conversation had taken a turn for the worse. Again. He should have known Laurel could give as good as she got. "I have not found the right person."

"I looked you up. There have been a number of women who would have liked to be your wife." Her smile was a teasing one.

"Do not believe everything you read, *habibti*."

"You still haven't answered my question about children."

He sat up. "I will not have any. It is not hard to get a woman to forget about marrying you when she learns that. I would guess the articles you read did not tell you that." For once the idea of never having children was painful. He looked at Laurel. She was the type of person who would make a wonderful caring mother. If only…

Tariq grabbed the bag and found his swimming trunks. He stood. "I am going for a swim. Come with me."

"I don't have a swimsuit."

"I bought you one." He pulled the bikini out of his pocket and dropped it on the blanket.

"I can't wear that!"

"Suit yourself." He gave her his best wicked grin. "You are always welcome to skinny dip. All I can tell you is that you are missing out if you do not come in." Tariq did not wait on her but headed to the water. He needed to get away from Laurel's probing questions and marshal his emotions. With his back to her he removed his pants and pulled on his swim trunks. He did not care about her sensibilities, he needed to swim.

He ran in up to his waist and threw himself headlong into the surf and a soothing rhythm of rapid strokes. When he had his libido in check he headed back to shore. Laurel came out of the crevice in the rocks with her shirt on and carrying her pants. Even from a distance he could appreciate her shapely legs. They were not long but he could imagine them tight around him. He needed to get control of the direction of his thoughts. He made a couple of deep, strong strokes as he watched her drop her pants on the blanket and walk to the water's edge.

Tariq called, "Are you coming in?"

"Eventually." She toyed with the hem of her shirt.

"It feels great." To give Laurel a chance to get over her nervousness, he turned and swam a few more stokes. By the time he slowed she was in the water. He drifted toward her. She'd shed her top. Little of her pink bikini top was visible, but what he could see was enticing. "What made you decide to come in?"

"If I wanted to swim I either had to wear the bikini or my clothes. I decided I didn't want to ride home in wet clothes. Especially if you had planned for us to stop along the way."

"You are very logical, Doctor. The bikini looks quite nice on you."

"What little there is of it!" She pulled on the straps, lifting what looked like lovely full breasts.

"From my vantage point you are very appealing." Too much so for his comfort. Buying the bikini might have been one of his worse ideas.

"When you talk like that I don't know whether or not to believe you. I think it might be the playboy Prince trying to charm me."

He was not sure she was wrong. "Are you a strong swimmer?"

"I can hold my own. I don't think you will have to save me."

Tariq would like to have an excuse to do CPR on her. This allure Laurel had over him was not only irrational, it was exasperating.

She made strong, steady stokes as they moved out into deeper water. Soon they slowed and floated.

Tariq shook the water from his hair. "You swim well."

She grinned. "It's all those years on the swim team at the community club after school."

"Now who is making fun of whom? I was assuring myself that I would not be in the papers for letting an American drown."

"Maybe I was trying to get you back." She swam away from him.

He followed. "What other hidden talents do you have?"

"I'm good at cards, paint some when I have time and read romance."

"Romance? Interesting." She just did not act on her romantic inclinations, it seemed.

"How about you?" She moved into sidestroke.

He did the same. "I like black and white movies, horses and American football."

Laurel gave him an approving nod. "Interesting. I would have never guessed."

As if in silent agreement, they started back to shore. Laurel lagged behind. When he could stand he looked out at her as she trod water. "Are you coming out?"

She acted unsure. Suddenly her expression turned to one of determination. Standing, she walked toward him with shoulders high and eyes focused on a point behind him. His heart bumped against his ribs. There was too much of sexy Laurel to contemplate. Water ran over her skin in sensual streams. How would she react if he used his tongue and followed one of them up her neck? His manhood pulsed to life. Laurel needed to dress and they needed to leave this beach right now.

Tariq strode out of the water, grabbed his jeans off

the sand and headed for their picnic spot. He quickly put their leftovers in the basket and set it aside. From the bag, he pulled out a towel for her. "Here. We need to change and go."

She reached for the towel, looking insecure and confused. "Uh...okay. Is there some hurry?"

"You need to get out of the sun."

"I could put on sunscreen." She reached down for her ever-present bottomless bag.

"Laurel!"

She looked at him, her lush behind still in the air. "You are the sexiest thing I have ever seen in a bikini. What little there is of it I would like to remove and have you here under the sun."

Her eyes went wide and her lips formed an O.

"I made a promise to you and I will keep it. To be friends. The problem is I am not feeling friendly right *now*. Get dressed, please. I will meet you at the car."

He turned his back, fearing Laurel would see just how aroused he was. How was he going to keep his hands off her for the rest of the day?

Laurel grinned as she made her way to the rocks to change. The need to skip almost took over. She hadn't missed Tariq's physical reaction. Female satisfaction filled her. She'd actually caused that response in such a virile man. After years of feeling inadequate it was empowering to know she wielded such influence.

She quickly changed clothes, but was tempted the entire time to watch Tariq do the same where he stood out in the open. Only she didn't want to get caught doing so. Pulling the band from her hair, she rubbed it dry. After rolling her nothing of a swimsuit in the towel, she headed for the car. Tariq waited.

"Your hair is down." His words were almost reverent.

Laurel pushed it over her shoulder. "It needs to dry. I'll put it up again when it does."

"I like it this way." He picked up a damp strand and let it glide over his fingers. "I've wondered more than once what you would look like with it loose. All freed and uninhibited."

"You've wondered about my hair?"

He appeared mesmerized by the threads he held. "And more than that."

Warmth crept through her that had nothing to do with the sun beating down.

Tariq's gaze met hers. "You do something to me, Laurel."

She did? Was he just putting her on? A man like Tariq didn't go for women like her. If they did it was to win a bet. "You don't sound glad about that."

"I'm not. I hadn't expected to feel about you the way I do." He studied her a moment then leaned toward her, only to abruptly straighten and back away. "We need to go."

Laurel blinked. Had he been about to kiss her? She almost staggered. *That* kiss she wanted. Could taste. Her body begged for it. "Okay."

He opened the door of the car.

"May I drive?" she teased, sure he was too alpha male to let a woman drive him around.

"Sure. Pull out into the road so I can get in without twisting myself into a knot."

Her mouth fell open. "You're actually going to let me drive?"

He shrugged. "Why not? You are a good driver, are you not?"

She shrugged. "I like to think so."

"Then there should not be a problem." Tariq handed her the keys.

Laurel looked at them a second then took them. She couldn't believe he trusted her enough to let her behind the wheel. She started the car and revved the engine. Sports cars had always appealed to her but she was too practical to buy one of her own. Then, too, as a research scientist she didn't make the money to own one. She grinned at Tariq. He smiled back, obviously enjoying her having fun. Other than her father, she had never known a man who liked to see others happy as much as Tariq did. Most of the men she knew were more concerned with themselves.

She made a tight turn to the other side of the road. "Hey, handsome, you interested in riding with me?"

Tariq released a full-bodied laugh and jogged to the passenger door. "I think I might have agreed to a speed demon getting behind the wheel." He climbed in. "Please be kind to me and my car."

"I plan to be." She gave him her best suggestive grin. Who was this risqué woman she was turning into?

As she drove off Tariq said in an odd tone, "I may hold you to that."

The car was as sweet to drive as it was in looks. Tariq appeared relaxed. He had shifted so he sat turned toward her with one arm along the door and the other resting across the back of their seats, his fingertips touching her shoulder.

"This is fun." Laurel glanced at him. He watched her

and not the road. What was he thinking behind those dark glasses?

"I'm glad you like it." His voice held pleasure, as if he was enjoying hers.

"A car like this, if I could afford it, isn't practical where I live. Too much snow and wind." She could imagine what she would look like driving a low-slung car in three feet of snow.

"You live here now. You are welcome to drive mine anytime you wish. A husband should share with his wife."

That sounded too generous. "You would do that?"

"Of course. Or we could get you your own."

"I won't be here long enough to justify having a car like this."

"So you are still intending to return to the States when we are both satisfied the lab is running as it should?" Tariq straightened and took his arm down from behind her.

"Or until I receive new funding."

"What I remember is that you said that but I didn't agree. You are needed here."

Laurel glanced Tariq's direction. His mouth was drawn into a tight line. "There are others that can do what you need as well as I can."

"I am not sure that is true." The words were sharper than she had heard from him in some time.

"If you could locate a replacement, I could train him or her. It would also assure that when I leave you won't be left without someone to fill the position." She couldn't stay here forever. This wasn't her home and she was becoming far too attached to Tariq. That couldn't continue.

He'd made it clear today that he didn't plan to marry or have children, both of which were important to her.

Tariq said nothing more.

Laurel concentrated on the road, but then stomped on the brakes. A man dressed in a well-worn full shirt and baggy pants stood in the middle of the road, waving his arms above his head, yelling something in Arabic. Before she could pull off the road Tariq was out of the car and running toward the man. They spoke rapidly. The man started up a path.

Tariq moved to follow while calling over his shoulder, "Bring my medical bag. It is behind the driver's seat."

He didn't wait for her to answer and started after the man.

Laurel pulled off the road as far as the shoulder would allow. She climbed out and found the bag. With it in her hand, she made her way up the narrow, steep and rocky trail with grass growing knee-high on the sides. Tariq and the man were nowhere in sight but she kept moving as fast as she could. The way was clearly visible but difficult to maneuver.

She reached a small, level pasture. From there Laurel could see Tariq's back in the distance as he ran under some mushroom-shaped trees. She picked up her pace and kept moving. Soon she entered the olive grove and moments later she came out into a small opening.

There stood a small single-level white house with a red clay tile roof. Beside it was a pen with a goat in it. Tariq ducked his head to enter a door in the middle of the building. She headed that way. At the entrance she paused, not wanting to barge into someone's home. After giving the door a quick knock, she continued into the dim interior.

It was a one-room house with a kitchen area to one

side and on the other a sitting and bedroom space. The place was neat and smelled slightly of smoke. Tariq and the man spoke rapidly in Arabic in the far corner where the bed was located. A colorful blanket hung from the ceiling as a room divider. Laurel joined them, placing the bag on the end of the bed.

When there was a pause in the conversation Laurel asked Tariq, "What's wrong?"

"His wife has not felt good for a few days. She passed out. He moved her to the bed before he went for help. He was walking to the nearest neighbor." Tariq opened the bag and pulled out a stethoscope.

"I'll check her temperature and blood pressure." Laurel found the thermometer and BP cuff.

Tariq spoke to the man again and he stepped back, giving Lauren and Tariq room to work.

Laurel stood beside Tariq. "Temperature one hundred and three point seven." Lifting the woman's arm, Laurel positioned the blood-pressure cuff. Tariq handed her the stethoscope, which she placed in her ears and found the woman's pulse. "BP is one-eighty over ninety."

Tariq continued to examine the woman as he said, "She should be taken to the hospital but there is no phone service. Since we can't, we should give her a thorough exam and see what we can find."

"Agreed." Laurel looked around. The one small window on that side of the room offered little help. "The light is bad."

He said something to the man, who nodded and hurried to the kitchen. "I asked if he had any candles." Tariq pushed the curtain against the wall as far as it would go. "You will need to do most of the examination. These older people consider their privacy and especially that of their women important. Husbands do not allow other men to touch their wife."

"I'll take care of it," Laurel assured him.

Would she have said that with as much confidence a few weeks ago? She was different. Coming to Zentar had changed her.

Their patient let out a moan. Hopefully she was regaining consciousness. "What's her name?"

"Melina."

Laurel spoke in a soft reassuring voice. "Melina, I'm going to have to move you. I'm sorry if it hurts. I promise I'll try to make this as painless as possible. I also have to remove your clothes."

Tariq stepped away. Laurel lifted the woman as much as she could and removed an arm from the sleeve of a full cotton dress, then did the same with the other.

The husband sat candles around the area. It helped some but the light was still poor.

With an amount of work that made Laurel break out in a sweat, she removed the woman's garment, always speaking to Melina as she worked. When she had Melina in nothing but her underclothes, Laurel proceeded to examine her. "I don't see any obvious problems on her head, arms or legs."

"Good." Tariq's voice came from close by.

Laurel rolled Melina to one side and checked her back, pulling the underclothing as far from the skin as the material would allow. Nothing. If she didn't find something obvious soon, it must be an internal problem. In these primitive conditions that would make the situation more difficult.

She eased Melina down on the bed again. Reaching

across her, Laurel rolled the woman toward her. Melina moaned.

"I'm almost done," Laurel comforted her. Shifting the woman's underclothes as much as possible again, Laurel checked her back for anything suspicious. Just under the woman's shoulder blade was a large angry-looking area. In the center the skin was raised, with an advanced infection. No wonder the woman was sick.

"I found the problem. She has an abscess. It's on her back." Laurel covered Melina's lower body with a blanket.

Tariq spoke to the man, who responded. Seconds later Tariq joined her, with the old man hovering nearby.

"Let me see," Tariq said.

Together they rolled Melina toward them. "That is ugly. It must be lanced and drained right away." He met her gaze. "You up for a little surgery?"

"I don't think we have a choice." Laurel helped him roll the woman back to the bed.

"We don't."

"We need to get her on her stomach and the rest of her clothing removed." Tariq picked up his bag and started going through it. "We will have to improvise. We cannot wait. It will take too long to get an ambulance to this remote area. This needs to be done now."

Tariq spoke to the man, who joined them. Tariq then said to her, "It will take all three of us to turn her. Her husband has agreed to help you remove her underclothing. Cover her with the blanket again."

They all did as instructed and soon had Melina in the necessary position.

Tariq spoke to the man and he left by the front door.

"I told him to heat some water." He looked down at the woman. "Do you want to handle the surgery or shall I?"

"I'll be glad to assist. I haven't done anything like this in a long time."

"We are thin on supplies but we will make do. See if you can find some clean cloths while I assemble what we need."

Laurel hurried to the kitchen. After a short search she located where Melina kept her dish towels. Grabbing the stack, she hurried back to Tariq. She placed them on the bed and then removed one off the top and spread it over the bed.

"Thanks," Tariq murmured his attention on the job at hand.

Tariq was impressed by Laurel's anticipation of what would be required She was thinking through the problem, not depending on him to make all the decisions. Laurel was far more capable than she let on. Or that he thought she would admit to herself. That guy in college had really messed with her mind.

It had been a long time since he had performed surgery, and he had never done it under such primitive conditions. Working in a small dark house in the middle of nowhere and with nothing but his medical bag contents for supplies was a stretch. What he feared was that the patient's condition would get worse if they did not do something immediately.

If only he could call an ambulance. But that would take over two hours to arrive. The road up the mountain it would have to travel was little more than a cart track.

As he assembled instruments Laurel redid vitals. "Her temperature is up."

The man returned with a bucket of water and was busy heating it on the wood stove.

"I only have a few alcohol and iodine wipes. We will use those only when absolutely necessary. What I cannot work out is what to use for the drain tubing."

"It's a little large but how about the hose on the blood-pressure cuff?" Laurel looked at him for a response. "We can always do BP by touch."

Tariq nodded. "That would work." He picked up the blood-pressure cuff and cut as long a length of tube as he could then set it on the towel beside his other instruments. "We need to sterilize everything in the hot water. We also need to wash Melina's back." He was talking to himself as much as to Laurel.

The man brought a pot of steaming water to the bedside and set it on the floor. Tariq asked for soap. The man returned with it. Laurel took it from him. Picking up a cloth, she bathed the surgical field. Tariq asked for a bowl and began sterilizing instruments as Laurel scrubbed Melina's back for the second time then wiped it with an iodine swab.

He met Laurel's gaze. "I have one set of plastic gloves. We each get one. That means we will have to think and act as one." Tariq handed her a glove.

"I understand."

"Are you ready?"

"As I'm going to be." She pulled on the glove with an unwavering look on her face.

"It is time. I will make the incision. You will need to mop up as we go. As soon as we can see, we will check for tissue damage then place the tube."

Laurel nodded. "I understand."

"Then we will begin." Tariq poised the disposable

scalpel over the swollen skin. Tariq nicked it. Melina groaned and Laurel dabbed as the infection flowed. Tariq enlarged the incision as Laurel grabbed another cloth. The smell of contamination filled the air. With the incision open, he placed the scalpel in the hot water.

"I'm going to press around the wound. We have to remove all the infection or we are doing no good." Tariq applied pressure with his glove-covered fingers. Melina let out a sob of pain.

Laurel mopped the exudate. Tariq continued until finally more blood than infected material covered the cloth. "I am going to open the site and see if the infection has affected the tissue. You hold one side and I will pull from the other. That should make it wide enough for us to see."

The old man brought another pot of water.

They did as Tariq had mapped out.

"It looks clean." Tariq glanced at Laurel to see if she agreed. She nodded. "Now we need to flush it and insert the drain." To the man he said, "We need a clean cup."

Seconds later the man had placed one in his hand. Tariq filled it with clean water. He checked the heat against his cheek. It should be close to room temperature before using it in the wound.

"Let's roll her on her side so it will drain well," Laurel suggested.

"Good idea. Roll her toward us, that way we can see better."

Happy with the temperature, he gently poured the water into the wound to irrigate it. The excess Laurel mopped up with a cloth. They continued the process for another five minutes.

Laurel dropped a wet cloth on the floor and picked up a clean one. "We shouldn't close it. Just pack it and they can close it after she has been started on an antibiotic at the hospital."

They settled the woman on her stomach again.

"I agree." Tariq removed his glove and pulled out packages of gauze squares. "Will you take care of packing while I reassure the husband?"

"I can do that." Laurel wiped her glove on the cloth then started opening a package.

A few minutes later Tariq returned to find the drain in place and the wound packed. "One of us is going to need to go for the ambulance while the other stays with our patient."

"That'll have to be you. I don't know the way back to the city and I don't speak the language." Laurel checked Melina's pulse at her neck.

"This is not how I planned our evening to go."

Laurel gave him a wry smile. "I have to admit it has been an unusual one."

"I will leave now so that I can return as soon as possible. I will only drive until I get phone reception."

She nodded, but looked a little unsure. Still, she said, "I'll be fine here."

He cupped her cheek. "You are a special person, Laurel. I would assist in your OR anytime."

She smiled. "Thanks. You weren't half-bad yourself."

Tariq returned the smile then headed toward the door, stopping just long enough to speak to the man.

Laurel had no idea how long Tariq had been gone. The old man had brought her a chair. After she had cleaned up, she sat beside Melina. The woman's temperature remained elevated and she had become restless. Laurel continued to take her vitals every fifteen minutes. The woman should be at the hospital, receiving IV antibiotics.

Today's adventure was just another one in the long line of reasons why she didn't belong in Zentar. Doing primitive surgery in a hovel of a house when she didn't speak the language was out of her comfort zone—along with living in a palace and wearing an ancient wedding dress, and the list seemed to go on. They were all reminders that this was a temporary stop on her way back to America. All she needed was for funding to come through.

The man said something and left at dusk. Laurel assumed he'd gone to see about the animals. It had turned dark and the candles were burning low by the time he returned. Still there was no Tariq.

Out of the silence came the sound of something whirling. The old man opened the door and looked out into the blackness. She joined him.

A bright light shone on the field on the other side of the trees. The noise grew and wind blew the branches. It was a helicopter. Laurel stepped out into the yard, watching as the dark machine hovered above the ground then settled.

This she hadn't expected. She'd been listening for a vehicle. How like Tariq to show up in the most dramatic fashion. But he'd come, as he had promised. Something that she learned about him was that he could be trusted to do as he said he would. That was the type of man she wanted in her life. Even if it was only for a little while.

Seconds later a figure came running toward her. It was Tariq. She knew his figure well.

"Laurel." He took her into a brief hug. Everything about him was warm, steady and reassuring. "How are things here?"

"Melina is still unconscious. Her vitals have been good, but she's in pain. It seems like forever since you left."

With his arm around her waist he led her toward the house. "I hurried as fast as I could. It occurred to me about halfway to the car that this place is so remote that a helicopter was the most efficient way to get here."

"Do you have one of those also?"

He grinned. "No, but I know someone who does. A couple of emergency staff are behind me with a stretcher. We will get Melina on the chopper and airlifted to the hospital. I also have somebody en route to drive her husband to the city."

Tariq spoke quickly to the old man and they entered the house. The paramedics with a stretcher in hand came in right behind them. She and Tariq stood out of the way as they worked. Soon they were carrying Melina toward the helicopter.

Tariq spoke to the husband again and they shook hands. All Laurel could do was give him her best reassuring smile. Tariq took her hand. She picked up his bag and they left. It wasn't until then that Laurel registered that the plan was for her to ride in the helicopter as well. She balked, jerking Tariq to a stop.

"What is wrong? Did you forget something?" Concern laced his words.

Laurel shook her head. "I can't get on a helicopter! I'll wait and ride down with the man."

Tariq took her by the shoulders. "Yes, you can. I will be there with you. I will not let anything happen to you." He gave her a quick kiss on the lips. "This I promise."

She studied him for a moment. Tariq had not let her down yet. She could trust him.

At her nod, he hurried her into the field. Tariq took his

bag and stowed it before helping her into the helicopter. She took a seat in the middle, not wanting to sit beside a window or the door. Tariq moved past her and settled in the seat next to the window. He buckled her in and then himself. Melina was secured in the area behind them with the two men attending her.

"I know this is only your second flight but it is more efficient for Melina."

"I know. But that doesn't mean I like it."

He gave her a reassuring smile. His arm came around her shoulders, pulling her against his firm side. He took her hand as the helicopter's blades began to turn.

Tariq spoke directly into her ear. "*Habibti*, I think you are very brave. I was proud of you this evening. You are very special to me."

If Tariq's intent was to take her mind off what was happening, it worked. In a daze of pleasure, Laurel squeezed her eyes shut and buried her face in Tariq's chest. They shifted to one side and then the other before the helicopter rose and moved off into the darkness. The steady thump-thump of Tariq's heart eased her fear. Laurel clung to him like the life support he was.

Thankfully the ride was a short one. The helicopter descended and finally rocked to a stop. They had only been on the ground a few seconds before Melina was unloaded and in the hands of waiting medical staff.

Tariq unbuckled and then helped Laurel. After he climbed out, he offered her his hand. They were on a helicopter pad outside what she assumed was the hospital. Tariq put a hand on her head and ducked his as they quickly moved out from under the still-rotating blades. He then led her inside the three-story building and down a long hall.

"We need to go to Emergency to give a report." Laurel worked to keep up with Tariq's long strides.

"We are on our way. I also want to tell them to expect Melina's husband. He is fearful and suspicious."

In the emergency department they both gave an account to the attending doctor of what they had done, and he appeared both surprised and pleased to see Tariq. Laurel informed the doctor of Melina's last vitals. Tariq then explained that the husband would be coming in and to see he had anything he needed.

He was not only generous where his family was concerned but his countrymen were as well. Why had she ever believe he was closed off emotionally?

They checked on Melina one last time. She was resting comfortably. Tariq directed Laurel toward the exit. "Nasser is waiting outside. I thought you would prefer not to ride home by helicopter." There was a teasing note in Tariq's voice.

She yawned. "You know me so well. I'm not sure you could convince me to get back into it."

He took her hand and kissed the back of it.

Warmth flowed through her. "Did the old man ever realize who you are?"

"I don't know."

Laurel watched as they approached the lit-up palace. Zentar was a wondrous place. She had gone from little more than a hovel to a castle in less than an hour. "What do you think he's going to think when he learns it was you?"

"He will be grateful that two doctors were driving by and his wife is alive."

Nasser pulled into the courtyard and they were soon inside the palace.

As they walked Tariq said, "You were great today. I am glad you were there with me."

"I'm sure you could've taken care of Melina without me."

"Maybe I could have, but it was nice to have your excellent skills as well." They stopped at her door. "You must be exhausted." He kissed her on the forehead. "Rest well, *habibti*. You have earned it."

Laurel watched Tariq walk to the door across the hall and open it. Her breath caught. She'd been that close to him all this time. How was she supposed to sleep knowing he was so near?

CHAPTER EIGHT

ON MONDAY MORNING Tariq expected to see Laurel in the dining room. He waited half an hour at breakfast before he asked one of the staff if he had seen her.

"I believe she ordered something sent to her room a number of hours ago, Your Highness."

"Thank you." Tariq stood with the intention of checking on her.

Less than a minute later he knocked on her bedroom door. There was no answer. Tariq knocked again and there was still no response. Where was she? *The lab.* He phoned Nasser. "Did you take Princess Laurel to the clinic this morning?"

"Yes, sir. Is there a problem?"

"No. Pick me up in five minutes."

"Yes, sir."

Fifteen minutes later Tariq reached Laurel's lab. There she was with her back to the door, filling a test tube. Tariq pushed the buzzer. She looked around and raised a hand.

Using the intercom, she said, "I'll be out in a minute."

He watched her remove her protective clothing. What he would not give to remove *all* her clothing. The taste he'd had of how beautiful her body was had haunted him the last two nights. He'd had big plans for the evening after their day together. They had been due to dine in the tower of the palace where the lights of the city could be seen. Then he had hoped that it might lead to her bedroom or his.

Instead, they had spent it attending to Melina. He did not regret that, was even glad they had been there, but his desire for Laurel had moved into an obsession. This morning's drive to see her was a fine example. He should be in his office.

Laurel greeted him with a smile. "Good morning. I didn't expect to see you here this early. When you said you would come I thought it would be more like lunchtime."

What was she talking about? Oh, the research on his family. He had said he would discuss that today.

"Come on, we'll go to my 'office'..." she made air quotes with her fingers "...and talk there. At least I can say I used it."

"That will be fine." She wore her hair up again. He longed to have that time at the beach back. Leaving her at her bedroom door that night might have been the most difficult thing he had ever done. He was also sorry that duties had taken him away from the palace the day before. "Your hair is up. I like it down." Now he sounded whiney, like he had not gotten his way.

"It's easier to fit under a cap if I pull it back. I've been thinking of cutting it."

"No!" He hadn't even had a chance to run his fingers through it.

She turned. "You don't have any say in that."

His gaze met hers. "I know, but I wish you wouldn't cut it. It is lovely."

Laurel shrugged. "I'll see. I checked on Melina this

morning. She's awake and doing well. They think she'll be well enough to leave today."

Tariq had not even given their patient a thought because he had been so consumed with thinking of Laurel. She was making a compete mess of his life, but for some reason he didn't mind as long as she remained in it. "I am glad to hear it. I had planned to go by the hospital this morning. Would you like to go when I do?"

"I don't think so. I have too much to do here after being gone on Saturday."

"You do know that it is permissible to take time off. Your work is important but life is as well." Why could she not see that she was missing out on living because she would not let go at all? She had been so much fun yesterday. Even while they'd cared for Melina she had been more open and alive.

"I like what I do."

"You might like other things as well." *Like me.*

They had reached her office and she took a seat behind the desk, leaving him a chair in front of it. This was a huge role reversal for him. As the Prince he was always afforded the seat of authority except with the King. One of the many nice things about Laurel was that she saw him as Tariq and not royalty. He slid into the chair.

She pulled a legal pad out of the top drawer and located a pen. "First I'm going to ask you a series of questions then we'll go back to the lab and draw your blood."

"What could you ask that you do not already know about my family history?"

"For starters I want to find out about your ancestors. I find that family members often forget about some while others remember others. I like to cross-check."

Tariq had never seen her so animated. He wished she was this excited about seeing him.

"Tell me about your mother's family. Brothers, sisters then go to grandparents."

Over the next few minutes he gave names, those he could remember, while Laurel nodded and made notes.

She tapped her pen on the paper then looked at him. "Do you know if any of them had hemophilia?"

He pursed his lips. "Um…one of my second cousins did. His mother, my great-aunt, is still alive."

Laurel sat forward. "She is?"

"Yes. She is part of a mountain tribe. I have not seen her in over a year."

"I would love to speak to her. Is that possible?" Laurel's eyes were filled with anticipation.

Tariq could not deny her this, or anything else for that matter. "I will see what I can do. I need to go up there anyway. I will look at clearing my schedule and maybe I could take you at the end of the week."

"That would be great!" She wiggled in her excitement. Would she react that way as he prepared to enter her? He had slipped over the edge.

Laurel continued to ask him questions but this time about his father's side of the family. Despite the subject, he enjoyed talking with Laurel. She asked intelligent and thoughtful questions.

She finished with, "Now it's time for your blood draw. Would you like to have it done at the clinic lab or for me to do it?"

"I have seen you in action. You may do it."

"Then we'll need to go back to my lab."

Tariq followed her there. He waited while she gathered what she needed in the small room. She put a tourniquet around his arm then located a vein. Her head moved close to his as she worked. "You smell like the gardenias that grow in the garden. Heavenly."

Her breath caught.

Tariq leaned closer. "I desire you, Laurel."

He felt a stick in his arm. He hissed and clenched his jaw.

"You shouldn't talk while I'm working." She released the tourniquet and watched the blood fill the tube. With that done, she placed a gauze square over the needle and pulled it out. She removed a length of tape from a nearby roll and applied it firmly over the gauze.

Tariq caught her hand and looked her in the eyes. "Just because you ignore what is between us, it doesn't mean it will go away."

A few hours later Tariq said to his office assistant, "Just make it happen. I will be gone the last three days of this week."

"Yes, sir. Is there anything else?"

"I would like the stables notified I will need Turo and Astor, trailered along with a pack horse and all the tack, ready to go at six in the morning on Wednesday. This afternoon I will provide you with a list of supplies I wish to take with me."

"I will see that all is taken care of." The man nodded and exited the office.

Tariq picked up the phone and autodialed the lab number. One of the staff answered and he asked for Laurel. He waited.

The woman's voice came back on the line. She sounded unsure. "I'm sorry, Your Highness, but she will not come to the phone right now. She will return your call later."

Tariq smiled. How like Laurel. When everyone else danced to his requests she acted as if he was no big deal. "Tell her that will be fine."

Hours later his secretary rang through. "The Princess is on the line."

Tariq picked up the phone, anticipation making his heart pound. He looked forward to hearing her voice. "Laurel."

"Hey. You needed me?" She sounded distracted.

He wanted to say in more ways than one, but refrained. "I have arranged for us to leave in two days' time for the mountains. You can be prepared by then?"

"Uh…yeah. I should be able to make that work." She paused as if her mind had gone elsewhere once more. "I'll put in a few extra hours here, but it'll be fine. Thanks for this, Tariq. I have to go." The phone went dead.

She obviously had not been as excited to speak to him as he had been to hear her voice. What did it take to get her attention?

Two evenings later Laurel returned to the palace just before bedtime. She'd come to expect that a dinner tray would be waiting in her room. She wasn't disappointed. Also there were a number of packages. A note in a bold script rested on top of one. It was from Tariq.

You will need these for our trip. See you at six a.m.

As usual he was very businesslike, even after their adventure the weekend before. As if in unspoken agreement they had both focused on their work. Laurel had required time to regroup and figure out her feelings. Apparently Tariq had needed to do the same. The problem was that hers were still an emotional jumble. Even when she had been asking him questions she could hardly focus for thinking about his sensual mouth as he'd answered.

Since their time together she'd thought of little else but him. Despite her inexperience, she had been well aware of where their day together had been going. The big question that kept rolling through her mind was whether she would have gone to bed with Tariq. Even days later she wasn't confident that she could have resisted him if he had asked. Would he have?

Now she'd be alone with him again. In the mountains, where she would be completely dependent on him. She'd have to keep her defenses up if she wanted her heart to survive. At least this time she knew the score. What would be the harm if she did let go? Tariq wasn't offering her anything, he had already made that clear. Why couldn't she have a wonderful memory to replace a horrible one? She had no doubt being with Tariq would be life-changing.

After all, she might be leaving soon. She had received an email from Stewart that afternoon. He had a good lead on funding for her and would know soon if it would come through or not. She hadn't been as excited at the prospect as she'd thought she would have been. Wasn't the funding and a way back to America what she had been hoping for?

But while she was here she would make the most of it. Going on this trip with Tariq was one more chance for her to compile information for her study. It must be difficult for a man of his stature to get away. Yet he had worked it out for her. With her quality staff, she would be able to leave them with a number of assignments so that her research would continue regardless of her absence. It would be the same when she returned to the States.

She'd not seen Tariq in the last couple of days. Outside their one brief phone call she had not spoken to him either. She missed him. The temptation to go for a swim in the hope he'd be there almost overcame her better judgment. She should focus on preparing for the trip.

Opening the packages, she found a heavy jacket lined with sheepskin. She ran her hand over the tooled leather on the outside. It was a much finer coat than she could afford. In a box was a pair of ankle boots with a soft interior. She slipped the moleskin shoes on. They fit perfectly and had the comfort of a cloud. In another were a couple of heavy flannel shirts and a red stocking cap with braided yarn hanging along the sides. She pulled on the cap and giggled at the sight she made, looking more like a little kid than a grown woman.

After bathing, she ate and climbed into bed. She needed her rest if she planned to handle the days ahead and her attraction to Tariq, which wasn't helped by the fact he was just steps away. How would he react if she went to him? Her eyes closed on thoughts of Tariq wearing nothing and leading her to his bed.

She couldn't remember her eyes even closing before there was a knock at her door. "Yes?"

"It is Nasser. It is six. The Prince asked me to see if you needed help."

Laurel had overslept. This wasn't a good way to start a trip with Tariq. If she had learned anything, he didn't like people not meeting his expectations. "Please tell him I will meet him at the car in fifteen minutes."

"Yes, ma'am."

As quick as humanly possible she washed her face and

applied sunscreen. This time she left her hair down but plaited it into a braid behind her head. Pulling on socks she'd brought from home, her jeans and a T-shirt with a flannel shirt over it, she put on her boots. She picked up her bag and stuffed the other things she needed into it. Snatching up her coat, she hurried to meet her husband.

Laurel opened the courtyard door with a jerk, then her mouth dropped open. A dual-wheeled pickup with a horse trailer waited. She had given no thought to how they were getting into the mountains but riding horses had never occurred to her. How like Tariq to keep that detail to himself. Once more she was out of her element. What if she couldn't handle the horse?

He came around the front of the truck. This morning he was dressed in a shirt much like hers, jeans, boots and safari-type hat. He was every bit as dashing as he had been in his traditional wear. What was she getting herself into?

"Horses?" She waved a hand toward the trailer.

"You said you rode."

Tariq made it sound like that was the answer to everything. "You could have told me your plans so I could at least be mentally prepared. I was a child the last time I was on a horse."

"What is the saying? It will be like riding a bike."

She climbed into the truck. "That's until I fall off."

Tariq stood in the open door, which put him at eye level with her. "I think not. You will be determined not to. The best way to the tribe is by horse. We will take it slowly and easily." He patted her leg then closed the door.

He was right. Just for the chance to talk to his elderly great-aunt she'd do whatever she had to, even ride a horse. The heavy truck rumbled in the early morning air as they drove way. She grinned. They must be an unusual sight, pulling away from the palace.

They continued out of the city on the same road they had used on the way to the beach but soon turned and headed toward the mountains. The sun and the gradient slowly rose as they went.

They had been traveling about an hour when she asked, "How far can we go in the pickup?"

"We have another hour to where we will leave the truck and trailer. I wanted to start early because it is easier on the horses when it is cool."

"And I overslept. I'm sorry."

He placed his hand over hers. She loved his touch. It would be one of many things she would miss when she left Zentar—and the funding seemed so close now. "You were tired. We are fine." Her hand remained under his as he continued, "It will get warm during the day but it gets cold at night. I hope you brought all that I sent you."

"I have it in my bag."

"Aw, the ever-present bag."

She glared and tried to pull her hand out from under his. He held it tight and kept his eyes on the road. "What do you mean by that?"

"You are not going to pull me into an argument this morning. It is too nice a day."

The man could make her so mad. If he wouldn't talk to her then she would take a nap. Being shaken woke her sometime later. Her head was resting against Tariq's shoulder. She quickly straightened. "I didn't mean to go to sleep on you, literally."

He smiled. "I did not mind. I wish it happened more often."

A flash of heat shot through her. If he kept saying

things like that, she would be at his feet, begging for his kisses. "You shouldn't say things like that to me."

"Why not? It is true. We will leave the truck here."

Tariq climbed out. She followed. He started unloading the horses.

"What can I do?" She wasn't going to stand there and watch while he did all the work.

"You can help me saddle them and load the pack horse."

Tariq had been correct. It did all come back to her. She remembered how to put the saddle on and adjust the cinch. "What are their names?"

"The bay is Astor. She is yours. The stallion is Turo."

When they were finished, Tariq gave her a kiss on the cheek as he passed. "You are a good help."

Laurel placed her hand over the spot. Tariq's praise made her glow. She couldn't keep from smiling. The man had such an effect on her.

Together they loaded the pack horse. In that process Tariq had to give her more instruction.

"What's all this?" Laurel asked as she removed another box from the back seat of the truck.

"Medical supplies. Twice a year they are taken to the village. I told the man who usually does it that I would take them this time. We will be doing a clinic tomorrow."

"*We* will?" She looked at him. "Are you speaking for me now, Your Highness?"

He met her gaze. "You know I don't like it when you call me that."

"Then maybe you should start asking and telling me things, and not act so high-handed."

He lowered his chin. "I will keep that in mind. Now bring me that box. We need to get started."

"Yes, *Your Highness*."

He glared at her and she grinned.

Thirty minutes later Laurel rode up the path behind Tariq, who was leading the pack horse. The sun was already beating down on her neck. They soon made a couple of switchbacks and moved into a stretch with rock both sides where it became much cooler. Tariq kept a slow, steady pace. They continued upward. Laurel contented herself with watching Tariq's broad shoulders and his skill with a horse. With the slightest movement of his legs his stallion responded. They had been riding sometime when Tariq called over his shoulder, "How are you doing?"

"I may not be able to walk in the morning, but I'm fine."

"I am sorry the path is so narrow that we cannot ride side by side."

"It's okay. I've just been enjoying the view." *Of him.* She left that off. Astor was surefooted and Laurel gained more confidence as they traveled. She did look around her when she could. The mountains were as Tariq had described them, harsh and rugged, but he was right, there was a beauty there as well.

The gradient grew steeper and more difficult as they rode. Laurel concentrated on the landscape. An occasional splotch of green showed here and there as a plant struggled to survive in the arid surroundings. A lizard ran along the rock then disappeared into a crack.

The sun hung high in the sky when Tariq led them into a level area. There were a few large mushroom-shaped trees making the space cool and refreshing. Laurel was surprised when she heard the sound of water. A small stream came out of a rock to form a pool below.

Tariq dismounted and Laurel followed suit. Her dismount was not nearly as graceful as his. It took her a moment to become steady on her feet. She patted Astor on the neck.

"Lead her over here and let her have some water, but not too much. We do not want her to founder." Tariq took Turo's reins.

"Founder?"

"When a hot horse drinks too much cool water."

"Well, a person learns something new every day." She followed Tariq.

After the horses had finished, they tied them up nearby and Tariq removed a small bag from the pack horse. They took seats on rocks near the pool. He removed some packets that included crackers, fruit and nuts, and handed them to her.

"There should be some bottles of water in here. There they are." Tariq handed one to her. "How are you doing?"

"It must show I've not ridden in a long time and even then, not much. Astor's a nice horse."

"I trained her myself."

Did the man's talents never end? "You did a wonderful job. How much further do we have to go?"

"At least another two hours. For the rest of the way I want you to be sure and stay right behind the pack horse. If you were to stray off the path it could be dangerous. Understood?"

She took a drink of the water. "Yes."

They finished their meal in silence and as soon as they were finished Tariq took her trash and stuffed it back into the bag. "If you are ready, we should go."

Laurel joined him at the horses. She winced at the thought of getting on again.

"Do you need help up?"

"No, I've got it."

"Aha, is that newfound confidence I hear?"

"Something like that." Laurel swung her leg over Astor and groaned.

They continued to travel. Tariq had not exaggerated his description of the landscape. They made one switchback after another, the going becoming harder all the time. When Laurel feared it would never end, they circled a large bolder and below them was a green valley with a stream running through it.

Tariq called over his shoulder, "We have arrived."

From the sky the village wouldn't have been visible because it blended in with the mountains and the landscape. The tents were the type with a high center pole and four corner ones, making the canvas look much like a circus tent.

"How did you know where to come?"

Tariq said over his shoulder, "Because in the spring this is where the tribe comes."

As they rode down there was a sudden shout and people came out of tents and left what they were doing to form a group. A thrill and trepidation raced through her. This was nothing she had any experience with. It was like going back in time.

"Were they expecting us?"

"Word travels even this far into the mountains. My countrymen live simply but they are not ignorant of the world."

As they rode in, people circled Tariq, trying to touch him. He dismounted and came to help her down. She wobbled and Tariq brought her against him. His warm musk smell surrounded her, making her feel more alive, further aware of his masculinity. She shivered.

"Nothing to fear. They are just excited to see us."

She stepped away. "I'm not afraid."

The crowd parted and an elderly man hobbled toward them. He said something in Arabic and bowed his head. Tariq responded then placed a hand on her shoulder as he spoke.

A sound of awe rose from the crowd.

Tariq said to her, "I told them that you are my wife. This is the leader of this tribe. He has welcomed us." The old man spoke again. Tariq translated. "He says they will have a celebration in honor of our marriage."

Once again she and Tariq were lying to people. She hated it but there was no way out of it now.

She forced a smile. "Please tell him thank you from me."

Tariq and the tribal leader lapsed into a discussion. When they had finished, Tariq took Astor's reins and handed them to a young man standing nearby who already held Turo's. Tariq then went to the pack horse and removed his medical bag. He returned to her and placing a hand at her waist he directed her toward the leader, who had started walking away.

"My great-aunt is very ill. She is too weak to greet us. He is taking us to her."

Laurel looked at him. "The one I want to speak to?"

"The very one."

The leader stopped in front of a tent and nodded before moving on. Tariq held the tent flap back for Laurel to pass.

"You go first. She will not know who I am."

Tariq preceded her. She entered right behind him. The

tent was lit by one large oil lamp hanging from the center pole. On a low bed of pillows lay a shrunken woman. Two women sat on either side of her. Tariq went to her, going down on his knees. He spoke softly then motioned Laurel forward.

"Belica says it is nice to meet the new Princess. She is surprised you are from another culture but wishes you happiness. She is willing to answer your questions."

"Please tell her it's nice to meet her as well. That I appreciate her willingness to help."

Tariq opened his bag. "Before we start the questions I am going to examine her."

Laurel stood by patiently while Tariq took the woman's vitals and checked her abdominal area. He soon finished. Over the next few minutes Laurel asked the same questions of Tariq's aunt as she had of him.

When the woman closed her eyes, Tariq stood and took Laurel's hand. "That is enough for now."

They exited the tent. The same young man who had led their horses away waited nearby. He bowed and spoke to Tariq.

"This way. Our tent is ready." Tariq followed the man.

"Tent? As we are staying together?"

Tariq looked at her. "Remember, we are married."

She couldn't think of a time she'd forgotten. "I'm well aware of that."

They were taken to a large tent off to one side.

"Whose is this? Are we taking someone's home?" Unease built in Laurel at the thought of sharing such close quarters with Tariq.

The man left them.

Tariq sweep his arm out indicating she should enter.

"It was put up just for us when they heard we were coming. We will also hold clinic here."

Inside the tent looked much as Tariq's aunt's had with the exception of the bright multicolored rug completely covering the floor. Piles of large pillows were set in a number of places. Off to the side was a low bed of pillows. Colorful draped material hung from the ceiling around it. The place looked as if the tribe had made an extra effort to make the space special. "I can see they go all out for royalty."

"This is to honor you. When I have been here before I have had a simple tent or stayed with my aunt."

Outside her family no one had ever made her feel included. The people of Zentar, even these simple mountain people, had worked their way into her heart. "It is beautiful. Like something out of the *Arabian Nights*."

Tariq went to the stack of supplies that had been placed in a corner near the entrance. He picked up her bag, offering it to her. She took it. Again he looked through the supplies and came out with a tube of cream. "You will find a fresh water basin on the other side of the bed." He gave her the tube. "You must be saddle sore. This will help. Food will be brought to us tonight. I have to go and speak to the leader about the clinic. I will return soon." Without a backward look, he left her.

Tariq had dreamed more than once of having Laurel to himself and tonight he would. But in those dreams he had her coming to him by choice, not because she had to share the same space with him. He could not go elsewhere to sleep because that would shame her in the eyes of the people. The best he could do was stay on the other side of the tent and pretend she was miles away. But that was never going to happen.

When he had insisted they marry he'd believed it would be no problem for him. He'd had zero personal interest in Laurel. Had not thought it would be an issue or change his life in any way. Nothing could be further from the truth. She had turned his world upside down. Where his life had revolved around his work, now he thought of nothing but Laurel. Surely if he could get her out of his system he could move on. Then he could look into finding someone to replace her, as she had suggested.

None of that solved his current difficulty of sharing a tent for the night with her and keeping his hands to himself. He would make it happen somehow. There was a promise between them. She deserved better than the way she had been treated before by a man. He refused to be considered part of that attitude.

Tariq returned to the tent to find Laurel asleep on the bed. He was both relieved and disappointed. She must be exhausted. They had had an early morning and it had been a long ride. Laurel had been amazing. For someone who had lived so closed off from the world she had not complained once. She never stopped astonishing him.

He had taken the time to freshen up in the stream instead of coming straight back to the tent in the hope the cold mountain water would settle his raging desire. Tariq looked at Laurel; unfortunately it had not worked.

A noise outside the tent entrance led him to look there. One of the village women held a tray of food in her hands. Tariq beckoned her in. She placed the tray on the low chest and left. Tariq debated whether or not to wake Laurel. Before he could make a decision, she rose.

"Tariq? Is that you?"

Laurel had changed her clothes. Now she wore a simple sundress with a flannel shirt over it, tied at her waist.

He almost groaned out loud when he saw her hair down around her shoulders. It shined in the lamplight. He was in trouble.

"You may want to put on heavier clothes. It will get cool tonight."

"I will. I'm starving now. Didn't I see someone bring a tray in?"

"You did. Come, we should eat." That was a safer subject than talking about her clothing.

"I'm ravenous."

Tariq knew the feeling. He picked up a couple of large pillows. Placing one on the right side of the temporary table, he threw the other on the floor across from it. "Our meal awaits."

Along with the food there was a bottle of wine.

Tariq reclined on his side on a pillow and she sat cross-legged on hers as they ate their meal of basic but substantial food.

"So what're the plans for tomorrow?" Laurel bit into a date.

How like Laurel to have to have her days planned. "You don't like surprises, do you?"

Laurel pursed her lips for a second then said, "If they are good ones."

"I think I will save my good surprises for another occasion. We will start seeing patients in the morning. Some will come from neighboring villages as well. I do not anticipate any challenges. Most of the issues will require simple care. If someone needs to have their clothes removed or we think there is a sensitive issue then we will bring them inside the tent. I will need to see the men and you the women."

For the same reason she was technically married to

Tariq they would be seeing patients in the traditional way. If she were truly his wife, Laurel would make it a mission to change that thinking.

"The language barrier will cause some difficulty. I will do triage and let you know what the issue is. You can handle it from there."

So now she was being relegated to being an assistant. Once again, she wished she knew some Arabic. "Is there no one who speaks some English here?"

Tariq's eyes widened in surprise. "Why?"

"I would like to work beside you, not for you." Who had she turned into? She hadn't ever made a habit of being aggressive until now. Most of her life she'd spent trying to blend in, causing no trouble. The idea that she had only started the assertive phase of her life with Tariq and the Zentaran people made her shudder.

"I can ask. You are right. You have proved over and over you are qualified. You should act as my equal. It would be good for the people to see that."

Heat flashed through her. He had captured her heart completely with that statement. She had never had higher praise from someone she admired more. Heaven help her, she was falling for Tariq. She looked away, hoping he wouldn't see how she felt. She murmured, "Thank you."

"You are welcome. I should have been the one to suggest it." He popped a grape into his mouth and chewed thoughtfully.

Laurel glanced at him. Those dark eyes had become hooded. She wanted to know what he was thinking. Then again maybe she didn't. What was she going to do? She had to get past this feeling. It had to go away. For days she'd been fighting against it. Maybe by the time they returned to Zentar City her funding would have come through. Sharing her research findings with Zentar would be part of the condition of her work. She would not leave the people, or the person, she'd grown to care about out of the equation.

They ate in silence for a few minutes. Tariq broke it with, "Tomorrow night the village will honor us with a dinner and celebration."

That she didn't need. Her fake marriage honored. It was difficult enough with how she felt about Tariq but to have it celebrated when he didn't feel the same way was too much. "You know I don't feel good about misleading the people."

"We aren't doing that because we are married." He didn't act concerned at all.

Laurel concentrated on her food. "You know that's in name only as well as I do."

"What is done is done. I will not insult them by refusing, and I will not let you either." He rose. "It is late. I will clean up and set this tray outside so you can get ready for bed. I will stay on a pallet on the floor for the night."

Laurel didn't question him further. His tone told her clearly the discussion was closed.

A few minutes later Tariq took a deep breath and entered the tent again. This would be the longest night of his life. He was tired, but not enough to keep Laurel's desirable body out of his mind. She had put him in his place about his plans for the next day. It seemed she had a talent for doing that. Few dared to try, and even fewer managed to do so. He needed more of that in his life. Someone who challenged him, made him look at ideas and situations differently. He liked Laurel too much. Slowly she had seeped into his world and started changing it. Could he ask her to stay forever? Make their marriage real? Did he want to?

No. He had promised himself a long time ago that he would not take a wife. Nothing had changed. He did not deserve happiness with his brothers' families dealing with hemophilia every day of their lives. Even if he considered Laurel a wife in every sense of the word, he wanted no children. Could he ask her to forgo them? It was best they keep their relationship business and not cross the line.

Laurel was already in bed with her back to him when he returned. A pile of pillows was arranged on the floor into a bed, with two blankets nearby.

He smiled. When had someone who was not paid to last taken care of him? "Thank you, *habibti*."

Tariq had no idea what time it was when he woke up to groaning and the chattering of teeth. What was going on? The lamp had burned low but he could make out Laurel curled into a ball beneath the covers.

Tariq shivered as he climbed out of bed. He reached for one of his blankets and placed it over Laurel.

"Tariq? I'm freezing." Her teeth chattered. "Keep me warm."

She didn't have to ask him twice. Thankfully he had pulled on baggy pants to sleep in so she would not be shocked by his nudity in the morning. He grabbed the other blanket off his bed and threw it over her before he slipped under the covers and pulled her against him.

CHAPTER NINE

LAUREL'S COOL CHEEK rubbed against his chest and her arm circled his waist as she snuggled against him. "You're so warm."

Tariq had gone from chilled to hot faster than his car could change gear. Getting into bed with Laurel might have been one of the worst decisions of his life, but it was by far the most pleasant. His arms wrapped around her. She was so tiny compared to him. His fingers slid over slick material. What was she wearing? Hadn't he told her to wear something warm?

She laid a leg over one of his, draping herself along him. How he was supposed to get through the rest of the night without having Laurel, he had no idea. She smelled of fresh air, clean water and desirable woman. Every part of him reached out to her. His manhood, large and needy, twitched with eagerness to find a home, yet Tariq lay there. He had promised. Laurel was the one who had to make the move.

A few minutes later her body stopped quaking.

"Mmm, you feel so good." Her hand drifted over his chest. His breath caught. She paused to tease the hair in the middle. A finger moved up to trace his beard before she cupped his jaw. "You're the finest-looking man I have ever seen."

"Laurel? Do you know what you are doing?"

"Dreaming?" Her hand traveled across his shoulder.

Tariq chuckled softly. "Then I am as well."

"You have dreamed of being like this with me?" Her breath floated across his skin, causing it to ripple.

"That I have, *habibti*."

Her hand stopped moving. "What is that you keep calling me?"

His gaze met hers. "My darling…person of my heart."

"I am your darling?" She sounded very doubtful.

"Almost from the moment I met you."

"I've never been someone's darling. I like it." Her hand returned to his chest to draw circles. "Will you say it again?"

"*Habibti.*" Tariq pulled her tighter for a second then released her. "As much as I enjoy holding you, I hurt with the need to have you. I cannot remain here like this. I promised not to pressure you. So if you are warm now, I will go." Being a gentleman might kill him. He would have to dress and spend the rest of the night outside.

"And if I ask you to stay?"

"I will—but know that I will also make you my wife in every sense of the word."

Heat roared through Laurel at the urgent note in Tariq's voice. His intent he'd made perfectly clear. He would hold nothing back if she invited him to stay. She couldn't resist the idea of removing an ugly memory and replacing it with a beautiful one. With Tariq she was sure lovemaking would be perfect and precious. A pleasure she could treasure for a long time after she had left Zentar.

She refused to continue to miss out on something wonderful out of fear.

She kissed his chest and let her hand drift to his hip bone. He hissed.

"Laurel," Tariq snapped. "Yes or no?"

Her finger dipped into his belly button and she looked into his eyes. "I used to wonder if I would ever be able to know what you felt."

Tariq turned on his side and brought her firmly against him, making her intimately aware of his hard desire for her. "Can you tell what I'm feeling now?"

She wiggled against him. "It's certainly clearer."

"And how do you feel?"

"Like a princess for the first time in my life."

That was all the encouragement Tariq apparently needed. His mouth found hers. His kisses were deep, hot and needy. He seemed unable to get enough of her. His hand fondled her breasts while he kissed her neck.

Laurel's body leaned into his of its own volition, as if it knew who and what it had been looking for. Her fingers ran through Tariq's hair as his mouth claimed a nipple through her gown. He sucked and teased until she groaned with delight and her center throbbed.

He pulled away and tugged at her clothing. "This has to go." She raised her arms and he removed it. "No wonder you were cold. There is nothing to this."

"It's the only nightclothes I own."

"I am going to contemplate that in depth later." Tariq pulled her to him and the blankets over them again.

He returned to lavishing her with attention. The unknown and unusual sensations shooting through her made her squirm. She was on sensory overload. Laurel could do little more that run her hands over his back and hang on. When he nudged her legs open and teased her center with his finger she jerked.

He whispered low against her ear, "Easy, *habibti*. I wish to touch all of you. Love all of you."

Slowly his finger entered her. Her breath came in gasps. Tariq removed it and she flexed her hips, wanting the sensation to return. He didn't disappoint. With a push and pull movement he had her going to a place she had never been before.

His lips found hers. He urged her to open for him. Their tongues met and mated. Laurel held his face as she returned his kisses. She wanted all of Tariq he would give.

Just as she started to believe she could take no more, he removed his finger. She moaned her complaint and disappointment. Her eyes widened as he kissed her thigh before settling between her legs.

Tariq looked at her briefly. "I must taste you." His mouth found her heated center and slurped before his tongue teased her most sensitive spot.

Laurel's back bowed, her hands fisted the blanket beneath her as she keened her delight. It rolled upon itself. Growing tighter, sweeter and more painful with every thrust of Tariq's tongue. She wasn't sure what was happening, but she loved every second. With eyes squeezed tight she focused on Tariq and his ministrations. Like a hot test tube bursting under pressure, she exploded into a thousand brilliant pieces.

Her hips rose and her head fell back as she floated in bliss. Slowly, she returned to reality.

Tariq, in all his beautiful glory, looked down at her. Her gaze met his as she laid a hand on his chest. She could read his feelings clearly in his eyes. He had opened himself completely to her. "Thank you."

"It was my pleasure. *Habibti*, I must be in you." He sounded as if he were in pain.

She opened her arms. "That's where I want you to be."

Tariq left her and went to his bag. He shoved his pants off and returned with his sheathed manhood standing tall. Her heart swelled. Tariq was all gorgeous male and he wanted her. As he came down over her, Laurel pulled the covers up over him, cocooning them in a world of their own.

"I can wait no longer." The tip of Tariq's manhood nudged her center. He came up on his palms, flexed his hips and pushed into her. Her breath caught. He pulled out, then entered again. Moving back, he thrust again, finding home. They waited. Laurel adjusted to the thickness of him.

Tariq made small plunges and eased back, going deeper and faster with each movement. His eyes remained locked with hers. His movements soon became thrusts. Shock registered in Laurel's foggy mind. The amazing sensation Tariq had created earlier built in her again. She gripped his forearms and held on for dear life as she tumbled over into oblivion. The last thing she remembered was the slight smile on Tariq's lips as he made one final plunge, then groaned his release.

Laurel woke from her dozing to Tariq gently cleaning her. He still wore nothing but she didn't mind. She started out of the bed. "You don't have to do that, I can get up."

He stopped her with a hand to her shoulder. "I would rather have you here warm and waiting for me." Tariq dropped the rag and climbed back into bed, tucking her close. "I did not hurt you, did I?"

"No." She looked at him in wonder. "It was perfect." Every minute had been.

"You were perfect."

"I don't believe that. I just hope I didn't ruin it for you."

He rose up on an elbow so that he was looking down at her. Cold air blew across her skin, making her shiver. He settled in again. "You have to be joking. You were everything I dreamed of."

"I was?"

"Why would you think differently?"

"The only other time I've been to bed with a man he announced afterwards, as he was dressing as fast as he could, that I was as cold a fish in bed as I was dull out of it."

Tariq's body tensed and his hands fisted. He used an expressive word she didn't understand but didn't think was nice. His body eased finally and he cupped her face in his hands. "Let me make this clear. You are neither dull out of bed nor in it. In fact, what we shared was the most amazing experience of my life." He kissed her sweetly, making her believe in the sincerity of his statement.

Laurel's heart swelled. If she hadn't been crazy about Tariq already she would be now. She moved so she lay along his body and he pulled the blankets over her shoulders. Shifting down until his manhood rested against her entrance, she smiled at him. "I bet I can do better the second time."

Tariq's hands came to her waist, lifted her and he slid into her. His voice was husky as he said, "*Habibti*, I am more than willing to let you try. But I doubt you can."

* * *

The next morning was the best of Tariq's life. He woke to a warm and compliant Laurel beside him, her head resting on his chest. He had the pleasure of watching her eyelids slowly flutter open. Knew the second she registered she was with him. There was wonder there, and something he did not wish to put a name to but felt as well. After a night with Laurel he had never been a more satisfied man.

She had given to him like no other woman ever had. Her responses to his actions had been affirming and exhilarating. All he could think about was having her again. What would it be like to have this sense of well-being every day of his life? But that was impossible. Laurel did not fit into his life plan. He would not question beyond what they had right now.

"Hi," Laurel said softly.

"Hello." He gave her a little squeeze and her smile broadened. "We had better get out of bed or someone is going to come in here to check on us. I do not mind being found in bed with you but you might not like it."

Laurel pushed away from him. He had a magnificent view of her beautiful, full breasts as she moved. He cupped one. "Perfect. So absolutely perfect."

She kissed him. "I'm not perfect. You just make me feel that way. For that I will forever be grateful."

This much emotion after only one night together disturbed him. They were headed down an uncertain road. "We should get started."

She rose from the bed, pulling a blanket with her.

Tariq wanted to see all of her. He wanted the bold Laurel in daylight he had experienced in the dark. "Let go of the blanket."

She gave him a timid look over her shoulder. "Aren't we in a hurry?"

"Not if it means you are going to try to hide from me." His gaze held hers.

"I'm not hiding."

"Yes, you are. Please let it go." He rose and started toward her. "I have touched all of you. Now I would like to see all of you. There should be nothing between us."

She slowly let the blanket go. It pooled at her feet.

He brought her into his arms and kissed her. "Thank you for trusting me. You should never hide yourself away. You have a light in you that should be allowed to shine."

Laurel clung to him. "Thank you."

He set her away. "We had better get dressed now."

"Okay. Will you see if there is food for us? I'm starving." She went to the basin.

He chuckled. Now she was the one giving the orders.

"What's so funny?"

"Look who's giving orders now." He pulled on his pants.

She gave him a sassy look over her shoulder. "You didn't seem to mind last night."

He chuckled. "I didn't." And he hadn't. In fact, he had loved it. There it was again, too many feelings. He went to the tent flap and found a tray of food waiting. Carrying it to the chest, he set it down there.

Laurel joined him. Instead of taking the pillow across from him, she pulled hers around so she could sit beside him. "I like being close to you."

And he liked having her there. They ate their meal in companionable silence. A couple of times Tariq caught her studying him. "Is there a problem?"

"I was just thinking how gorgeous you are. You're the most handsome man I have ever seen."

He had been told that he was nice looking before but somehow it mattered more coming from Laurel. "Thank you. You are lovely yourself."

"Oh, no, I'm not even in the same ballpark as you. The first time I saw you I thought you were the most handsome man I had seen, but now I know it's both inside and out. Which makes you even more attractive."

Now she was embarrassing him, which did not happen easily. "I think you are special as well." His mouth found hers. They broke apart when someone called from outside the tent entrance. "He said there is a queue waiting for us."

"Then we should get busy."

"That we should." Tariq helped her to her feet.

Over the next few hours they saw patients as quickly as they could. Tariq had requested someone who spoke English to help them. A young man assisted Laurel.

They had been seeing patients for a couple of hours when Laurel called to him. He looked away from the patient he was seeing. "Yes?"

"When you have a second, could you give me a second opinion?"

"One moment." Tariq liked it that she valued his thoughts. At one point in their relationship he hadn't been sure she held them in much esteem. He also found he enjoyed working with her. Laurel was efficient and gentle, and truly seemed to care about his people.

Tariq finished with his patient and stepped over to where Laurel stood. Her patient was a young mother who held a small child of about two in her arms. The translator asked the mother if she knew what the child had been drinking.

He gave Laurel a questioning look.

"I think the boy may have worms. Have you ever seen them before?"

Tariq gave the mother a reassuring smile. "No. All my knowledge is from a textbook."

"Mine too. But that's all I can come up with for a diagnosis. The mother states that the boy's stools have been runny, that he wakes often during the night and she is having difficulty keeping him from putting his hands in his diaper."

Tariq ask the mother to remove the boy's diaper. Together he and Laurel examined the boy's bottom. It was an angry red color.

"Has he been eating well?" Tariq asked the mother.

"No."

"Where are you getting your drinking water from?"

"From the storage bag beside our tent," the mother answered.

"What did she say?" Laurel demanded. She gave him a determined look. "Translate, please!" She seemed frustrated not to be able to understand things herself.

Tariq repeated what the woman had said.

"You need to explain to her that she will need to dump the water and clean the container with hot water. That pinworms are very contagious. She will need to clean her tent. Even better, she needs to move to another tent. Not share one, and bring nothing with her until the old one is clean. Do you have any medicine to give her?" Laurel was in doctor mode.

"I do not, but I will send a tribe member down to meet someone who will bring it to him."

"Good. Make sure she understands that they should bathe right now and clean their clothes as well."

"I will explain. You have made a diagnosis I am not sure I would have arrived at. Well done."

She sighed then smiled, a look of satisfaction coming over her face. "Thank you. I'll see another patient at your station while you finish up here." She did not wait for him to reply before she walked off.

At noon they took a short break for lunch. Once again one of the women in the village brought them a meal.

"Interesting morning?" Tariq asked.

"Yes. I've done more clinic work in Zentar in the last few weeks than I have done in years. I have found I missed it. I think I'll start doing at least one day a week in a clinic when I return home. It'll keep me in touch with why I went to medical school. To help people."

Home. A muscle in his jaw jerked. She was still talking about leaving Zentar. Leaving him.

It was mid-afternoon and Laurel had just finished with her latest patient when Tariq called her.

"Come here a moment. I have a patient I think you would like to meet."

She joined him along with a man who looked around thirty years old.

"Laurel, I would like you to meet Uric. He has hemophilia."

She nodded. "Hello Uric. I'm Dr. Martin. It's nice to meet you." Tariq translated. She understood when he corrected her name to Dr. Al Marktum. She still wasn't used to calling herself that. After last night she truly was his wife. She still glowed from their time together.

Laurel looked at Tariq. "Does he mind me asking him

some questions and examining him? You will need to translate."

"Yes, that is fine."

Over the next half an hour she asked questions with Tariq's help and took notes. "Would you ask him how he has managed to survived to adulthood living in the tribe? I know he must have been hurt at some time."

Tariq nodded. When he had finished talking to the man he turned to her. "He was born in the city. He joined the tribe later in life. He keeps a supply of factor. If no one brings him a supply he goes down for it. He only takes factor if he has fallen or cut himself."

"Ask how his joints feel and if he will walk to the other tent and back."

Again Tariq translated. "He does have pain after long walks. Especially if it is cold. It has become more frequent."

Laurel watched the man walk away, paying special attention to his knees. "So he does have the deterioration of the joints that I expected." She watched carefully as the man returned to them. "Would you ask him if he would be willing to come in for X-rays when he comes to the city again?"

Tariq relayed her request. "He said he will but it will be months from now."

"Tell him that will be fine. And thank you." She smiled at the man. But she might not be here when that happened. If her funding did come through, she would be gone. Sadness came over her. Tariq had said nothing about their relationship becoming a real one. She couldn't base the rest of her life on one night of passion. It took more than that. She turned to him. "Even if I am not here to see him, will you see that his test results are sent to me?"

Tariq studied her a moment with his now expression-less eyes and spoke to the man, who returned a toothy grin and hobbled away.

She and Tariq finished with the last few people wait-ing and stored the few supplies they hadn't given away.

"What will happen with these?" Laurel placed her hand on the boxes of supplies.

"We will leave them here. They will be used. Come, we need to get dressed for the celebration." Tariq headed for the tent and she joined him.

Laurel entered behind Tariq to find two royal blue tra-ditional gowns with silver braid down the front openings hanging on a tent pole hook. Sitting on the chest was a matching headdress for him, and another that was much like the one she had worn at their wedding. The clothes were extraordinary. She ran her finger along a section of the braid then looked at Tariq.

"The women of the village started working on these as soon as we arrived. They are our wedding gift from the village. We are to wear them tonight."

"They are absolutely gorgeous." She couldn't believe the generosity of these people.

Tariq picked up his bag. "I need to check on my aunt then I'm going to the stream to wash up. So you will have some privacy."

Laurel had just pulled on the gown when he returned.

"There should be a belt for yours," Tariq commented as he put his bag down.

Laurel look through the material on the bed and found the belt. It was embellished with silver as well. She tied it at her waist.

Tariq came to her. "Let me help you." He removed the belt and wrapped it in and out, creating a pattern.

She looked at the top of his head. "If you have to give up being a prince, you can always go into dressing women."

Tariq straightened and gave her a pointed look. "I would much rather undress them. One in particular."

Heat shot through her. He stepped away and the air around her cooled.

Laurel pulled on the long flowing jacket with full-length sleeves. When it came to the head covering she needed help once more. "I don't know what I need to do here either."

Tariq helped her put it in place. The material reached below her hips. He stepped back and gave her a full-body look. "You make a beautiful Zentaran princess." Tariq kissed her lightly on the lips.

After their night together she didn't feel as much like a fraud, but still she didn't belong here. She was an outsider. Had become a princess under pretense. She might like the people, but would they ever embrace her? Would Tariq? They were good in bed but that didn't mean they could have a marriage. Could she be who he needed beside him always?

Tariq quickly finished dressing and they stepped outside the tent. The young man from the day before waited. He led them through the tents.

She touched Tariq's arm. "Where is he taking us?"

"To the leader's tent. Just do what I do and you will be fine."

She would try. Insulting these kind people wasn't something she wished to do.

At the tent they were greeted by the leader. People

stood as they entered. Tariq spoke warmly to everyone. She smiled and nodded. They were shown a place of honor in a circle of pillows where Tariq helped her to sit. The others only sat after she and Tariq had taken their places. The people looked as if they were dressed in their finest. The occasion was as special for them as it was for her.

She need to learn the language. That thought had never passed through her mind before. Would she ever consider staying in Zentar if Tariq asked? Become part of his life, his world? Laurel looked at the handsome, incredible man next to her. Could she?

Tariq glanced at her while talking to a man. He finished his conversation and turned his attention to her. "Is something wrong?"

What could she say? Nothing and everything was wrong. "No, I was just thinking how special all of this is. And my gown. Please thank the tribe for me."

Tariq squeezed her hand and spoke to the leader.

Young women carried food around on trays, offering it to the guests, while others poured drink from pottery containers. After the meal had been served a group of singers performed and then some young girls danced. Laurel was enchanted. She loved every minute of the evening. What if she did belong here? What if she became the Princess in truth? Could she make a life here? Would there be a real place for her? Or was this just a short-lived dream, one that would slip through her fingers?

She all but floated back to their tent. It had been an almost flawless day. The only missing piece had been genuine commitment between her and Tariq. As soon as they were inside their tent, Tariq brought her tightly against him. "All I could think about all evening was coming back here with you." His mouth joined hers and any of her anxiety was overshadowed by the heaven that was being in Tariq's arms.

Tariq hated to leave the cozy bed and warm woman nestled against him the next morning but they had to return to the city. Laurel complained a bit but soon started moving. She had satisfied him more than once during the night with an impeccable blend of timid and bold and generous and demanding. He could not have asked for a more desirable partner.

They left on their trek back down at daylight. A number of the tribe were there to see them off. When they came to a semi-flat spot Tariq made the excuse that the horses needed to rest from their weight so they should walk. Really all he wanted to do was have a chance to touch Laurel. They held hands as they strolled for a while.

Around noon they arrived at the pool where they had stopped before and had lunch. By late afternoon they were back at the truck. Laurel helped with the horses and sat next to him with her head against his shoulder and arm intertwined with his as he drove. They spent the return ride talking about their trip and what more could be done for the mountain tribe.

Even the short time with Laurel gave Tariq a good feeling deep inside. He wanted more of them. The sun had set before they drove into the palace courtyard. She spoke softly to Astor and they went inside.

Tariq placed his hands on her shoulders. "I hate it, but I must check in with my office." He gave her a kiss. "I will be as quick as I can."

"Okay. I will miss you." She brushed a hand over his beard.

An hour later he was still at his desk. It appeared there was no end to what he needed to get caught up on. *Miss you,* Laurel had said. When had someone last said that to him? Pushing back his chair, he headed for his room to clean up. Would Laurel be waiting up for him?

Wearing nothing but knit pants, he stepped across the hall and lightly knocked on Laurel's door. There was no answer. Disappointment flooded him. Was she asleep? He knocked again. Nothing. Even if she was asleep, he was not going to bed alone.

Tariq entered. Laurel lay sleeping across the top of the bed. He gently scooped her into his arms and strode across the hall.

"Tariq?" Her arms came around his neck. She kissed his jaw.

"Habibti."

"What're you doing?"

"Taking my wife to my bed, where she belongs."

"Mmm, that sounds nice." She snuggled against him. *His wife.* It did.

CHAPTER TEN

LAUREL'S LIFE HAD turned into a picture-perfect cycle of waking in Tariq's arms, spending her day at the lab, and returning far before midnight, to join Tariq for dinner and a swim. He then took her to his bed and heaven once more.

They didn't discuss their feelings or the future. That suited Laurel. She was content to bask in the feeling of being wanted, included. For so many years she had been the outsider. Now she was part of the royal family here, had her work and, most importantly, was the center of attention of a man she admired. Maybe with time Tariq would realize how he felt. There was no doubt she was in love.

They had been home from their trip for a week when the intercom in her lab buzzed. She placed the test tube she had been holding in the rack. "Yes?"

"There is a call for you from the United States."

"Please ask them to hold. I'll be right out." Laurel headed to the door. In the outer chamber, she picked up the phone. "Dr. Al Marktum."

"Laurel, is that you?"

Stewart. She had started thinking of herself as an Al

Marktum. It came off her lips without thought. "Stewart, is that you?"

"Yes."

"It's so good to hear from you." Maybe if she kept him talking he wouldn't ask any questions about how she had answered. "How have you been?"

"I'm fine." He sounded unsure as if quizzical about their conversation. "I have some news for you."

Had the funding come through? It would be bittersweet if it had. Could she leave Tariq? Heart beating faster, she asked, "You do?"

"You have the funding. But I also found out something I think you should know."

"That's wonderful news about the funding." She didn't feel that way.

"Laurel, you should know that the Prince sabotaged you getting funding in the States."

Her hands shook. "He what?"

"He put out the word that you were going to Zentar before you had even agreed. No one offered you funding because they believed you no longer needed it."

It had happened to her again. She had been misled and used. All this time she'd believed Tariq was different. No! Had convinced herself he was different. Her initial impression had been right all along. He was no better than Larry. Tariq had wanted something and he'd done whatever it had taken to get it, regardless of how she might feel.

"Laurel, are you all right?"

"Yes." To her astonishment, her voice was firm, resolute even. "I'll see you soon. I'm excited about the funding. Thank you for letting me know."

She hung up and called Nasser. "Please come get me now."

When they arrived at the palace she asked him to give her directions to Tariq's office. Although he looked perplexed and concerned, Nasser did as she asked. Minutes later, Laurel stalked into the outer chamber of Tariq's office. His shocked assistant just stared at her wide-eyed.

"Does the Prince have anyone with him?" she snapped.

Apparently the assistant was so astonished to see her he answered with a shake of his head.

She kept walking toward Tariq's office door.

The man rose behind his desk. "You cannot just go—"

"Try to stop me." Laurel turned the knob and pushed the heavy door open.

Tariq looked up. Disbelief then a smile came over his face. "Laurel, this is a nice surprise. Is everything all right?"

Laurel walked right to his desk, placed her hands on it and leaned toward him. "How dare you?"

"I am sorry, Your Highness," his assistant said.

Tariq waved him away. His eyes had gone emotionless. "How dare I do what?"

"You saw to it that I had no choice but to come to Zentar. You put the word out that I was coming here so that no one would offer me funding. You manipulated me. Worked me like a puppet."

Tariq stood. "It was not like that."

"Then tell me how it was." She straightened as he circled the desk to stand in front of her.

"I needed you here. It has not been that bad, has it?" He reached for her.

She stepped back.

"That's not the point. You turned my life upside down

for your own advantage. You had no right. On top of that, you convinced me I needed to marry you to do the work I wanted to do. It has all been a lie. You…" she pointed her finger at him "…are no better than Larry was. You wanted something and my feelings didn't matter." To her satisfaction, Tariq looked as if she had slapped him.

"It was not like that! Maybe I did let a few people know I wanted you for my lab. That is all. I never used you to win a bet. My country needed you."

"So that gives you the right to do whatever it took to make that happen? Even disrupt my life?"

"What life? The one where you lived in a glass room all the time? Or the one where you never used your skills to actually interact with patients? The one where you were too afraid to let people get to really know you?"

Laurel's stomach churned. "As opposed to yours? Where you carry guilt around like a boulder on your shoulders for something you had no control over. Or deny what you want most in the world—children. You hide behind your job and position, so you are safe from having feelings on a personal level."

Tariq took a step back. "That is enough."

"Don't go all 'Your Highness' on me. It won't work. What you did was wrong. It can't be changed now but I'm done here. I'm done with the lab, Zentar and you!" She headed for the door.

"Laurel, you cannot just leave like that. What about us?"

She whirled, glaring at him. "There is no us! There never was. It's been about you all along. About your lab, your country, your needs. I'm done providing you with all of that. It's time I see about me. Send me the annulment papers—oh, yeah, that would be divorce papers now, wouldn't it? I'll gladly sign them."

Three weeks later Tariq sat in the King's office during a meeting of ministry heads. His mind wandered back to the day his life had become one of misery. He could still hear the sound of his office door slamming behind Laurel, actually flinched at the memory. As happy as he had been during the weeks Laurel had been in his world, he now lived in the depths of despair. Somehow she had become ingrained in his life, to grow into the light he revolved around. He was paying dearly for his actions now.

Shame heated his face. He had let her down like no one ever had. She had believed in him. It had shone clearly in her eyes. Her love for him, which he had stupidly refused to acknowledge, had sparkled in them as well. She had tried to hide it but on more than one occasion when she'd thought he was not paying attention it had been brightly visible.

Laurel loved with all her heart and being. He had learned that early in their relationship when she had spoken about her family. He'd had a taste of that sweet, cleansing water and he craved it again. He not only wanted Laurel, he needed her.

She had been right when she'd spat those words at him. He had become so used to getting his way he gave no thought to what it did to other people. The need to divest himself of his guilt had driven him all these years. He was a doctor and intelligent, no longer a boy trying to understand why his brothers were going through something horrible while he was not. Yet he had let it dictate his life. Let it drive him to do something he regretted and was ashamed of. Because of it he had even indirectly forced a woman to marry him.

With Laurel he'd had laughter, been challenged. He had become a different man. Just watching her experience something new had given him joy. She'd teased him and taught him not to take life so seriously. If there was an emergency, her level head was the one he wanted helping him.

As impossible as the days were, the nights were far worse. His body craved Laurel's touch. He swam more laps than he would have thought humanly possible and still was not tired enough to dislodge the ache long enough for him to sleep. He needed her warm body against his to get through the night. Since it was not there, he spent hours walking the halls or in his office. When he could he took Turo out for a ride but nothing seemed to ease the pain.

"Tariq, what do you think?" The King's question brought Tariq back to the present.

His head jerked up. "I am not sure."

"We are going to close this meeting for now," the King said with a hint of irritation in his voice.

The others walked away from the table. Tariq moved to follow.

"Tariq, I wish to speak to you." There was no room for argument in his brother's voice.

Tariq settled in his seat again.

After all the others had left and the door was closed behind them, the King sat again. "I am going to say this as your brother. You work is suffering. I cannot tolerate that, for the sake of the country."

Tariq sat straighter. "It is handled."

"Is it?"

His brother watched him too closely. "You know I supported you about the lab. I understand better than most the need for the work done there. I also understand why you wanted the best of the best."

Tariq started to speak. His brother held up a hand.

"I know you hate the disease as much as I do. I also know you feel guilt that you do not have it. I am older, I could see the fear on your face when Rasheed or I had a problem. It scared you as much as it did us. I also know you felt left out. Neither Rasheed nor I ever resented you for not having hemophilia. We were glad you did not."

These things they had never spoken of before. Uncomfortable with this frank discussion, Tariq shifted in his chair.

"I could not have been happier when you took a wife. I was surprised but happy also. I feared you never would because you were so driven by your work and the need to find a cure for hemophilia. I worried you would never take a chance on having children, or know the joy that having a family brings."

Tariq looked at him in surprise.

"Yes, I knew. I've known since we were young. I overheard you telling Rasheed that night in the hospital."

Tariq had said that to Rasheed after he had been admitted after a fall. Tariq had had no idea anyone else had been around.

"When you married Laurel I hoped you had changed your mind. I was greatly disappointed when she left. What I do know is that she was good for you. I do not know what happened between you two. I am not sure I want to know, but I will tell you this—life is too precious and fragile to waste, and we know that better than many. In the state you are in, that is what you are doing."

"May I say something now?" Tariq looked at his brother.

The King stood. "No, I am not finished yet. As your King I command you to let your guilt go and fix the problem with Laurel."

Tariq waited for him to say more and when he didn't he asked, "Now may I speak?"

"Yes."

Tariq stood as well and went to his brother, hugging him. "May I use the jet?"

Laurel had set her lab schedule and stuck to it since she had returned to the States. Eight hours a day and no more unless she was performing a special test. Having that much time on her hands outside work had been difficult at first. There was too many hours available to think about Tariq but she needed to find balance. That started with setting work boundaries.

She had already found a clinic that was willing to let her work one day a week seeing patients. Her family was pleased with her decision to spend more time with them as well. She had even accepted an invitation to go bowling with some of her lab mates, to their great amazement. The night had been entertaining but her heart hadn't been in it. She missed Zentar. Nights in the garden. Swimming. The lights of the city. If she admitted the truth, she missed Tariq. Desperately.

That awful day she had gone to Tariq's office she had left it to pack her bags and called for a palace driver to take her to the airport. The only thing she had taken with her that she hadn't come with was the blue gown the villagers had given her. She had been unable to just leave it behind.

At the airport she had been met by Nasser. He had told her he had been instructed to escort her home and that the royal jet was waiting. She had refused him but had soon found out that it would be the next day before a commercial airline was flying to the States. Reluctantly, she'd agreed to use the jet.

She had been nervous about flying but it had been overridden by the anguish she'd felt. How could Tariq have done that to her? Especially after she had told him about Larry? As soon as they'd been in the air, and not wanting Nasser to report back to Tariq, she had locked herself in the bedroom and cried until the jet was far out over the ocean, then had slept. She hadn't come out until it was time to land.

As Laurel had left the plane Nasser had said, "It has been a great honor to know you, Your Highness."

She'd kissed him on the cheek. "Thank you, Nasser, for being a friend."

He'd nodded and she'd gone down the steps, leaving what little remained of Zentar behind her forever.

Just as she had done all those years before, she turned to her sister for a shoulder to cry on. She stayed on through the night. Laurel told her about how Tariq had tricked her into taking the job and about their pretend marriage.

"You *married* him?" Sharon squealed. "You are a princess. I can't believe that my sister is a princess."

"I won't be for long. He will send the divorce papers soon." That thought made Laurel even sadder.

"Did you live in the palace?"

"Yes."

Sharon leaned toward her. "Was it fabulous?"

Laurel had been happy there. Far more than she had been in her apartment. "It was."

"What are you not telling me?" Her sister put her hand over hers.

"Nothing."

"I know you too well to believe that. Give."

"I fell in love." It made it much more painful to admit it out loud.

Sharon brought her into a hug. "Oh, honey. I'm sorry."

Laurel returned the embrace.

"Did you tell him?"

"No." Laurel sniffled.

"Then it was his loss. He isn't a good guy anyway." Sharon patted Laurel's back.

She pulled away. "Yes, he is! He loves his country and family. Because of him I rode a horse, slept in a tent. I took time off to discover a market, swim in the sea. I learned to live, not just exist."

"It sounds like you changed a lot in a few weeks."

"Being with Tariq changed me," Laurel said softly. Far more than she had realized or imagined possible.

Sharon shook her. "But he still didn't treat you right."

"No, but he did that for unselfish reasons. To help others."

"You do realize you have been defending the man you ran away from, don't you?"

Her sister was right, but it didn't matter. What had been between Tariq and her wouldn't have lasted. It would have had to end sooner or later anyway. It was just as well that it had happened when it had.

* * *

Over the next few weeks Laurel worked to stay busy. The less time she had to think about Tariq the better. When her mother called and invited her to an impromptu family dinner, she readily agreed, not wanting to spend any more time alone than necessary.

As she arrived at her parents' house she saw none of the vehicles of other members of her family. There was one unknown car sitting across the street. A shiny red sports car that made her think of Tariq. She refused to let her sadness ruin her time with her family.

Putting a smile on her face, she stepped up on her parents' porch. There was laughter coming from inside. She knocked on the door then entered. "Hey, I'm here. Who robbed a bank and bought that nice car?"

All went quiet. There was no one in the living room so she continued toward the dining room.

Tariq stepped into the doorway. Heat flashed through Laurel and her heart did a tap dance. He was dressed in a collared shirt, jeans and loafers and he had never looked better. Her mouth went dry and her heart raced. She grabbed the back of a chair to steady herself. "It's your car. What're you doing here?"

"Actually, it is *your* car, if you want it." Tariq's eyes didn't leave her.

"You came all this way to give me a car?"

"And I needed to speak to your parents, but more than that I missed you."

Did she dare get her hopes up? Could she live through heartache like that again? "You do? I'm surprised that a Prince of Zentar would stoop to making house calls." Her words were harsher than she'd intended, especially when all she really wanted to do was run into his arms. "I'm sorry, Tariq. That was just plain mean."

He winced. "I deserved it. And more."

Her mother appeared behind Tariq. He stepped out of the way and she came to Laurel, giving her a hug.

Her father joined them and did the same thing. "Hi, sweetheart."

She watched Tariq. His gaze didn't waver. What was he thinking?

"Why don't you two go out back and talk?" her mother suggested.

Her father nodded.

She looked from one parent to the other. Seeing no help there, she resigned herself to spend time alone with Tariq.

"Please, Laurel?" Tariq was asking. That was a rare occurrence.

"Come this way." Laurel led the way through the dining room into the kitchen and out the back door. She stopped in the center of the fenced yard and turned to face him. "Why are you here, Tariq? And involving my parents?"

"I did not think you would let me come to your apartment so I asked your parents to help me talk to you."

"What do you want to say that hasn't already been said?"

"That I apologize for the way I treated you, manipulated you. It was wrong. I will never do that to you or anyone else ever again. You were right. I have let guilt rule my life and actions. It turns out that my brothers never blamed me. It was only me blaming myself. I will continue to make finding a cure for hemophilia a priority but not over living my own life. I am even considering children."

What a wonderful father he would make. This strong, self-assured man had humbled himself, admitted his weakness. "I'm glad to hear that and I forgive you. I owe you an apology as well."

"There is a great deal of that going around today."

"I guess there is. When you can't face who you have become, that's what happens. You were right. I've spent years hiding behind, first, books, then what happened in college, then my work in the lab. Because of you and going to Zentar I have started really living. I have set work hours and found a clinic that needs my help. If it hadn't been for your highhandedness, that would probably never have happened. I will always be grateful to you for that."

"Thank you for telling me. I was afraid you would hate me forever."

"I could never hate you." If she wasn't careful she'd be telling him things she should keep to herself. "I still don't understand why we're having this conversation in my parents' backyard."

"I wished to meet them. To explain what happened and mostly to apologize for my dishonesty. They deserve to know why you came to Zentar and that you marrying me behind their backs was my doing, not yours."

She stepped toward him. *How could he?* "You told them we married?"

"I had to if I wanted to ask for their blessing."

Laurel looked at him in disbelief. "What are you talking about?"

He took her hand. "That I love you and want you to be my wife, *habibti*. Always."

Surely this was a dream. "Tariq, are you sure you're not just doing this to be honorable?"

He chuckled. "How like you to question someone telling you that they love you." Tariq pulled something out of his pocket and went down on one knee.

Her breath caught. The ring was beautiful.

"It was my mother's. I failed to give this to you when you agreed to marry me, but I want you to have it now. Laurel, will you remain my Princess?"

She threw herself into his open arms. "Forever."

* * * * *

THE SURGEON'S
CONVENIENT
HUSBAND

AMY RUTTAN

MILLS & BOON

For my mom.

My heart will never be the same.

I love you.

CHAPTER ONE

Anchorage, Alaska

Sleep. I need sleep.

Ruby was exhausted. She'd just flown to a bush camp at the DEW Line and then back again because of an injured tourist who had been mauled by a bear. They had managed to get the tourist out of the bush camp and to Wainwright, but there had been no surgeon there at the time.

So Ruby had done the surgery. She had stabilized the man and then, with a couple members of her team, she'd brought him back down after the surgery. The Air Ambulance wouldn't have been able to handle it. The man had needed surgery before he could travel. He would have died on the trip in the Medevac.

This was why Ruby loved her job so much. This is what she lived for. Saving lives on the frontier.

Still, she was beat tired, and very thankful for the midnight sun of the summer. Her internal clock was a bit off, and all she wanted to do now was go home and have a rest. She thought it was morning, but she couldn't be quite certain. And she was pretty sure there was something that she was supposed to do today.

Only she couldn't remember what.

"Dr. Cloutier. I was just looking for you!"

Ruby groaned inwardly and turned around to see Jessica Atkinson, the hospital director at Seward Memorial, and her voice screeching through the fog of her exhaustion reminded her of what she'd forgotten.

Oh. Right.

It was not that she didn't like her, but she was just so exhausted, and she'd completely forgotten about today. Today was the day her husband Aran, Jessica's son, was coming to Anchorage after his honorable discharge.

How could I forget?

She hated herself for forgetting that piece of information. So she plastered on the best, most energetic smile that she could.

She and Aran had been residents together, and when Ruby had had to return to Canada, which had meant giving up all her plans to implement a wilderness trauma team based out of Anchorage, it had been a huge blow. That was when Aran had suggested they get married— so she could stay and finish her work while he enlisted in the Army.

At first Ruby had been against a fake marriage. She hadn't wanted to endanger her plans or Aran's career, but Aran had insisted.

So five years ago they'd got married, and a month ago she'd received word that he'd been injured while on a tour of duty and, after a period of recovery in Germany, would be honorably discharged to his home in San Diego.

She hadn't gone down there because she'd been so busy with her rounds here up north, and she regretted not going. And, judging by the stern look on Jessica's face now, she should *really* be regretting her choice. It had been five years since she'd seen Aran. He'd been her friend, or the closest thing she'd had to a friend, and he'd done her a huge favor.

"Jessica, I haven't seen you in a while. How was your trip to San Diego?" Ruby avoided asking about Aran. She was worried that he was more injured than the initial reports had let on.

"Good, but hot. I much prefer the north." Jessica hesitated, then said, "I'm hoping you can come to my office. I have to talk to you about something."

A shudder ran down Ruby's spine when she saw how uneasy Jessica was. It must be something bad that Jessica wanted to tell her. She had always been pretty good at reading people—it helped when she was dealing with patients, because not everyone told the truth, and helped especially when she was having to deal with people who lived in the bush and didn't have much trust for people who lived in the city.

Or tourists who got drunk and baited a bear.

And, even though Ruby wanted to tell Jessica no, she couldn't. Ruby still felt so guilty about not going down to San Diego to see Aran, even though Aran had sent her an email and told her it was okay that she didn't come. That he didn't mind and knew her work was important.

She should have ignored that and gone anyway.

"Sure." Ruby stifled a yawn and fell into step beside Jessica.

"I know you're tired, Ruby," Jessica said sympathetically. "I heard that you just got back from Wainwright and brought in a bear attack patient?"

Ruby nodded. "A drunk tourist who thought it would be great to get a close-up selfie with a bear, and a bear who thought, *Oh, here's an easy meal.*"

Jessica shook her head and then opened the door to her office. "When will people learn?"

"Never!" Ruby said as she followed Jessica into her office.

"Have a seat."

Jessica walked around and sat down on the opposite side of the desk and Ruby's stomach twisted into a knot. The last time she had been in this situation she had learned that her work visa was ending and that she was going to be sent back to Canada.

As much as she loved her home in the Northwest Territories, the government there didn't have the money or the manpower to fund Ruby's big aspirations to bring more medical care to the north. Her hope was to one day go back and have the territorial and federal government see what she had done in Alaska. She was getting closer now, but five years ago she hadn't been ready.

Ruby was having an extreme sense of déjà-vu and she didn't like it too much. "Jessica, you're making me a little nervous," she admitted.

"It's nothing bad. Well, *I* don't think it's bad..." Jessica trailed off.

"But I'll think it's bad?"

"You might not be happy about it. I know how particular you are about your team."

That wasn't a good start.

Ruby *was* particular about her team. Working in extreme weather under difficult circumstances and in difficult terrain took a very special kind of person and Ruby was picky about that.

She stiffened her spine and crossed her arms, bracing herself for the worst. "Okay..."

"As you must know, Aran has been honorably discharged from the Armed Forces after he suffered a leg injury."

It was a dig at her and Ruby knew that. She deserved it. "Yes. I do know."

"Aran is your *husband*," Jessica reminded her gently.

"I know, Jessica, and I'm sorry I didn't go down to see him. My work… I had a lot of rounds to finish and…"

Jessica raised her hand. "I get it. I respect it. And Aran understands too. It's just…this whole fake marriage thing…"

"Has Aran found someone else?"

Ruby knew it was possible. Aran was handsome and charming. If she was a different person she might have fallen for him. Every time he walked into a room she could see the dreamy expressions cross women's faces.

She was pretty sure she'd had the same wide-eyed look a few times when she'd used to see him, but she'd kept him at a distance. They'd been work friends—nothing more.

And, since she'd been the only female resident he hadn't slept with during their residency, she had often been paired up with him.

She'd thought his proposal for a fake marriage before he'd left a bad idea, but he'd convinced her it would be fine…

"You're insane." Ruby shook her head and tried to walk away from him.

Aran jogged up beside her and flashed her that bright smile that always melted so many hearts. Including hers, sometimes, but she'd never let him know that.

"So you've told me before," he said. "I'm not wrong about this, though."

Ruby stopped and crossed her arms. "A marriage of

convenience? That's something that's only done in the
movies or romantic fiction. In real life it's fraud!"

"It's not fraud."

Aran took her hands in his and she tried to control
the tremble of excitement he caused in her by his touch.

"We're friends."

"Work friends."

He sighed. "We like each other, at least."

"I'll give you that." She smiled. "What do you get out
of doing me this huge favor right before you ship out?"

"I'm doing this for you. I believe in you and you'll
owe me one."

"Okay. As long as you're sure."

"Positive. Will you marry me, Ruby Cloutier?"

Ruby shook the thoughts away. She had been attracted
to him, but she didn't want any kind of relationship. Her
"marriage" to Aran had stopped a lot of friends from
trying to set her up. Which had been great. Still, if Aran
found someone else she couldn't blame him. She couldn't
give him what he wanted.

Can't you?

"Does he want a divorce? If that's what this is about
it's no problem. Honestly, I've thought about getting it
done and over with, but I've been so busy…"

Jessica shook her head "It's not that—and anyway you
still don't have a Green Card. Immigration will want to
interview the both of you now that Aran has been honorably discharged."

"Then what is this about?" Ruby asked, hoping she
didn't come off sounding too testy. But she was exhausted
and just wanted to get to the point.

"Aran is coming here to work and I want him on *your*
trauma team."

Ruby blinked a couple of times. She wasn't certain that she heard Jessica clearly. "What?"

"He has military training and he's a perfect fit."

Only he wasn't. Aran was a fine surgeon, and military training *was* an asset, but she remembered how much he hated the north. How he'd complained bitterly during the winter and through the darkness. He wasn't suited to living up here. He'd told her so enough times.

Maybe he's changed.

Ruby bit her lip. "I vet my team very closely. We all have to work together seamlessly. Aran didn't seem interested in what my team does when I first talked about it. He supported it, yes, but didn't ever seem keen on being a part of it."

It was a nice way of saying she'd thought Aran wouldn't be able to hack it.

Jessica folded her hands across the desk. "It's the only way I can get him to come home. He will be on your team. You have a spot…"

"No offense, Jessica, but I was going to interview someone else for that position."

"Ruby, you can do this favor for me. I've been able to facilitate your stay in this country, and I'm the one who fights with the rest of the board about keeping your vital services. Like you, I think it's important that your venture expands and that you're able to teach your services across the north. Too many people die needlessly because there is no access to healthcare or mental healthcare."

Ruby's mind drifted for a second. Jessica was right. Too many people died because they couldn't get help right away. Just like her father. Her father who had taught her everything about the north…

"Momma, what's wrong?" Ruby asked, peering through the doorway from the kitchen to the front hall.

She could see her mother leaning against the door, her hand covering her face, her shoulders shaking. Beyond her stood two RCMP officers, their faces crestfallen.

"Momma?" Ruby asked again.

Lieutenant Alexander looked at her. He was her older brother's best friend and his eyes were full of tears. He would tell her the truth. Ruby was a big girl of twelve.

"Ruby, it's your papa. There was an accident at the mine..."

Ruby took a deep breath and tried to shake the memory away.

This was why she was doing what she was doing, but she was selective about who was on her team and who wasn't. Part of her didn't want to take on Aran because she knew how he hated the north, but another part of her realized he was a man with military training.

Although the leg injury worried her...

Sometimes her work took them out into the wilderness, and they had to hike from where they could land the plane. And then there were natural disasters. If he couldn't keep up, then what would happen?

"Okay," Ruby said cautiously. "But he knows that this is *my* team, right? He knows that I'm in charge? The Aran I remember from our resident days was very headstrong."

Jessica nodded and smiled. Ruby could see the relief on her face.

"Yes, he knows that."

"When does he arrive?"

"He'll be here in five minutes. I know you're tired..."

"It's fine," Ruby said, though really it wasn't. She

needed to sleep. She'd been up too long, But she had to stay and talk to her husband of five years.

That thought made her chuckle to herself.

She was *really* tired.

There was a knock, and then the door opened and Ruby turned in her chair, expecting to see the same man from all those years ago.

Instead it was a very different man from the one she'd last seen five years ago who walked through the door.

It was shocking what war could do to change a person. The jovial, confident and arrogant man she had known was gone.

Aran was thinner, and instead of the short, buzzed and clean military hair he'd had on their wedding day his dark brown hair was longer, and there were a few grays mixed in there. A scar ran down the side of his face— faint, but still somewhat fresh. The cleft in his chin was hidden by a short-cropped beard and his bearing was not so ramrod-straight as it had once been. He seemed to bear his weight on his left and favored the right leg.

It threw off warning bells. If he couldn't physically handle working on her team he'd be useless to her. Still, Aran was handsome as ever—like on the first day she'd met him. In spite of herself, her heart skipped a beat...

"Dr. Cloutier, you will work with Dr. Atkinson on post-operatives."

Ruby groaned and looked through the throng of residents. Figured that she would get the new guy. The son of the president of the board of directors. She'd heard he was cocky and privileged.

And then she saw him.

He was the most handsome man she'd ever seen. And when those blue eyes settled on her, her pulse kicked up

a notch. She had to control herself. She wasn't going to
fall for his charms.

"Hi, Dr. Cloutier. I'm Dr. Atkinson." He held out his
hand.

She crossed her arms and looked him up and down,
but she said nothing. Just grabbed the charts she'd been
assigned and walked past him. She didn't have time for
any of the kind of games he had to play.

"Okay, then. You're a bit of a hard nut to crack," he
said, keeping up with her pace.

She rolled her eyes and handed him a pile of charts.
"Here are your cases."

"Thanks," he muttered, and then stood in front of
her. "Look, I think the key to a good medical partner-
ship is to at least be friends. We can be civil to each
other, can't we?"

Ruby felt guilty for being so cold to him. She was so
used to pushing people away. "I suppose... I'm sorry."

He smiled brightly at her. "There—that's better."

She narrowed her eyes and shook her head. "Just do
your job and do it well, then we won't have a problem."

"Aran, glad you could finally make it."

Jessica got up and went to embrace her son. He hugged
her back, but Ruby could tell that it was grudgingly. In
fact, it looked as if her touch caused him pain.

Jessica moved away. "Have a seat, Aran. I was just
talking to Ruby about you joining her trauma team."

Ruby watched as he limped to the chair beside her and
took a seat. He winced slightly as he sat, but didn't look
at her. He was obviously annoyed she hadn't gone down
to San Diego, despite what he'd told her. Still, it was the
discomfort he was in that worried her. Military man or

not, if he was this stiff, in this much pain, he couldn't be on her trauma team. He wouldn't be able to keep up.

"I'm sorry, Jessica," Ruby said.

"For what?" Jessica asked, surprised.

"Aran, you're an excellent surgeon, and your military training would be an asset, but clearly you're not healed enough to be on my team."

She glanced over at Aran and saw he was finally looking at her. His expression was that of a broken man who had seen too much violence. She felt bad, she truly did, but he *had* to be able to handle tough situations. Extreme weather...rough conditions... And she wasn't certain that he could. She hated hurting him like this, but he just wouldn't be able to handle it.

"I can move fine, Ruby. I was just on a very long flight from San Diego to Juneau, then a flight to Anchorage and a cab ride here. Once I start moving I'll be able to perform my duties adequately," Aran said stiffly.

"Ruby, the board of directors wants Aran on your team. It would be in your best interests—"

"I'm sorry, Jessica." Ruby stood up. "He needs to be in better physical condition. I'm sorry."

Ruby couldn't look at Aran as she left the office. And she didn't get very far before she felt a hand slip around her arm and turn her around. It was Aran and she was surprised.

"Is this fast enough for you?" he asked.

She could see the anger in his eyes. She shook out of his grasp. "So I misjudged your physical endurance..."

"Yes, I'm stiff. Yes, I'm still recovering from my injury. But I can keep up with the work on the trauma team. I can help your team if you just give me a chance." He

scrubbed his hand over his face and his expression softened. "Besides, you owe me this. You owe me a favor,
remember?"

Aran held his breath as he looked down into the dark
black eyes of his wife and now potentially his boss. When
he'd been injured and honorably discharged, he'd been
surprised when his mother had showed up in San Diego.
She'd never left Alaska—not even when her marriage to
his father had been at stake. His mother loved the north.

He'd been glad she'd come, but he'd been disappointed
that Ruby hadn't shown. Even though he'd told her she
didn't need to come, he'd thought they were friends as
well as fake spouses.

He'd always cared for Ruby. Always had a soft spot
for her, always desired her. But she'd never been interested. So he'd befriended her. The only woman he'd ever
befriended who hadn't turned into a short-lived romance.

Ruby was different from other women he knew. She
always had a wall up. So when she hadn't shown up he'd
hidden his disappointment. Ruby reminded him of his
mother. Always bound to the north and her work. That
kind of woman was a kind that he didn't want to get attached to. Yet, he had married Ruby anyway.

He was crazy.

So he hadn't expected his mother to come down to
San Diego. And he definitely hadn't expected his mother
to offer him a job.

When his mother had offered him a chance to work
on an elite trauma team—like working on the front line,
but without enemy fire—he'd felt a faint glimmer of hope
again. It had crushed him completely when he'd been in-

jured and unable to go back to the front line, and working in a military hospital was something he didn't want to do. He liked to be out in the field, saving lives.

Of course when he'd heard that the leader of this team of trauma surgeons, paramedics and nurses was none other than his fake wife, he'd almost thought about backing down. He knew Ruby wouldn't like it.

He didn't know much about her, because she never let anyone in, but he admired her tenacity—which was why he'd proposed to her. He'd wanted her to make her dream become a reality and he'd valued their work friendship.

It hadn't hurt, either, that Aran had always thought she was one of the most beautiful women he had ever laid eyes on, and for one brief moment in that time just after they were married—just before he shipped out—he'd wished that he could get to know her better. Wished he had more time to bring down those walls of hers.

He had been hoping that their years apart would have changed the attraction he felt for her. Only they hadn't. She was just as beautiful and feisty as ever. With those dark eyes that seemed to pierce right through his soul, her pink full lips, and the black hair that was really a rich dark brown and shot through with hues of auburn.

But she was unobtainable to him, and he knew that a relationship with a woman so connected to her work and to the north would never work out for him.

Now he was really wishing he had said no to the offer of working up here in Anchorage. He should head back to San Diego.

You made your bed. Now lie in it.

Ruby shook out of his grasp. "Fine. I will give you a chance. But if you can't keep up then I'm sorry but I can't use you on my team."

Aran nodded. "Fair enough."

"Are you going to keep up with physiotherapy?" she asked.

"Yes. I'm about to head there now, and then on to Human Resources."

"I'll walk with you and explain a bit about what I'm doing."

He nodded. "Okay."

Ruby walked slowly. He appreciated that she was trying to be nice, but it was actually harder on his leg than walking quickly.

"We *can* speed it up, you know."

"What?" she asked.

"It's actually better for stretching out the muscles if we move a bit faster."

"Sorry." A blush tinged her warm tawny-colored cheeks.

"It's okay. I've been adamant about getting back into fighting form. I didn't want to lounge away in a hospital bed for long."

She nodded. "Do you mind if I ask exactly how it happened? I was told it was an IED, but nothing else. They didn't give me any more details."

Yes, I do mind.

Only he didn't say that out loud. He hated talking about it—but he didn't have to talk about everything that had happened the night he was injured. He just had to talk about his leg wound. She didn't need to know the rest and he wouldn't tell her. That was *his* business and he wasn't going to let it interfere with his work here. He was going to make damn sure of that.

"No, I don't mind. I was transporting some wounded

soldiers to a field hospital and there was an IED explosion."

Cold sweat broke across his brow and he hoped she wouldn't notice. He had thought he was over the initial trauma of talking about it, after he'd recounted what had happened countless times to his superiors and his counsellors during his recovery, but telling Ruby changed the game, and he wasn't sure how he felt about it.

He hoped that she wouldn't pry further. He really didn't want to talk about it, and just thinking about the incident was making him a bit dizzy.

"I'm sorry," Ruby said, and didn't ask anything further. "Well, keep up with the physiotherapy."

Aran nodded curtly. "I will."

"I don't know what your mother has told you about the team I've put together..." She trailed off.

"I remember your ideas for it from back when you were first talking about it."

The blush crept into her cheeks again. "You do?" she asked in amazement.

"I thought it was a good idea—which is why I offered to marry you so you could stay here. I still think it's a good idea. You've done a great job."

"Thanks," she said.

He nodded curtly and looked away. He couldn't let himself get sucked into her life. She was off-limits. Every relationship was off-limits. He didn't have it in him to pursue one. Not until he got his life back on track.

"Look, I know that it's physically taxing. You've said as much. But I won't hold you back. I have a lot of expertise working in some of the roughest conditions and working with minimal resources to save lives. I would like to continue that work. It's my passion."

A smile tugged on the corner of her lips and made his pulse race. He liked it when she smiled. Since he'd met her all those years ago he hadn't seen her smile genuinely once. Her smiles on their wedding day had been forced and for show.

This smile—it was genuine. It was as if she understood him.

"It's mine as well." She cleared her throat and looked away, the smile disappearing. She stopped, pointing at a door that led to another hall. "Physiotherapy is down the hall. Third door on the left."

Aran nodded. "Thank you."

"Sure." She turned to leave.

"Ruby, maybe…" He couldn't believe what he was about to say. "Can I take you to dinner tonight?"

CHAPTER TWO

"What?" Ruby couldn't believe what she was hearing.

"I asked if I could take you, my wife, out to dinner?" His blue eyes were twinkling and he was smiling at her.

"Dinner?" she asked, a bit dumbfounded.

"You know—where people share a meal? We *have* had dinner together before, if you recall."

"I hardly call a sandwich in the cafeteria after doing a round when we were residents a *meal*."

"Well, then, it's time to rectify that, don't you think?"

"Do you think that's wise?" she asked, stunned.

"You *are* my wife," he teased.

She took a step closer and lowered her voice. "In name only. We're friends, but…really that's all."

"Yeah, but you haven't gained your citizenship yet, have you? Also, since you haven't mentioned divorce…"

Ruby bit her lip. He was right. She had been granted a temporary stay in the country while Aran served, but soon they would have to be interviewed about their marriage before she could obtain citizenship. And then they would have to wait some more time before she could divorce him without it looking suspicious.

Once she got her citizenship she could go back to Canada and visit her relatives.

Do you really want to?

She tried not to think about going back. When she went back to her community it was great to see her mother and her brothers, but it always reminded her of her father's death. How they hadn't been able to get him the help he needed in time. He had died of such a simple thing. If he had been in a city, or had had quick access to a hospital, he would have lived.

She missed her home. She missed the summers spent on the McKenzie, or boating and swimming on Great Slave Lake. She missed flying her brother up to Great Bear Lake to fish and watching muskox across the tundra.

But Ruby didn't want to go back until she was able to fulfill her dream. Completely. Everyone in the north—Alaska, Yukon, Northwest Territories and Nunavut—needed resources. More lives could be saved. And in order to do that she needed dual citizenship.

Aran had done her a huge favor. The least she could do was have dinner with him, she decided.

Big mistake.

All those old feelings she'd had for him—the ones that she'd thought locked away—came rushing back. He was still as charming as ever. Which was why he had been somewhat of a playboy when they were residents. She hadn't been immune to him. She'd just kept him at a distance to protect herself.

Having dinner with him now wasn't exactly keeping her distance from him, but… "Okay. Sure. I suppose we could," she agreed grudgingly.

"Great. I'll see you about six?"

She nodded. "I'll meet you at the front entrance. Right

now I have to check on a patient, and then I'm headed home to sleep."

Aran nodded and then opened the door, disappearing down the hall toward Physiotherapy. Ruby breathed a sigh of relief and rubbed her temples, trying to will the stress headache that was building up to dissipate.

She didn't like to date.

She didn't want to settle down with anyone.

In her job, her life was on the line. She was put in perilous situations. That was no way to raise a family.

Aran was making her question her plans in a way she didn't like. She had been attracted to him once but she'd hoped over their years apart those feelings would change.

They hadn't.

And going out to dinner with him would probably be a big mistake.

She was *not* looking forward to it.

Not even a little?

There was a part of her, deep down, that was. Her job was the most important thing but, whether she liked to admit it or not, she was lonely. It was just a dinner out. What harm could that do?

Ruby looked at her watch. It was a quarter past six and still there was no sign of Aran. It was frustrating. She liked to be punctual. She liked things done a certain way. Aran was late.

So that hadn't changed. Aran had always used to run late for rounds.

She glanced at her watch again.

"A watched pot never boils." That was what her grandmother always said. Her grandmother also always said that Ruby was in a rush to do everything all at once and

do it right away. Maybe she was right, but Ruby had learned that you didn't get very far in life just by sitting around or running late.

It was a bad habit of hers to watch the clock, but watching the clock was important when it came to surgery and saving lives.

A minute could mean life or death. It had been a matter of minutes that had cost her father his life. The delay of the Air Ambulance by that one minute had meant her father didn't have a chance, so Ruby was slightly obsessed with timing.

It didn't do her any good when she was waiting for other people, though. Like now, waiting on Aran to arrive…

"Sorry I'm late," Aran said from behind her, causing her to jump because she hadn't been expecting him to sneak up behind her. He cocked an eyebrow. "You're a bit jumpy?"

"I didn't see you coming." She took a deep breath and tried to calm her racing heart. "Where did you come from, anyways?"

"My cab was late. I had to go back to my hotel room and change."

"Your hotel room? Aren't you staying with your mother?"

"No," Aran said quickly. "I've learned that my mother and me should *not* live together. I haven't lived with her since I was about eight."

"You had your own place at eight years old?" Ruby teased.

"No." He chuckled. "My parents divorced and I lived with my father. My mother would come down to see me, and when I came up to Anchorage to see her my dad would usually stay in town so that I could stay with him."

"Wow!"

Ruby knew Jessica was divorced, but she'd assumed Aran had stayed with her. And then she remembered Aran had told her he was from San Diego when he was doing his residency, and said how much he loved Southern California.

They'd been friendly with each other, but she was realizing now she really didn't know much about him—and that worried her.

Why had she ever agreed to this sham of a marriage? She shouldn't have, but Aran had been so persuasive. So insistent.

"You okay?" Aran asked.

"Why?"

"You seem a bit tense."

"I'm fine. Sorry, I forgot you said you were from San Diego. I forgot you didn't grow up here."

And it was mistakes like this that made her worry about what they'd done.

"Don't get me wrong—I love my mom. It's just she does certain things a certain way."

"Oh… That's not going to bode well for us, then," Ruby teased.

Aran cocked an eyebrow. "Why's that?"

"I am a bit of a stickler when it comes to doing things a certain way—like being on time." She pointed to her watch and hoped he'd get her joke. She was relieved when he smiled.

"I think it'll be fine." He shoved his hands in his jean pockets. "Where do you want to go?"

"There's a little crab shack down by the water. Do you like crab?"

He nodded. "I do—and it's been some time since I had Alaskan crab."

"Good. I can drive—or we can walk? It's not far from here."

"A walk would be nice. Lead on, Macduff."

She hadn't heard anyone say that to her in a long time. Her father had used to say it all the time, and it brought a memory flooding back to her.

"And where did you see this footprint, Ruby?"

"In the woods. Just before the ice road."

"The ice road is closed and that's all muskeg."

"I know, Papa. I didn't go traveling through that. I was on my way back from the corner store and I saw the footprint. I want to show you."

Her papa smiled. "Okay, show me. Lead on, Macduff."

They walked the way she had taken back from the corner store. She always listened to her parents and kept to the paths she'd been taught to. She knew not to wander in the woods because of bears and other wild animals—not that many would be out in the middle of the day in the summer. Usually the heat and the bugs drove the animals further into the woods. Animals were most likely to come out during the early morning or when it briefly went to dusk.

It was a short walk along the well-worn path from her parents' place, and they stopped when Ruby found the strange footprints she'd never seen before.

Her father knelt down. "Ah, this is a wolverine."

"A wolverine?"

"Yep—and they're nasty. You did good, showing this footprint to me." Her father stood. "Let's go inform the

elders and make sure that the other kids keep away from this area. The wolverine has obviously found a food source and will come back, like a bear. A wolverine would attack a young child if it was hungry enough. Remember that, Ruby. Remember that sometimes in the north it's a battle of survival. Eat or be eaten. But you must also respect the land."

"Right, Papa."

"What?" she asked quizzically now, trying to shake the memory away.

Her father had never learned a lot of stories, except what he had been taught when he had been forced to attend a school far from home. The residential school was something he didn't like to talk much about to her. It had been an awful place where his culture and heritage had been forced out of him. Where his language had been stolen. All he had known was what the priests and nuns had taught him, but her father *had* liked Shakespeare.

"It's 'Lay on, Macduff'," Aran remarked offhandedly as he held open the door for her. "'Lead on' is a popular misquote."

"I know. It's just… I haven't heard someone say that in a long time. The way my father said it." She cleared her throat and tried not to let emotion overtake her. She didn't have time to deal with her grief or her sadness.

Aran didn't say any more as they walked down the street from the hospital to the waterfront.

Because it was summer, it was nice to have sunlight so late. It made for pleasant evenings. And it was nice to have the sun because in the winter the sun wouldn't be around long, and there would be a period of time where it just stayed dark, especially the further north you went.

"How long have you lived in Alaska now?" Aran asked.

"This is my sixth year."

"Right!" He chuckled. "We got married five years ago—right after our residency finished. I'm sorry I forgot."

"Well, now I'm going to have to hold it against you."

"Hold what against me?"

"Forgetting our anniversary," she teased.

He shook his head. "So, where in Canada are you from?"

"Behchokǫ̀."

His eyes widened. "I have *no* idea where that is."

Ruby laughed. "Well, it's just outside of Yellowknife, in the Northwest Territories."

"I *do* know where that is. So you're from the north? That makes a lot of sense of why you love it up here."

She nodded. "I went to university and then medical school in London, Ontario. That was a hard transition. I much prefer the north over the city. Although Anchorage is a city, so it must be the north I love."

She was rambling. She knew that. But she really didn't know what else to say to ease the awkward tension that had fallen between them.

"I prefer the south," he said.

"Then why did you come north?" she asked.

"My mother had an opening for a residency."

"I *know* that. That's how we met."

"Right…"

"I mean now…besides our marriage, I guess."

"It's *because* of our marriage," Aran stated, making her blush.

"Oh?"

"Also it's an opening now I've been discharged from the army."

"And your father? How does *he* feel about you moving near your mother?"

Aran's expression hardened. "My father died just before I was deployed."

"Oh, I'm sorry."

And she truly was. She knew what it was like to lose a parent when you were young. It sucked. And she felt bad that she hadn't known that, since they'd got married right before he'd deployed.

Of course. Now it made sense why he'd been so distant during their wedding...

"Look, if you don't want to go through with this it's okay," Ruby offered. Aran was not his usual jovial self.

"No. It's fine," he said quickly.

But he didn't offer a reason why he was so cold. So preoccupied.

"Is it something I did?"

"No," he said tersely.

Before she could back out the court reporter came out into the hallway. "Dr. Cloutier and Dr. Atkinson?"

Aran took her hand and led her into the judge's chambers.

He looked down at her. "Why are you smiling like that?"

"Like what?" Ruby asked. A smile tugged at the corner of her lips.

"Relax. It's okay."

Only it wasn't okay. He'd married her when he'd been grieving. People made a lot of mistakes when they were grieving. Life was like a blur. And when you lost a parent it was as if a piece of your soul had been gouged out from you and you had to relearn the world without that vital piece there. Even twenty years later she was still mourning the loss of her father. She was still grieving him, even though she kept it to herself.

They didn't say much else as they walked the rest of the way to the crab shack. When they got down to the docks the familiar scent of Old Bay seasoning, melted butter and salt water hit her and her stomach growled in response. It had been a long time since she'd come down here and had some Alaskan King Crab. She'd been so busy at work.

Aran held open the door for her and they took a seat in the screened porch that looked out over the Cook Inlet.

"I don't think I've ever been here in all the times I've visited Anchorage," Aran said, looking around.

"Your mom never brought you here? It's an Anchorage institution, apparently."

"This is not my mom's type of place. Brown paper tablecloths, crab and beer... Yeah, so not her thing."

Ruby laughed. "Well, I'm not having any beer tonight. I have a patient to check on when we're done."

"Right—this is the patient who was brought in this morning from up near Wainwright?"

"Yes..." Ruby sighed looking at the menu.

"What can I get you folks today?" asked a waiter, coming up then and interrupting their discussion of the patient.

Which was fine. Ruby really didn't want to talk about her patient at that moment. She was worried about him. He wasn't doing well.

"I'll have an order of crab legs and an iced tea." She handed the menu to the waiter.

"Same," Aran said and handed his menu back.

"Great! I'll be back with your drinks in a moment."

An awkward tension settled between them. She saw Aran was picking at his napkin. What had happened between the two of them? They'd used to be so comfortable around each other. They'd used to be able to work and converse easily.

Of course that had been when they were just friends and not husband and wife. And, really, they hadn't talked much about anything besides work.

"He's not doing well. My patient," Ruby finally said, breaking the tension.

"Oh...?"

"I think an infection has set in. I started a round of rabies shots, obviously, but..."

"Go on," he urged, interested.

"I'm not going to talk about the nature of a bear attack in a restaurant. It was pretty bad. I'm actually surprised that he made it to Anchorage."

Aran nodded. "Yeah, it's best not to talk too much about that when people are eating."

"He's in the ICU, but I have a feeling I'm going to have to open him up again and see if an abscess has formed."

The waiter appeared again just then, with their drinks, and there was a slightly horrified look on his face at hearing the word "abscess." She tried to stifle a laugh.

"Enjoy," the waiter said quickly, before leaving.

Ruby chuckled and Aran smiled.

"See what I mean?" she said. "That waiter was grossed out."

"He did look a bit green around the gills," Aran said looking over his shoulder. "Remember that time when we had to take those first-year medical students on rounds?"

Ruby groaned. "Oh, don't remind me. That was so awful."

"I dragged one young man into the operating room and there was that infected bowel..."

"No, you really need to stop!" Ruby laughed. "That was awful."

"Well, it helped him decide that surgery was not his cup of tea."

Ruby nodded. "It did—and he looked just as green as that waiter."

Aran nodded. "So, who pilots your plane while you're saving lives?"

"Me. I do."

"You're a pilot?" Aran asked, stunned.

"Yes. You seem surprised."

"I haven't met many women pilots. Logically, I know they exist. I've just never met one."

"Well, I grew up in a community where for a long time the only access in or out during different parts of the year was via plane."

Aran cocked an eyebrow. "What do you mean?"

"Up until 2008 the side of Great Slave Lake I lived on could only be accessed in the summer if you drove your car onto a ferry or in the winter when the river froze and you drove your car across it."

Aran's eyes widened. "You mean people drive across ice?"

"Have you never heard of an ice road? They have them up here in Alaska."

"No. I haven't."

Ruby chuckled. "You really are a southern boy."

"So, now you have a bridge?" he asked.

"Yes, there's a bridge crossing the river now, and those communities aren't landlocked during certain seasons. See, when there was ice breaking up the ferry couldn't run, and of course you couldn't drive across it. And ice road seasons are becoming shorter. Still, there are many other places that rely on bush planes to service their communities. When I was old enough I started to take flying lessons. I wanted to be a pilot. My older brother is a bush pilot."

"Is he a doctor too?"

"No!" Ruby smiled as she thought of the time her older brother had been fishing and got a splinter. He had passed out when she'd had to remove it. "He turns green much like the waiter."

Aran laughed softly. "You're pretty strong-willed. It's one thing I've always liked about you."

"I'll take that as a compliment."

"Do."

His blue eyes twinkled and she could feel warmth flooding her cheeks. She looked away.

"Why don't you tell me about your time in the Army? You never did say much about it the few times you emailed."

His expression hardened and he went back to fiddling with his paper napkin. "We don't need to talk about that."

"I think we do," Ruby said. "I'm very selective about my team. You know that I am. I need to know about your time overseas so that I can ease my anxiety about the nepotism your mother seems to have imposed on me. Also, if the Immigration people come… I mean…we're *married*. We've been married for five years and I should know about what happened to you in those years."

Ruby had a point, but it didn't mean that Aran liked it. The military had been so important to him. His father had been in the military too, but he had been a doctor who worked on base and never served time overseas, like Aran had. It was another reason why his parents had split.

His dad had loved the military life and his mother had not. She'd loved Anchorage. She'd loved the hospital that she'd helped build from the ground up and she wouldn't leave Alaska for anything. Not even for her child.

Aran understood her love for her career now. Especially since he'd been mustered into the Armed Forces and become a military surgeon. He'd loved serving his country. It had been the most important thing to him.

But now it was gone.

He couldn't serve.

So, no, he really *didn't* want to talk about it—but Ruby was right. They could get into a lot of trouble for what they'd done. A marriage of convenience so that Ruby could stay in the country and work…so that his mother wouldn't lose Ruby's contribution to what she'd sacrificed everything for. And that was Seward Memorial.

Aran had done it for Ruby, though. He'd agreed to the marriage because of Ruby and her passion for her work.

"I really can't talk about where I was. It was a war zone. It is still a war zone."

Ruby nodded, but persisted. "Tell me more about the IED blast?"

Sweat broke across his brow and he took a sip of his iced tea. He tried to stop the thundering in his ears as his pulse quickened. He closed his eyes and tried to drown out the sounds of the blast.

Pain.

Aran woke up lying in sand. He couldn't move his leg. He cursed and tried to orient himself to his surroundings. The sun was bright against the sand and the air was filled with smoke and gasoline.

Oh, God.

He looked around to try and find members of his unit,

but all he could see was the truck on its side, on fire, and bodies scattered around the dunes.

"Yuck!"

Aran's eyes snapped open and he saw a look of horror on Ruby's face. "What's wrong?"

"Pass the sugar."

Aran slid the sugar shaker toward her and Ruby dumped some sugar in her iced tea.

He couldn't help but chuckle.

"You have to ask for sweet tea," he gently reminded her.

"I know and I always forget. In Canada, iced tea *is* sweet tea." Ruby stirred her drink and took a sip. "Better."

The waiter returned then, with their food, and he was eyeing Ruby with interest and fear. "Is everything okay, miss?"

"Fine," Aran said. "She just wanted sweet tea. Canadians—what can you do?"

Ruby's eyes narrowed and Aran tried not to laugh. He couldn't remember the last time he'd really laughed and enjoyed himself. There had never been much time when he was at the front. There had been too many broken soldiers to mend. Wounded civilians too. It had all been just a big mess.

The waiter left.

"I don't think he's coming back to this table in a hurry," Ruby teased as she cracked open a crab leg.

"I agree. We've scared him off."

Ruby nodded.

"Do you know when Immigration will be wanting to interview us?" Aran asked in a hushed tone.

"No. I assume, though, now that you're back in

Alaska and honorably discharged, it will be sooner rather than later."

Aran nodded. "I'm willing to make this work you know."

"Our marriage?" she asked.

"Right. So that you can get your citizenship, I mean. I still believe in your work like I did five years ago."

She blushed again. "Thank you. I appreciate that. It means a lot to me. I have a lot of big plans, and Seward Memorial is the first step in making them a reality. I really do appreciate the favor. The sacrifice you made."

"Thank you," he said. "And I really do admire the work you've done and the team you've set up."

"You don't need to patronize me," she muttered.

"I'm not. It's true. What you're doing for people who are out there, away from a hospital... It's important. You're out there saving lives."

She nodded, but didn't say anything further, and he couldn't help but wonder what had changed. Had he said something wrong?

Aran thought it best not to press it.

They ate in silence.

When they were finishing up Ruby's pager went off. She wiped her hands and looked at it, frowning when she saw the message.

"Shoot," she mumbled.

"What's wrong?"

"My bear attack patient—he needs surgery. It's just what I thought. I have to get back to the hospital." Ruby motioned to the waiter.

"Can I help you, miss?" the waiter asked.

"The bill, please."

"Separate or...?"

"Together," Aran said.

The waiter nodded and disappeared.

"Aran, you don't…"

"I asked you out to dinner. This is my treat. You go back to the hospital and I'll meet you there. I'd like to help. I'd like to learn how you do things."

Ruby's expression softened. "Thank you—and, yes. Of course. Come to the operating floor and we'll get you scrubbed in."

"Okay. I'll see you there."

Ruby slid out of her chair and moved quickly through the busy restaurant.

It was not a long walk to the hospital, he thought. But his leg was a bit stiff. Yeah, it helped to move it, but he had been doing too much today to be able to show her that he could keep up. So he was going to take a cab back to the hospital.

Hopefully the pain would subside a bit so that he could be in the operating room with her, because that was the last thing he needed anyone to see.

He didn't need anyone to see his pain.

CHAPTER THREE

RUBY WAS HOPING that Aran would show up soon, because in another minute she wouldn't be able to wait any longer and she'd have to go and scrub in. Her patient from Wainwright was in the operating room and being prepped for surgery.

Come on Aran. Don't be late this time.

Ruby tied back her hair and then put on a scrub cap. As she tied it on Aran appeared, in scrubs, and seemed ready to go.

Thank goodness.

"I was just about to scrub in," she said as he moved past her to grab a scrub cap.

"I know. That waiter was slow."

He winced slightly and it made her uneasy.

"Are you okay?" she asked.

"Fine. A little stiff, but I can handle the operating room. It's an infected abscess, yes?"

"As far as I know. My plan is to go in and remove what I can of the infection, then pack him and place a drain. That bear tore open his abdomen and I'm not so sure it was completely clean."

"Jeez…" Aran said. "He's lucky to be alive."

"Yes—and this is why drinking and hunting don't mix."

"I thought most camps up there were dry?" he asked.

"They are. He snuck some beer in. The State Troopers are involved, and there are fish and wildlife troopers dealing with the bear. Unfortunately the bear loses completely, because he'll be destroyed. Once they have the taste for... Well, the bear might come back to the camp and it would pose a threat."

Ruby did feel bad for the bear. It wasn't the bear's fault that it had attacked. The man had been reckless and stupid. He'd done something illegal by bringing alcohol to a dry camp. To survive up in remote locations like that you needed your wits about you.

Eat or be eaten. That was what her father and her older brother had taught her about surviving in the north. They'd told her to trust her instincts and be wary of strangers as well. Ruby totally relied on her instincts. They'd saved her countless times.

They walked to the scrub room and started scrubbing in.

"Just follow my lead," Ruby said.

"I have put together men who were in worse shape than this patient," Aran stated.

"I'm sure, but this is *my* patient and my operating room." She shook her hands before drying them off with a paper towel. She slipped on a paper mask and headed into the operating room, where a scrub nurse was waiting to help her on with her gown and gloves.

She didn't doubt that Aran had worked on worse cases, but Ruby liked control, and this was her patient and her OR. She was going to do things *her* way.

She took a calming breath. A little moment of meditation before she approached the operating table. She could hear the door behind her open—the door to the scrub room. She knew that Aran was getting into his gown and being gloved.

She wasn't sure how this was going to work out, and she was sort of kicking herself for inviting him into her operating room. She liked to work with surgeons she knew. Surgeons she'd worked with before. Aran might be an excellent surgeon, but he was still an unknown factor in the calm and order that she demanded in her operating room.

This was why she was one of the best trauma surgeons in the north. This was why she led such an elite rescue team. Because things were done her way, in her fashion.

It worked.

It saved lives.

She took her place at the operating table while a resident read off the chart.

"Patient is Albert Weinstein, thirty-three. The surgery is to remove an abscess that has formed on his abdominal wall secondary to an…"

The resident cleared her throat and Ruby knew she was having a hard time reading it because it was a pretty vicious injury.

"Evisceration," Ruby stated.

The resident nodded. "Evisceration that was repaired by Dr. Cloutier in Wainwright. Patient was deemed stable to travel and be placed in the ICU at Seward Memorial. The patient's white cell count has increased, and he spiked a temperature this afternoon. This led to a CT scan that confirmed an abscess has formed."

"Thank you, Dr. Marks," Ruby said.

Aran stood on the opposite of the table. "Ready, Dr. Cloutier?"

Ruby nodded at him and looked down at her patient. *Foolish man.* Well, whether he was foolish or not, she was going to save his life.

Ruby finished her chart, even though her shoulders were aching. She had managed a small nap when she'd got home, before she went out to dinner with Aran, but her body was telling her that it hadn't been enough.

She rubbed her eyes. She needed to finish her work here and then find a place to crash. Even though she should go home, she didn't want to leave her patient. She wanted to monitor him closely while he was in the intensive care unit. So she needed to be close by, just in case anything happened to him.

"Hey," Aran said as he approached the charge desk.

"Hey." She nodded, not looking up from her work.

"Your patient's family is here—and his brothers who were up at the hunting camp too. They're looking for an update."

Ruby sighed. This was the part of the job she hated. She hated having to deal with the families of her patients. Good or bad, she just found it difficult.

"Okay." Ruby finished off her chart and set the binder back behind the ICU charge desk. "Where are they?"

"In the waiting room. You want me to come with you?" he asked.

"No, it's fine."

"It doesn't look fine. You look like you'd rather do anything but talk to the family."

"Well, that's the truth. Especially when I don't have any answers."

Only that wasn't completely it. Talking to families was hard when you were a trauma surgeon most times anyway, but it also evoked something in her. Something she didn't like to think about.

She remembered what it had been like, walking down the halls of Stanton Territorial Hospital in Yellowknife so that they could view her father. How the doctor there had tried to offer his condolences to them. But all Ruby had been able to see was her father, lying there under a white sheet. His eyes had been closed and he was gone.

Just gone.

The one person who had always been her rock was no longer there.

It was a pain that haunted her still. And when she had to tell family members that their loved one was really ill and might not make it, or that their loved one had passed away, the pain in their faces brought it all back.

It was the worst part of the job for Ruby. If she didn't have to deal with the families, it would be so much better.

Ruby walked numbly toward the quiet room where her patient's family had been told to wait for her. Her pulse was racing as she saw a little girl, clutching her mother's hand. The little girl looked to be about twelve.

Just like she had been.

Oh, Creator.

"Hey, are you okay?" Aran asked.

Ruby nodded. "Just give me a moment."

"Sure."

She could hear the sympathy in his voice.

"I don't envy you. I never had to do this in the Army. I would patch the soldiers up and get them stable enough to travel to a military hospital. I didn't have to contact significant others or children about their loved ones."

Ruby nodded. "I hate this part."

"What about when your patients live? Surely you don't mind delivering *that* news?"

"I don't like interacting with families at all—but, yeah, when they live and pull through that is so much better." She took a deep breath.

"Do you mind if I come in with you?" Aran asked. "I haven't done this in a while—not since I was a resident, and even then it was in a military hospital. I'd like to see how you handle it."

"Sure. Let's go."

Aran opened the door for her and Ruby walked into the room. The family stood, but their gazes didn't go to her—they focused on Aran.

"How is he, Doctor? How is my husband?" asked the woman holding the little girl's hand.

Aran glanced at Ruby. "You'll have to ask his doctor. This is Dr. Ruby Cloutier—the one who brought him down from Wainwright—and she's his surgeon."

Everyone turned and looked at her.

Her pulse began to race as they looked at her with disbelief. It wasn't the first time someone had looked at her like that and it wouldn't be the last. She was short and she was a woman. People always assumed it was a man who was the surgeon and not her.

"Yes, I'm Dr. Cloutier, and I did the first surgery on Mr. Weinstein in Wainwright."

"How is he?" his wife asked.

"Stable, but..." Ruby trailed off as she looked down at the little girl staring up at her. It broke her heart. "He's in the intensive care unit. Mrs. Weinstein, I can have a child life specialist paged and then I can talk to you about your husband's condition."

"Mommy...?" the little girl asked.

Mrs. Weinstein nodded. "Yes, that's probably for the best."

Ruby nodded and quickly left the room to page someone to take the child to a play area. It wasn't long before Bonnie, a child life specialist, came down to the quiet room.

Ruby led Bonnie over to the little girl. "This is my friend, Bonnie, and she's going to take you to do some crafts while I talk to your mom, okay?"

The little girl nodded and took Bonnie's hand as she was led from the room.

"How bad is it, Doc? I'm his brother and I remember you from the camp."

Ruby glanced up at the man. "It's bad—and you need to prepare yourself. I'm not going to lie. Your husband's condition is severe, Mrs. Weinstein. I was able to repair the damage to his internal organs and stabilize him before flying to Anchorage, but he's developed an infection and an abscess has formed. Right now he needs to stay in the intensive care unit while the infection drains and while the wound is open and packed."

"Oh, God..." Mrs. Weinstein sat down.

Ruby wanted to chastise her patient's brothers about safety, and drinking while dealing with large predators, but she didn't. She fought the urge.

"We're not from Alaska," Mrs. Weinstein stated. "We're from Kansas. Can we get him transferred there?"

"Eventually," Ruby said. "We can't move him right now. If we do, he will die."

"He can't stay here. He *has* to come home," Mr. Weinstein's brother insisted. "When can we move him?"

Only he wasn't looking at her. He was looking at Aran again, which infuriated her.

"He can't be moved," Aran stated. "Did you not clearly hear what Dr. Cloutier said?"

"We'll stay," Mrs. Weinstein said with resignation. "We'll stay until he can be transferred to Kansas."

Ruby nodded. "I'll send in a social worker to help you with arrangements and someone will take you up to see him shortly."

Mrs. Weinstein nodded and Ruby took that moment to leave the room and catch her breath as well as control her anger. This was why she hated dealing with families. They couldn't think rationally.

But there was a side of her that sympathized with them. You didn't think rationally when you were grieving. She got that. She understood that well.

"Dr. Cloutier?"

Ruby turned to see a nurse coming toward her. "Yes, Janet?" she said.

"There's a call for you on line three. It's a man from the United States Citizen and Immigration services."

"Immigration?"

It took a moment to let the word really sink in. Her stomach dropped to the soles of her feet.

"Immigration…" Janet said nervously.

Ruby's stomach sank. "Thank you, Janet."

Janet nodded and headed back to the charge desk.

Ruby groaned as Aran came out of the waiting room. He'd stuck around, waiting for the social worker to arrive.

"What's wrong?" he asked.

"Immigration is calling me."

Aran's brow furrowed. "They want to check up on us, I suppose."

"Yeah…" Ruby sighed nervously and began to wring her hands.

"Well, you should take the call."

Ruby nodded, but she really didn't want to.

They made their way into an empty doctors' lounge and Aran locked the door behind them. She just stared at the phone flashing, her heart racing as she picked up the line.

"Dr. Cloutier speaking."

"Dr. Cloutier—this is Agent Bolton of the United States Citizen and Immigration Services, about your Green Card application."

"Yes?"

"We've been informed that your husband, Dr. Aran Atkinson, has been honorably discharged from the Armed Forces and has since returned to Anchorage. Is that correct?"

"Yes, he arrived yesterday." She was glad her sleep deprivation hadn't deprived her from remembering that it was early the next morning.

"That's great. We'd like to set up a time to come and meet both of you in the next couple of days—at your convenience. We'd like to do a last interview and some paperwork before we can approve your Green Card and citizenship."

"Sounds great. Why don't you email me a few dates and I'll arrange our schedules?"

"Perfect. We look forward to meeting you both, Dr. Cloutier."

Ruby hung up the phone and felt as if the room was

spinning. This was why she should have said no when Aran had suggested marriage to her five years ago.

"Well? Do you know what they want?" Aran asked.

She nodded. "I do. They probably know that you're not living with me. That you've checked into a hotel."

"Right…"

Ruby sighed. "They want to meet with us both—probably at *our* house."

"Did they *say* our house?" Aran asked.

"No. They didn't. But it really doesn't make sense that a husband and wife live apart, now, does it?"

"You're right."

"They want to meet us at our convenience." Ruby bit her lip nervously.

"Okay. So we'll set up a time, right?"

Ruby nodded. "I think we need to do a bit more than that, though."

"Oh?" Aran asked.

She couldn't believe she was about to say this, but to make this work it was the only solution—even if it was a dangerous one.

"I think you need to check out of your hotel and move in with me."

Aran wasn't sure if he was hearing Ruby correctly. Had she actually just suggested that he move in with her? He had planned to get his own place in Anchorage. He didn't have plans to live with *anyone*—not even the woman who was technically his wife.

He was better off alone—especially since the accident. He had really bad bouts of night terrors and he didn't want to scare Ruby or even to have her know. He didn't want anyone to know. The only person it affected was him.

Living with Ruby?

That was *not* a good idea.

He didn't want to get married—ever.

You are *married, remember?*

Well, he didn't want to get emotionally involved with anyone. Not after seeing what had happened to his parents. Not after living through that IED explosion. He didn't have any desire to be with anyone. He was better off alone.

Moving in with Ruby was a bad idea. Why had he offered to marry her in the first place?

You believed in her. You still do.

But he was supposed to be still serving overseas. He wasn't supposed to be here, broken and no longer doing what he loved.

"Aran?" Ruby asked, breaking his chain of thought.

"What?"

"I said I think you should check out of your hotel and move in with me."

"That's what I thought you said." Aran ran his hand through his hair.

"It would look better if we were living together since we've been married these last five years."

She bit her lip, and he could tell that she wasn't exactly thrilled with the prospect.

"It's not permanent. It would just be until everything's cleared up and we can divorce."

Say no. Say no.

Only he couldn't. She was right. The most logical thing to do was move in with her. Even if he thought it was the worst idea ever. He wasn't emotionally in the right place to move in with any one.

Not after what had happened overseas.

Not after his whole unit had been wiped out and he'd been the only one to survive.

Even his survival had been pure dumb luck, and there were days when he wished he *hadn't* survived.

Don't think like that.

Aran closed his eyes and took a few deep, calming breaths as the negative thoughts threatened to take over, as the post-traumatic stress started getting to him.

"Aran? Are you okay?" Ruby asked cautiously.

"Fine." Only he wasn't.

"You're sweating."

"I'm fine," he snapped, and then scrubbed a hand over his face.

"Is it because of my suggestion? I know it's a big deal—and, trust me, I'm not a fan of it either."

"It's not your fault." Aran sighed. "It was at my suggestion we got married and now we have to live with the consequences. You're right. It makes sense that we move in together."

She nodded. "So is that a yes?"

"Yeah, I'll move in with you."

What had he done?

CHAPTER FOUR

THE NEXT EVENING, after their shifts in the emergency room, was when the big move was going to happen. Not that it was really a big move. Aran didn't have much to pack from his hotel room. The rest of his things, and some of the things he'd been left by his late father, were in storage back in San Diego.

Aran's stepmother had the majority of the stuff, and Aran's half-siblings had all had things left to them, but Aran hadn't wanted to bring the few things he'd been left up to Anchorage, because he wasn't sure how long he would stay here.

So he packed what he had and shoved it into his Army duffel bag.

Ruby was waiting in her car. He'd told her there was no point in her coming in and helping him. He threw his duffel bag into the back of her truck and slowly climbed into the passenger side of the cab.

"You good?" Ruby asked, and her voice rose slightly.

He could tell that she was just as uneasy about this as he was.

"As good as I'll ever be," Aran admitted.

"Okay. Let's go." Ruby pulled the stick and put the truck into gear. He could hear the drive shaft grind and the truck lurch.

"You know how to drive stick?" he asked, amused.

"Yes. That's all I've ever driven. But this truck needs work and I haven't had time to get it to the shop."

"It's an old truck."

Ruby glanced at him briefly. "So?"

"So you're a surgeon—a *well-paid* surgeon…"

"Who has bought her own bush plane… Well, with help from the hospital," Ruby interjected. "The plane and its upkeep is where I spend my free money. I need to have the best plane in order to save lives in the bush."

"Ah…"

Ruby smiled. "I will admit I'm a better pilot than I am a driver."

"Well, I can take a look at your truck when I get a day off, or something."

"You know how to fix trucks?"

Aran shrugged. "My dad and I restored an old Trans Am, and I did some tinkering when I was overseas."

"I would appreciate that."

Then Ruby moaned.

"What's wrong?" Aran asked.

"We were friends for…what?…like, a year before we were both at the end of our residency and yet we know nothing about each other."

"Well, we hung out in a group, and really all we talked about was medicine. You wanted it that way, usually."

"Right…"

He could hear the nervousness in her voice.

"Hey, we haven't set a date for the interview. Let's take this chance to get to know each other beyond the hospital."

Ruby nodded. "Okay. Because I'm worried no one will believe we're married."

"Ditto."

Ruby glanced at him. "What did you tell people about me?"

"What?" he asked. "What do you mean?"

"What did you tell people about your wife—which is me?" she teased.

"I told people that you were a surgeon. A talented surgeon in Anchorage. Sometimes there wasn't a whole lot of time to chat…"

"We're under fire, Captain!" Aran shouted.

"Get the wounded out of here. Pack them and transport them."

Aran nodded and went about packing the wound of the soldier he'd been working on. He taped over the open wound so that nothing would get in there. Or nothing more. Because they were working on these wounded men in a tent, in the middle of the desert.

He shook away that memory.

"So, what did you tell people about *me*?" he asked.

"Most people at the hospital know who you are."

"Yes, but you always made it clear you were only interested in surgery. How did I win you over? Was it my charm? Was it my good looks?"

Ruby chuckled. "Something like that. Yes, I guess you can say people were a little shocked, but since your mother was thrilled about it they really didn't question it. We were always working together and butting heads. I guess a lot of the staff thought it was inevitable."

Inevitable.

Before the war he'd thought that might be true, but right now he wasn't so sure.

It wasn't a long drive from his hotel to her home. She lived just outside of town, down a windy dirt road off

Glen Highway Number One, in the middle of a copse of hemlock and black spruce. It was a small log cabin, like something out of the frontier days.

"This is a nice place," he said, and he meant it.

He had always been partial to log homes—especially log homes that were outside the city. He loved San Diego, and being close to the beach, but he preferred the mountains. He loved spending time up in Yosemite, and had climbed El Capitan twice. Of course that had been when he was younger and his leg hadn't been mangled to heck, with pins holding the remnants together.

"Thanks."

She pulled out her keys and tossed them to him. He caught them easily.

"Just go on in. You can use the guest bedroom on the main floor. I'm going to chop some wood for the night."

"You chop wood too? Are you some kind of lumber jill?"

She picked up the ax and looked confused. "No, but I've been chopping wood since I was able to swing an ax."

"Next you're going to tell me you built this home."

"No. *That* I didn't do. When would I have had the time?"

She winked and he couldn't help but smile.

Aran watched her walk away, admiring the sway of her hips and carrying the large ax as if it weighed nothing. Her black hair was tied back. She was tough. He had to give her that. And her toughness, her indomitable spirit, attracted him.

He admired her. Still. Time hadn't changed that fact.

He unlocked the door to her house and stepped in. The place was sparsely decorated, but it was modern, mixed with the rustic feel of a northern cabin, and most important it was comfortable. It was way better than a hotel room.

He set his stuff down on the bed and then heard a dog barking wildly outside. He moved quickly, his pulse quickening, hoping it wasn't a wolf or a coyote—even if the bark didn't sound particularly vicious.

Aran found the back door that led to where Ruby was chopping wood. He was about to call out to her, but then he saw what was barking and relaxed.

There was a dog house outside. And a long chain. The barking dog in question was bouncing from the top of his dog house to the ground and happily wagging his tail. It was a beautiful sled dog, with white and black fur. Its eyes were brilliant blue and the tail that was wagging back and forth was quirked up in a question mark.

"You okay?" Aran asked.

The dog's ears perked and its eyes focused on him. It didn't growl, but Aran knew it was on alert.

"Chinook, it's okay. This is Aran. He's a *friend*."

As soon as Ruby said "friend" Chinook came bounding over and sniffed him cautiously—but only for a moment before the question mark tail began to wag.

"You can pet him," Ruby said as she set up another log. "He's friendly and very well trained."

Aran reached out and the dog closed his eyes and leaned into the head scratch. Aran couldn't help but smile. When Chinook had had enough, he bounded down the back steps and ran around the yard, barking happily.

"When did you get a dog?" he asked.

"About two years ago."

"He's beautiful."

"I know. He's pretty special. He keeps me company."

"I'm glad you're a dog person," he said.

"I never did understand that."

"What?" he asked.

"Dog person or cat person. How could you *not* be a dog person? Dogs are awesome. Cats are cool too. Why does it have to be one or the other?"

"You're right. I don't get it either."

"This is why we're friends."

"I thought we knew nothing about each other?" he teased.

"Right." She continued chopping wood while Chinook trotted back for more petting.

"You're not worried about your dog running out onto the road?" Aran asked.

"No," Ruby said. "He knows his territory. He has a long chain and he protects the property when I'm gone. He prefers the outdoors. Alaskan Malamutes do. I tried keeping him inside and it was a disaster."

She brought the axe down, splitting the wood.

Aran sat on the back steps. "Sure you don't want help with that?"

"No, I'm fine. I can do it on my own."

"You like to be in control, don't you?" he asked.

"Don't you?" she asked, before bringing the ax down again, splitting off another piece.

"I do."

"When you grow up in the north you have to be in control. It's a hard life." Her expression changed and she set up another log.

"How do you mean?" he asked.

"It's cold," she stated.

But he had a feeling that she was hiding something. There had been other times in the past when he got too close to something and she'd thrown up a wall. What was she hiding?

Of course he was hiding things too. He was hiding the horror he'd experienced on the front. Hiding the pain and scarring of his leg. Who was he to judge?

"I know that. Although it's not that cold right now." And then he slapped his arm where a mosquito had landed. "Buggy, but not cold."

A slight smile quirked on Ruby's lips. "It's better when you get closer to the city. A lot of people make their way down to the city. To die."

He was confused by that statement. "What do you mean, people go to the city to die?"

"There's more resources there. When it gets too hard to live on the land they go to the city to die. You have to be healthy to live in the remote areas of northern Alaska and Canada. One small mistake and your life could be over. That's how my father died."

She brought the ax down and Aran noticed she brought it down harder.

So that was it. That was what she was hiding.

"So that's why you're a trauma surgeon?"

She glanced at him. Her dark eyes flashed with anger and annoyance. He'd hit a nerve.

"Don't try and figure me out."

"I can't help it. Patients don't always tell you the whole truth," he said. "It's my job to figure it out."

"Yeah, I guess," she remarked as she set down her ax and collected up the wood she'd cut.

Aran got up and helped her pick up the wood, following her inside, where she set it next to the fireplace. She knelt down and Aran handed her the wood so she could stack it neatly.

"Sorry about your dad," he said.

She shrugged. "It was a long time ago. I don't really want to talk about it."

"Isn't this the kind of stuff that we *should* be talking about?" he asked.

"What do you mean?" Her dark eyes were flashing again in annoyance.

"This Agent Bolton is going to want to ask us in-depth questions about each other. Fine, we live together, but how well do we know each other?"

"Married couples have secrets. They don't always know everything about each other."

She was right about that. He only had to look at his own parents for confirmation of that.

His dad had been up in Alaska on vacation when he'd met his mother, and it had been love at first sight. Although in reality probably more like lust at first sight. They'd married after a week of dating and the next month his mother had discovered she was expecting him.

Aran's father had tried to like Alaska, but he hadn't been able to stand the cold winters, and Aran's mother had been focused on her job with the hospital board of directors and research grants. Aran's father had raised him.

And then they'd got divorced. Aran's mother had tried to take care of him, but Aran had been left alone with nannies and babysitters all the time and he'd hated it. So he'd been sent to San Diego to live with his father.

It had been the best thing for him. He'd had a good life there. He didn't know his mother that well, and he wasn't close with her, but he'd loved living with his father and then his stepmother.

But Ruby was right. His parents had rushed into marriage and hadn't known anything about each other. They'd acted on impulse and look how that had turned out.

Didn't you act on impulse in agreeing to marry Ruby before you shipped out?

"I think secrets are a dangerous thing," he stated. "I think we should try to get to know one another the best we can."

Ruby didn't look convinced. She finished stacking the wood and stood up. "You hungry?"

"Sure."

"Good. I'll make something."

She went into the kitchen and Aran sighed. He was trying to help her. Why was she being so stubborn? What was she hiding about her father's death?

You're hiding something too.

Ruby didn't really want to think about her father and how he'd died. That was how she got through the days. She didn't exactly bury the grief that she carried around, but she'd learned to compartmentalize it so that she could continue with her life.

If she didn't do that it would eat away at her. She would break down. And there was no time for that. There was no time for emotions.

Even after all this time the grief was still there. That gnawing pain that ate away at her very soul. It was an ache that she'd got used to. So, no she didn't want to talk about it.

Not with Aran, not with anyone.

That was her pain to bear. It had nothing to do with her Green Card.

It was what had shaped her. What had made her who she was today.

She opened the fridge and frowned when she saw there wasn't much. Actually, there was nothing but some orange juice and an onion.

"What are you going to make with such a variety of ingredients?"

She glanced over her shoulder to see Aran standing there. His eyes were twinkling and she couldn't help but laugh. "I've been busy."

"Does pizza come out this far?" he asked.

"Yes." Ruby picked up her phone. "Any particular kind of pizza?"

"Nope. I'm not picky."

Ruby called the local pizza place and ordered her usual and some drinks, as she didn't think that orange juice and pizza would go together particularly well. "Should be here in about an hour," she said as she set the phone down.

She leaned across the island counter. Aran had taken a seat on one of the barstools on the other side of the island and was facing the bank of floor-to-ceiling windows that faced out back.

Chinook was bouncing back and forth like a lunatic and she couldn't help but laugh at his antics. When she had time off she liked to take him on a hike down to the lake, so that he could go swimming and stretch his legs. In the winter she'd often set up a small sled and run him around.

"Your dog is a bit crazy," Aran said.

"I like a bit crazy."

He grinned at her. "Why doesn't that surprise me?"

"And what's *that* supposed to mean?" she asked, straightening up and crossing her arms.

"You're as bad as those smoke jumpers who fight forest fires."

"Hey, I know a lot of those men and women. In fact one of my nurses is a former fire jumper. He's a valuable asset to my team. One I picked out specially."

"I know—and I'm one you didn't get to pick out."

"Right. I was forced to add you to my team."

He looked at her. "Just like I was forced to ask you to marry me to keep you here."

She pursed her lips together. She couldn't really argue that point. She didn't like it too much, but it was true. He had done her a big favor. She really owed him one but she was completely stressed out by this whole charade.

"I'm thankful for that, you know, but the north is harsh."

"Look, I know you don't think I understand the north, and maybe I don't, but my training speaks for itself. I've worked in harsh conditions and under fire."

She didn't doubt him. During the surgery he'd done well. There'd been a few things he'd did that she hadn't exactly agreed with, but that was a matter of preference. It hadn't endangered the patient. Still, she didn't know him as he was now. She didn't know much about him. They had to change that.

"How do feel about flying?" she asked.

"Like in an airplane?"

"No, in a glider," she retorted.

"Well, if you mean your bush plane, not a jet plane, then I would be fine. I've never been in a bush plane, but I'd be willing to fly in one."

Ruby smiled. "I'm due to make a trip up to Whitehead tomorrow. It's a routine check on a nurse practitioner who's in the village. I'd like you to come."

He nodded. "Sure. I'd like that."

Ruby smiled. "We might have to do some minor surgeries. The nurse practitioner saves up routine operations for when I come. For any big surgeries that need to be done in a hospital she either calls me or the Air Ambulance to fly the patients out."

"Minor? So, like gall bladders or things like that?" he asked.

"Yes. Is that a problem?"

"Nope. It sounds good. I look forward to flying with you."

"Good."

Although she wasn't too sure about this either. She wasn't sure how it was going to go tomorrow, and she wasn't sure how well they were going to work together. But it was better that she tested it out this way instead of being thrust into an emergency situation with him, where everything might potentially fall apart and cost lives.

There was a knock at the door and Chinook went around the front to visit Sam the pizza guy who was very familiar with Chinook and his behavior. Sam was her neighbor, and he often took care of Chinook when Ruby had to fly out to remote locations.

"Hey, Doc," said Sam when she answered the door. "Bigger order. You have company?"

Leave it to Sam, who had been operating his pizza place in the area for a long time, always to poke his nose into everyone's business.

She really didn't want it to become neighborhood gossip that her husband was back, or that she was even married. But then a thought occurred to her that maybe this *would* be a good thing. It would solidify their fake marriage for Agent Bolton when he came to check up on them.

"I do have company, Sam." Ruby stepped back and Aran stood up. "My husband has been serving overseas the last five years and he's finally come home. Sam, I'd like to introduce you to my husband, Dr. Aran Atkinson. Aran, this is Sam, and he's the local pizza guru for this part of Anchorage."

Sam stood there, stunned, holding the pizza, but then he smiled brightly and extended his hand. "It's a pleasure to meet you, Dr. Atkinson! Wow, that's a long call of duty."

"It was, but I'm home now. For good."

Ruby could tell that Aran felt slightly uncomfortable. he *was* back in America for good—but home? This wasn't his home. How could he say that?

Home was where the heart was, and Ruby had the distinct feeling that this wasn't where Aran's heart was.

"You've been discharged?" Sam asked.

"Yes. I was injured overseas and I'm back now to work at the hospital. I still want to serve—just serve the good citizens of Anchorage."

Sam beamed and handed Ruby the pizza. "This is on me."

"Sam, you don't have to—"

Sam held up his hands. "No. I insist. It's my pleasure to welcome back Dr. Atkinson after sacrificing so much for our country. I'll leave you two alone. Welcome home, Dr. Atkinson."

Aran nodded.

Sam slipped away and Ruby shut the door, stunned that Sam had fallen for their ruse so easily. Usually he had a lot more questions, especially when it came to what Sam felt was his role as protector and knowledge-keeper of the neighborhood. More like gossip rather than knowledge.

And she was also stunned by the fact that she'd just scored a free pizza from him.

"I set his broken leg once and didn't even get a free pizza," she said, setting the box down on the island.

Aran chuckled. "War hero. I guess that's a perk I wasn't quite expecting. I hope it's good pizza."

"And if it's not?" she asked as she opened the box and drank in the scent of melted cheese, sausage and Italian herbs.

"I don't care if it's good or not. I haven't had a pizza in a long, long time." Aran picked up a slice and took a bite. "That's *good* pizza."

"Homemade is so much better than the big chains. There's a lot of great small restaurants throughout the north that are just Mom-and-Pop type places and they make the best food. There was this great café in Yellow-knife I loved going to. It served the best Arctic Gray-ling sushi."

Aran cocked an eyebrow. "Arctic Grayling *sushi*?"

"Oh, yeah. Nothing quite like getting fresh Arctic Grayling right out of Great Slave Lake."

"Hey, in San Diego we have great seafood and authentic Mexican food. Not that junk you get in chain restaurants either. Have you ever had a fish taco?"

"No. I can't say that I have."

"That's a good taco."

"I'll take your word for it, since I doubt I'll ever go to San Diego." And then she mentally kicked herself, because she'd had a chance to go there and hadn't taken it.

"Never say never. You might one day."

Heat bloomed in her cheeks. "Well, I'm glad you like the pizza."

"So, you obviously told more than just the people at the hospital about me?"

"Yes. Sam has a son and he was always trying to fix me up with him. You got me out of many, many pity dates."

"Pity dates?"

"What else would you call them? Dates for a single woman who never goes out and always works...?"

"I doubt they were pity dates, Ruby. There's so much more to you and I think they saw that."

She blushed again and looked away. She wasn't used to compliments.

They sat in silence. Ruby was tired, but she had to take Chinook down to the lake and let him have a good run or he would howl all night.

She grabbed her sweater and bear spray.

"Where are you going?" Aran asked, watching her.

"I have to take Chinook down to the lake for a swim and to stretch his legs. He needs to run off his energy. This is the problem with having a sled dog for a pet and working odd hours."

"I'll come with you, if you don't mind," Aran said.

He made his way to the guest room and came back with a flannel jacket. She noticed he was limping slightly, and was worried that the walk would be too much.

"Are you sure you're going to be okay?" she asked.

"I'll be fine. Besides, there's no backing out now. Chinook looks raring to go."

Aran nodded at the window and Ruby saw Chinook with his face against it, smearing up the outside with his nose and tongue. His blue eyes were bright with excitement.

She chuckled. "Okay, let's go before he dirties up the entire pane."

Ruby locked up and they headed outside. Chinook started barking and hopping around excitedly as she led Aran down to the path, through the forest that led to the lake. Chinook soon took off, but he never went far.

"So, if Chinook needs so much exercise, and you keep such odd hours, why did you get him?"

"No one wanted him," Ruby said. "He was supposed to be a champion dog for the Iditarod team, but he was injured on the first leg of the race. He'll never race again. If you watch him closely you can see that he has a slight limp in his giddy-up."

Aran cocked his head. "Yeah, I can see it now."

"I didn't want to see him put down, or have him waste away somewhere. The owner of the team didn't want to pay for the surgery to fix him, so I did. And he's been my pal ever since. He's well trained and he watches my place. He's happiest outside in his dog house, but on bitter nights I bring him inside. When I'm away for long periods the neighbors come and walk him, and in the winter we do some mushing down on the lake when it freezes over."

"You run a dog sled?" he asked in amazement.

"Only a small one. I like the Iditarod. It's kind of fascinating and it's a big deal up here."

"So I've heard. I've never watched it."

"You should. If you're going to stay up in Alaska you need to immerse yourself in all her excitement."

"Alaska is exciting?" he asked in disbelief.

"Yes," she said, beaming up at him.

"You told me the north is hard."

"It can be, but it's an amazing place. There's no other place I'd rather be."

There was a splash as they rounded the last bend and they saw Chinook happily splashing in the lake, barking and chasing fish. Aran chuckled and wandered down to the shore. She could tell that he was taking in the sight around him. The mountains framing the lake. The tall spruce trees. The quaking aspens rising and climbing up the mountain, each of them tall and slender, their leaves stretching as far as they could to grasp the short bursts of sunlight during the winter months, before darkness descended and the temperature was brutal.

If only he could see it in the fall and the winter, when the Aurora danced across the sky. That was her favorite time of the year. She closed her eyes and pictured the blue, green and purple lights dancing overhead. The hum that they generated in the silence of darkness...

A gunshot rang out and Chinook barked, his fur standing on end. Ruby spun around and saw Aran was completely on edge.

"What was that?" he asked.

"I—" She was just going to say that she didn't know when another shot rang out, followed by screams. Aran's jaw clenched.

"It's not hunting season," Ruby said.

She gave a quick command to Chinook and the dog came to her side. She cocked her head and listened. She could hear someone coming.

She gripped her bear spray tighter and waited. Aran was stiff as a board and his eyes were fixated on the bush behind them as the sound of someone running came closer. Chinook growled low.

Please don't be an angry bear. Please don't be an angry bear.

"Help!" A man burst through the brush, blood all over his face and hands. "Help, my buddy's been shot!"

CHAPTER FIVE

WHEN ARAN HAD heard those shots fired his heart had stopped. The world around him had frozen and his body had coiled tight, like a spring that was ready to snap. Immediately he'd been taken right back to when the fight had broken out—just before the IED explosion had injured him and wiped out his unit...

"We're under fire!"

Aran craned his head back to see the driver radioing for help. His pulse thundered in his ears and he turned back to the patient he was transporting. The soldier with the open abdomen that had now been packed. The man whose life was in his hands.

Bullets bounced off the metal, and behind him he could see a Jeep burst into flames as it hit an IED.

He trembled—and then felt the world beneath him crumble...

Seeing the confused and dazed hunter come crashing out of the bush brought him back to reality.

"Slow down and tell us where he is," Ruby said calmly.

Aran glanced down to see Chinook standing next to him. The dog was no longer growling, but he could tell he was completely on guard, his gaze focused on the distraught hunter. Or he could only assume he was a hunter, given the camo the man was wearing and the fact that they'd heard gunshots.

"He's not far away. We were in the woods hiking and Zeke thought he saw a bear."

"Okay," Ruby said. "Take us to him and we'll see what we can do, Mr....?"

"Mike," the man said breathlessly. "My name is Mike."

"Okay, Mike. Lead the way."

Mike started making his way up the trail and Ruby turned and gave Aran a strange look. Aran had the feeling that Mike and Zeke shouldn't be out hunting, especially so close to town. Chinook's hackles were still raised. The dog was on alert and Aran was thankful that he was with them.

It didn't take them long before they found Zeke, his back against the tree and holding his side. Even from this distance Aran could tell the man had a collapsed lung, just by the way he was struggling to breathe and the color of his skin.

"I found help, Zeke!" Mike said.

Aran knelt down. Ruby gave a command to her dog and Chinook immediately lay down, but he was ever watchful.

"Mind if I look?" Aran asked, before he even tried to remove the man's hand from the wound.

"You a doctor?" Zeke asked through labored breaths.

"I am."

Zeke nodded. Aran inspected the wound. He'd seen this before. Gunshot wounds were common at the front.

"Okay, Mike, do you have something like a piece of material that you can apply pressure to?" Aran asked.

Mike nodded and dug in a rucksack, pulling out a clean shirt. "Will this do?"

"That's good." Aran took the shirt from Mike and held it against the wound. "I need you to stay with me, Zeke. I'm going to send Dr. Cloutier here to get some supplies from her house and call the paramedics."

Ruby nodded. "I know what you need."

"Good. Hurry," Aran urged under his breath.

"Chinook—come," Ruby said.

Chinook got up and followed after her.

"Am I going to die?" Zeke asked.

"Not if I can help it," Aran said. "I was at the front line and I saw guys in worse shape than you and they pulled through."

"You're Army?" Mike asked.

Aran nodded. "Yes."

He could tell they were both relieved. It gave Mike and Zeke some comfort and it would help them relax, before what Aran knew he would have to do to ensure that Zeke survived transport to the hospital. It was not going to be pretty.

"What were you out hunting for?" Aran asked.

"Well, we weren't *hunting*," Mike said quickly.

"You're certainly outfitted like you were."

"We were practicing. We're going on a hunt when the season opens. We're headed further up north, to a camp, and we're going to stalk big game. We thought we'd check out some of our gear on this trail. My summer place is just the other side of the lake. Zeke thought he saw a bear…"

"I panicked," Zeke said. "I've never hunted before."

"I think your hunting days might be over," Aran remarked.

Zeke smiled weakly. "I think you're right."

It wasn't long before Aran heard an engine and he

looked down the trail to see Ruby driving a small ATV with a sled hooked to the back, like a gurney. He was impressed. She really was ready for anything out here.

"The ambulance is on its way, but the paramedics can't get out here. We need to stabilize him and then take him back slowly on the gurney."

"Good thinking." Aran glanced at Mike. "I need you to do me a favor, Mike."

Mike nodded. "Sure."

"I need you to hold this shirt and apply pressure while Dr. Cloutier and I get everything ready—okay?"

Mike looked unsure, but nodded. "Okay."

Aran showed him how to apply pressure and then let Mike take over before going to see what Ruby had brought. He was hoping she'd brought a surgical kit.

"You *did* bring the right kit," he said with relief, under his breath.

"This is not my first rodeo," she stated.

"How long until the paramedics get here?" Aran asked.

"Thirty minutes. We'll hear the sirens. The highway isn't far from here."

Aran opened the surgical kit and saw everything he needed to insert a chest tube.

"Does he really need a chest tube?" Ruby whispered, as if reading his mind.

"He has a collapsed lung and a flail chest," Aran said. "We need to do something to relieve the pressure."

"I don't have anything to sedate him. His body has been under a lot of stress, and this is going to add more."

"I'm aware," Aran said. "I've done this countless times before, in worse conditions and under gunfire. I can handle this."

Ruby didn't look so sure. "Should we get him on the gurney before we do this?"

Aran nodded. "It would be best. He won't feel like moving much after I do it."

Ruby pursed her lips together and nodded. "You get the stuff ready and I'll help him up."

Aran went through the surgical supplies and pulled out everything he needed while Ruby instructed Mike on getting Zeke strapped into the gurney.

"He's ready," Ruby said.

Aran slipped on rubber gloves and knelt down to the gurney. "Zeke, you need a chest tube. Your lung has collapsed and this will help you, but I'm not going to lie— it's going to hurt something fierce."

Zeke closed his eyes and nodded and Mike worried at his bottom lip. Aran didn't want to sugarcoat how much it was going to hurt, but the guy was young, healthy and strong. If Zeke got the help he needed then he should fully recover, but in order to get that medical attention Aran had to do this.

Now.

"Mike, I need you to help hold Zeke," Ruby instructed. "We have to keep him still while Dr. Atkinson works."

"Sure thing, Doc." Mike followed Ruby's instruction.

Aran cut away the shirt to expose the side of Zeke's chest and use an antibacterial wipe on him.

"Okay, Zeke... Hold him tight, Mike," Aran warned. Mike closed his eyes and nodded.

Aran swiftly inserted the chest tube while Zeke screamed and cussed.

"Good job, Zeke," Ruby said gently. "Good job."

Aran taped up the chest tube and made sure it was secure.

"Dang it, Doc. That more than just hurt..." Zeke said

weakly, before his eyes rolled into the back of his head and he passed out.

"He needs to get to the hospital."

"Dr. Franklin is on duty," Ruby said. "He's waiting for him."

Aran nodded. "Let's get him to the road."

They finished securing Zeke and then Ruby got on the ATV and gently pulled Zeke's gurney closer to the main road by her home. By the time they got to the road they could hear the sirens and see the ambulance coming up the road.

"You okay?" Aran asked Mike, who looked a bit pale.

"Yeah. As long as Zeke will be okay I think I'm good."

"Still, you should go with him and get yourself checked out. It looks like you hit your head," Aran said, inspecting Mike's temple, where there was a laceration.

"Okay, Doc. What about our shotguns?"

"That's for the State Troopers to take care of. They'll be here soon. They have to investigate every gunshot wound, even if it's accidental," Ruby said.

Mike nodded. "Okay."

The ambulance pulled up and the back was opened. A young man jumped out, followed by a young woman.

"Hey, Ruby!" the male paramedic said brightly.

"Hi, John," Ruby said. "Dr. Franklin is waiting for this patient. Thirty-year-old male with a gunshot wound in the upper right quadrant. Suspect flail chest and a chest tube inserted in situ."

John nodded and with his partner got Zeke off the makeshift gurney onto theirs, where they could assess him.

"This is the patient's friend, who was with him. He has a laceration and I suspect a possible concussion," Aran said. "If you could take him too?"

John nodded. "Sure thing, Dr....?"

"Dr. Atkinson—Aran Atkinson."

John's eyes widened and he looked at Ruby. "Your husband?"

Aran could see the blush bloom in Ruby's cheeks. "Yes."

John smiled brightly. "Pleased to meet you, Dr. Atkinson."

"Same." Aran nodded curtly.

The State Troopers pulled up behind the ambulance then, and Aran took a step back. Ruby went over to talk to the troopers about what had happened and where to find the firearms. Aran was still having a hard time believing that the two men were just out on a practice hike, and he hoped that they hadn't actually killed any game—because if it was off-season they would be in serious trouble.

At least that was his understanding. He knew from his father that Alaska had strict hunting laws and that it had state troopers who were game wardens and totally focused on protecting fish and wildlife in Alaska. Plus, Ruby had found them over the border of the Chugach State Park. That was another big no-no.

Aran had no idea she lived so close to the park.

Ruby came back over to him and stood next to him. "Good job back there, inserting that chest tube."

"Thank you," he said, and he was pleased to receive a compliment from her.

"You kept your wits about you out there."

He pursed his lips. He wasn't sure he'd completely kept his cool. It had been hard for him. He hadn't been in a situation like that since the front line and it had been hard—but he'd managed it.

Though right now he could do with a stiff drink, or maybe a good night's sleep. He wasn't sure. All he knew now was that he was crashing down off that adrenaline high and he didn't want Ruby to see it.

"Thanks." He scrubbed a hand over his face. "Since the paramedics have it under control, do you mind if I go lie down for a bit? I'm feeling tired. It's been a long day."

Ruby nodded and handed him her house keys. "Sure."

"Thanks."

Aran turned around and made his way up the drive to Ruby's house. His body was shaking and he was sweating, even though it wasn't particularly warm out. He had to get out of sight and get this under control before Ruby saw.

Before Ruby knew what ate away at his very soul.

Something had changed in Aran's mood after Mike and Zeke's care had been taken over by John's paramedic team. She knew that he had been in an IED explosion that had damaged his leg and got him discharged from the Army, but she couldn't help but suspect that he had some post-traumatic stress from that situation.

Who wouldn't?

When the ambulance had left the scene, and the State Troopers had collected the firearms and what they needed from her, she headed back up to her place. It was getting close to midnight, although with the presence of the sun it was hard to tell.

Once they passed the summer equinox the sun wouldn't be up so late.

Of course she didn't mind the sun so much—it was the near constant darkness in the winter that drove her slightly squirrelly. That was one thing about going to university in southern Ontario that she had appreciated. Sure, it was dark and cold in the winter, but the sun stuck around a heck of a lot longer than it did up in Yellowknife.

She fed Chinook and made sure he was snug for the night, then headed inside. The house was quiet, and she found the dishes had been done and the kitchen was cleaned up.

That was nice of him.

His door was shut, and if he was smart he was fast asleep. Which was what she should be. She had to fly then up to Whitehead tomorrow and run a surgical clinic for Lacey, the nurse practitioner there.

She finished locking up and was about to head upstairs to her loft when she heard a low murmur of cursing that was laced with a healthy dose of pain.

She crept toward Aran's door and knocked gently. "Aran?"

"I'm fine," he snapped from the other side, but it didn't sound as if he was fine at all.

"I don't think you are."

"I am."

Ruby rolled her eyes. "I have some acetaminophen or ibuprofen if you need it?"

She heard him groan and then move across to unlock the door. The moment he opened the door she could see the pain etched on his face. He was wearing a T-shirt and shorts and the muscles in his leg looked hard and stiff.

"Well, you might as well come in and see the mess for yourself," he said with resignation.

Ruby slipped into the room as Aran sat down on the edge of the bed. His leg was out straight. His hands were gripping the edge of the mattress so tightly that his knuckles were white.

"Do you mind?" Ruby asked as she knelt down in front of him.

He shook his head.

She reached out and touched the scars. It had been a deep wound and extensive surgical work had been on the leg. She was almost surprised that they hadn't amputated.

As if reading her mind, he said, "I wouldn't let them take it. There are pins, and I thought they would be better."

Ruby nodded solemnly and gently began to work on the tight muscle.

"That feels great," he murmured, his eyes closed.

She watched his face relax and could see the aging his work on the front line had caused him. The lines in his face, the bit of gray in his dark hair... Still, he was as handsome. She'd always thought he was handsome. If only she...

She shook that thought away. There was no *if only*. She didn't want a relationship. This fake marriage was as close as she was going to get.

"I think you overdid it out there."

Aran nodded and let out a deep breath as she worked the tight calf muscle in his leg. "I know—that's why I came back. I had a quick shower and then fell asleep—that is until the pain from my leg woke me up."

"It was a five-kilometer hike out there. That's a lot."

He cocked an eyebrow and looked at her. "You took me on a five-kilometer loop?"

"I didn't intend to, but our friends Mike and Zeke had other plans."

Aran groaned. "I didn't realize."

"Yeah, neither did I."

"That feels good," he murmured.

"You already said that," she said gently, but she was pleased that it was relaxing him.

"So I did—but it really does feel good. Thank you."

She looked up at him and caught his gaze. Those blue eyes were fixed on her. He was relaxing under her touch and her pulse quickened as he watched her. The heat crept up her neck into her cheeks and she knew that she was blushing again.

She hated that she blushed around him so much. What *was* it about him?

You're attracted to him, numbskull.

"I like it when you blush," he said.

"You…what?" She didn't look at him, kept focused on her work.

"Sorry. But from the first moment I saw you, you came off so harsh, so cold. It's nice to see this side of you."

"What do you mean?" she asked.

"That first day I showed up for my residency… I introduced myself to you and you just looked me up and down and said nothing."

"You were the competition," she teased.

"Ah, so *that's* why you were so cold."

"Exactly." She continued her massage. "You know, I like this new side of *you* too."

"How do you mean?" he asked.

"When I first met you, you were a bit of an arrogant ass."

"Was I?"

"You were the son of the president of the board of directors. You had swagger. That's another reason I was so cold to you. I thought you'd had an easy ride."

Aran chuckled. "Right. Sorry about that."

"And *I'm* sorry I assumed you were a spoiled, pompous jerk."

"Well, I was a bit arrogant."

"Just a bit." Ruby smiled and shrugged. "Well, you did me a solid. I owe you for that."

"I take payment in massages. You're quite adept at it. It feels great."

"So you said—twice," she replied.

Her pulse was racing as he closed his eyes and relaxed under her touch. She liked that she was giving him relief, but this was not keeping her distance from her convenient husband. Because that was what he was. He was her fake husband. He wasn't her real husband. Their marriage might be legal on paper, but that was it. Aran was a friend and nothing more.

A friend she was completely drawn and attracted to.

She cleared her throat and looked down at the floor. "I still think you should take some ibuprofen—and I can get you a heated pad. You need to alternate hot and cold."

Aran nodded. "That's probably for the best."

She finished up and stood. "Do you think you'll be able to fly tomorrow? A bush plane is pretty compact."

"I should be fine," he said tersely, and then he sighed. "Look, I'm sorry, but the last thing I want to do is let this keep me from my work. My work is all I have. I know that you understand that."

And she did. Her career and Chinook were all she had.

She did it to honor her father. To give to others who might not live without her help. And she could tell that was important to Aran too. After the way his leg had been pieced back together she understood why he felt he needed to work, that he couldn't give up. And she admired that. She truly did.

"I do understand that. I'll get you that ibuprofen and the heated pad for the night, so that you'll be able to accompany me up to Whitehead tomorrow morning."

Aran's shoulders relaxed. "I appreciate that, Ruby."

She nodded and slipped out of the room, shutting the door behind her. Usually she kept guys at a distance. It had been nice telling people she was married, but knowing she was not really married. Aran was a good excuse to keep men at an arm's length.

She'd had a few boyfriends when she was younger, but nothing serious because she hadn't wanted to tie herself to someone who didn't understand that her job came first. That her life living in the north and saving lives was all that mattered to her.

And she didn't want to leave anyone behind. She didn't want to leave a child or a husband to grieve over her if she died on the job.

The problem was, Aran understood that.

And that was a scary prospect indeed.

CHAPTER SIX

ARAN DIDN'T LOOK RELAXED, but he was trying his best to make himself comfortable in the cockpit of her bush plane. When he'd got up that morning he'd still been moving quite stiffly, but when she'd offered to help him he'd turned her down.

And that was okay by her.

She hadn't got much sleep because she'd thought about Aran all night. She'd thought about the way he'd looked at her, and she'd imagined what it would be like to be taken in his arms. To be kissed. To be with him the way she'd always wanted to be with him.

She'd never desired anyone like this before. It scared her how much of an effect he had on her. How he *got* her. How he understood.

But she couldn't let herself think like that. They were in a marriage of convenience. Once she'd got her Green Card and an acceptable time had passed they would get a divorce and they could both move on with their lives.

What if he stays in Alaska? That's not moving on.

She shook that thought from her mind and focused on her flight path. They were flying over the end of the tree line, where the Alaska forests gave way to the endless majestic tundra of the far north.

Aran craned his neck so he could get a better glimpse out over the horizon. "Not much further?" he asked over the mic.

"Not much further," she said. "How's your leg?"

"Stiff, but I'll be fine once I can walk around and stretch it out."

Ruby nodded and adjusted her instruments, descending a bit lower. She was getting closer to the small gravel air strip that was just outside Whitehead, a tiny community at the edge of the Beaufort Sea. She could see the sea at the edge of the horizon. Just a thin silver strip that got wider the closer they got to their destination.

The community bordered the edge of Alaska and the Yukon Territory in Canada. It was as remote as remote could be, and at the top of the world, although in Canada there were even more remote communities.

"Do you know what surgeries we're going to be doing up there?" Aran asked.

"A cholecystectomy, for sure, but I'm not sure of the others. We'll assess all who come in today. We'll see everything. That's the thing with visiting these outposts—you get a variety."

"N539BY, this is WHX. You're clear to land on the runway," the voice over the radio crackled.

"This is N539BY. Roger that, WHX. We're readying to land. Dropping landing gear," Ruby responded.

"Roger," the air traffic controller responded.

"I guess they don't get many visitors up here," said Aran.

"They get cargo planes. How else are they going to get fuel and food?"

Ruby began her checks and prepared her plane to land.

She lined up with the gravel airstrip just as the wind picked up, blowing in off the Beaufort Sea.

"Whoa..." Aran muttered.

"It's okay. We'll crab it in," she teased.

"What?" Aran asked.

"Crabbing is when we go in sideways instead of straight—that way the wind won't flip the plane."

His eyes widened as she adjusted her instruments and brought the plane down sideways toward the runway, before straightening and landing with just a slight bounce as the plane ran the distance it needed to slow down. She brought the plane around toward the hangar, where a group of community members were waiting.

"Good job," Aran said.

"You were white-knuckling it a bit there!"

"Maybe..." He chuckled. "Just a bit."

"Trust me."

Aran cocked an eyebrow. "Really?"

She grinned. "Just be mindful of the bears."

"What?"

"Polar bears. It's summer. The come inland when the ice breaks up."

"Great," Aran muttered. "Is this the excitement you were talking about earlier?"

She laughed. "Just a touch of excitement mixed with caution."

Being at the top of the world meant that polar bears were often a threat in the summer months. With the ice broken up, and so far out, polar bears came inland, and there were always lookouts to make sure they didn't come too close to town.

Ruby shut down the plane and opened the pilot's door. Already the side door was open, and all the medical supplies she'd loaded up were being offloaded by Lacey's staff at the clinic.

Mitchell, an elder of the community, came forward.

"Ruby, it's good to see you again," he said.

"Glad to be back, Mitchell. Is Lacey waiting for me at the clinic?" Ruby asked.

"You bet she is." Mitchell's gaze fell on Aran. "Who is this? This isn't John or Dr. Franklin. And definitely not Lindsey, your nurse."

Mitchell was teasing her, and Aran laughed.

"No." Ruby swallowed the lump in her throat as she tried to figure out how to explain who Aran was. "This is Dr. Atkinson. New to the team, but also my..."

"I'm her husband," Aran said quickly, and smiled brightly.

"Oh! You were overseas, yeah?" Mitchell asked.

Aran nodded. "I was. But I'm home now, and looking forward to working with my wife both at the hospital and on her team."

Mitchell smiled and nodded. "Good to have you back. And good to have two surgeons here today, yeah?"

"For sure."

Ruby's stomach twisted in a knot. It was hard to tell these people she worked with so closely that she was married. She'd told them before, but now that Aran was standing here it was a little bit harder—because it was a lie. She hated lying. She hated lying to Mitchell and everyone else in Whitehead. She hated that this whole marriage was a fraud.

It doesn't have to be a lie.

She ignored that thought.

"Why don't we head to the clinic before Lacey starts to worry."

"I've got my truck. The bears have been bad this summer, so it's best we drive to the clinic—unless you have a high-velocity rifle to scare them off?"

"What?" Aran muttered under his breath. "You weren't joking, then?"

"Polar bears are dangerous predators," Ruby whispered back. "It's eat or be eaten."

"I see."

"No, you don't want to see *that*." Ruby shuddered. "That is not pretty."

"I'll take your word for it," Aran said dryly.

They followed Mitchell to his truck and Ruby was crammed between Mitchell and Aran. She was used to being crammed into a truck with Mitchell and John, or Lacey, but she wasn't used to being flush up against Aran.

"I'm not hurting your bad leg, am I?" Ruby asked as she tried to position herself so she wouldn't hurt him.

"No, it's fine. You're nice and soft."

His blue eyes were twinkling and he smirked. She realized then that he was trying to get her goat since they weren't alone.

She rolled her eyes and tried to angle herself away from him. Aran moved and rested his arm on the back of the seat, so that he almost had his arm around her, forcing her to move into the crook of his elbow.

"Cheap move!" Ruby teased.

Aran chuckled softly as Mitchell fired up the old truck and headed away from the tiny airport and across town.

Most of the homes there were built up on stilts because of the permafrost and the tides from the Beaufort Sea. Whitehead was right on the coast, near an inlet, and there were a lot of traditional fishermen who made their livelihoods out on the water.

There weren't many vehicles in town. Most people got around via ATV in the summer or snowmobile in the winter.

Even though it was the end of June there were still patches of snow on the ground, covering up the rock and lichen that grew over the tundra this far north.

The houses were painted in bright colors, and as Mitchell drove through town people came out and waved. They were happy to see Ruby.

Whitehead was far away from any other town, but it was a friendly place. It struggled with the same issues that other places did, but Mitchell was passionate about taking care of the people.

Ruby's father had been very involved in the council and making sure that the people in her own village had what they needed. Residential school may have broken him in some ways, but in others it had taught him the meaning of keeping family and community together, of healing and making sure that everyone was taken care of. Of making sure to reclaim what was once lost.

"This is a nice place, Mitchell," Aran said, but Ruby wasn't completely sure that he meant it—because Aran came from San Diego and had told her that he preferred the south over the north.

"Thanks," Mitchell replied. "We work hard and we work to take care of each other, but there are some things we can't do—and that's why we appreciate Lacey and doctors like you and Ruby coming up here and helping us out."

Mitchell pulled up to a long building that was partly

built into a side of a hill and partly on stilts. There was a long wooden ramp for wheelchairs and stretchers.

"Here we are," Mitchell announced as he opened the door and climbed out. "My boys should be along soon with the medical supplies."

"Great. Thanks, Mitchell," Ruby said.

Aran slid out and Ruby was glad to have her own personal bubble back and intact. Now, if she could just calm her nerves a bit, she would be good to tackle whatever today threw at her.

The door to the clinic opened and Lacey stepped out—with a very round belly.

Ruby's eyes widened. "You're *pregnant*?"

Lacey grinned. "About twenty-nine weeks. Over the danger zone."

Ruby gave her a hug. "I had no idea. You were away and I dealt with another nurse practitioner the last time I was here."

"I was in Anchorage for a couple months on a course, and getting checked out. I hope my replacement did good?"

"She was fine," Ruby replied. "What does Jack think about being a dad?"

Jack was Lacey's husband and the village State Trooper, who kept the peace and made sure fishing and gaming laws were respected. Also, when convicts were released they would often return to their own communities, and Jack made sure that they met the conditions of their parole. He didn't just serve Whitehead, but traveled by bush plane to several other communities that dotted the Beaufort Sea coast.

"He's thrilled—but he wants me back down in Anchorage to give birth. He's worried. *I'm* not worried. We have a midwife up here besides me." Lacey looked past Ruby. "Who's this?"

"This is my...my husband, Dr. Aran Atkinson."

Lacey's eyebrows shot up. "Wow!"

Ruby shook her head and Lacey covered her mouth.

"Sorry, pregnancy brain," she apologized. "It's nice to meet you finally, Aran. Ruby has told me a lot about you."

Aran cocked an eyebrow and chuckled. "Has she? It's nice to meet you too, Lacey."

"Let's get inside and I'll fill you two in on what's going to happen today."

"Sounds good."

Ruby glanced back at Aran, who was still chuckling to himself, and couldn't help but laugh. She didn't know exactly why Lacey had said that to Aran. All she had ever told her about her husband was that she was married and he was overseas, serving.

Lacey had been something of a matchmaker when Ruby had first met her. In fact, Lacey had been trying to set Ruby up with Jack—but Ruby had known the moment she'd met Jack that it was Lacey he truly wanted. Another time when her fake marriage to Aran had come in handy. Once people knew you were married they stopped trying to fix you up with every single guy in a hundred-mile radius.

The clinic was warm and quiet, but Ruby knew that wouldn't last long. As soon as the doors opened, in an hour, the clinic would be packed.

"You guys can set your stuff down in the staff lounge." Lacey pointed to a door behind the desk. "I just have to get some of the charts ready. I'll come back in ten minutes and we'll go over the day's work."

Ruby opened the door to the lounge room and peeled off her coat. Aran followed her in.

"I have a question," he said.

"What's that?"

"What exactly have you been telling people about me? I mean, everyone I've met knows exactly who I am and is excited to meet me..."

"What do you mean, what have I been telling them? I've told you what I've been saying."

"And what *is* that again?" he teased.

"That you served overseas and your name."

"That's it?" he asked, and there was the smug smirk she remembered.

"Yes. What's your point?"

"Lacey hearing 'so much' about me."

And there was another saucy smirk on his face.

Oh, Creator.

"Again, I only told her your name, the fact you were a surgeon in the Army, who your mother was, and that you were overseas. Also that we did a year of residency together."

Aran looked a bit disappointed. "That's it?" he said again.

"What else was I going to tell her?" Ruby asked, and then she lowered her voice. "I didn't tell them that our marriage was a sham and that we barely knew each other."

"We know more about each other now, after only a couple of days."

Ruby cocked an eyebrow and crossed her arms. "Oh? Enlighten me."

"You know I come from San Diego. You know that I haven't seen much of Anchorage and don't know much about the north. And you know the damage done to my leg."

"And I know you're a pretty good surgeon."

Aran smiled and his expression softened. "See? Those are things. But I was kind of hoping that you'd told some juicy lies about me."

Ruby tied back her hair into a bun and then pulled her scrubs out of her bag. "I'm not a good liar. I give this tight smile and just kind of stare off into space while I try not to sweat."

He chuckled. "Yeah, I've seen that expression before. You were wearing it the day we got married."

"What?" she asked.

Aran grinned and she laughed out loud.

"I did *not* grin like that," she said.

"You *so* did."

Ruby rolled her eyes. "I suppose I did. That was a very uncomfortable situation."

And she remembered how, even though she knew now that he had been upset about his father's death, he'd taken her hand and calmed her down, and how much she'd appreciated it.

"Agreed." He pulled out the set of scrubs he'd packed and then slipped off his shirt.

Ruby tried to not watch him as he changed, but she couldn't help it. He wasn't as ripped as he had been before he'd shipped out, but he was still a well-built specimen.

She could see scars from the shrapnel littering his side. He hadn't told her much about the IED explosion, but from the way his leg had been damaged and the scars on his torso it seemed he was lucky to have survived.

The thought of him almost dying caused her anxiety.

What if he had died? How would she have got her Green Card?

And then she felt bad for thinking so selfishly about herself.

As if he knew she was staring, he glanced over his shoulder. "What?"

"Your scars. That must've been one of heck of an explosion."

His jaw tightened and he pulled his shirt down over his head and covered them up. "Yeah."

She'd obviously touched a sore spot and she couldn't blame him. She couldn't even begin to fathom what it would have been like and she knew that she wasn't going to press him on the matter—just as she didn't want him to press her on the matter of her father's death.

They finished getting changed in tense silence and Lacey came back to the room with a pile of charts.

"You two ready? Our cholecystectomy patient is ready to go!"

"Yeah," Ruby said.

Aran just nodded, and then they followed Lacey out of the lounge area to start their long day of surgeries and consults.

Aran was exhausted. He hadn't pulled such a long day since before his injury. He'd done that surgery with Ruby when he'd first arrived in Anchorage, but that had been just one surgery. Then there had been the flail chest in the woods but, again, that had been one isolated incident.

It was a much different thing seeing case after case and doing many minor day surgeries to save the people of Whitehead a very expensive trip down to Anchorage or Juneau.

His leg was aching too, but there had been a lull, so he quietly slipped away and made his way back to the lounge. There was a comfortable-looking couch there, and after he'd grabbed himself a cup of lukewarm coffee he sat down and leaned his head back.

Ruby hadn't been joking when she'd mentioned that it would be tough work. Now he understood his limitations.

He'd had physiotherapy, and had been cleared to do surgery, but he should've eased himself into it rather than thinking he could just go back to the way he'd always done things.

He hated that the injury was preventing him from just getting back into the swing of things as he'd always done.

One thing that had made it easier was working with Ruby and Lacey. They both ran a tight ship and he appreciated that. Lacey's staff were well equipped to handle day surgeries and that was impressive.

It wasn't just the people in Whitehead who were utilizing the clinic today—they were flying in from all the other isolated little communities.

Lacey had handled the day-to day-appointments, while Ruby and he handled what Lacey couldn't.

"How are you holding up?" Ruby asked as she came into the room and poured herself a cup of coffee.

"A little sore, but I just need ten minutes and I'll be back at it."

Ruby leaned against the counter and took a sip of coffee. "I think we're done."

"Don't say that."

"Why?" she asked.

"Inevitably when a doctor says that there will be some crazy emergency."

Ruby chuckled softly. "Not here. No other flights are

coming in and Lacey is dealing with the last of the regular check-ups."

Aran scrubbed a hand over his face. "I hope you're right."

"As soon as my last patient comes out of the post-anesthesia recovery room I'm going to suggest high-tailing it out of here. I've been watching the radar and there's a nasty storm coming down from the mountains. I'd like to get back to Anchorage tonight."

"Because of Chinook?" Aran asked.

"No, he's fine. Sam will check on him. But if it's a bad storm we could be stuck for a couple of days. The temperature has dropped outside."

"You're not seriously telling me it's a snow storm?" Aran asked in disbelief. "It's *June*."

"Yeah, exactly. It's June. Stranger things have happened."

"Okay, then, I'll go get..." Aran trailed off as Lacey came in. He could tell by her pained expression something was wrong.

"Hey, guys. It's Mitchell..."

"What about Mitchell?" Ruby asked.

"Appendicitis. It's bad. His son Max just brought him in."

"Okay." Ruby finished her coffee.

"See?" Aran said, and he finished his coffee and got up.

"You were right." Ruby stretched. "You okay to handle this?"

"I'm good. Maybe we can stabilize him with some antibiotics and fly him down to Anchorage?"

"Hopefully—and hopefully before the storm hits." Ruby tossed her coffee cup in the garbage. "You ready?"

Aran nodded. "Yeah, as ready as I'll ever be."

He followed her and Lacey as they made their way to an empty exam room. The last of the post-operative patients were being taken care of and discharged. As soon as he walked into the exam room and saw Mitchell he could tell that this appendicitis wouldn't be stopped with simple intravenous antibiotics.

The man's appendix was about to rupture.

Ruby took the chart from Lacey and shook her head gently, showing him the last recorded temperature.

"It's high," Aran said quietly.

"I did an ultrasound and the appendix is enlarged. He is unable to pass gas and his blood test shows a high white blood count," Lacey said.

"What's wrong with my dad?" Max asked.

"Appendicitis," Ruby said. "Mitchell, were you feeling this bad this morning?"

Mitchell winced. "I thought I had some indigestion, but it just got worse as the day went on."

Ruby looked at him. "Well, what do you think, Aran?"

"That appendix needs to come out before we can fly him down to Anchorage."

"My dad has to have *surgery*?" Max asked, shocked.

"Yes," Aran said. "He needs that appendix removed. If it isn't it could burst and be fatal for him."

Max nodded, but looked worried. "I should get my mom. Dad, you going to be okay?"

Mitchell nodded. "I am. Be careful, yeah?"

"I will."

Max left and Lacey began prepping a bag of antibiotics and getting Mitchell some pain medication.

"Lacey, can you prep Mitchell for surgery and we'll get the operating room ready?" Ruby asked.

"Of course, Ruby."

Aran followed Ruby out of Mitchell's room.

"I don't think we're going to beat that storm. And even if we did, I wouldn't want to risk transporting Mitchell to Anchorage this late in the evening."

"Agreed. So we stay here and hope that the weather clears in the morning?"

Ruby nodded. "There's no other choice. That appendix is going to rupture before we can get him to the hospital and that's much worse than getting stuck in Whitehead for a couple of days."

"Okay, well, let's get that appendix out." Aran winced slightly. His leg was bothering him. "I'm going to take some ibuprofen and I'll meet you in the operating room."

"Okay."

Aran headed back to the lounge to grab some medication, just so he could make it through this last surgery. As he got to the front of the clinic the light disappeared and the wind shook the building, rattling the windows as the snowstorm darkened the sky.

He'd never seen anything quite like it before. And he worried that it might be more than just a night that they were stuck in Whitehead.

CHAPTER SEVEN

RUBY WAS TRYING not worry about Aran as he stood on the other side of the operating table. She could tell that his leg was bothering him, but he was still focused on his work and she had to admire him for that.

There was a lot she liked about him. She'd forgotten what he was like. How much she'd missed him—how much she'd missed working with him.

She definitely needed his help in operating the laparoscope to remove Mitchell's appendix. Lacey was sitting next to Mitchell's head, monitoring him, and her anesthesiologist was making sure that Mitchell stayed under.

Ruby kept her attention on the screen in front of her as she navigated through Mitchell's peritoneum to find the nasty little appendix.

"There it is," Ruby said confidently.

It was red and swollen. A couple more hours and she had no doubt that it would burst. Long before they'd be able to get to Anchorage.

"Looks bad," Aran said.

Ruby nodded and adjusted the laparoscope so she could remove the appendix and invert the stump into the cecum. "With the storm raging outside, there's no way we would've made it to the hospital. I'm wondering how long he's been masking his symptoms…"

"I don't know," Lacey piped up. "He's pretty good at hiding things like this. He doesn't ever want to be a bother and he doesn't want to take off time from work."

"Ah, that sounds like Mitchell for sure."

Ruby finished removing the appendix and sealing off the wound. Mitchell would still have to go down to Anchorage and be on intravenous antibiotics for a few days, to make sure that no abscess formed and he didn't get a post-operative infection. Post-operative infections were uncommon, but with something like the appendix Mitchell would have to be closely monitored.

Aran took over to help remove the instruments and close up the wound.

"Good job, Doctors," Lacey said. "I am *beat*."

"You need to rest," Ruby remarked as she cleaned up.

"Yes. Thankfully Joanna the night nurse will be on duty soon, to monitor all the patients and be here in case of any post-operative complications."

"We'll be here too," Ruby said. "We're not flying out in this weather. Is there a couple of rooms we can use for the night?"

Lacey gave her a strange look. "A couple of rooms? Don't you two want the same room?"

Ruby's heart skipped a beat and she could see Aran's spine stiffen as he finished bandaging Mitchell.

"Oh…yeah, right. I'm just tired." It was an excuse but she hoped that Lacey bought it. "One room is all we need."

"I understand that," Lacey remarked as she made some notes on Mitchell's chart. "Besides, we only have one extra room at the moment. Good thing you two are married!"

"Yeah, good thing…"

Ruby glanced at Aran. He wasn't looking at her, but she could tell by the way his body had tensed that he wasn't exactly thrilled with the prospect of sharing a room with her. She only hoped it had a set of bunks or a couple of beds, like on-call rooms usually had.

After they'd finished with Mitchell, and made sure that he was stable in the post-anesthesia recovery unit, with Joanna the night nurse and Mitchell's wife Kayla, Lacey showed them to the room that was used for locum medical staff.

"It's a small room, but it has a double bed."

Lacey opened the door and Ruby's heart sank when she saw how tiny the room was. The double bed filled the small space. There really would be nowhere to escape Aran. And if someone found him or her sleeping on the couch in the lounge they would question why they weren't sleeping together.

It's only sleeping.

They had slept in the same on-call room before.

Yeah, but you never shared a bed with him.

"This is great. Thank you," Aran said cordially.

Lacey nodded. "I'm just down the hall. With Jack out of town I'd rather stay close to the clinic."

"That's a good plan," Aran replied, because Ruby was clearly still too stunned to say anything.

"Night!"

Lacey turned and headed down the hall. When she was out of sight Ruby groaned.

"What're we going to do?" Ruby asked.

Aran ushered her into the room and shut the door, closing it behind him. "What do you mean, what're we going to do? We're going to lie down and try and get some sleep so that we can transport Mitchell to Anchorage tomorrow."

"We have to share a *bed*!"

"So?" Aran asked.

"We've never done that before!"

"We're married," Aran stated.

"Yeah, but still…" Ruby rubbed her temple. "I'm freaking out over this."

"Why?" he asked. "You're safe with me."

"I know. I just hate all this deception. I hate this immigration interview looming. I hate it all."

"I know," he said softly. "Me too."

"I know…sorry. I'm tired."

"We both are."

Aran glanced down at the small double bed, which was placed up against the wall. There was just enough space to walk in and out of the room. That was it. It was a place for people to rest their heads at night. Nothing more.

"Which side do you want?" he asked.

"I think, given your leg, you should have this side. You're, like, six foot, and you're going to need extra space. I'm more compact at five-five. I can cram into the corner."

Aran looked relieved. "Thanks. I didn't particularly feel like cramming myself anywhere."

Ruby kicked off her shoes and then crawled across the creaky bed and tried to make herself somewhat comfortable before Aran got in.

"You ready?" he asked.

"As ready as I'll ever be."

He chuckled and sat on the edge of the bed to remove his shoes. Then slowly he lay down, trying to stretch out his sore leg.

Ruby giggled.

"What?" he asked.

"Your foot touches the door and your head is at the wall!"

Aran craned his neck to look and then shrugged. "I've slept in tighter spots than this."

The wind howled outside. It was a deafening sound as it hit the corrugated steel buildings and whipped across the tundra.

Aran shuddered. "A snowstorm in June..." he mumbled.

"Get used to it," Ruby replied.

"It sounds a bit like a sandstorm, to be honest. Had a few of those when I was serving. At least snow melts—sand just gets into everything. Even the patients you're working on."

"I can't even imagine."

"Don't try. It's awful."

Ruby couldn't sleep. All she could do was stare up at the ceiling and count the marks on it. She knew Aran was awake too, because of the way he was breathing. It wasn't steady and even. And his body was still tense, as if he was trying to give her space.

"I think I prefer snow," she said, breaking the tension.

"What?" he asked.

"Well, as you say, snow melts. Sand stays and shifts around. It never leaves. Although there are times in the winter when the top layer of snow blows and shifts like the desert. You get white-out conditions—not because it's fresh snow, but blowing snow when there's no trees to break it."

"That would be neat to see."

"Not if you're driving in it."

She remembered the few times her older brother had had to stop on the highway between Yellowknife and Enterprise because the snow had been bad. He always had emergency gear in the back and he always knew the good places to stop.

Their father had taught him that. Taught him how to survive. Because he had run away from residential school. He'd been lucky to make it when so many didn't. Her dad had been going to show her too, but he'd never got around to teaching her. He'd died before he got the chance.

So she'd taken it upon herself to learn. She'd taken it upon herself to learn a lot of things. All the things her father had promised to teach her.

And now, as she thought about her father, all she could see was his body on that cold metal table. His eyes closed, no life left in him. Just an empty shell.

No.

She was not going to think about that. Not here.

"I could survive a snowstorm, but not sand," she said offhandedly, breaking the tension and trying to shoo away the memories of her father.

"You've taken survival courses?" he asked, intrigued.

"To live and work in remote areas you need to. You need to know how to survive on the land."

"We took some as part of our training. But I wouldn't mind a refresher on surviving here in the winter."

"I can show you," she offered, pleased that he wanted to learn. She'd always thought of him as a soft southerner, but maybe she was wrong. He was proving to be anything but the spoiled, privileged, arrogant man she'd thought he was when she'd first met him all those years ago.

"Would you?"

"Of course. If you're going to be part of a medical team, you need to know."

He turned and looked at her. His face was so close to hers.

"Thank you."

"No problem." She stifled a yawn.

"You should try to sleep. *I* can't fly the plane tomorrow."

She smiled. "I know. I'm just not used to sharing a bed with anyone."

"I'm not used to this constant daylight. Although the storm helps to darken the room a bit."

"You get used to it. It's why I have blackout blinds."

"I still can't sleep. I'm exhausted, but…"

He trailed off and then turned his head away. She could tell that something had changed. That he'd been going to say something and thought better of it.

It's not your business.

Although she couldn't help wonder what it was. She didn't want to pry. Well, she *did* want to pry, but she wasn't going to. She couldn't get involved with him. Sure, he was her husband, but it was just until she got her Green Card.

Still, there was a part of her that wanted to know more about him. There was a part of her that was comfortable being around him. She hadn't been as lonely since he'd shown up. It was nice having someone to talk to instead of Chinook.

"Count sheep?" she suggested.

"That never works."

"How do you know? Have you tried?"

He glanced back at her. "No—have you?"

"No."

"Then why would you suggest it?"

Ruby shrugged. "Everyone suggests it."

"So, that makes it a certainty that it will put me to sleep?" he teased.

"No, but it's been common knowledge for a long time. Sheep are kind of boring, right?"

"Why are we having a conversation about sheep?" he asked.

"I don't know—probably because you won't stop talking."

"Sorry about that." He groaned and rubbed his eyes.

"I can't sleep either," she said. "I'm tired, but I really can't sleep. I'm not used to sleeping next to someone."

"So you keep saying."

"Sorry." Heat bloomed in her cheeks. "Not even Chinook sleeps with me."

Aran rolled over and propped himself on one elbow. "You've never lived with anyone?"

"My parents and siblings. And I had a roommate in university, but we didn't share a bed."

"No, I mean…a boyfriend or a fiancé or some other significant other?"

Heat bloomed in her cheeks. "I've had boyfriends, but never long-term. So, no, I've never slept in the same bed as anyone."

Ruby was not used to talking so intimately with someone. Not even with her girlfriends. And she didn't have many of those because her career was her life. She didn't make much time for her friends, and eventually some of those friends had stopped inviting her to places.

Even if she did go out, she didn't really open up about her life. Keeping to herself was a way to compartmentalize her feelings, so she could keep focused on her work.

It was why any relationships she'd had had never lasted. Men said she wouldn't open up. That she was too focused on her work.

It had never really bothered her.

Until now.

"You're blushing again," he said softly.

"I don't talk about my personal life."

"I remember. You were always all business. Which is why I liked you so much."

"Right…"

Her heart had fluttered when he'd said he liked her. *Don't think about it. You're friends. That's all.*

"Why did you like me," she asked, "if I was all business? I saw you with others…you know…before we were married."

"You were driven and focused. I admired that. And, to be honest, I thought you were a challenge I wanted to take on. I don't think that way now."

"A challenge?" she asked, annoyed.

"Yeah, but once I got to know why you were so focused and what you wanted to do I didn't think that way anymore. You were not just someone I wanted to conquer. I learned that lesson fast. Instead I wanted to be a part of your work."

Her heart skipped a beat again.

You're treading on dangerous ground.

She couldn't let him get too close. She had to keep him at a distance. But it was nice lying here in bed and talking to him. To have this moment of connection.

"I should know some personal facts before this Agent Bolton comes and talks to us," he said.

"If I open up are you going to open up?"

"Sure. If I think you need to know," he stated.

"Ditto."

"So how do we do this?" he asked.

"We play fifty questions."

His eyes widened. "Fifty?"

"Or the amount of questions until we get bored and/ or fall asleep."

Aran sat up and she did too. They were sitting cross-legged across from each other.

"What do we start with?" he asked.

"Favorite color?"

"Green," he said. "Yours?"

"Red. Now you ask a question."

"I don't know…" He ran his hand through his hair, as he often did when he didn't know what to say or was annoyed.

"Just think of one," she said.

"Uh… I'm not good at this. I don't want to do this."

"This was your idea, pal. You wanted to get to know me."

He ran his hand through his hair again. "What drink would you be?"

She looked at him like he was crazy. "What *drink* would I be? Don't you mean what drink do I like?"

"No, what drink would you *be*. If you weren't human, what drink would you be?"

Ruby sat there, stunned. And then she saw a strange smirk on his face. She flicked him on his good knee.

"Ow—what was that for?" he asked.

"That's a stupid question."

"No question is stupid." His eyes were twinkling.

"That one was."

Aran laughed softly. "Sorry."

"I don't know how we're going to convince this Agent

Bolton that we've been properly married for five years and that we know each other well—especially when we can't seem to relax around each other. The only time we're relaxed is in surgery, and I hardly think Agent Bolton will want to do his interview in the operating room."

"I know one way," Aran said softly.

Her pulse began to race. "Oh?"

"Well, we can kiss and break the tension that way."

Say no. Say no.

"Okay."

Her voice went up one octave as she said it. What was she thinking? This was a bad idea.

Except she was curious. She was attracted to him and she had always wondered what it would be like to kiss him—just once. And he was right. It might ease the tension between them.

"You sure?" he asked.

She nodded. "You're right. We have to be more comfortable around each other and a kiss is a pretty easy way to do that. Let's do it."

"Relax," he whispered, and he reached out and touched her face.

Just the simple touch made her stomach flip-flop with anticipation.

"I'll try." But she couldn't look at him, and she was sure that her cheeks were bright red. She'd kissed guys before—what was so different about this?

You're not in control.

Aran inched closer to her and tilted her chin so she was forced to look at him. She wanted to look away, but she couldn't.

"It's okay," he whispered.

Ruby relaxed, mesmerized by him. His gentle touch was electric, igniting every nerve-ending under her skin. Her heart hammered against her chest.

With that simple acknowledgement that it would be okay he'd cast a spell over her. So much so she felt she was losing control—something she usually kept a tight rein on.

But she didn't care.

It was okay.

He cupped her face, his thumbs brushing her cheeks, and no matter how much the rational side of her wanted to fight it, she couldn't. For the first time in her life Ruby gave over control to a man, when *she* was usually the initiator of any intimate moments. This time she just reveled in the sensation, in the desire that Aran was stirring in her.

She closed her eyes and let him kiss her. His lips were gentle against hers. And then the kiss deepened and she welcomed it. It had been so long since she had been kissed by a man or had any kind of physical connection with another person.

It was intoxicating. The simple act of human contact with a man she desired was creating a hunger, a need to have more.

Aran wrapped his arms around her and she forgot everything else as she melted against him. In that brief moment he made her feel safe…he made her feel alive.

What are you doing?

As his hands moved down her back she realized this was dangerous territory. She pushed him away. "I can't. We can't…not here."

"You're right," he murmured, and pulled away. "I'm sorry. I… I'm sorry."

"Don't be sorry. It was nice."

He nodded. "Yeah…"

She bit her lip. Her body wanted more, and her pulse was still racing, but this was not the place to do anything more than kiss.

Aran stood.

"Where are you going?" she asked.

"I need to take a little walk, and then I'll do a round on the patients. You rest."

Before she could stop him he'd opened up the door and slipped out into the hallway.

Ruby lay down. There was no way she was getting any sleep now. Not with the taste of Aran on her lips, her blood thrumming in her veins and her body craving more than just a simple kiss.

CHAPTER EIGHT

ARAN TOOK A long walk to try and calm down. He had wanted to kiss Ruby for a long time, although he'd never intended for it to go that far. But the moment he'd tasted her sweet lips he'd just wanted more.

What were you thinking?

It was taking all his willpower not to go back to her and throw himself at her feet. He was attracted to her.

Usually when he was attracted to someone he saw them a few times and then it was done. The romance had run its course.

Women didn't understand his devotion to his work and that was fine by him. He didn't want to be tied down. He didn't want a family only to have it broken.

And he was too broken himself.

The problem with Ruby was that she did understand his devotion to work. That was her passion too and that made him want her even more. She was smart, funny, strong, beautiful and independent. There was so much he loved about her.

He liked working with her and he wanted her. He'd always wanted her.

What was supposed to have been a simple kiss to break the tension had turned into something he hadn't expected. Something he hadn't prepared for mentally or emotionally. It had woken something inside him.

He'd thought maybe the kiss would break him of the hold she had on him, but he'd been so wrong. It had fired his blood. Made him feel alive. It had made him feel as if he was his old self again.

But he wasn't. He would never be the same person he was before. That IED explosion had shattered him. It had broken him. And Ruby deserved so much better than the pieces of him that were left.

He'd taken a walk so that she could get some rest and be able to fly them out of Whitehead if the weather had cleared in the morning. He sincerely hoped that it would.

He went back to the room and quietly opened the door. Ruby had curled up in the middle of the bed and was sleeping soundly. A smile tugged at the corner of his mouth. She looked so peaceful.

Good.

She needed the rest. It had been a long, busy day and flying up to Whitehead from Anchorage had meant that they'd started early. Ruby had definitely clocked up over eighteen hours and she needed sleep.

He was okay. He was tired, and a bit sore, but there were many nights when he couldn't sleep. When his PTSD was working in overdrive and the nightmares just wouldn't stop. He could sleep later. He didn't have to fly a plane back.

She looked so peaceful there and he wished that he could hold her.

He wished he could do more.

You need to back away.

He shut the door. The couch in the lounge room would

be the perfect place to crash. If anyone asked he'd just tell them Ruby snored.

Aran chuckled silently to himself, thinking about how Ruby would react to that. He headed into the lounge and stared at the couch.

You've slept on worse.

"Dr. Atkinson?"

Aran spun around to see the night nurse, Joanna, standing behind him.

"Yes?"

"It's Mitchell. He's spiked a fever and I can't get it to go down. I've given him the maximum amount of antibiotics I can."

"I'll be right there."

Joanna nodded and Aran washed his hands in the lounge's sink and took a deep breath to calm his nerves. He wasn't a stranger to post-operative infection and fever. Especially in situations where the wounded patient was maxed out on medication and they were waiting for transport.

He just hoped that this storm would clear so they could get Mitchell down to the larger hospital which would have access to different kinds of antibiotics and a larger staff on call. He was glad that Whitehead was equipped to deal with small surgeries, but some things were better left to a hospital.

He'd learned from working on the front line that some things just couldn't be done, and that was when you just basically did what you could to keep your patients alive until they could be shipped out. Even that was a case of throwing the dice...

He walked into the room and saw that Mitchell's heart-rate was up. He was pale and looked as if he was having trouble breathing.

"Did you run a culture of his blood?" Aran asked as he pulled out his chart.

"I did. His white cell count isn't elevated that high. He's feverish, but I don't think it's sepsis."

"I agree," Aran said.

He set the chart down and examined the wound. It was healing well and there was no sign of infection there. He moved back the sheet and saw red in Mitchell's legs. It was warm to the touch.

"Look at this, Joanna. What do you see?"

Joanna leaned in and examined it. "Deep vein thrombosis?"

Aran nodded. "Could be. Does Mitchell have a history of blood clots?"

"Not, Mitchell—but his mother did. She died of a pulmonary embolism three years ago."

"Do you have a Doppler?" Aran asked.

"We do."

Joanna left the room and Aran monitored Mitchell's pulse-rate. It was high, and Aran had no doubt that what Mitchell had was thrombophlebitis. And since they didn't have a CT scanner here the Doppler would have to do. If it was a pulmonary embolism they would have to get him back to Anchorage to do an angiogram.

Aran hoped that Whitehead stocked a supply of heparin. If he could get some heparin into Mitchell that would at least help until they got back to Seward Memorial.

Joanna returned with the Doppler.

"Here you are, Dr. Atkinson. The weather looks to be clearing. Not much snow has stayed—it's been pretty much blown away and the temperature is rising."

"Good—because we really need to get Mitchell down to Anchorage."

Mitchell moaned, but he was pretty much out of it—which was good. The poor guy had been through the wringer today, and all while putting on a smile. Aran would never understand that—hiding symptoms—but then he knew there were people out there who thought every ache was cancer. Still, the pain Mitchell must have been in would have been more than just a slight ache.

"Do you have any heparin here in Whitehead?" Aran asked.

Joanna nodded. "Of course."

"Good. Can you ready a dose, please?"

"Right away, Doctor."

Joanna disappeared out of the room again and Aran prepped the Doppler to examine Mitchell's leg. The more Aran thought about it the more he realized that the Medevac should be called in.

Ruby had the means to transport their patient, but with a deep vein thrombosis and a family history of pulmonary embolism the last thing Aran wanted was to take a risk flying Mitchell in Ruby's plane.

The larger Medevac would have more staff. It was a helicopter, and it would get Mitchell where he needed to be with the right stuff on board.

Joanna returned with the dose of heparin—and it was at that moment that Aran found the clot in Mitchell's leg.

"Thank you, Joanna. We need to get a hold of the Medevac. This can't wait until Dr. Cloutier can fly him down. He has to get out of here *now*."

"I'll call them, Dr. Atkinson. And Mitchell's wife too."

"Thank you. I'll stay with him."

Joanna nodded and Aran administered the dose of

heparin, hoping that it would help until the nearest Medevac could get in to Whitehead and take Mitchell to a hospital that would help him.

Even if it wasn't Seward Memorial.

Ruby woke with a start.

The room was brighter, but she realized that she was sleeping in the middle of the bed and that Aran wasn't in the bed with her. She sat up and looked on the floor, the small little laneway from the door to the bed. Thankfully he wasn't there either.

So I didn't knock him to the floor. That's good.

She tied back her hair and then glanced at her watch. It was nine in the morning. She'd slept way past her alarm.

Ruby scrambled out of bed and pulled the blinds. There was melting snow, blue skies and sunshine. At least the runway would be clear and they would be able to fly back to Anchorage. She was just mad at herself for being late. She *never* slept in.

She cursed under her breath, annoyed, but pulled herself together, slipped on her shoes and headed out into the hall. The clinic was quiet, but it was Saturday so that wasn't unusual. She found Aran in a waiting room chair, his head on his hand and sleeping.

Lacey rounded the corner. "You're awake!"

"I didn't mean to sleep in," Ruby said. "Sorry."

"Aran said to let you sleep. That you needed it."

Ruby glanced at Aran. He looked completely uncomfortable in that chair. "How long has he been there?"

"About an hour. He was up waiting for the Medevac to come and take Mitchell to Juneau."

Ruby's eyes widened. "Juneau? I was supposed to fly him down to Anchorage."

Lacey sighed. "Mitchell developed a post-operative fever last night that Joanna was unable to bring down with ibuprofen or antibiotics. His pulse-rate increased and she was worried. She found Dr. Atkinson leaving your room and asked for help. He found thrombophlebitis in Mitchell's leg and, given the family history of pulmonary embolism, he felt it would be better if the Medevac helicopter came and took him. There's another storm rolling in—this time off the Bering Sea. It's headed straight for Anchorage, so the Medevac decided on Juneau."

"Oh…" Ruby glanced at Aran.

She was annoyed that Mitchell—*her* patient—had been sent away without her knowing and that he wasn't going to be at Seward, where she could continue to monitor him, but she completely understood why Aran had done what he had.

Mitchell would need to be monitored in case the blood clot in his leg broke off and headed to his lungs or heart, which would be fatal. Medevac had more team members with them then she did. In the same shoes, she would have done the same thing.

"Kayla, Mitchell's wife, couldn't go on the Medevac so she's hoping you can take her to Anchorage. Her sister lives there, and from there they'll travel to Juneau."

"Of course. Can you let her know that I'm leaving within the next hour? As soon as I get my flight plan logged."

"I will. And thanks again." Lacey headed back to the exam rooms.

Ruby took a deep breath and leaned against the wall.

Why hadn't Aran woken her? How had she slept through the Medevac team coming?

She felt guilty that she'd let Mitchell down. That she

hadn't been the one to make the call. She'd known Mitchell for five years. She'd treated him for other ailments and she'd been the one to try and help his mother before the pulmonary embolism had killed her so suddenly. She felt bad that she'd slept through all this.

She hated losing control.

She hated that she hadn't been awake.

She hated that Aran had totally thrown her world upside down.

"Hey…" she said gently, leaning over and nudging him.

Aran jumped with a start and Ruby jumped back, surprised by his response. His eyes were wild, and for one brief moment it looked as if he didn't know where he was. As if he was on the defensive.

"Aran, it's just me."

It took a minute or so, but his wide eyes narrowed and his body relaxed. "Sorry," he said and covered his face with his hand. "Sorry. I guess I was… I was sound asleep."

There was an edge to his voice and she didn't quite believe that she had just startled him. It was something more than being startled. There was panic, a fear just behind his eyes. As if he had post traumatic stress disorder.

She wouldn't be surprised, given his experience with the IED explosion.

"So Mitchell was flown to Juneau?" she asked.

Aran stifled and yawn and nodded. "Yes. I'm sorry, but he had to be sent out of here to get proper help."

"I understand. I just wish you'd woken me up."

"Why?" he asked. "I could handle it."

"He was *my* patient."

Aran stood up. "I understand, but it's all taken care of."

"I know—and you did the right thing. Just next time wake me up and let me know."

"Wait," he said. "You're bothered?"

"I would've liked to have known."

"And what would waking you have done? He still would have had to be transferred out, with a larger team who could take him to a proper hospital. Once I gave the Medevac team an update they took over. All I did was stay up and wait for them."

"I still would've liked to have known," Ruby said sternly.

Aran shook his head. "You really don't like relinquishing control, do you?"

"He was my patient. I am the leader of this team…"

"I did right by *your* patient, and now he's off to a better facility. I don't know why you're picking a fight. If it's about last night…"

"It's not," she said quickly, but it was. She was picking a fight because she'd been so afraid at how close he'd gotten to her. How he had affected her. How his kiss had made her forget all the rules she'd put in place when it came to relationships.

She didn't want anything except casual, and there was no way you could do *casual* with someone you worked with. Getting involved with the man who was your convenient fake husband was also not casual, and she didn't want to get involved with Aran when their marriage wasn't even real and had a time limit.

Ruby understood the idea of sharing that kiss, but really it had been a bad idea all around and she shouldn't have let it happen.

"We have to get back to Anchorage. The weather has

cleared and we're going to take Mitchell's wife down so she can get a flight to Juneau."

She didn't wait for a response from him—just turned on her heel and left to get everything ready. She had to call in her flight plan and have someone get the plane prepared. She had to gather up what gear was left and make sure Lacey had arranged for someone to get them to the airport.

She didn't have time to deal with the emotional crisis that Aran had stirred up in her.

She didn't have time for any of it.

She only had time for her work.

The flight back to Anchorage was somewhat awkward. Ruby felt bad that Kayla had to be a part of it, but Kayla was mostly worried about Mitchell in Juneau and the flight down to Anchorage. Ruby knew that Kayla hated flying, and that she rarely left Whitehead, but thankfully the flight was relatively smooth.

When they landed in Anchorage, Kayla's sister was waiting at the airport in the charter terminal, near where Ruby stored her plane. Ruby told Kayla to give Mitchell a big hug and said that she'd see them soon enough.

Then it was just her and Aran.

As they walked out to her truck she felt bad for the way she had treated him. She felt bad for trying to pick a fight with him. He'd done the right thing, and if the situations were reversed she would have done the same.

She'd just been scared.

"I'm sorry," she said after he'd climbed into the passenger side.

"For what?" he asked.

"For snapping at you about Mitchell. You did the right

thing. And you're right—I like control. I hate losing it, and I hate when I'm not involved with my patient's diagnosis from beginning to end. But there are some things I *can't* do, and it's hard for me to let my patient's care fall into the hands of other competent surgeons. So I'm sorry."

His eyebrows arched. "Thank you. Apology accepted."

Ruby nodded. "We should get to the hospital. I was supposed to start rounds three hours ago."

"Yes... Well, I was supposed to start in the middle of the night, but look how that turned out."

Ruby started the truck and headed out on the highway to Seward Memorial. The weather was bad in Anchorage, but at least it wasn't snow. Just rain.

It was a short drive to the hospital, and when they got there Jessica was waiting for them. Ruby was surprised to see her when they got off the elevators from the main entrance to the trauma floor.

"There you two are!" Jessica said impatiently.

Ruby could tell that she was completely agitated and she saw that Aran's spine had stiffened, his body tensing in light of his mother's anxious behavior.

"I sent you a message. A storm waylaid us in Whitehead," Ruby responded calmly.

"I know," Jessica replied. "And I completely understand that. The thing is the U.S. Citizen and Immigration Services *doesn't*. Agent Bolton has been here since this morning and he's a bit annoyed that you're not here."

"Agent Bolton?" Ruby asked. "I told him to send me some dates to set up a time. He didn't."

"This is a surprise visit," Aran said. "I've heard of them before."

"Well, he's in the boardroom—waiting. You two need to go meet with him."

Ruby's stomach twisted in a knot.

Oh, Creator. How am I going to handle this?

"It'll be okay," Aran said calmly. "We'll present a united front. Just don't plaster that fake smile on your face like you did on our wedding day."

Ruby chuckled nervously. "I'll try not to."

"What fake smile?" Jessica asked.

"This one."

Ruby plastered on the smile which had been on her face the day she'd married Aran. The smile that she so often used when she was in an uncomfortable situation. Aran was laughing silently to himself and shaking his head, but Jessica looked less than impressed.

"You two have to pull it together!" Jessica snapped. "This is serious."

"I know," Ruby murmured.

It was a huge risk for all of them. She should never have agreed to it in the first place. She should have said no to Aran.

Only when she'd said yes she had heard her father's voice telling her to say yes, and she'd just closed her eyes and taken the plunge into the unknown.

Jessica pursed her lips together. "Just try and keep it together."

Ruby nodded and Jessica stormed away. "This was a bad idea," she whispered. "I thought our marriage was a good idea at the time. I wanted to stay in the country. But I shouldn't have said yes."

Aran sighed. "I asked you because I wanted to do it for you. I believed in your work. I still do believe in your work. This isn't all your fault. We both agreed to this and we'll face this together."

"Right," Ruby agreed. She took a deep calming breath and stared at the door. "We can do this."

"We can." He took her hand. "Come on, Mrs. Atkinson."

"That's *Dr.* Mrs. Atkinson, buster," she teased, and Aran laughed.

His blue eyes were twinkling and it reassured her. He took her hand, just as he had on their wedding day, and it calmed her.

Aran opened the door to the boardroom and Agent Bolton, who had been pacing by the coffee table, stopped and turned. He didn't look particularly threatening. He was a man in his mid-fifties, in a suit, and he looked like someone you could trust—which was probably exactly what he needed to look like.

Someone you could really open up to.

Someone who was good at catching lies.

It'll be okay.

She and Aran were friends. They weren't strangers. There was some intimacy. They were in this together.

Though she still really didn't completely understand why he'd done it.

Don't think about it. Focus.

"Dr. Atkinson and Dr. Cloutier, I presume?" Agent Bolton asked.

"Yes," Ruby answered. "Sorry to have kept you. We weren't expecting you."

Agent Bolton smiled, but she could tell that the smile was not sincere. It was business, and it was calculated.

"That's fine. We do like to do preliminary surprise checks on our applicants before the official interview. I thought you two would be here in the city. Not up near the Canadian border."

"You mean in Whitehead?" Aran asked.

"Yes," Agent Bolton said. "Whitehead is not far from the Yukon—where your wife is from."

"No, Ruby is from the Northwest Territories. Behchokǫ̀. Which is, I believe, near Yellowknife and one territory over."

Ruby breathed an inward sigh of relief at Aran's quick thinking.

Agent Bolton grinned again. "So it is. Why don't we have a seat?"

Aran pulled out a chair for Ruby and she sat down. She could feel her palms sweating and was glad when Aran put himself between her and Agent Bolton.

Agent Bolton looked unassuming and friendly, but right now Ruby was not a fan of his, and she was pretty sure that he wasn't a fan of hers.

"What were you two doing in Whitehead anyhow?" Agent Bolton asked.

"I was making my quarterly visit to a clinic up there. They have a nurse practitioner, but I fly my team in with me and we do all the medical procedures the nurse practitioner can't. I usually only go up there for a day, but a storm hit after I'd had to perform an emergency appendectomy and it wasn't safe to fly."

Agent Bolton nodded. "How admirable of you. That patient has been transferred here?"

"Juneau," Aran said. "During the night the nurse on call asked me to come and check on him. As my wife is the pilot, and needed her sleep, I ascertained that the patient had developed a blood clot and called for the Medevac service to transport him to the nearest hospital."

"It's a good thing that storm hit, then," Agent Bolton remarked.

Ruby gritted her teeth. She didn't like the way this agent was operating. "A very good thing," she said.

He nodded and opened the folder that sat on the table. "I have your file, Dr. Atkinson, about your service here for the last five years. Five years is a long time for a newly married couple to be apart, don't you think?"

"Yes," Ruby answered. "We wanted to marry because we were in love."

"Right," Aran said. "I didn't want to leave my girlfriend behind when I shipped out, so I made her my wife. She understood that I needed to serve my country, and she was focused on her career here."

"How long was it before you decided to get married?" he asked, and he looked at both of them.

"We dated for a year," Aran said.

"A year?" Agent Bolton asked.

"We were surgical residents together. It's how we met." Ruby smiled at Aran. "You grow close to a person when you work a forty-eight-hour shift together."

Aran grinned back at her, making her pulse slow. It was calming and reassuring.

"As soon as I knew I was going to get shipped out I asked her. I wanted her to be my wife. Sometimes you just know—and I knew. I knew from the moment I met her that she was the one."

Ruby's stomach did a flip-flop and she blushed.

Agent Bolton nodded. "But a long-distance relationship? That doesn't always work."

"I know," Aran answered. "It didn't work for my parents, but for me it was right. Ruby loves it here in the north. She's from the north, and I completed my training at Fort Irwin in San Bernardino."

"I thought you were from San Diego?" said Agent Bolton.

"My father is from San Diego, and I grew up there. My mother lives in Anchorage and I visit her here—but I'm sure you have my military records and can see where I completed my basic training."

Agent Bolton shut his folder. "Okay, then. Well, I won't take up more of your time right now. I'll come back in a week and we'll do separate interviews then, and a joint interview before I determine whether or not a Green Card will be issued to Dr. Cloutier."

Ruby stood, and Aran did as well.

Agent Bolton got up and shook their hands. "See you both next week. I'll call and arrange a day, so you two won't be off on a jaunt somewhere in the bush. Good evening, doctors."

Ruby watched him leave the boardroom and when he was gone sank down into her chair, resting her head in her hands.

"Whew! That guy was intense," said Aran.

"So it wasn't just me that was unnerved by him?" Ruby asked.

"No. He's good at his job."

Ruby shuddered. "I thought he might be a serial killer or something."

Aran chuckled. "No. He's probably got ex-military, though. It wouldn't surprise me if he's a Marine, or something like that. Most of those agents have military training."

"Well, we should go home and talk about next week." She didn't want to say too much because she was suddenly feeling slightly paranoid that the boardroom might be bugged. "Besides, I need my own bed tonight."

"Agreed."

They got up and left the boardroom in silence. She was still trembling when they walked down the hall toward the attendings' lounge. As much as she wanted to go home and formulate a plan, she was still on duty. She had to calm down so that she could focus on her patients.

It was for them that she was doing this.

It was for her patients—for all the lives that could be saved because of her work. Just like Mitchell. He had a fighting chance because she had been there to do his appendectomy. Aran had given him a further chance by being there and finding that thrombophlebitis. Because of their work Mitchell was in Juneau and alive.

Even though she was scared about what had just happened with Agent Bolton, and about having to see him again, she was glad she'd done it.

If she wasn't here to help, who would?

No one had been there to help her father when he'd needed it the most.

She was not going to let that happen to another family.

She was not going to let anyone die if she could help it.

Even if it meant faking a marriage to a man who made her want to lose control completely.

It was close to midnight when Ruby and Aran finally stumbled back to her house. Sam had taken Chinook over to his place and left a note, but Ruby was tired and it was too late to go over there and get him. She just wanted to sleep in her own bed and try to forget about the events of the last couple of days.

"I think before we go to sleep we should figure out our story," Aran said as he took off his shoes.

"Really? I'm exhausted. I've flown down from Whitehead. Been grilled by a government agent. And worked a five-hour shift at the hospital."

"I'm tired too, Ruby, but we need to strategize. I don't know why you insisted on waiting so long to talk about it."

"We were at work…and I thought the place might be bugged."

Aran laughed softly. "Okay…well, we're home now. Let's come up with something."

"I liked your off-the-cuff explanation about a long-distance relationship. And how we dated in residency."

"Well, we knew each other then, and we did work all those awful shifts together," he stated.

"I know. It was perfect."

"Yeah, but now they'll ask us things like what side of the bed do you sleep on? Where did you honeymoon? How many windows in your bedroom?"

Ruby rubbed her eyes. "Wait—did you just say how many windows in the bedroom?"

Aran nodded. "I've heard that's been asked before."

"Well, I can easily answer that. My bedroom is a loft. It's all skylights."

"How many?"

"Four." She frowned. "No…wait…"

"You don't *know*?"

"I don't lie there and count my skylights."

Aran rolled his eyes and headed to the stairs.

"Where are you going?" she asked.

"To see how many skylights are in your loft."

Ruby crossed her arms and waited for him to come back down.

"You were right. There's four," he said.

"See? You know…this is the most bizarre conversation ever."

"I think our conversation about sheep and what kind of drink we'd like to be was weirder," he teased.

"Right, I'd forgotten that."

"You never did answer that question."

"And I won't. It's still the weirdest question ever. What kind of *drink* would I be? *That's* weird."

He smiled—that handsome devilish smile she liked so much.

"So, besides us dating in residency, let's figure out our proposal story. Our current one is just me offering to enter into this marriage—it's not really great. How did I do it?"

Ruby could feel her blood heat. She didn't really want to talk about this with him. It came dangerously close to the territory they'd found themselves in when they were in Whitehead. When he'd suggested they kiss.

Just thinking about that kiss made her body thrum with excitement. She was trying to forget about that kiss, but she couldn't.

The sooner she got her Green Card the better.

Really?

"I think you got down on one knee," she said quickly, and walked over to the cupboard to make herself a cup of the decaffeinated tea that always relaxed her and put her to sleep. She set down a mug and filled up her electric kettle.

"That's it?"

"Why does it have to be elaborate?" she asked.

"What if they ask specific questions? Like where I did it?"

"By a lake," she said quickly.

"What lake?"

Ideally she would have loved to have been down by the shores of Great Slave Lake, or beside the McKenzie River, where you could see the Deh Cho Bridge. She loved being by water, which was why she bought this house.

"My lake. I bought this house before I married you. Maybe we were out on a walk and talking about your deployment and you got down on one knee and asked me."

His expression softened. "See—was that so hard?"

"Yeah, it was."

"What do you mean?"

"I don't *do* this," she said quickly. "Relationships are not my thing. I'm not good with relationships. I never wanted to get married. The only thing I ever wanted was my career. That's it."

"I feel the same way," Aran said. "I didn't want to get married either. But marrying you was a convenience for both of us. It gave me an excuse not to get involved with anyone and it gave you a chance to get a Green Card. For better or for worse we're in this together, and we need to convince that agent that we married for love."

"How many relationships have you had?" she asked as her teapot whistled and she flicked it off.

A strange expression crossed his face. "What do you mean?"

"How many girlfriends have you had in the past?"

"A couple—but once they knew I never wanted anything serious they left. And that was fine by me. What about you? Did you leave behind someone in Canada?"

"Not really. It was the same thing. I just wanted casual and had no real time to date. A lot of men didn't like it when I took the initiative. They didn't like me being in control." They also hadn't liked how emotionally unavailable she was.

He smiled, and his eyes twinkled as he moved closer. "I don't mind that you have control."

Her pulse began to race and she knew that she was blushing again. Every part of her was crying out to kiss him. To give in to what he was making her feel. But she couldn't. This marriage of convenience was nothing more than a business arrangement when she came right down to it—and she never mixed business with pleasure.

Even if she wanted to.

But it had been so long since she'd been with someone. Since she'd had human contact...

"It's late. I think I'm going to drink my herbal tea and just read in bed for a bit."

He nodded and rubbed the back of his neck. "Right. That's a very good plan."

"I'll see you in the morning?"

Aran nodded and headed to his room. "Yes. Have a good night, Ruby."

"You too."

She went up the stairs and heard his door shut. She let out the breath she realized she'd been holding and tried to calm her nerves.

What was it about him that made her run so hot and cold? She felt as if she was losing all control around him. Being around him made her do things and say things she'd never thought she would say or do.

And she should've known. The moment he'd walked into the hospital and introduced himself to her during their first shift together she should've realized that he was nothing but trouble.

And trouble was exactly what she didn't need.

She only *wanted* it.

CHAPTER NINE

ARAN GOT UP early and went outside to chop some wood. It had been cold in the night and there was no wood by the fireplace because they'd been trapped in Whitehead. It was still kind of damp and drizzly, but he didn't mind going out and chopping some wood.

Besides, he couldn't sleep anyways.

All he could think about was Ruby.

That kiss that they'd shared in Whitehead just kept playing over and over in his mind. He'd kissed other women, but somehow that simple kiss had stuck with him. And he wanted to do more than just kiss her.

You don't want a relationship and neither does she. What could it hurt?

And it was true. Ruby had told him herself that she didn't want anything serious beyond their sham of a marriage. She was only legally bound to him because she wanted a Green Card.

That was it.

He knew that she was attracted to him, and he was attracted to her. *What could it hurt?* The thing was, he knew that if he indulged then someone was going to be hurt by this and he didn't want that to happen.

Aran had seen what had happened to his father when

his parents had divorced. It had nearly broken him to leave his wife behind in Alaska. Aran's mother had always told him that she'd married his father out of lust, that they'd rushed into it and hadn't really talked about what they wanted, but that was not how his father viewed it.

Aran's father had loved Jessica.

Sure, he'd found love again, with Aran's stepmother, but he'd been broken for so long, pining after Jessica.

Aran never wanted that. He never wanted to feel that way and he certainly didn't want anyone to feel that way over him.

He liked Ruby. She had a bit of a tough exterior, but she really cared for people. She wanted to help people and give them everything she could. She was dedicating her life to them, flying out and rescuing people from natural disasters and accidents. Or flying to remote communities and doing a job that no other doctor or surgeon wanted to fill, because no one really wanted to live out in the middle of nowhere in one of the world's harshest climates.

Aran admired her for that.

He wished that he could stay on after they were divorced, but once this whole thing was over with he was going to return south and try to get a job somewhere. Anywhere. As soon as he got his PTSD under control.

He almost had it under control.

Who are you kidding?

He brought down the ax in one swift movement, splitting the log in two. It felt good to swing the ax—it helped him forget how he'd jumped at Ruby when she'd woken him in the clinic. For a brief moment he'd been back on the front line, lying on a stretcher after having being found in the wreckage after the IED explosion.

He could still feel the pain in his leg. The agony. And his leg gave a twinge when he thought about it. He wished that he hadn't been pieced together the way he had been. He wished that they had just taken his leg.

Then he remembered Ruby's gentle touch. Her delicate hands on his leg, working the muscles, and how good it had felt. How she made him forget about the pain. How she'd made him forget about the horrors of the front.

He winced as he picked up the logs from where they'd fallen and started a little pile.

"It'll take you all day, doing it like that."

He looked up to see Ruby leaning against the open back door in flannel pajamas, holding a cup of coffee. The steam was rising out of the top and melting away in the damp mist that clung to the trees surrounding her cabin.

"I don't like leaving a mess," he joked, and then he picked up another log.

He was trying not to look at her in her pajamas. He had never realized how sexy plaid flannel pajamas could be.

Get a grip.

Except he couldn't shake that image of her touching him. Touching the most vulnerable part of him, easing his pain with her gentleness. And how he'd wanted to reach down and kiss her, to bring her as much pleasure as she'd brought him.

He wanted to taste her lips again. He wanted to get lost in her arms.

He wanted to bare everything to her.

"I hope I didn't wake you with the wood-chopping?" he asked, trying not to think about what was under those pajamas and how much he wanted to find out.

"No, I was up," she said. "I did wonder who was chopping my wood. Why *are* you chopping my wood?"

"It was cold in the night and I couldn't sleep."

"Nightmares?"

A shiver ran down his spine and he hesitated. "Why would you say that?"

"I heard you," she said gently.

"Sorry." He felt bad that he'd woken her.

"Is it PTSD?"

"No," he snapped.

"Come on—I can see you're still suffering with the after-effects of what happened to you. You don't need to hide your post traumatic stress from me."

He didn't say anything. He didn't like her talking about it. He didn't want to talk about it with her. He didn't want to let her in. But the thing was the more he was around her the more she just wiggled her way in.

And you want to know what she's hiding from you.

"You going to pick up Chinook this morning? I kind of miss him." He was changing the subject and he didn't care. He only hoped that she didn't keep pressing him on the matter.

"No. Sam is going to keep him for a couple more days." She took a seat on the step and took a sip of her coffee. "I got a message in from Dr. Franklin. There's a typhoon blowing in and threatening the Aleutian Islands. It's wreaking havoc in the Bering Sea."

"Typhoon?"

"They're rare, but they *can* happen in southeast Alaska. Dr. Franklin wants to have a meeting and get a plan in place to fly in extra supplies and make sure we're here and ready to help the people who live along those islands."

"Will your entire team fit in your plane?" he asked.

"No, Dr. Franklin will fly another plane and I'll load up mine. We can fly together. Dr. Franklin is from Unalaska, which is part of the Aleutian Islands. He wants to make sure that everyone is taken care of there. He'll be heading out right away—we'll follow."

"Okay. Sounds good."

Aran finished his wood-chopping while Ruby sat and watched.

"That's a couple of storms and a typhoon since I started here. Maybe it's a sign," he said.

"A sign of what?" she asked.

"That I should leave Alaska," he teased.

Only he wasn't really teasing. It was best that he leave.

Sure. Run away again.

Ruby smiled. "No, it's common for early summer. The winter is worse for the islands, when the Aleutian low pressure sits there. We have a lot of bodies of water converging and meeting up. The Beaufort Sea, Bering Sea, Gulf of Alaska and the Pacific. And then you add in mountains and permafrost... Yeah, it can be a bit unpredictable."

"Just a bit!"

Ruby stood. "Keeps it interesting, though. There's coffee in the house when you're ready."

Aran nodded and watched her make her way inside. Watched her walk away. Her hair was down and loose and she looked totally relaxed and comfortable. She was *comfortable* around him. When had that happened?

And then he realized that he was at ease around her too—for the most part. He wasn't at ease when he thought about the taste of her lips or how she'd felt pressed up against him.

He finished with the last log and then set the ax into the wood block. He scooped up all the pieces he'd chopped and carried them inside.

Ruby was puttering around in the kitchen and listening to Queen. A smile tugged at the corner of his lips as he watched her dance. She was so sexy. Everything about her made him want her more. No other woman had ever gotten to him like this.

All that worry he'd been feeling fizzled away as he watched her.

She spun around and crimson bloomed in her cheeks when she saw him standing there, watching her.

"Queen?" he said quizzically as she pulled down a frying pan.

"Yeah, it's Queen. You don't like Queen?" she asked, ignoring the fact that he'd caught her awkward dancing.

"Sure—I just never would've pegged you for a fan."

"And what's a Queen fan supposed to look like?" she teased.

"You've got me. I don't know. I just never would have thought you were one."

"I *love* the immortal Freddie. Plus, I like listening to them when I cook."

"What're you cooking?" he asked.

"Scrambled eggs. Want some?"

"Sure."

Aran slowly knelt down. He was a bit stiff, but he managed to hide the pain he was feeling from Ruby because she was distracted by making breakfast. He stacked the logs neatly.

"Well, at least I now know what you wear to bed and that you listen to Queen while you cook."

She glanced over her shoulder as she cracked eggs into the frying pan. "And what music do *you* like?"

"Country."

"I like that too."

"You're an eclectic music listener, are you?"

"Yeah, I like what I like and it's all over the board. But I only listen to certain music at certain times. Like rock or metal while I cook—but metal from the seventies. And when I drive it's usually The Hip."

"Yeah... I'm just a country fan. I don't mind Queen, though."

"Good, because I'm not turning it off."

She finished scrambling the eggs while Aran washed his hands and sat down at the kitchen island. She dished out a plate of scrambled eggs and he poured himself a cup of coffee.

"Thanks," he said as he sat down to eat his eggs.

"Thanks for the morning wood."

He almost choked on his eggs. *"What?"*

She flushed pink and groaned. "Oh, Creator! That's not what I meant at all."

He chuckled. "That's okay. I understand what you meant and it was no problem."

"We have *got* to get over this awkwardness. I mean, we're friends, right?"

"Yeah, sure."

Only he didn't think of her as a friend. And he really didn't *want* to think of her as a friend. He wanted to think of her as more than that, only he couldn't let himself. It wasn't fair to her. There was nothing he could give her.

"I'm going to get ready for the day. I want to get to the hospital and help Dr. Franklin plan before he gets agitated that I'm not there."

"Sounds good. I'll be waiting."

Aran watched her disappear up the stairs and finished his breakfast in silence. He had to pull himself together. They could be friends and they could work together. Nothing more.

There couldn't be anything more between them.

She was kicking herself for saying that.

Thanks for the morning wood? How could you be so silly?

It had taken her off-guard to wake up to the sound of wood being cut, and when she'd gone downstairs to see a shirtless Aran cutting up firewood it had made her think about a lot of inappropriate things.

He might have an injury, but he was still a strong man. A capable man. Not the man she'd thought he was when they'd first met. The arrogant playboy who'd got on her nerves but whom she'd never been able to shake. This man—he belonged here. It was as if he fit right in with her life and that thought scared her. There was no room in her life for anyone but herself and Chinook.

Oh, really?

She jumped into the shower and heard the ax again. She looked out the small window and watched him out there again as the water ran over her. Her blood heated and she turned the cold water on, hoping it would clear her head of all the naughty thoughts of Aran running through her mind.

Thoughts of him scooping her up in his arms and carrying her to the bed...of herself running her hands over his chest and tasting his kisses again.

She cranked the cold water up some more, hoping it would work.

It didn't.

"Dr. Franklin, you're taking the team and getting set up in Unalaska. Dr. Atkinson and I will bring the rest of the supplies and meet you there by the end of the day." Ruby went down her check list for the meeting. "Do you have your flight plan?"

"Yes." Dr. Franklin pulled out the printout of the plan he had submitted.

Ruby looked it over. "Going a little bit out of the way?"

"The weather system is bringing a low, which is strange for this time of year. I want to avoid it if at all possible. I flew planes through the Aleutian Islands long before I became a doctor," said Dr. Franklin. "I want to get there and set up in the emergency shelter before the storm hits."

"Okay—well, you have your team. You're taking John and Lindsey. I'll file a flight plan to join you later. When you arrive tell me what you need and I'll bring it along with me."

Dr. Franklin nodded. "Sure thing, Dr. Cloutier."

"Okay, let's get this done, then."

Franklin, John and Lindsey got up to start work. Ruby had to stay behind and finish her rotation on the trauma floor. They would arrive before the storm made landfall.

Aran had sat quietly in the meeting not saying much. He looked a little tired and she wasn't surprised, since he'd told her that he hadn't slept much the night before. Not that she'd slept much either, knowing he was having nightmares, and she couldn't stop thinking about this morning, with him at the wood pile.

Once the others had left her office she sat down on the edge of her desk. "You okay?"

"What?" he asked, as if he had been zoning out.

"You look like you're ready to fall asleep."

"Yeah, I feel like I *could* sleep." He scrubbed his hand over his face.

"Why don't you have a rest in the on-call room? I need you with your wits about you when we head to Unalaska."

Aran pursed his lips together, much as his mother did when she was about to deliver bad news or when she was unhappy or worried. "I don't know if I should go."

"What do you mean?" Ruby asked, confused.

"A typhoon? Getting stuck somewhere with you for a couple of days?" Aran said. "We haven't talked about the kiss since it happened and I don't like this awkwardness."

A blush crept up her neck. "It won't be like White-head, Aran. Franklin, John and Lindsey will all be there. And Unalaska is bigger than Whitehead—there are other small communities surrounding it and people will be coming to the storm shelter. I need you up there. I need all hands on deck."

"Well, if that's the case..."

"It'll be fine. We're not going to do that again. We're not going to..."

She couldn't even bring herself to say it—because she *wanted* to kiss him again. Even though she knew it was a bad idea, she still wanted it.

She wanted more from him.

She might not have had a lot of relationships, or anything meaningful, but he was the first man she really desired. The first man who had stirred something deep down inside her.

Still, she couldn't let herself give in to temptation. She'd promised herself that. The kiss had been a one-time thing. It had been done in order to break the tension between them and that was it.

"We could be doing medical procedures. It won't be—"

"Yeah," he said cutting her off. "You're right. We have to stop being so awkward around each other."

"Exactly."

They had been doing fine until that kiss. Perhaps this was karma's way of paying her back for this deceitful marriage?

"So what do you need me to do?" he asked.

She handed him a sheet. "Get the medical supplies ready. I'm doing a first round of those patients who are still in the emergency room. Then the surgical patients and then I'm free."

Aran nodded. "I'll get these ready for you."

"Meet me down in the ambulance pod in three hours. An ambulance will take us and the supplies to the airport in no time. I'm going to file a flight plan now and then do my rounds."

"All right. I'll see you then."

Aran left the office, and once he did she was finally able to relax a bit after thinking about him and her in Whitehead.

She had to get better control over herself. She wasn't doing a very good job.

When she'd woken up that morning to Dr. Franklin's email, she had not expected to find Aran outside chopping wood. She had watched him from the kitchen while her coffee had been brewing.

She'd been completely mesmerized by the way he moved. How easily he had split the wood. How Alaska seemed to suit him, even if he *did* insist that he much preferred the south. It was as if he belonged with her.

And all she'd been able to think about was how he'd made her feel. How she'd wanted to continue that kiss. How she'd wanted to lose control over him.

She hated the way he affected her so much.

Maybe you should've sent him with Dr. Franklin?

The problem was that Dr. Franklin didn't completely trust Aran. None of the team did. It was better that Aran came with her. He was still on probation.

Ruby had no doubt that after this mission the other team members would see what a valuable asset he was to the team and then they would all feel comfortable working with him. They would trust him.

In order to make a team like hers work there had to be a high level of trust. If there was no trust then it was doomed to fail from the start.

The team had to believe there was complete trust between her and Aran—which there was. But Aran and her were married. Married couples were intimate, not awkward around each other. At least all the married couples she knew…

Aran did exactly what was needed and got all the supplies. Ruby's rounds took longer because an accident came in. Someone had collided with a moose on the highway and she was called in to emergency surgery.

When she got out she saw Dr. Franklin had landed in Unalaska and had forwarded a list of supplies he needed.

It was a lot more than they'd thought. Apparently the last shipment of the most vital medical supplies hadn't come in on time. So she spent an hour trying to collect everything from the list that she could, so they could prepare for the typhoon when it made landfall.

Aran was loading up the rig when she arrived.

"You're late," he said.

"Emergency trauma came in. Someone hit a moose on the highway. And then Dr. Franklin sent his list and it turns out that Unalaska needs some more supplies." She lifted one of the kits into the back of the rig. "I then had to adjust our departure time because we're leaving later. I just hope the weather holds."

"Me too."

They finished loading and then got into the back. The ambulance driver raced them to the airport with the sirens blaring. Ruby was glad of that, because right now it was a race to get to Unalaska before the typhoon hit.

Her plane was ready and waiting and Aran and the ambulance driver helped her load up. She could see dark clouds far across the horizon. Anchorage was supposed to get the tail end of the storm. It would be heavy rainfall and some wind, but nothing compared to Unalaska and the rest of the most westerly tip of the Aleutian Islands. When the Bering Sea became stormy it became a dangerous place.

Once the plane was loaded she prepared for take-off and was given clearance right away, because her flight was considered an emergency. It was a smooth takeoff, but it wasn't long before she realized that they hadn't beaten the storm and she was flying straight into it. The turbulence became wicked.

"I think we'll have to turn back," she shouted into her microphone.

"I think you're right," Aran responded.

He looked a little pale as the wind jostled the plane around. He was nervous and she couldn't blame him—she was nervous too.

She made her course correction and had just started to turn and head back to Anchorage when the engine light came on.

Oh, Creator. No.

"What's wrong?" Aran asked when he noticed the flashing lights and alarms.

"I lost an engine. I'm going to have to make an emergency landing. There's an old town not far from here that has an old airstrip."

"What do you mean, an old town?" he asked, and she could hear the panic in his voice.

"No one lives there anymore, but there are buildings and a runway. It's used in emergency situations like this. It'll be okay," she reassured him. "We're fine. We're just going to land. Hang on."

After a few tense moments Ruby caught sight of the airfield that was always maintained. The town was an old ghost town, but often bush pilots that had been chartered by hunting outfits used this airstrip to drop off guides who would take parties into the wilderness to hunt. Especially in the summer.

She turned her plane sideways and made a tight crab landing on the gravel strip that ran alongside a riverbank. Her plane sputtered as she made the landing and then came to a halt, with the other engine giving up and starting to smoke.

Ruby breathed a sigh of relief—and then cursed under

her breath as she climbed out of the plane and went to look at the engine. She could see a leak and she cursed again.

The wind was strong and howling down off the mountains into the little valley where they had landed. She could see the storm clouds moving in fast. They were close to the Aleutian Islands and right in the path of the edge of the storm. It wasn't raining yet, but the temperature was dropping with the low pressure moving in.

It wasn't the rain that bothered Ruby at the moment, but the wind speed.

"What're we going to do?" Aran shouted over the wind.

"We'll cover my plane and then seek shelter in the old airport. It's an emergency shelter and it's kept stocked. We'll have to wait out this storm and then radio for help. With a leak in one of the engines I can't get this plane off the ground."

"And what about Dr. Franklin?" Aran asked.

Ruby sighed. "He knows what to do. We'll get this plane fixed and then we can help with the clean-up after. As much as I hate this, there's nothing else to do."

She pulled out a tarp from the back of her plane and began to lash the covering down. The last thing she needed was the storm doing even more damage. After she'd finished securing it she jammed blocks under the wheels and hoped to heck that the plane would withstand the winds that were now whipping down through this wind tunnel of a ghost town.

When she was done the rain came down in a sheet, soaking them instantly. They ran for the shelter of the metal U-shaped airport. There was an old transistor radio for emergencies, but best of all there was a wood stove in the center of the room.

With the temperature dropping the rain had felt like knives cutting at her skin. Her teeth were chattering as she helped Aran collect wood from the lean-to attached to the entrance so they could start a fire.

It wasn't long before they had a nice fire going, but they were still so soaking wet there was no way they were ever going to warm up.

She knew that they had to get out of their clothes.

Aran was already peeling off his wet clothing and hanging it on the line that ran across the room. He glanced at her, shivering. She knew she needed to get out of her own clothes, but she didn't want to do that in front of him.

"I'll get it."

He went to the storage locker and brought back some Army blankets. He strung them up, making a room divider, and stepped onto the colder side, leaving her by the stove.

"Get undressed and wrap a blanket around you. It's not ideal, but you really don't want to catch pneumonia, now, do you?"

"No," she said through her chattering teeth.

She quickly began to peel off her clothes and hung them on the line. The rain pelted like hammers against the metal roof while the wind howled like a banshee. It made her shiver even more, listening to it.

In all her years in Alaska she had never been in a typhoon before. They were rare. They never got typhoons in the Northwest Territories. The worst storm she'd ever been in had been a bad thunderstorm in Southern Ontario when she was going there to university, but that had been nothing compared to this.

And it was amplified by the fact that she was stuck in a small room, powerless to help her team and getting naked in front of her fake husband.

She knew one thing. It was going to be a very long night.

CHAPTER TEN

RUBY WAS HUDDLED on the floor and trying to keep warm. The wood stove was great, and did the job of heating the whole small space they were sharing, but it was nothing like a good crackling fire.

The makeshift wall parted and she saw that Aran had a blanket wrapped around him. He sat down close to her, next to the wood stove. The wind was howling outside and the rain was lashing the side of the building hard. Ruby trembled again.

"Did you take off everything?" Aran asked.

"Yes, but I can't seem to get warm." She pulled the blanket around her tighter.

Aran scooted closer and leaned against her, trying to give her some of his body heat. She was nervous about how close he was, knowing that the only thing between them was a couple of blankets.

Thinking about that made her tremble—not from the cold, but from something else.

Even though she shouldn't, she leaned her head against him. It felt nice. It made her feel safe, even though she was afraid about what might happen if she just let him in. If she gave in to all the strange emotions that he stirred in her.

No one had ever affected her this way. Aran made her feel alive. She wanted him, desired him, and she cared about him.

She'd never cared about someone this much.

She'd never *wanted* to care about someone like this—especially after she'd watched her mother grieve over her father for years. Her mother never had got over Papa.

Ruby let out a long sigh. The thought of caring about someone so much, loving someone so much and losing them, was unbearable.

On those days when she lost the battle with death and lost a patient she'd see the pain in the family's faces and know what they were feeling. She knew that pain, and she didn't ever want to experience that kind of trauma again. It was too hard. It was too much.

But being around Aran stirred up feelings that she'd never thought she'd have and it was scary how much he affected her.

"What're you thinking about?" Aran asked gently.

"What?" she asked.

"You let out a sigh."

"I was thinking of my father. I was thinking about when he died."

"Tell me about that," he said softly.

She didn't want to. She'd never talked about it with anyone before and she was terrified. But a little voice urged her to tell him. To let it out. To free herself from the burden she had carried around for so long. Alone.

"He was killed working in a diamond mine where there were no roads. There were no medical staff at the mine—which was a huge no-no. There was a winter storm that slowed getting help up there, and by the time the air ambulance got to him he was gone. If he'd have had the same injury in a city, or if medical staff had been there, he would've lived."

"I'm sorry to hear that. It explains why you're so dedicated to your job. That's admirable."

"Thank you." Tears welled up in her eyes as she thought about her father. "I never talk about him with anyone."

"Thanks for talking about it with me."

She nodded. "I saw the pain my mother went through, losing him. They were best friends. You know, they both went to the same residential school and they just formed a bond there. To survive. They lost track of each other when the last of those schools was shut down and they were sent back to their parents. My mother came from a reserve in northern Alberta and my dad was Bechokö, but they met up again when they were given the chance to go to college. My parents both wanted to better themselves, and to forget about residential school and everything they'd lost. Anyways, long story short, they got married and had kids. Papa taught me so much and then… I watched my mother grieve him and I just… I couldn't ever…" Tears slipped down her cheek. "It's not easy for me to let someone in."

Aran nodded. "I understand. I watched my parents go through divorce and I watched my dad grieve. My mother wasn't dead, but it was a different kind of loss. I knew I never wanted to go through that. I have no interest in that kind of pain. Of course, who does?"

"No one does."

He nodded. "And I'm still not whole. Not whole after what happened to me at the front line. I'm not going to tie someone down. I'm not going to make someone else suffer because of what I do."

"I understand. Probably more than most."

He nodded. "Yeah. I know you do."

She smiled and Aran leaned in and wiped the tears from her cheek with his thumb. The simple touch made her body tremble with delight and she reached out and touched him. "I'm glad you're here with me."

"I'm glad I'm here too."

And before she could stop herself, before she let the controlled and rational side of her take over, she kissed him.

The blanket slipped down off her shoulders as Aran kissed her back, his fingers moving to her hair. She moved closer. She knew she shouldn't reach out and kiss Aran again, but she couldn't help herself.

Right now she wanted to lose control. She wanted to *feel*. She wanted this. She chose this. She couldn't fight it anymore. She wanted Aran as she had never wanted another man.

It was overpowering. Primal.

It thrilled her.

Made her feel alive.

How long had she been so numb? She didn't know. All she knew was that Aran made her feel something she'd never felt before, and even though it scared her she couldn't stop.

"Ruby," he whispered against her hair. "Are you sure? I can't promise you anything beyond what we have now."

"Yes. I'm sure. And you know I can't promise you anything either, but I *want* this, Aran."

"I want this too. I have since the first time I met you and you looked me up and down with such indifference."

"I was your challenge," she teased. "Sorry."

"No, you were more than that. It wasn't that. You were

strong and I admired it. Never be sorry for that, or for who you are."

Ruby pulled him down to the floor and Aran laid kisses on her lips, her neck and lower. His strong hands roved over her body, igniting the flames that burned in her veins.

"Ruby, you make me feel like I've never felt before."

He brushed a kiss against her lips, lightly, then deepened the kiss into an urgent need that made her body sing. They were skin to skin, pressed against each other, and it felt so right. She opened her legs to let him settle between her thighs. She arched her hips, wanting to feel all of him.

"Ruby," Aran moaned. "We have to stop."

"Why?" she asked.

"I don't have protection."

"It's okay. I'm on birth control. Don't stop. Please don't stop." She just wanted to have this moment and she didn't care about the consequences.

"Are you sure?"

"Yes. Are *you* sure?" She bucked her hips and he groaned.

"God, yes."

"How much do you want it?" she teased.

Aran kissed her again, his tongue pushing past her lips, claiming her. He ran his hands over her, driving her wild with need. Ruby pulled him closer and wrapped her legs around his waist.

"You're so beautiful. From that first moment I saw you five years ago I've wanted you," he murmured.

His hands slid between them and he began to stroke her. Ruby cried out at his touch. She wanted so much more. She wanted Aran to be inside her, to take her and claim her. She just wanted to forget everything. She wanted to forget her lonely life. Forget the storm that had forced them to land. Forget all the rules she'd put in place to protect her heart from pain—the rules that guarded her heart from feeling any kind of love.

She wanted to forget it all and have this moment with him.

"Ruby," Aran whispered. "You feel so soft. I want you."

"I want you too." She kissed him. "I've always wanted you…since I first met you."

Aran slowly entered her, filling her, and her body shuddered in pleasure. Being joined with him was exactly what she needed. What she wanted. She moved her hips, urging him to move faster, but Aran took his time and it drove her wild.

She wanted him hard and fast. Her instinct was to control him even now, to take control over the situation as she always did, but Aran was in control. It scared her, but she let all those inhibitions melt away. Aran was controlling the pace and he was taking his time and it drove her wild.

She moved in time with him. Her eyes locked with his in the dim light. The only sound was their breathing, their little cries of pleasure. The storm and everything else that weighed them down were miles away.

All she had in this moment was him.

It was just the two of them.

"Come for me…" He whispered the command. "Come for me, Ruby."

"I don't want this to end."

She arched her body to press herself against him, tighter, and he trailed kisses down her neck, his hands cupping her breast.

"Come for me," he repeated. "Let it go."

And as she let him control the moment she could feel her body succumbing to the sweet release she was searching for. The release she so desperately needed and wanted.

It was unlike anything she'd ever felt before. Her body tingled as pleasure overtook her and she cried out, digging her nails into his back as she came around him. She wanted to hold on to this moment. Never to let go.

As her body drifted down from her release his rhythm picked up and he thrust hard and fast, seeking his own. She moved her hips, wanting him to come. Now she had some control over him, urging him on, and with the subtle movements of her hips it wasn't long until his own release came.

Aran rolled away and she curled up against him. He put his arm around her, holding her close, and then pulled a blanket over them as they lay on the floor next to the wood stove. She laid her head on his chest and listened to the reassuring sound of his heart.

They said nothing. There was nothing to say. No promises had been made and she didn't want them. Or she thought she didn't. This had been about human contact. That was it.

Really?

She shook the thought away. She wouldn't allow it in. She didn't want to feel anything more than what they had shared here, this night. Their marriage wasn't real and it had a time limit. Tonight had been about human contact, warmth and comfort. Just two lonely and broken souls reaching out to one another.

That was it.

She knew that, but there was a part of her that wanted more. A part of her that had never been here before. A part of her that wanted just a fraction of what her mother and father had had—which scared her.

It was the part of her that wanted love.

That wanted happiness.

That wanted more than just convenience.

Aran listened to the even, steady breaths of Ruby as she slept. He liked that she was curled up against him.

He had risked all his self-control, every part of him, when he had moved to the other side of the curtain.

He had rationalized it by telling himself he was just trying to survive. He was just trying to keep her warm. That was all. They were both cold and the last thing they needed was hypothermia while they waited for help out in the middle of nowhere.

She had looked so beautiful, sitting there. Her soft, silken hair curling as the heat from the wood stove dried it. Her body glowing in the light. And then she'd reached over and kissed him.

The moment she'd kissed him he'd been a lost man. His body had burned with need and he'd wanted her. He'd wanted her for a long time.

It had thrilled him that she'd wanted him too, though he'd been nervous. He'd wanted to be with her, but he hadn't wanted to hurt her. All he could give her was this night. He wouldn't burden her with his pain, with his hurt, with his ghosts.

Being with her and having nothing between them was more dangerous than being out in that storm.

So he had been nervous, but he hadn't been able to pull himself away when she'd told him she wanted him just as much as he wanted her. Her hands on his skin had made him feel as if he was on fire. Her lips on his had made him ache with need.

He'd forgotten what a woman's touch felt like.

He'd forgotten what passion tasted like.

He wasn't even sure that what he'd had before had ever been like this. He couldn't recall ever wanting a woman so much that it had taken every ounce of his control not to rush through it.

It had never burned so slow as it had with Ruby.

What he'd shared with her tonight had been something completely different. He had been completely lost to her.

And, God help him, he wanted more.

Only he couldn't have more.

He wouldn't put his heart at risk—especially with someone who didn't want commitment either.

Love just brought pain.

Who said anything about love?

The thought caught him off-guard. He shouldn't have given in to Ruby. He should have held back when she'd kissed him.

But when it came to Ruby and her heady kisses he was a lost man. He couldn't help himself. So he wanted more. But it just wasn't meant to be.

Even if it could never happen again he would always care for her. He would always cherish this shared night together.

His heart was guarded, just as much as hers was, but it had been wonderful even just for a moment to share something so deep and intimate with her. To have that connection with someone.

It saddened him that it had just been a brief moment, and it frightened him that it didn't feel like enough. Deep down, he knew that if he didn't put some distance between him and Ruby he would never be able to let her go. He knew he would always want more.

CHAPTER ELEVEN

THE SOUND OF the radio crackling woke him up and he shivered, realizing that the fire in the wood stove had gone out. There was silence except for the sound of Ruby beside him, sleeping still.

Aran got up and peered out the small window in the radio room. The storm was over. There were a few downed trees, and it was still raining, but not heavily. The runway, at least, was clear of trees.

He padded back into the other room and found his clothes were dry. He slipped them on.

Ruby stirred then. "What's going on?" she asked drowsily.

"The storm's over and the radio is back on."

"The radio is on?" She sat up and wrapped a blanket around herself, running into the other room to call for assistance.

After Aran was dressed he grabbed some more wood from the woodpile. Thankfully there were a few embers that were still burning and it wouldn't take much to get a full fire going again. He knew how to do that.

Ruby came back into the room. "I got a hold of someone in Anchorage. They're sending out a mechanic to take a look at the plane and hopefully we can get air-borne again and fly to Unalaska."

"Were you able to contact anyone there?"

She shook her head. "No, but I know that they've been looking for us since we didn't arrive. Anchorage was very glad to hear my call signal."

He nodded. "Good. I'm sorry I let the fire die out. Are you cold?"

"A bit—but are the clothes dry?" she asked.

"Yeah."

"I'll just get dressed."

Ruby slipped past him and went behind the curtain to get dressed. He tried not to think about her, naked behind that curtain, but try as he might images of her in his arms last night flashed through his mind.

He closed the door to the wood stove and then moved to the cabinet, where he hoped there would be some canned food. He opened the door and was met with nothing.

"Rats," he mumbled.

"What?" Ruby asked, pulling down the curtain now that she was dressed.

"I was hoping for some food."

"Check the gear bag I brought in last night. There's some freeze-dried survival food in there. It's not the best, but you won't starve eating that."

"I know. I've lived on it before."

He picked up her gear bag and set it on the worktop. He found the stash of freeze-dried food. All they needed was to add some water.

Ruby found the kettle that went on the stove. She filled it with water and set it on top.

"What would you like for breakfast?" Aran asked as

he went through the selection—which wasn't much. He kept digging and then pulled out a bag. "How about a breakfast skillet? Hash browns and scrambled eggs mixed with sausage?"

"Sounds good. At least that's a breakfast type of food. There should be instant coffee in there too."

Aran dug down further and found it. "We're all set."

"I like to be prepared. It's the Girl Guide in me."

"Is that like a Girl Scout?" Aran asked.

"Yep."

Ruby used a towel and picked the kettle off the top of the stove. Aran divided up the freeze-dried contents and added water to rehydrate it. It didn't look appetizing, but Aran was pretty sure he'd eaten worse. And the coffee might be instant but, again, he wasn't going to look a gift horse in the mouth.

"Well, I guess if one of the questions is how we spent our honeymoon…"

Ruby blushed and then laughed. "Yeah, I suppose you're right. Jeez, you could've picked a nicer place."

Aran smiled, and was relieved that she was joking. Maybe this would be okay. Maybe this would work even if he wanted to be more than friends.

But he couldn't promise her anything. He couldn't promise her forever.

Why not?

"I hope Dr. Franklin and his team managed okay," Aran said, changing the subject so that he wouldn't have to think about it.

"I hope so too. And I hope the typhoon wasn't as strong as they were predicting and that it just dissipated over the islands and into the Bering Sea. They're so rare here, and usually by the time they reach Alaska they've lost steam."

"Roger, bush camp base. Can you hear me?" The radio crackled.

Ruby got up and ran into the radio room. "Roger that, BX7935. We can hear you loud and clear."

"Bush camp base, I've got a fix on your location and I'm just circling to make a safe landing. See you short."

"Roger." Ruby craned her neck to look out the window.

Aran could hear the plane coming in. Hopefully it wouldn't take too long to fix up the plane and they could get out of here and back to work.

He knew that Ruby was anxious to find out what had happened to Dr. Franklin and the others in Unalaska. And Aran was anxious to put some distance between them and this cabin where they'd been alone.

He needed to throw himself back into work and get his mindset back on track. Then he could put what had happened behind him. They could move forward, as the plan had always been.

Who are you kidding?

"You're all fixed, Dr. Cloutier," said Stewart, the mechanic. "You're lucky that you were able to land safely. I'm glad this didn't happen out over the water when the storm was at its worst."

"Me too, Stewart. I'm still annoyed that it happened at all. There's supplies I needed to get out to Unalaska. Do you know how they fared?"

"Typhoon was pretty strong when it made landfall on the leeward side of the island. I'm hoping it just blew over, but I know they lost power and communications for a while. I can tell you that Seward Memorial was quite worried about you two when your plane didn't check in and Unalaska reported you missing."

"It was a bad situation all around." Ruby finished going over the plane. "I appreciate it, Stewart. I owe you a drink for coming out here and fixing my plane."

"Sounds like a plan. Come on, Rick. We have to get back to Anchorage."

Rick, the pilot of the other plane, nodded to Stewart and shook Aran's hand. Ruby walked back to where Aran was standing and they waited until Stewart and Rick's plane had taken off toward Anchorage.

"You ready?" Ruby asked.

"More than ready."

Ruby grabbed the gear she'd brought inside and Aran made sure the fire in the wood stove was out and that everything was back the way it should be, just in case someone else needed a place to stay in an emergency.

They loaded the gear into the back of the plane and Ruby took her place in the cockpit. She was glad to get back into the sky. It was still drizzly and gray out, with the after-effects of the typhoon that had blown in, but it was nothing like yesterday. And at least there was no fog.

She just hoped that she'd have a clear place to land in Unalaska. But Unalaska Airport—or Dutch Harbor— was better than this one, and they would have lights and an air traffic controller.

She just hoped that Dr. Franklin, John and Lindsey had managed to fare well without them...

It was just a short plane ride from where they'd spent the night to Unalaska.

"That's the Bering Sea, over there," Ruby pointed out.

"Not far from Russia, then?"

"Nope." Ruby smiled. "I'm glad the weather is cooperating, but the sea is a little choppy."

"I don't aim to go swimming," Aran joked.

"Me neither."

As they approached the airport Ruby made contact with the air traffic controller and was given clearance to land. It was a little windy, but she was able to bring the plane down gently and taxi to the location where she'd been told to park.

When she got out of the plane Dr. Franklin was waiting with a truck.

"Thank God you two are okay," he said as he came up to them.

Aran opened the hatch and helped to offload the supplies.

"Yeah, I lost an engine and I was forced to land at that old abandoned airstrip that serves as a bush camp starting point. You know the one?" Ruby said.

Dr. Franklin nodded. "Good. I'm so glad. The supplies are needed. There were some injuries when the typhoon hit, but nothing serious. The town fared well, but we're still out of power. We're mostly camped out in the town's recreation center. There were also some strong storm surges and there's quite a bit of damage from that. We could use your help, though. John was trying to help some civilians and he dislocated his shoulder."

"Ouch. Did you reset it?"

Franklin nodded. "I was able to get an X-ray before the back-up generator was damaged by a storm surge. He's on some strong painkillers, so it's been just me and Lindsey running the show all night. We're waiting for the National Guard to get in and help restore power."

"Well, Dr. Atkinson and I are here now."

And apparently they were there in the nick of time.

She could see that Dr. Franklin was exhausted, and she was worried about John. He would be out of action for some time.

They finished loading the supplies into the truck Franklin had borrowed and then climbed in and headed toward the recreation center.

There were downed trees and flooding near the water. Ships in the harbor had been damaged and some had been capsized. Fishing and crabbing were the main industries in Unalaska and a lot of livelihoods and money would be lost.

It was a slow and bumpy ride, but it didn't take them long to navigate the debris on the road to the recreation center. Lindsey was waiting with a group of residents, who let out a cheer when Ruby climbed out of the truck.

Ruby could see Lindsey visibly relax as she came over to give Ruby a hug.

"I was so worried about you," Lindsey said. "I know you're a good pilot, but that was a wicked storm."

"I only caught the tail-end of it. I had an engine failure and had to turn back."

"Good thing you did," Lindsey said. "It's been a wild night, and with John injured it's been a hard slog for Dr. Franklin and me."

"We're here now," Aran said as he picked up one of the boxes and followed Dr. Franklin inside.

"Right," Ruby stated, and grabbed a couple of gear bags. "We're here now, so you can get some rest. Show me what you've set up and we'll get right to work."

There weren't many really bad injuries, but more people from the smaller outlying islands were being brought in by boat.

While Dr. Franklin and Lindsey rested Ruby and Aran took over seeing all the patients. Ruby didn't have to explain anything to Aran about how she usually ran a makeshift medical clinic in the aftermath of a natural disaster. His Army training meant he knew exactly what to do.

And now she was questioning herself as to why she'd been so against him in the first place—why she'd wanted to hire and train someone herself. That would have taken time, and they wouldn't have been able to treat as many people as efficiently as they were now.

She watched him work on the other side of the gymnasium and couldn't help but smile. He was the perfect ying to her yang. They worked so well together.

You don't want love, remember? You don't want a relationship.

She tore her gaze away. What had she been thinking? Why had she given in to her needs and kissed him? She was putting her heart in jeopardy. She didn't have it in her to leave herself open to the possibility of pain. The possibility of losing someone.

Really?

The thing was, a part of her wanted to explore that with Aran. Maybe, just maybe, it would be worth the risk if she had someone like Aran by her side...

"Dr. Cloutier, there's been an accident with the crew clearing off a section of road near the mountain. There's been a rock slide and there's an injured man up on the pass."

"Your husband died from crush injuries. If we'd only got to him sooner, Mrs. Cloutier."

She could hear the doctor's voice in her head. She could hear her mother crying and it made her heart skip a beat—because that was something she didn't want to think about.

Not right now.

Not here.

"Okay," she said quickly, shaking the ghost of the memory away. "Okay."

Aran was looking at her and she could see the concern on his face. She waved him over and he came as quickly as he could.

"Is everything all right?" he asked.

"Get a trauma kit ready. Prep it for a crush injury. There's a man who has been caught in a landslide and he needs medical attention. We need to get up there as soon as possible."

"Sure."

Aran disappeared into the annex where they were keeping the supplies. Ruby collected up some other gear that they would need and then called the airport to ready a flight plan back to Anchorage.

She was not going to let this man die here.

She wasn't going to let him die like her father.

By the time they had collected everything they needed it was raining as the tail-end of the typhoon drifted through.

The crewman who had come to get her drove Aran and her toward where the landslide had happened.

Come on.

Every second that passed made her all the more anxious. When her father had died his life had hung in the balance for a matter of minutes, so the longer it took them in the rain the more upset she was, thinking that they weren't going to make it in time.

Don't think like that.

She couldn't let herself think like that. This was why she had developed her trauma team—this was why she'd become a surgeon. She'd left the north to head to a larger city that had been overwhelming and strange just so that she could return to the place that was home and save others.

No one had to die needlessly.

There were flares on the road, visible even through the sheets of rain that were falling.

"We're here," the crewman said. "Be careful, though. With this rain we're at risk of another landslide."

Ruby nodded and grabbed a gear bag, and Aran followed closely behind her. The rain jacket she'd borrowed from the recreation center did nothing, really. She was still getting soaked as she followed the other members of the road crew around the rubble to where lanterns were lit and a tarp had been erected.

Ruby's heart sank when she saw the man.

No.

She looked over at Aran and saw his jaw was clenched. He gave a slight shake of his head and pulled her aside.

"What do you think?" she asked, but she already knew the answer.

"There's nothing we can do. Look at the rocks on his body. We remove those rocks and he'll bleed out. His crush injuries are probably severe."

"Probably," Ruby snapped. "We don't know for sure."

When she looked at the man under the rubble all she could see was her father's face looking back at her and a lump formed in her throat.

Papa.

"The most we can do is make him comfortable until he passes," Aran whispered.

"I'm going to do everything I can to save him."

"Ruby, it's a lost cause," Aran said. "Even on the front lines we knew when it was time to let go."

Ruby ignored him and moved toward the man. "Gerald, I'm here."

Gerald, the man who was trapped, barely looked at her.

"Gerald? I'm Dr. Cloutier and I'm here to help."

"Oh. Okay." Gerald was shivering and looking around him.

"Can you feel anything, Gerald? Are you in any pain?" Ruby asked, kneeling next to him.

"No," Gerald responded. "No. Not in pain. Just want to get out of here. I have some errands to run."

He was delirious. Ruby glanced out of the corner of her eye to see that Aran was speaking gently to the foreman. She was angry that he was giving up hope. That was not what *she* did. She saved lives. She didn't just walk away.

"I'm glad you're not in any pain," Ruby whispered.

"Who are you?" he asked again.

"I'm Dr. Cloutier, but you can call me Ruby."

"Ruby...that's a pretty name."

"Thank you."

She set up her equipment. She had pain medication, but she wanted to save that for when they moved the boulders. She glanced up at the rubble and could see the size of the rocks that were pinning him down. Her heart sank.

His spine was most likely shattered, which was why he wasn't in any pain.

"I can't see!" Gerald called out in a panic. "I can't see."

Ruby choked back the tears that were threatening to overtake her. "It's okay, it's raining and it's pretty dark.

Why don't you close your eyes and try to rest? We'll get these rocks off you in a moment."

"Okay." Gerald closed his eyes.

"There was nothing to be done, Mrs. Cloutier. His spine was crushed."

Aran came and stood close to her. "Ruby?"

"No," she whispered to him. *"No."*

Aran sank down beside her.

Gerald's breathing became labored and she watched him slip away. Hot tears slid down her cheeks as Gerald took his last breath on the side of the mountain.

"Time of death: twenty-thirty," Aran stated.

The men on Gerald's crew took off their hats and looked solemn.

"You can dig him out now," Aran said gently.

Ruby cursed and stormed off into the rain. She walked away from where everything was happening. She had to put distance between herself and that senseless, pointless death.

Tears streamed down her face and she just stared up into the rain.

"Ruby…?" Aran said.

"Leave me alone!" she snapped.

"Ruby, there was nothing—"

"Don't tell me there was nothing we could've done. We had everything to save that man. *Everything!* We're both surgeons. I could've taken him to the rec center and had him stabilized. I had my plane ready to take him to Anchorage. He should've survived. My father had *nothing*! That's why he died. That's why he died and that's why I've given my whole life to the north—to saving lives so that people like my papa and Gerald don't have to die!"

"We're not God, Ruby. We can only do so much."

"You'd given up on him before we even got to him. Admit it."

"I won't!" Aran said hotly. "But when I saw him I knew there was no saving him. Ruby, his spine was crushed. There's no way he could've survived that."

"Every minute counts. If you had been quicker..." She regretted the words as soon as they'd slipped out of her mouth.

His eyes narrowed. "If my leg hadn't slowed us down? Fine—blame me. But nothing could've saved Gerald. And probably not your father either, given the fact it sounds like he died of a crush injury as well."

Ruby slapped him. "Don't you *dare* talk about my father! You don't know anything about it. You don't know anything about *me*!"

Aran touched his face. "You're right. I don't. But this marriage isn't real and soon enough we can go our separate ways."

He turned around and left her standing in the rain, weeping.

Weeping for her father, weeping for the patients she couldn't save, weeping for all she'd given to the north and how she could never save her father's life no matter how much of her life she gave.

Her father was never coming back and she was alone.

CHAPTER TWELVE

THE FLIGHT BACK to Anchorage the next day was solemn and quiet. Lindsey had decided to fly with Ruby, and Aran had stayed behind to help with John, who was still in a lot of pain from his dislocated shoulder. He also wanted to help Dr. Franklin load up his plane.

Aran had mentioned to her that he thought that John might need surgery. After he had spent the night helping the road crew dig out Gerald's body and bring him back to town.

Lindsey slept on the way back, and Ruby couldn't blame her. Not really. She wished *she* could just sleep away the last couple of days.

They landed in Anchorage and it was only thirty minutes after that when Dr. Franklin landed his plane. An ambulance was waiting to take John to the hospital.

Aran barely looked at her.

She'd hurt him.

But he'd hurt her too.

They'd hurt each other.

It was only supposed to be a marriage of convenience—it wasn't supposed to form itself into anything else. But she had developed feelings for him. She had thought it was just attraction, but she admired him. She admired his strength, his tenacity, his tenderness.

She wanted so much more than just a fake marriage with him. They'd risked everything and for what? A Green Card? It seemed pointless.

She might want him to be more than just a convenient husband but she had ruined that now, and she knew that he didn't want to stay in the north. He didn't want to be really married to her, and she wasn't going to hold him back.

The right thing to do was to let him go. He had done her a huge favor, but that was all it was. All it could ever be.

This whole time she'd been trying to protect her heart from getting hurt, and instead she'd set herself up for pain.

Her phone buzzed and it was Jessica. Agent Bolton was ready for their final interviews and was on his way to the hospital.

Ruby sighed.

Aran came over to her. "Did you get my mom's message?"

"Yes."

"Ready to get this over with?" he asked.

"Yes. I'm ready for this to end."

A strange expression crossed his face. "Right."

They rode back to the hospital in silence, and when they got there went straight up to the boardroom and sat next to each other, waiting for Agent Bolton to arrive.

"Ruby…"

"You don't have to say anything, Aran. For what it's worth, I'm sorry."

"I'm sorry too," he said gently.

The door opened and Agent Bolton stepped in. He smiled—and then frowned when he saw them. "Is everything okay, Doctors?"

"We lost a patient last night," Ruby muttered. "It was a bit difficult. He was a well-liked member of the Dutch Harbor community."

"It's affecting my wife particularly hard, Agent Bolton, because her father died in a similar circumstance when she was twelve." Aran glanced over at her. "That's why she's here, doing what she does. She doesn't want anyone to lose a loved one because there wasn't medical help when it was needed."

Ruby felt tears stinging her eyes as he spoke. She wiped them away.

"But even though I had everything there to save that man's life, I couldn't," she whispered. "Aran has been trying to teach me that there are some cases beyond our control, and that's sort of the curse of medicine. When it's beyond our control to save a life."

"I'm afraid the storm also triggered my post-traumatic stress disorder and brought back a lot of memories from the front."

Ruby knew Aran was saying these words to her, not Agent Bolton.

"So it's been a bit of a hard night for both of us."

"I can see that," Agent Bolton said gently. "And I can see that you two work very closely together. So I'm pleased to inform you, Dr. Cloutier that the United States Citizen and Immigration Services has granted you your Green Card."

Agent Bolton pulled out an envelope and slid it across the table to her.

"Congratulations, Dr. Cloutier. We're pleased to accept you as a citizen."

Ruby stared at the envelope in disbelief. She could go home. She could visit her mom and her brothers. She could visit her papa's grave. It was all she'd ever wanted... but somehow it wasn't everything.

It would mean the end of her marriage to Aran.

She looked over at Aran, who was staring at his hands, and wished that she had a little bit longer to get to know him. She wished she hadn't been so stubborn.

"Thank you," she whispered. "Thank you, Agent Bolton."

"You're welcome."

Agent Bolton stood up and left the boardroom. The silence in the room was so thick you could cut it with a knife. Ruby just stared at the envelope in disbelief.

"How long do we wait?" Aran asked.

"For what?" Ruby asked.

"You know for what," he said.

"A few months...no longer than that," she whispered.

Aran nodded. "I'm glad you got what you wanted."

"Thank you."

But even though she'd got what she wanted, her priorities had changed. She wanted Aran. She wanted what her parents had had.

Yesterday Gerald had died up on that roadside and, yes, it had crushed his family—but at least he'd *had* a family. He'd had someone to love him.

It had been the same with her parents. Her father's death had devastated Ruby's mother, but they'd had love. They'd shared love. They hadn't been lonely.

And this life that she had created, trying to protect her heart, had actually done more damage than good. She was alone and there would be no one to cry over her if she died. There was no one to share her life with.

She didn't want to live her life like that. She didn't want to live her life in fear any longer. She wanted Aran in her life and she wanted him as more than a convenient husband. She wanted him as a *real* husband.

"Aran…" She trailed off.

"A few months is good," he said quickly. "I want to return to San Diego."

"Oh," she whispered. "Right."

Her heart might have changed its mind about taking a chance on love, but she was a fool to think that Aran had. There had been no change of heart for him on that roadside. As far as he was concerned his job was done. She had her Green Card and that meant he was free.

"I think… I think I'm going to head for home." Ruby walked past him and didn't offer him a ride. She didn't think that he would come with her anyways. "I'm sure Sam is ready to get rid of Chinook."

Aran gave her a half-smile but wouldn't meet her eyes. "Right. I'll see you later?"

"Right."

Ruby left the board room as quickly as she could, clutching the Green Card. This was what she'd signed up for in the beginning. She'd always known there was a time limit to this marriage.

She just hadn't expected that she would fall in love with her fake husband.

She hadn't thought that she would fall in love at all.

Stop her!

That was what Aran's mind was screaming as he watched her leave the room, but he couldn't. He didn't want to be hurt by her rejection. That was why he didn't get involved in relationships. This was supposed to be just a simple marriage of convenience and it had been for so long, when they were apart, but now, after spending a short time with her, he was a lost man.

He'd known that the moment he'd seen her again. The moment she'd stood up to his mother, saying that she didn't want him on her team.

Ruby's words had hurt him at first, but after he'd calmed down he'd realized they were just words. He might have post-traumatic stress disorder from the IED explosion that had destroyed his career in the Army, but he wasn't the only one who was living with unresolved trauma.

Ruby had faced her demons last night when Gerald had died.

It hadn't just been about Gerald dying; she had been reliving what had happened to her father. She had given her whole life to stop others from dying like her father had—so much so that she'd never really dealt with the pain of losing him.

She'd avoided facing the reality of what had happened by trying not to let it happen again. But it wasn't lack of medical services that was the reason her father had died. It was the fact that his injuries hadn't been as simple as she'd thought as a child. They'd probably been just as catastrophic as Gerald's.

So he didn't hate her for lashing out at him. He hated himself for letting her into his heart, because now it was over. She had what she wanted. She didn't need him anymore.

Was that really accurate?

Aran had been so afraid of repeating what had happened to his parents. Maybe he'd really never accepted their divorce? The fact that his father hadn't been able to stay living in the north because his career was important, just as his mother's career was important to her.

His own career in the Army was over. He had accepted his discharge. So why was he so adamant about leaving Alaska and going back south? He had a couple of half-brothers and a half-sister there, but he could always visit them. What else did he have down there?

Nothing.

Here he had the chance of something more, if he could just reach out and take it. He wanted to be with Ruby. He cared for her...he was falling in love with her. And it wasn't just lust—he'd gotten to know her.

If it didn't work out, then it didn't work out. But he would never know unless he actually tried. If she didn't love him, if she didn't want anything more from him, he would move on with his life—but he had to try. If he didn't he'd always wonder if he'd let go his one and only chance to be happy. His one chance to shake away the loneliness he felt.

Aran got up and ran after her as best he could with his leg aching.

"Ruby!"

Ruby turned around and he could see the tears in her eyes.

"Aran...?"

"Wait for me."

"What?" she asked.

He caught up with her and touched her face. "I love you."

Her dark eyes widened and welled with tears. "What?"

"I know. I know... But I've fallen in love with you. I

know I told you that I couldn't make you any promises, and I still don't know…" He was rambling. He ran his hands through his hair. "I love you and I want to make this work."

"What about going back south? What about…?"

"I don't care."

"You told me it didn't work for your parents," she whispered. "How can it work for us?"

"Because I don't *have* anything in the south. My career is up here. I want to be here for you. I don't want to end this, Ruby. I want a chance to make things right."

Tears slid down her cheek. "I want to make this work too."

"You do?" he asked in disbelief.

"I love you as well. I was so afraid of falling in love because I was so afraid of what might happen to me if I lost the love of my life. I saw the way my mother mourned and I swore that I would never feel that way. But you made me realize that a life without love is not worth living. A marriage of convenience is not a marriage that I want to have. I want a *real* marriage. I want to love and I don't want to be alone anymore. I'm so tired of being alone. I didn't realize how alone I was until I met you."

She reached out and touched his cheek.

"I love you, Aran."

He pulled her into his arms and kissed her urgently. In that kiss he tried to convey all the emotions she'd brought out in him. How she had made him feel again. How she had brought him back to life. How she had *saved* his life.

"You've saved my life, Ruby Cloutier. You have saved *me*," he whispered.

She sobbed against his neck. "No. No, I didn't save you. *You* saved me."

They kissed again. Her arms moved around him and he never wanted to let her go. He was terrified about what the future held, but somehow the future that had looked so bleak when he had been discharged from the Army was looking brighter.

He hadn't realized how much of a fog he'd been living in until he'd seen her again. She had been the light waiting for him at the end of a very dark tunnel—just as he had been the light for her. They were guiding each other through the fog, showing each other the way home.

Jessica came down the hall. She was wringing her hands, but stopped when she saw them together.

"She got it?" Jessica asked.

Aran nodded and grinned down at Ruby. "She did."

Jessica let out a sigh of relief. "I'm so glad."

"And there's something else too, Mom," Aran said.

"What?" Jessica asked.

"We've decided to stay together and give this marriage a shot."

Jessica's eyes welled with tears and she smiled. "I'm so glad to hear that."

"Are you?" Aran asked.

Jessica nodded. "I messed up so bad with your father. I've always regretted that... And I've seen the way you two work together here and on the team. I'm so happy."

"Mom, it wasn't just you. It was Dad too." Aran stepped closer to his mother. "I'm sorry that I've blamed you all these years."

Jessica broke down in tears and he embraced her.

"I love you, Mom," Aran whispered. "I'm sorry for all the years that I didn't tell you that."

Tears slid down Jessica's face. "I love you too."

Ruby came forward and Jessica and Aran held onto her too.

Aran knew he had everything he could ever want in that moment. He'd been given a second chance. A way to make amends. And there was no way he was going to mess this up.

This time their marriage would be more than just a convenience. It would be a privilege.

His life started here—with Ruby.

EPILOGUE

One year later, north shore, Great Slave Lake

RUBY GAZED UP into her husband's eyes as they stood on the north shore of Great Slave Lake. It was a bright sunny day, although there was a bit of a haze in the sky from some of the faraway forest fires that weren't uncommon for August in the Northwest Territories.

Aran was holding her hand as one of the elders from her village blessed their union. She was wearing a white gown, but it was a pretty simple gown, and it didn't hide the fact that there was a slight swell to her belly—she was five months pregnant.

Aran winked at her and she laughed softly.

Behind them sat the closest of their friends and family.

Her mother was crying softly and her brother sat next to her. Jessica sat next to Ruby's mother, and Aran's stepmother had flown up from San Diego. Lacey, Jack and their little girl Emily had flown down from White-head.

Mitchell had sent a card, as had Sam, who had promised to watch Chinook while Ruby and Aran enjoyed their honeymoon at a small fishing lodge up in Great

Bear Lake for the next few days. Ruby was looking forward to relaxing there.

And beyond those few special guests who had come to witness their wedding vow renewal was a small table that held two precious photos. One of her papa and one of Aran's father.

It was everything she'd ever wanted. Because she'd never thought that when she'd married Aran six years ago she would one day be standing here, so close to home, pregnant and vowing to love him for real.

And she did love him.

She loved him with all her heart.

"And, in a renewal of your vows, do you, Aran, take Ruby to be your wife?"

"I do," Aran said, and slipped the ring he'd bought her on her finger.

"Ruby..."

The elder turned to her and spoke to her in her father's traditional language of Chipewyan. She'd had to relearn it because she'd never spoken it again after her father died, and relearning the language that had been lost to her had been like a rebirth.

It had righted a wrong.

"I do," Ruby answered, in both Chipewyan and English. She slipped the ring she had gotten for Aran on his finger.

"Then I am proud to announce the renewal of your vows, Aran and Ruby. May your lives be truly blessed."

Aran cupped her face and kissed her gently. Then he reached down and touched her belly. "My life is already blessed. I love you, Ruby."

"I love you too, Aran."

And she kissed him again. Surrounded by love, filled

with love, and hoping for the brightest future possible. Even if that future was uncertain she was willing to face it—because she was no longer alone.

* * * * *

MILLS & BOON

Coming next month

FROM MIDWIFE TO MUMMY
Deanne Anders

Lana opened her door and stared at the chaos of her living room. Every toy Maggie owned had to be in that room plus what looked like half the clothes from her dresser. She leaned down to pick up the large stuffed elephant in her way then froze. Stretched out on her couch was a sound asleep Trent. He held her sleeping daughter on top of him with one of his arms laid protectively around her. While a wide awake Trent with his powerful frame and those mesmerizing blue eyes of his was a seductive temptation even to her, this version of the man took her breath away. Thick, dark lashes lay resting on copper toned skin, while lips usually turned in a smile relaxed into a soft invitation. She'd felt those lips against hers. She bent down closer. Had they really been that warm, that firm?

Bright blue eyes stared up at her and she jerked away from him.

Heaven help her, had she really been about to kiss him?

No, of course not. She'd never do anything like that.

Lifting Maggie up into her arms, she held her tight against her racing heart as she carried her into her room and laid her in her crib. She took a minute to catch her breath then walked back into the living room where she found Trent sitting up and rubbing the back of his neck.

"I can't believe you did that," he said.

"What?" she said. Her heart sped back up. He'd caught her.

"You got her to stay in her crib," he said.

She watched him walk toward the door, shoulders slumped and feet all but dragging, and she said a silent thank you to a sleeping Maggie.

"Just one of those tricks you learn when you're a mother," she said.

"You're a good mother, Lana," he said. "I just want you to know that. This isn't about me not thinking you can take care of Maggie."

"Then what, Trent? What is it about if not what's best for Maggie?"

She stilled as Trent's hand came up to her face, running the back of his hand down one cheek, then cupping her chin. He pulled her to him and laid a kiss so soft on her lips that she wondered if she'd imagined it. He pulled away, a half smile on his lips, and walked out the door.

Continue reading
FROM MIDWIFE TO MUMMY
Deanne Anders

Available next month
www.millsandboon.co.uk

COMING SOON!

We really hope you enjoyed reading this book. If you're looking for more romance, be sure to head to the shops when new books are available on

Thursday 30th May

To see which titles are coming soon, please visit

millsandboon.co.uk/nextmonth